CHAOS

IN MY WAKE

By A.V. Shener

Printed in the United States of America

Ebook ISBN 978-965-92994-0-9
Paperback ISBN 978-965-92994-1-6

First Printing, 2022

This is a work of fiction. Names, characters, events, and incidents are the products of the author's imagination. Most places referenced in this book do exist, but the author has taken liberties when depicting their locations. The town of Hudson, NH is the main location of this book, and it's a much smaller town in real life. Any resemblance to actual persons, living or dead, or actual events is purely coincidental.

CONTENT WARNING

This book is not for the faint of heart. It is intended for mature audience only, and contains graphic violence and explicit sexual content.

Part One
A Slippery Slope

1

I wasn't surprised he was here. Although he hadn't tried contacting me in the past month, his presence constantly lurked in the back of my mind. I didn't count on him banging on my door in the middle of the night, though.

"Matt, open up! Don't make me break down this door!"

I looked out my window, considering making a run for it through the rusty fire escape. But I didn't have enough money and couldn't count on Hudson's lackluster public transportation at this hour.

"Matt!"

He was going to wake up the entire building. I jumped to my feet and hurried into the living room, my heart pounding in my chest. With a shaky hand, I unlocked the door.

Jeff Holden stormed inside and elbowed me out of his way. I checked that none of my neighbors came out of their apartments, then quietly shut the door behind me, making sure to keep it unlocked.

Jeff glanced around with a wrinkled nose. "You're living in a dump."

I would have been offended if it wasn't true. "I'm working on an upgrade, but these things take time."

"*Too much time*, in your case." He strolled around and picked up my Simpsons figurines from the shelf. A pang of panic hit my chest when he held the small, plastic red couch in his massive palm. It was the only souvenir I'd kept from my childhood home after I'd been forced to put it up for sale.

"Why didn't you call?" I asked, feeling the last remains of sleepiness fading away now that cold dread was taking over.

"Our last couple of calls haven't exactly been productive." He passed the Simpsons between his hands like a hot potato, his unblinking eyes boring into me.

I blurted, "Paying you back is the only thing on my mind, I swear."

With a snort, he put the Simpsons back on the shelf and took off his leather jacket. He looked the same as I remembered with his shaved head, square jaw, and a nose that had been broken too many times. The snake's head tattoo on his neck always made me nervous. I figured he was about ten years older than I, in his early thirties.

It was hard to believe I'd once thought of him as my savior. Now, he was the boogeyman who haunted my dreams.

"Want some coffee?" I turned toward the kitchen, hoping to lighten the mood.

He grabbed my arm. "I'm not here for your hospitality."

"Listen, you know I'm always paying you back."

He yanked my arm, and the pain shot up my neck. "Don't give me that crap. When you do bother paying, it's barely enough to cover the interest rate."

That interest rate was like pouring water into a bucket riddled with holes. Every dollar I managed to scrape up went into that endless pit. "How much do I owe you now?"

He let go of my arm. "A hundred and two grand."

The words circled in my head until they registered. "Christ. Are you for real?"

"Painfully real. Do you have my money?"

"I...well, no."

For a second, he seemed pleased with my answer, although I must have imagined it. He went and sat on the couch. The cushions were so worn out it seemed that he was sinking into them.

"How long has it been since we started this mess?" he asked.

"Eight months." It felt like a lifetime. A growing debt can make time fly like a rocket, yet the fear made every minute stretch forever.

Jeff nodded, his face thoughtful. "Eight months... remind me, how many jobs have you had during this time?"

"You know it's hard to find a good job in Hudson. I should move to Portsmouth."

He shook his head. "We've been over this before, and the answer's still no."

"But it will be way easier finding a job over there." It would also give me a chance to start fresh, away from people I didn't want to see and memories best left buried.

Jeff said, "I'm not letting you out of my sight. For that,

I need to trust you, and you haven't been trustworthy." He spread his arms on the back of the couch like he was claiming ownership. "You've got beer?"

"Yes." I hurried to bring him a beer from the fridge, hoping the alcohol would make him less prone to violence. The microwave clock showed it was 3:00 a.m.

Jeff took the beer and drank while watching me with his dark eyes.

I crossed my arms and waited for him to leave so I could go back to normal breathing. I had nightmares that played out alarmingly close to what was currently happening, and they never ended in my favor. I almost wished for him to go ahead and hit me, to get this anxiety session over with.

"You've decorated the place?" Jeff's eyes flicked around the room as he sucked on the can.

"Decorated is too strong of a word."

He pointed at the two pictures of angels I had hanging on the wall. "What's the deal with those?"

"A gift from my neighbor. She said they would protect me." I mostly needed them to cover the cracks on my walls, but they weren't enough to cover everything.

"And how well are they protecting you?"

"Considering you're here, not very well."

The corner of his mouth twisted into an ugly, crooked smile. "Don't blame the angels for your mistakes." He put the can on the table and came to stand behind me, sending ice fingers of anxiety across my shoulder blades.

He said, "Did you think that I turned into a saint who no longer gives a damn about his money?"

"I don't think you're a saint."

I flinched when he put his hands on my shoulders, half expecting him to choke me. I glanced around to mentally mark what I could use to hit him with, but I failed to find a good enough option.

Jeff calmly said, "I came here because there might be a way for you out of this mess. Listen carefully like your life depends on it, okay?"

My mouth felt too dry. I was used to his threats, but this time they carried a sense of fatality I hadn't heard before. "Okay."

He turned me around to face him. "You're never going to pay me back."

"I—"

"Shhh. Now you listen. Since you're not going to pay me back, we'll need to be creative, and it just so happens I have a creative solution."

I couldn't remember a time when the word 'creative' made my stomach turn like it did now. "Go on."

"I recently started working with a scientist named Albert Lesko. He used to work in the pharmacy field and got laid off after playing with some stuff he wasn't supposed to."

"What stuff?"

"Doesn't matter. He wants to keep working on his projects, and for that he needs someone to help him out." He poked my chest with his finger. "You will be that someone."

I rubbed the back of my head. "What kind of help does he need? I know squat about these things."

"I don't know the specifics, just that he needs help

testing some of the things he's been working on."

A shiver of unease ran through me. "How exactly am I going to help him test anything?"

He looked into my eyes, and the room suddenly felt a few degrees colder. "You know the answer."

I took a step back, alarm bells ringing. "Hold on now. I'm not a monkey."

He came closer. Despite being my height, his mere presence had a way of shrinking me. "Don't lose your shit. He's willing to pay a thousand bucks for every time you two meet in his lab."

I allowed myself to momentarily toy with the notion of making so much money in such a short time, but nothing in life was free—I'd learned that the hard way.

I said, "Listen, if this guy's willing to pay me—"

"Pay *me*, not you."

"Fine. If he's willing to pay you so much for my help, that means we're talking about some serious stuff. *Dangerous* stuff."

"This guy is not some psycho; he used to be a big deal back in the day, helped develop some medicines and stuff."

"Doesn't mean he hasn't gone nuts since then."

His eyes hardened. "What I'm offering you is a solution to the biggest problem you have, probably the *last* problem you're going to have. And it's not like my neck isn't on the line here as well."

"Your neck?"

"I was instructed to find someone for Albert to work with, and it wasn't debatable. Since you have everything to lose, I'm going to take a chance and give you this opportunity."

He made it sound like I was being offered a prize, but that prize might as well have been a bomb. "Listen, I'm going to pay you back, it's just taking me longer than I hoped. If we could—"

Before I knew what was happening, he moved his hand toward me. Something cold pressed against my throat. I looked down carefully to see him holding a knife. My brain filled with images of my blood soaking into the peeling laminate floor. My body left to rot, only to be found once the smell reached the hallway.

Jeff's voice was disturbingly calm as he said, "the best thing about ending you will be not having to listen to the piles of crap coming out of your mouth. You're shaping up to be a lost cause, Matt. I'm offering you a way out of this mess."

"The knife makes it feel like a demand."

"I have over one hundred thousand reasons to demand this from you."

I looked into his eyes and found cold determination. He wasn't going to leave until I agreed to his messed-up offer.

I nodded carefully. "I hear you."

He moved the knife away. "Do we have a deal?"

I stalled before answering, hoping that somehow an idea would pop into my head and prevent me from being a part of this. Jeff raised the knife again.

"Yes! We have a deal."

"Good. Albert will come here tomorrow at one o'clock to meet you. Be polite and respectful. Don't give him any trouble."

"You've already told him he could come here?"

"Call it a leap of faith. And there's one more thing. Working with Albert will help cover your debt, but your interest will make it hard to reach the finish line."

"Then let's stop the interest."

He snorted. "Now why would we do that?"

"Because working with some scientist on God knows what is more than enough."

"Maybe, but that's not your call."

"I'm not going ahead with this if it won't solve the problem."

"Relax. There's a way." He cleared his throat and looked hesitant, which made me nervous since Jeff Holden didn't do hesitant. "If you laugh at what I'm about to say, I'll break your face." He let out a breath. "I need your help with hooking up."

He said it so fast I wasn't sure I heard him right. "Say what now?"

"Hooking up. I need you to go out with me and help break the ice."

The thought of a night out with Jeff was hurting my brain. "Why do you want my help with that?"

"I need someone who'll take this seriously and knows what he's doing."

"Well, thanks, but what about Tinder?"

"I hate those things."

"So wouldn't it be easier, you know, paying for it?" Even though he looked like a villain from a James Bond movie with his broken nose and weirdly small eyes, he seemed to have enough money to pay for sex.

"I don't want a woman to be there because I paid."

"How am I supposed to make that happen?"

"Like I said, you and I will go out together. You'll get the conversation going, then steer it forward. Doing it solo has been...unsuccessful."

"How did you date women in the past?"

He remained quiet.

I cleared my throat. "I see. Well, listen, let's try it out and see how it goes."

"If I'm stopping your interest, I'll need a more solid commitment."

"I can't just wave my wand like a matchmaking fairy."

"If you want to stop that interest, you better wave that wand."

I wasn't so arrogant to think that I could score any girl in the world, but I was aware of my good looks. Between playing Cupid and keeping that damn interest from growing, it was a no-brainer. "Fine. I'll do it."

He scanned my face closely like he was searching for a lie. "Good." He walked past me and put on his jacket. The snake's eye on his neck seemed to be looking directly at me. "We'll go out tomorrow night to see what you've got." He came to stand in front of me. "Give me a smile so I know we're good."

"I don't feel like smiling."

I flinched when he pressed his warm thumbs to the corners of my mouth and pulled my lips to the sides in a fake, wide smile. "That's better."

He was about to open the door and leave when I said, "Wait."

He turned around. "What is it?"

"Can..." I cleared my throat. "Can you spare me some

cash?"

"You've got to be kidding me."

"I'm late on my bills."

"So?"

"I won't be much help to you if I freeze to death."

"I'm tempted to test that," he said, but still pulled out his wallet and took out three fifty-dollar bills. "Enough?"

"Yes."

He held the bills for me to take, but just when I was about to, he let them fall on the floor.

"Go on," he said. "Pick them up."

I stopped myself from calling him a bastard as I leaned down to pick up the bills. By the time I got back to my feet, he was gone.

Back in my bed, I stared at the streetlights dancing across the ceiling. Currents of unease swam up and down my body, keeping sleep out of reach. The deal Jeff had shoved down my throat could end up being a golden opportunity to clear up my debt and finally start fresh. Up until now, the possibility of that happening seemed depressingly far-fetched. Yet I couldn't shake the feeling that this whole thing was going to blow up in my face.

2

The first time I noticed something was off with Dad was during my first semester break, when I was back home and was about to head out to meet with friends. He was sitting alone in our wide living room, the burning fireplace being the only source of light.

There was a sense of heaviness in the air as I stepped inside the room. An almost empty glass sat next to Dad, most likely not containing water. He was an occasional drinker, but rarely alone.

He turned his head when he heard me approaching, gave me a smile that was absent from his eyes. "You're heading out?"

"Yep. Nick's picking me up."

"Make sure he doesn't drink."

I glanced at the glass next to Dad and nodded. "I will. You're doing anything?"

"Nothing exciting. I'll probably read and call it a night."

"Cool. So, is everything okay with work?"

I caught a quick twitch above his upper right eye. Someone else would've missed it, but I was watching closely for that incriminating twitch.

"Why are you asking?"

"Thought I heard you getting angry at someone on

the phone the other day."

He waved his hand dismissively. "Don't read too much into it." He shifted in his chair. "A couple of deals fell through in the last minute, but we'll bounce back."

I had nothing to do with the family business, never took on any of the load and responsibility, but it was always *we* when he spoke about it. Dad's shoulders were stiff, and I caught a thin line of concern between his brows.

"You sure?" I asked.

"Matt, when did I ever fail you?" There was a challenge in his voice.

"What? Never."

"That's right. So there's nothing for you to worry about. Focus on doing good in school, and by school I don't mean fraternity parties."

It might have been selfish of me, but I jumped at the change of topic. "Gee, Dad, just send me to a convent why don't ya."

He laughed, which was the reaction I was hoping for.

"Us Evans boys need to keep our charm on a tight leash," he said with a wink.

"Yeah, it's like a super power. All the responsibility."

He laughed again, and it felt that my work here was done. I leaned down and gave him a peck on the cheek, which I hadn't done in ages. This time the smile reached his eyes.

As I stepped outside, I had no doubt there was nothing to be worried about.

*

I woke up from a troubled sleep at noon, feeling that I hadn't slept at all. Assuming Jeff's visit last night hadn't been a bad dream, that Albert guy was due to arrive soon. I got out of bed and went to take a shower. Since I was living on the third and top floor of a shitty building, the water pressure ranged between mild and a trickle. This morning, I was blessed with mild.

Under the stream, I ran my hand across my neck, where not too long ago a knife was pressed against my skin. I knew Jeff meant business, but things had a tendency to become clearer when you're a cut away from a gruesome death.

Once I was done with the shower, I got dressed and crashed on the couch with my morning Doritos. I went with an extra spicy flavor to help me wake up faster. Looking at the ceiling, the water stains resembled clouds while the cracks resembled lightning. I used to worry the ceiling might collapse on me someday, but now it felt like a possible escape from my growing list of problems.

I opened my phone and went through my regular job boards. I was searching for positions fit for people who haven't finished college and had very short experience running a business into the ground. Like the day before, my options were bleak. I sometimes managed to score remote gigs doing sales or customer support online, but the money was miles away from what I needed to make. Until six months ago, I'd delivered the Carriage Towne News to subscribers around town like I was twelve and saving for an Xbox. When I was asked to expand my route to include my old neighborhood of Hudson Village, the thought of running into anyone I knew was so petrifying that I fought with the manager and lost my job.

I had been dead serious last night when I asked Jeff to let me move away. Hudson was a nice place to raise a family, but the wrong place to find a well-paying job with my lackluster work experience.

After more than twenty unproductive minutes, I left the job searching alone and moved to check out my Twitter feed. It was the only social network I was still occasionally checking since I couldn't stomach seeing how great everyone was doing on Instagram and Facebook while I was struggling to keep a roof over my head.

The breeze from the open window rustled the tips of my hair. The buzzing sounds of activity from the street slipped into my apartment. Growing up in the northern part of town, the only sound to reach my room had been the steady flow of the Merrimack River.

I shut my eyes and tried to envision what it would feel like to wake up in the mornings without worrying about money and how the hell I was going to put my life back in order. If that Albert guy was my best chance of getting Jeff off my back, I needed to start thinking of him as an opportunity, not a threat.

A knock on the door brought me back to reality. I quickly checked myself in the mirror and wiped Doritos crumbs from my shirt and lips. I opened the door and blinked in surprise. In my head, I had an image of an older guy with gray hair and a white lab coat. In reality,

Albert seemed to be about forty, his hair was black, and his navy blazer looked way too preppy for this neighborhood. He was also rather skinny and short, which boosted my confidence.

"Hello," he said. "You must be Matthew."

"It's Matt. Come in. Want something to drink?"

"Water would be nice." The tone of his voice was deep like a radio host. He sat on the couch and the springs creaked to make it clear he was now in a shithole.

I gave him a glass of water and sat on the only chair I had. "Are you from around here?"

"You mean from New Hampshire? No, from New York. I moved here a couple of years ago for my work. Hudson provides the type of peace and quiet I was lacking back in the city."

"If by 'peace and quiet' you mean 'mind-bogglingly boring,' I get you."

He chuckled and put the glass on the table. "You didn't like growing up here?"

I shrugged. "I guess it was all right." More than all right, but the last year had taken its toll on my perspective of my former life. Once something gets so deeply tainted, it doesn't matter how good it looked before—you're stuck with a stain.

Albert rubbed his palms on his knees before saying, "It's nice to finally meet you."

"Finally?"

"Well, I first heard about you around a month ago, but only yesterday morning Jeff called to tell me the good news."

A month? That explained why I barely heard from

him lately. Knowing I had been targeted for this gig in advance wasn't good for my anxiety.

Albert asked, "Did Jeff explain to you why I need your help?"

"He said you need me for testing some medical stuff. Sounds pretty crazy, to be honest."

He opened and closed his mouth before saying, "I don't believe my work is crazy."

"I didn't mean it like that." But in a way, I did. "Sorry if I was blunt."

He managed a smile, but it seemed forced. "You can be blunt, Matthew—I mean, Matt. Honest communication is very important in our case." He straightened and said, "We've gotten ahead of ourselves. Let me give you some background into why we're here today."

I leaned back in my chair. "Shoot."

"I was fired a while back from a leading pharmaceutical company. This had nothing to do with the quality of my work and everything to do with how old-fashioned my supervisors were. From their point of view, there was no reason to push the envelope, as if the problems I was trying to solve were going to miraculously solve themselves. I tried to stand my ground, but we had a falling out, and they ended up letting me go."

I couldn't shake the feeling that he was overly simplifying the truth. To *push the envelope* could mean a lot of things.

I asked, "Couldn't you go work for another company?"

"I tried, but they made sure to spread lies about me, and..." He took a deep breath. "Let's just say that going to work somewhere else and still be able to continue with my projects isn't possible. After all this time, I do believe that what happened was for the best. *Live free or die*. Isn't that the New Hampshire motto?"

"Yes. We're dramatic like that."

He smiled and seemed more at ease. I wondered how long he had been waiting for someone like me to come along. But I was more curious about something else. "How did you end up working with Jeff?"

"I haven't worked with him directly until recently. The ones I initially reached out to got me in touch with him."

"Who are they?"

He shook his head. "I'm afraid my dealings with them will remain private. But now that I have gained my professional freedom, your part starts." He drank the rest of his water. "I've developed different types of substances and techniques, and I'm past the stage of trying them out on animals. It's time to try them on a human being." He watched me closely, the only other human being in the room.

I tried to keep myself composed, but my heart was beating faster. This entire conversation felt wrong because he was using logical words to cover for something so profoundly irrational.

I asked, "Aren't there people who *volunteer* for stuff like this for money?"

"Well, I'm not interested in counting on strangers with my work."

"I'm a stranger."

"True, but the circumstances are different."

"Because I don't have a choice?"

He shifted uneasily and avoided my eyes.

"Sorry," I said. Jeff's warning about causing problems played in the back of my mind. Albert and I might have been sitting here having a civil conversation, but I was fully aware of the high stakes involved.

"That's all right," Albert said. "I'm not expecting you to come to my lab with a smile every time. In truth, I'm curious as to why you and Jeff are involved with one another."

"I tried to save my dad's company after he died, and for that I needed money."

He pondered my words and slowly nodded. "I'm assuming Jeff wasn't your first option."

"More like the last. I probably should've given up after the fifth bank showed me the door."

But it wasn't that simple. I'd grown up knowing every person who worked at my dad's company, had celebrated with them every new granite distribution deal like I had something to do with it. They used to call me the company's mascot, but that mascot had ended up letting them down when it mattered the most.

I said, "It felt wrong letting everything my dad had worked for disappear." Maybe I should have kept my mouth shut about my reasons for dealing with Jeff, but it felt good being honest with someone about my life.

Yet you didn't tell him the full reason, did you?

"I see," Albert said with a nod. "I'm sure your dad would have appreciated your efforts."

He wouldn't have. He would have told me to stop being so goddamn stubborn and move on with my life. Unfortunately, I didn't inherit his practicality.

Albert said, "There's one more thing I'd like to put on the table." His voice went deeper as he leaned forward. "Some of the things I've developed are meant to be used by the military."

"The...military?"

"Indeed. I used to work with different military officials back in the day, and they were not pleased to hear I had to stop my work. They couldn't hire me directly because that could have attracted the wrong kind of attention, but they are currently my main source of funding. That is why secrecy is of the highest importance here."

This whole thing was getting weirder and weirder. I moved uneasily in the chair. "Military stuff? That's heavy."

"If by *heavy* you mean vital to our country, then yes, it is."

There was an edge to his voice, and I decided to let it go for now. I tapped my knees. "So...now what?"

He glanced at his watch, and I hoped we were done for the day, but then he said, "I will need to have a thorough examination of you in my lab before we'll do any real work together. But since I'm already here, I would like to use this opportunity to have a quick look at you."

"Aren't you looking at me now?"

He smiled. "That's not what I meant. Please remove your clothes."

"Uh, what?"

"Before we can work in my lab, I need to make sure there aren't any noticeable issues that might get in the way. If there are, I will be risking my privacy in vain. You may stay in your underwear."

Despite his attempt to make this sound logical, a bad feeling grew in my stomach. Even after our polite conversation, there were still gaps in my understanding of what I was supposed to do for him. I thought of prying him for more information, but Jeff's menacing voice played in my brain, warning me to go along.

I stood up with a sigh and took off my clothes until I was left in my boxer briefs. Albert stood up and came closer. I stared at the small window in front of me, which offered a not-so-great view of the building next to mine.

Albert paced around me like he was about to buy a cow in the market. "I don't see any obvious defects on your body."

"You sure know how to make a guy feel special. Can I put my clothes back on?"

"Not yet. It will only take a few more minutes." He took a step closer. His cologne smelled expensive. I noticed a bit of gray in the hair on his temples. I stopped breathing when he put his cold hand on my shoulder.

"Please relax," he said. "I have no intention of causing you any pain."

He peeked into my mouth and ears, then pressed my stomach and chest. He asked me to move my head in different positions and stretch my arms. It went on for about five minutes until he casually moved his hand

and closed it around my crotch.

Before my brain could figure out what my body was doing, I shoved him back, causing him to fall on the floor. Looking down at him, I knew I'd made a mistake.

"Shit. Let me help you—"

"No. Get away from me." He stood up and fixed his glasses.

"Don't touch me like that without asking."

With a flushed face, he said, "I think we might have a problem here, Matthew."

"Matt."

"Maybe Jeff wasn't clear with you about our agreement, but I was told I'd have no limitations regarding my work."

Hearing him put it like that clenched my stomach. "Listen, I don't know what Jeff told you, but—"

He raised his hand to shut me up. "I will not stand here and talk about my agreement. It was already discussed thoroughly."

"Not with me it wasn't."

He let out a sigh like speaking with me was pointless. "I will let Jeff know about this."

I was about to ask him to keep this between us, but I wasn't willing to show him how scared I was of Jeff. "Do what you want. The door is that way." I began putting my clothes back on, my pulse refusing to settle down.

Without another word, Albert left.

I sat on the couch for a few minutes and stared at nothing, my leg bouncing nervously on the floor. *What the hell just happened?* I debated whether I should call Jeff before Albert got the chance, but I couldn't bring myself to listen to any more of his threats. There was no way he was going to take my side in this.

I decided I couldn't stay in my stuffy apartment anymore and boil in dread, so I changed into my running clothes and headed out to escape my thoughts.

*

It was a relatively warm day and the sky was empty of clouds. Winter was right around the corner, but Hudson was still covered in different shades of orange and yellow. I'd seen my share of America in my time off before college, and nothing came close to New Hampshire in autumn.

Leaves crunched beneath my feet as I entered Merrifield Park. A family of squirrels ran away as I made my way toward the trail surrounding the lake. I started running on my usual route, trying to clear my head and focus on the music in my headphones. But my brain was having none of that. Worries about what might happen next kept nagging at me like mosquitoes. I decided to call Jeff once I was back home instead of drowning in anxiety.

After an hour, I dragged my sweaty self to buy a well-earned pizza with a coupon I'd cut out of a local newspaper. I strolled around the lake as I ate and watched the ducks lazily swimming by. Even close to my struggling neighborhood, it was easy to find beautiful places like this park.

I was about to head back when I suddenly heard, "Matt? Is that you?"

I turned around. The pizza started climbing up my

throat. *This cannot be happening.*

"It is you!" Sharon walked toward me, flushed after a run. She still looked great with her long blond hair, green eyes, and perfect figure.

I stood motionless, my mouth open and my heart beating fast. She came up and hugged me. I was too numb to hug her back.

With her hands resting on her slim hips, she said, "It's so weird seeing you here. I didn't think I'd run into anyone I know. You come here often?"

"Yeah. Haven't seen you here before."

"I was getting sick of running around Benson Park. Too many people there wanted to stop and chat. I mean, come on, can't you see I'm running here?" She gave me a once-over. "It's been forever since I last saw you. You're looking good. Does this mean you're done with the not-having-any-money thing?" She whispered that last part like we were talking about hemorrhoids.

I rubbed the back of my neck. "Oh, you know how it is. Working on it."

She looked around with a little frown. "Do you live around here?"

"Me? No, c'mon. In this area?"

She laughed and lightly touched my arm. "Right, we all have our limits."

Keeping a smile on my face was torture. I wanted to leave, to get the hell away from her. We dated in high school but broke up shortly after prom when she caught me with a college girl at a party. That hadn't been my finest hour, although I wasn't exactly sober that night. Despite the drama, Sharon seemed to have gotten over it rather quickly, and we continued being friends.

Years later, when I desperately needed money to keep a roof over my head, I turned to my friends for help. Sharon was the only one who agreed, but her help came with a price. She offered me to go down on her for thirty minutes in exchange for two hundred bucks. It just so happened that was how she'd caught me with that college girl all those years before. Karma was apparently a bitch named Sharon.

I'd told her to forget about it and keep her dirty money. But two depressing days later, when I wasn't sure I could afford to pay for food, I decided to forget about my self-respect and gave her a call. Afterward, I begged her not to tell anyone about what we did. She promised this would be our little secret and I had nothing to worry about.

A few days later, I got wind something was up when friends began avoiding me. I dug around and found out that pretty much everyone I knew had heard about what I'd been desperate enough to agree to. One of my friends had been clueless enough to accidentally send me a text message with a list of things I was allegedly willing to do for money. "*Matt Evans's Special Rates*!"

It was obvious the same people I grew up with were not the kind of people I needed in my life. Some had tried to downplay it, but a line had been drawn between us and there was no going back.

"Are you doing anything now?" Sharon asked and ran her fingers through her hair. "We can go grab coffee or maybe go to your place..."

The possibility of sex was tempting, but simply

standing next to her was a loud reminder of how much her actions had hurt. Not to mention she never apologized.

"I have better things to do," I said. "It was cool seeing you, though. Enjoy your run." I walked away from her stunned face with my head held high. It wasn't the big revenge I dreamed of having, but it was enough to brighten my day.

3

My good mood lasted until I reached my apartment and opened the door. "What the—?"

Everything was trashed. My couch, my table, my chair, and even my TV was now broken. I stood at the entrance and couldn't move, a hollow feeling growing in my chest. It had to have been Jeff's doing or one of the guys who worked for him.

I hurried to check the small cabinet under my broken TV and carefully took out my parents' photo album. If anything had happened to that album, I didn't know what I'd do. My mom had died from a simple operation gone wrong when I was four, and these photos were my only way of remembering her.

I carefully put back the album and glanced around the room. "Oh, shit! No, no, no." I hurried to pick up the broken Simpsons couch from the floor, my fury making me dizzy. The couch was split in two. Lisa's head was squashed after being stamped on.

I let the pieces fall on the floor, feeling that I'd lost more than a mere toy. I went to check my phone. A voice message from Jeff was waiting.

"Last night I was clear with you, Matt. Be polite, I said. Don't give Albert any trouble. And what did you end up doing? Fucking everything up! You should be glad what happened to your apartment didn't happen to your face. Be ready at ten. I'll come pick you up."

I slumped down on the floor, my broken belongings surrounding me in a circle of guilt. Before I could control myself, my throat seized up and a sob escaped my mouth.

I should have given up on Dad's company when I had the chance. Instead, I'd set out to score a loan from every bank in southern New Hampshire. They all looked at the numbers, looked at me, then not-so-politely declined.

I'd heard about Jeff from a guy in my neighborhood who I later discovered was a small-time criminal. If I hadn't been so thrilled with having someone finally willing to loan me money, I would have figured out something was off with Jeff's offer. The weight of my guilt for not being there for Dad had squashed my common sense and guided my decisions. Once I realized how fast his interest was growing, I was already drowning.

Like shoving candy into the mouth of a crying baby, the smell of weed calmed me down. I got up and trudged to my bedroom. Luckily, Jeff hadn't trashed this room; it was as ugly as it had always been, with water-stained walls and an old, squeaky closet.

I suddenly remembered my escape folder. If Jeff had happened to have seen it, I was a dead man walking. I hurried to the closet and shoved aside the dirty clothes I used for cover. I found the blue folder at the bottom of the closet, then picked it up and browsed through the familiar pages. Everything seemed to be in order—

every map, bus line, and note I'd made with important information meant to help me escape and disappear. I also kept copies of all my personal documentation in there. It had been silly making an actual folder in this day and age, but it had given me a bit of optimism in the last depressing months.

I wasn't yet willing to split town, even after the situation had drastically escalated in the last twenty-four hours. To escape with no money would move me from one mess to another, and I didn't want to look over my shoulder for the rest of my life.

I carefully put the folder back in the closet before climbing out the window. Caleb was sitting on the fire escape of the building next to mine, wearing his usual faded crimson robe. He was about seventy and one of the few black people I ever saw around Hudson. He was also rather blind and most likely a bit crazy.

"You all right, Matt? I heard all these noises earlier. Were you renovating?"

"That wasn't me."

"Oh. Then whoever it was, he was not happy with the way you decorated your place, I can tell you that much."

I sat on the stairs. "You heard it when it happened?"

Caleb blew out smoke and nodded. "My eyes are shit, but my ears are fine, thank you very much. Whoever did it was hella pissed off."

"Yeah, he was."

"Must be a total nutjob to be pissed off with a nice fellow like yourself. Here, take some of this. No better medicine after a good cry."

"Wasn't crying."

He snorted. "Never bullshit a bullshitter. I can hear you sniffling. Ain't nothing wrong with crying—just ask any reasonable baby."

I took the joint from between his thin fingers and filled my lungs with sweet weed. Nothing made me happier these days than a joint I didn't have to pay for.

Caleb asked, "You know who did that to your place?"

"Yes."

"Did you call the cops?"

"No. I'll handle it."

"Hmm. You think the asshole's gonna come back?"

"Oh, he'll come back." I glanced at my watch. "We're going out in about six hours."

Caleb turned his body toward me. "The fuck you just say?"

"It's a long story."

"Long or short, doesn't matter one bit. You need to find friends who won't break your furniture." His voice went low. "Not breaking each other's furniture is the basis of every good friendship."

I snickered. "Yeah, I'll look around for better friends."

Caleb knew I was broke, but never asked how I was planning on getting my life back in order, which was all I was looking for in a friend these days. He let me smoke the entire joint by myself, and by the time I was done, my thoughts felt covered in soft clouds. It was a temporary armor, but I cherished it.

I thanked Caleb and staggered back inside. The thought of cleaning my apartment crossed my mind, but I ended up going straight to bed to escape my sour mood.

*

Opening my eyes to the setting sun, it took me a few seconds to remember why I was sleeping at this hour and what I was supposed to be doing later tonight.

A cold breeze blew in from the half-open window. I caught a sniff of a salmon being cooked and wondered whether Molly from downstairs would save me a piece. I would have been living on snacks and sandwiches if it weren't for Molly.

I reluctantly entered the war zone that was my living room, then spent the next hour and a half cleaning and throwing things away. By the time I was done, the place was spotless yet noticeably bare. I'd only moved here after my pitiful credit score prevented me from renting anything better. And even then, the lease required me to always pay for six months in advance, which swallowed the rest of my savings like a hungry whale.

I didn't have a lot of time to get ready but being late wasn't an option. I showered and spent ten minutes trying to decide on what to wear. Knowing what was at stake tonight, I couldn't afford to mess this up. I ended up going with my favorite jeans and a buttoned-down navy shirt that was a bit tight but the right kind of tight.

Jeff knocked on my door a few minutes past ten, wearing black like usual. He scanned my apartment and nodded. "You should clean my place next."

"You fucking broke all my stuff!"

He raised a warning finger. "Watch your mouth. You had it coming."

"You gave Albert the wrong impression about what he can and cannot do."

"Oh, did I?"

"Grabbing my junk wasn't a part of the deal. You need to tell him that."

"I can't tell him what to do because he doesn't work for me. I just make sure he gets what he wants as long as he pays on time." He took a step closer. My muscles tensed up, but I stood my ground. "I told you, very slowly—so you could understand—that you mustn't cause him any trouble. He's paying a lot for your help, and he's going to get his money's worth." He held my chin, his minty breath tickling my nose. "Are the words coming out of my mouth getting through your thick head?"

I shook my head from his grip. "I get what you're saying, but you broke things I cared about."

"Listen to me." His voice was a tad gentler. "The amount of money you've risked today is worth a lot more than your cheap stuff. Do better next time, and you and I will have no more drama. I'm not getting a kick out of being an ass."

I had a hundred cynical responses, but I settled for a silent nod.

Jeff gave me a once-over. "Shouldn't you be showing more skin? We're going to a club, not a reception."

"You didn't tell me where we're going."

"I'm telling you now."

If I was going to dance, a t-shirt would have been best, but I didn't have a clean one left. "What I'm wearing is fine."

"If you say so. Come on, let's see what you've got."

We left my apartment and got into Jeff's BMW. It felt like an expensive cage with a profound scent of leather. We drove on Ferry Street, which was deserted at this hour, then continued to cross the old bridge above Merrimack River, leaving Hudson behind us in favor of slightly bigger Nashua.

We kept driving further away on a dark road with thin traffic, and I realized I had no idea about our destination.

I asked, "What club are we going to?"

"Apollo."

"Never heard of it."

He shrugged. "Good music."

"Cool. So...you grew up around here?"

"No."

"Oh. Well, I did. My parents moved here from Boston after they got married. Where are you from?"

"Philly."

"I've been there once. Took a long road trip after high school. Why'd you leave?"

He sighed. "I wanted a chance to sit in the car with people who were trying to make pointless small talk. Looks like I got my wish."

"I see." I couldn't care less about his life, but nervousness made me babble. Back in the day, I'd considered myself a smooth talker when it came to women, but my self-confidence was currently at an all-time low. I'd also never needed to sweet talk my way for another man's benefit.

I gathered the courage to ask, "What if it doesn't

work out tonight?"

"What do you mean?"

"What we're trying to do isn't science. I can't be one hundred percent sure I'll be able to get you what you want."

He remained quiet for a long minute, then the car slowed down until we stopped by the side of the road. There was barely any light around. Even the moon was hiding behind the clouds.

Jeff turned down the radio and narrowed his eyes at me. "You're having second thoughts about our agreement?"

"What? No, it's not that. I was just…you know, trying to make sure you're aware that these things aren't foolproof."

"You have a job to do, and making excuses isn't part of it. I've no intention of going to sleep tonight without getting some action."

"Yeah, for sure. Forget I said anything."

He stared at me for a long moment before saying, "Glad we could clear this up."

I rolled down the window to let the cold wind calm my rapid heartbeat. We were driving on a road I'd used to take to Southern New Hampshire University in my old life. A billboard for a college hockey game reminded me of the times Dad had driven to see me play, even when I was only there to warm the bench.

When we finally arrived at Apollo, the parking lot was packed. Drunks were roaming around like zombies. We ended up parking far from the entrance. Once we entered the club, waves of techno music crashed against my eardrums.

Jeff led us toward the bar, cutting his way through the crowd like he owned the place. People got angry, but one look at his neck tattoo caused a sudden change of heart.

At the bar, Jeff ordered a beer for himself and a cocktail for me. We drank without speaking as we scanned the crowd. There were two main dance floors, each illuminated with different sets of changing lights. I checked out the girls and wasn't thrilled to see them dancing in packs. Hitting on one would be an even bigger challenge with her friends watching me closely.

"What sort of girls are you into?" I asked Jeff through the pounding music.

"Huh? Oh." He put down his beer and chewed on his thin bottom lip. "They don't have to be beauty queens, but don't go for the easiest one you can find. And it might be smarter to get two instead of one."

"Two? Why?"

"Easier for us to switch."

I leaned closer since I wasn't sure I'd heard him right. "What did you say?"

"Switch. You do one, I do the other."

I stared at him, unsure of what to say. This curveball was the last thing I needed.

Jeff frowned. "Problem?"

"I thought it was about getting someone to go home *only* with you."

"Do people usually hit on someone for somebody else without looking like creeps?"

"But that was the whole damn point!"

He shrugged and looked away.

My skin grew hot. The thought of having sex next to him felt wrong in every possible way, but a part of me could see how it might be easier selling Jeff as an extra rather than the main dish.

I glanced at my watch. It was past 11:00 p.m. I finished my drink and said, "I'm going in. You're staying here?"

He nodded and leaned back against the bar. "I'll be here." He patted me on the shoulder. "Go on, let's see what you've got."

I took a deep breath and made my way toward the crowded dance floor. I should have worn something else; the air system in this place was a joke, and I already felt myself getting sweaty.

I found a place that was not too crowded and waited for the right moment to start dancing. Minutes passed and I remained glued to the floor, insecurity planting roots inside me. Everyone around looked like they were having a blast while I couldn't help but feel like a creep lurking in the shadows. My mouth was getting dry, my heart beating fast.

Someone suddenly tapped my shoulder. I turned around and saw a guy I couldn't remember ever knowing his name, but I did remember him from one of my classes at Southern New Hampshire University. We started talking despite the loud music, and once I let it slip that I was dancing solo, he invited me to come dance with his friends.

It was definitely less awkward dancing with other people, and I remembered how much I used to love dancing back when the world made more sense. The fun came to a crashing halt when I suddenly locked my eyes with Jeff. His angry face stopped me dead in my tracks, making me realize I'd let myself get sidetracked.

I hurried to the restroom to wash my face, ignoring the strong smell of urine. My shirt was glued to my skin, but my adrenaline was still high. I turned around to leave and crashed into Jeff. He grabbed my arm and dragged me to one of the stalls.

"Jeff, wait. I—"

He slammed the door behind us and smashed his fist into my stomach. The music in the background swallowed my shout.

"Having fun?"

I shook my head and held my stomach. "I didn't forget."

"You've been fucking dancing like it's your prom!"

"I needed to get into the mood." It sounded lame even to me.

"I don't give a fuck about your mood. Do your job and stop messing around." He started opening the buttons of my shirt. "You're sweating like a pig. I told you to wear something else."

"I'm sorry."

He grabbed my jaw, the anger in his eyes feeling worse than a punch. "Final warning," he said and stormed out.

I went to wash my face again, my hands unsteady. A guy with pointy hair finished peeing and gave me a sympathetic look in the mirror. "Problems with your boyfriend?"

"What? Hell no."

I hurried back to the club.

*

My first attempt was with a hot, older woman, but when I suggested leaving together with a friend of mine, she called me a pervert and left. Next came two loud girls who liked the idea of having another guy join us. When they asked who this guy was, I waited for a moment when Jeff wasn't looking, then pointed at him. The girls exchanged concerned looks and said it wouldn't work.

I looked over at Jeff and couldn't blame them. With the snake tattoo on his neck and a constant mean look on his face, it was clear why he struggled to attract normal women. Only tonight, his problem was my own.

It was getting close to 1:00 a.m. and the place started thinning with every passing minute. My panic reached its peak, making it hard to think. I was about to switch to full-on begging mode when salvation came with a hand on my butt.

I turned around to see a beautiful blonde standing in front of me. Before I could speak, she started kissing me. Her breath smelled like whiskey and strawberry bubblegum. She broke the kiss and got right to the point in a delicious French accent. "My sister and I watched you earlier. You're looking for sex, right?"

It was embarrassing to hear how blunt I'd been acting, but wounded pride was better than a wounded face. I glanced aside at her brunette sister. They looked similar but not twins. "Yeah, I am. You see my friend over there? It's his birthday and we're looking to celebrate. You two should join us."

She glanced at Jeff with a frown, then told me to wait while she went to her sister. They talked for what felt like a long time while around me more people were leaving the club. I was about to give up hope when they both suddenly started walking toward me. The brunette gave me a long once-over and shrugged. "Yeah, fine. Let's go."

The blond quickly added, "Can your friend just watch? He's sort of scary."

"What? No-no. C'mon, it'll be fun. He's a kitten. And besides, it's his birthday wish." I used my pleading face.

She sighed and tucked her hand in the crook of my elbow. "Fine."

We went over to the bar, and Jeff blinked in surprise when he spotted us, almost spilling his drink. I felt like a winner, like I'd finally managed to kick my bad luck in the ass. Jeff asked the girls if they wanted something to drink, they said no, and we all began walking toward the exit.

The cold air outside caught me by surprise, and I hurried to button up my shirt. The two sisters walked behind us, speaking French.

Jeff quietly said, "You did okay."

"I know, right? Those two are hot."

"They are. It shouldn't have taken you so long, but next time you'll try harder."

Thinking of going through this anxiety session again was an instant downer to my good mood.

I suddenly heard from behind, "Guys, wait."

Jeff and I both stopped and turned around. We were a few feet from the car, and the entire area was deserted.

"Everything all right?" I asked.

The blond held her sister's hand and looked uncomfortable. "We talked about this again, and we don't think it's a good idea. No offense."

"But—"

"Ladies," Jeff said, his voice higher than usual. "I think you should give us a chance. It's late, and we're all obviously horny."

God, words weren't his friends.

"Yeah...we're gonna go," the blond said and took a step back with her sister.

Jeff cleared his throat. "You're missing out. Matt here is the best fuck around."

Despite the cold, my cheeks warmed up.

"Is he now?" Both identically crossed their arms.

"You bet." Jeff stood in front of me and started unbuttoning my shirt.

"What are you doing?" I hissed.

"We need to convince them you're good enough to be worth it." He finished with the buttons and stood behind me, pulled the shirt off my shoulders and let it fall on the ground.

I stood frozen in place, unable to look the girls in the eyes. I never felt more self-conscious in my life.

"What do you say?" Jeff tried to sound relaxed, but there was an edge to his voice.

"Hot," the blond said. "But we still need to—"

"He has a great cock."

"Jeff!"

"Drop your pants and show them."

"What? No way."

"Show. Them."

I turned around to face him. "I'm not doing that here. It's freezing, and it's messed up."

His eyes blazed as he grabbed my belt. "I didn't wait all these hours for nothing. Show them, or we'll have a problem."

I shook from both cold and fear, his threat floating between us. Protecting my dignity would end up with me being beaten up in front of those girls who wouldn't be much help. I grumbled and turned around, my eyes glued to the ground. My hands shook as I started opening my zipper. If my face were one degree hotter, my cheeks would've melted.

"You two are crazy," the blond one said in disgust. "You need to work on your issues. Anyway, we're out of here." To Jeff, she said, "Happy birthday."

I remained open-mouthed and watched them go back to the club, taking with them my hopes of catching a goddamn break. "I'm sorry," I said and rubbed my face. "I tried."

"Put your shirt back on and get in the car." The calm in his voice worried me more than his shouts could have.

I put on my shirt and slipped into the car, the heat from the AC defrosting my body. We started driving and Jeff didn't turn on the radio. The silence was heavy, pressing against my chest. It was too much for my fragile nerves.

"Jeff, I'm sorry it didn't work out. Those two totally

led us on. Maybe it's a French thing."

He shrugged. "You tried. Shit happens."

A wave of relief rushed through me. "Thanks for understanding. These things are way trickier than I remembered. We'll have better luck next time."

"Good." He glanced at me and then back at the road. "And since I have you here, I'll still be getting some action."

"Well yeah, and also—wait. What?"

"You heard what I said."

"Yeah, but I don't understand."

"Don't see what there's to understand. I told you earlier I have no intention of ending the night alone —I was clear about that. So tonight, I'll have to compromise." He snorted. "Although it's apparently my birthday."

I hesitantly asked, "What do you want me to do?"

"You have a mouth and a pair of hands—use them."

I forced a chuckle. "Good one."

He shook his head. "Wasn't trying to be funny."

I watched his face, hoping and failing to find cracks in his stoic stare. "Listen—"

"Choose your words carefully."

"I am, but I'm not going to do this…this thing you're talking about. There's no way in hell."

He didn't respond, just kept looking straight ahead. I didn't know if I should speak or wait for my refusal sink in. Before I could decide, I got slammed against the door when he sharply turned the wheel. "Jeff!"

He drove like crazy on a dirt road. I braced myself against the dashboard, sure we were about to crash into a tree or a deer. He suddenly stopped the car with such force, I would have been thrown through the windshield if it wasn't for the seat belt. Clouds of dust rose around us, blocking the view of the trees and sky. I breathed fast, my hands gripping the dashboard like a lifesaver.

Jeff said, "Get out."

I rubbed my bruised chest. "What?"

"Get the fuck out!" He put his hand under the seat, and I was sure he was going to pull out a knife.

"Jeff, let's talk about this. I—" It wasn't a knife; it was a gun.

"Out!"

I fumbled with the door handle and considered making a run for it, but I was sure to get lost. I got out as Jeff came to stand in front of me, the gun in his hand. I couldn't help but take a step back.

"You're trying to run?" He aimed the gun at my face.

"I'm not!"

"Go over there." He pointed to an area in front of the car. I walked without breathing with him following closely behind. The night air was freezing, clinging to my bones.

"Stop," he said. "On your knees."

"What are you—?"

He pushed me down. Little rocks dug into my knees and the car lights burned my eyes. The realization that these might be the last moments of my life sank in.

"Got something to say?"

I shook my head, my brain empty of words.

"Back in the car, you were talking about not wanting

to do something. Care to remind me?"

I didn't, but he was holding a gun, so it was clearly his show. "You said…you *implied* that you want me to suck you off later."

"And?"

"That's messed up."

He smashed the back of his hand across my face, sending me down on the cold ground. My ears rang like a foghorn went off inside my brain. I moved my mouth to make sure my jaw was intact.

"You're unbelievable." He spat on the ground. "It's like you're programmed to screw things up. I should just end you now and save myself a world of trouble."

I turned on my back. My eyes landed on the gun aiming at my face. It wasn't smart to get angry at the man who was about to shoot you, but my self-control was hanging by a thread. "I don't know what the hell you want from me. I was *this* close with those girls earlier. Maybe do something about that tattoo on your neck to make it a bit less goddamn hard."

Jeff rubbed his face. "Shut up and lie still." He crouched next to me. "Open your mouth."

"What?"

"Open it or I'll break your teeth!"

Every nerve in my body trembled, a collision of fear and fury. Looking at the gun moving closer to my face, I used my remaining common sense and opened my mouth.

Jeff slowly slid the barrel between my lips. The cold taste of iron took over my tongue, the tip of the barrel pressing against my throat. I breathed through my nose and fought the need to gag, wondering if I'd feel anything once he pulled the trigger. My brain would probably explode before I'd notice anything.

When Jeff slowly began moving the gun back and forth, it took me a few seconds to realize he was fucking my mouth with the barrel.

"See that? You're a goddamn pro." His breath puffed out in white clouds.

The back of my throat filled with saliva until I managed to swallow without choking. Minutes passed and the cold leaked into my bones, making me forget what warmth felt like. The next time Jeff pulled the gun out of my mouth, I yelled, "Stop! What the hell's wrong with you?"

He moved the gun close to my face, then the world shattered when he fired.

I screamed. My ears rang so loudly I feared my brain might split in two. I rolled to my side, my knees to my chest.

"For Christ's sake, calm down." Jeff put a hand on my shoulder. "You've got the message?"

I could barely hear him, but I managed a quick nod.

"Fine. Let's get back and—wait. What's that smell? You pissed yourself?"

I was about to say, "Hell no," but there it was—a warm wet feeling spreading across my crotch and scorching me with shame. *Shoot me and be done with it.*

Jeff sighed and stood up. "I'll put a towel on the back seat. Get yourself together and head back to the car." He walked away, the sound of his shoes on the ground getting weaker.

I took a deep, cold breath and pushed myself up from the ground. Small stones fell from my clothes as I walked in my piss.

Jeff waited next to the back of the car. He told me to turn around and roughly wiped the dirt away.

"Get in."

I sat on a towel, the heat in the car a blessing on my skin. I wanted to throw away my jeans and underwear but sitting naked was not a good idea. Jeff got in and watched me in the rear-view mirror.

"My ears are ringing," I said.

"Because you don't have a brain between them. Take this." He gave me a bottle of water and I gulped it down.

When we started driving, I leaned my head against the window, shut my eyes, and focused on inhaling and exhaling while the metallic taste of the barrel still lingered in my mouth.

4

The drive felt endless. My head bubbled with ominous thoughts while the heat in the car dried the degrading wetness from my crotch.

Jeff lived on Jamesway Drive, a relatively new neighborhood on the west side of town. I remembered the locals being up in arms back in the day from having tall buildings "polluting the scenery."

The elevator took us to the tenth and top floor, opening into a stylish hallway with pictures of meadows and still-life flowers. The quiet and the cleanliness carried an eerie feeling, although I was probably nervous enough to feel that way about anything.

Jeff opened the door with both a key and a digital code. Inside, the apartment caught me by surprise. Almost everything was either black or white, elegant without trying too hard. The place was huge, the living room bigger than my entire apartment. The kitchen was state-of-the-art, and the entire side of the living room was one big window. A wide wooden bookcase was packed with old-looking books.

"I didn't think you were living in a place like this."

Jeff stood in the kitchen, pouring himself a glass of red wine. "Where'd you think I live?"

A cave, I almost said. "Never mind. Do you have clothes that I could borrow?"

"Yes. The bathroom is the second door on the right."

His bathroom looked suspiciously clean. When I took off my dirty clothes, it struck me that everything was clean because Jeff had planned on having a girl in here right now.

The room had a bathtub. I hadn't been in one for over a year, but taking a bath now wasn't a good idea. My eyes looked bloodshot in the mirror, the green in them almost unnoticeable. I had a bruise on my right temple and a red mark on my stomach. How had this night turned into such a colossal disaster?

I stepped into the shower. The hot water untangled my muscles but did nothing to ease my stress. I was in the middle of washing the soap off my skin when the bathroom door suddenly opened. Jeff's silhouette appeared on the other side of the glass door.

"Brought you clothes," he said and left.

I turned off the water shortly after, then put on the clothes he'd brought. The "clothes" were only long pajama pants.

"In here," he called when I got out of the bathroom.

The door of the last room was slightly open. Jeff was standing in front of a big closet, taking off his clothes until only his underwear remained. The green snake was wrapped around his torso in a death grip. Someone put a lot of thought into this tattoo; the scales looked alarmingly real. I spotted something odd on his abdomen. "Is that...?"

"Yes."

"Who shot you?"

"Doesn't matter. He's not a problem anymore." He went over to the bed, which was big enough to fit three people, then dimmed the lights and lay on his back.

"Come here."

"Jeff, please."

He sighed. "You fucked up one time too many. Get your ass over here and make me forget about this disappointing night."

I was stubborn—too stubborn for my own good—but even I knew when the battle was lost. I stopped next to the bed and didn't know what the hell I was supposed to do.

"Get in."

I took a deep breath like I was about to dive into the ocean, then lay on my back and stared at the ceiling with my hands on my stomach and my body tense. I couldn't stop thinking of every mistake I'd made that led me to this pitiful moment. *Am I making you proud, Dad?*

"Should I slap you around to get you in the mood?" Jeff pulled down his underwear.

I'd hoped he was only trying to scare me, but this was the real, R-rated deal. I moved to lay on my side, and there it was—Jeff's cock. Like me, he was cut. I tried to picture putting it in my mouth, and a wave of nausea ran through me.

Do it already. It's not a snake.

I raised my hand and held Jeff's cock in my shaky palm. It was warm, not yet hard. I began stroking him. It felt different and yet familiar.

"Harder," Jeff said. "I'm not fragile." He was lying with his eyes closed, face relaxed. I kept stroking him, feeling him hardening in my palm. I forced my eyes to look at anything that wasn't the naked body lying next to me.

"Enough," Jeff suddenly said. "Use your mouth."

"It seems you're enjoying my hand plenty."

"Matt…"

Goddammit. I closed my eyes and leaned my head toward his cock. I caught a sniff of his musky scent and unintentionally gagged. I swallowed spit and tried again but got the same result. "I'm gonna be sick."

"Jesus Christ."

My stomach painfully cramped. "I'm not faking."

He growled and looked me in the eyes for a long, stressful moment. Finally, he said, "Just keep stroking. Damn you."

Feeling so relieved my head spun, I gave him the best hand job I possibly could. Five minutes later, while my arm was already strained, his body began shaking. There was something deeply unnerving about watching a guy's face so closely when he was about to shoot. Jeff came all over his stomach with a deep moan I didn't want to ever hear again. I managed to stay clear of the landing zone, but my hand got disgustingly sticky.

Jeff slid his hand under the bed and pulled out wet wipes. I took some and cleaned my hand while Jeff cleaned himself.

"Can I go wash my hands?" I asked.

"Go on."

I walked over to the bathroom and washed my hands with a lot of soap. Back in the bedroom, Jeff was lying with his hands behind his head.

I stood by the entrance. "It's almost morning. I'm going home."

"No. Albert's expecting you later today, and he lives closer to me than to you."

"Do you have a spare room?"

"I use it for a gym. Get in."

With a sigh, I climbed onto the bed. The mattress felt better than what I had in my apartment, but Jeff was lying too close for comfort. I tried to clear my head, but my mind was being held captive by dark thoughts. *What happened here could be the beginning of something much darker.* I had no guarantee my next attempt would end up better since Jeff would still be Jeff next time around.

I cleared my throat. "I have something to say."

Jeff grumbled, "You usually do. Make it short."

"I'll try to make sure next time will turn out better, but even if it won't—I can't do this again. What we just did, I mean. It's not right."

After a long moment of silence, he said, "I went to prison a while back."

I frowned. "Okay..."

"I fucked guys there. It was the best way to make someone understand that you own him." He turned his face toward me, eyes covered in shadows. "I own you, Matt, but I didn't fuck you tonight, although that would have been reasonable considering what you were supposed to set up. For your sake, you better chill out and not overthink it."

If he said those things to make me *chill out*, he failed miserably. My skin turned hot as my pulse quickened. I couldn't stay there; I needed to breathe fresh air and be away from him. "I want to go home."

"Enough."

"I'm not a prisoner. I'm leaving." I started getting up, but Jeff grabbed my arm.

"You fucking did it this time. Get down to sleep on the floor."

"What?"

"Get down on the floor. No pillow and no blanket." I began to open my mouth, but he squeezed my arm harder and hissed, "One more word. Come on, give me one more word."

I didn't give him any more words. A cold shiver ran across my skin, making me feel like we were back in the middle of nowhere and he was once again aiming a gun at me.

He let go of my arm, and I slid down to the cold floor, knowing my body would be a mess if I slept like this for more than an hour. It was somewhat symbolic to finish one of the most degrading days of my life sleeping on the floor.

Worked up as I was, I was also so deeply exhausted that even the cold, hard floor couldn't keep me from eventually falling asleep.

5

Pain shot through my side with the first movement I tried to make. I stopped moving and listened to the rain pouring heavily outside while my brain gradually became functional. I forced myself to sit with a hiss of pain, then got up and stretched, bringing much-needed blood into my stiff muscles.

Jeff's bed was empty. The thought of what had almost happened there earlier made me consider sneaking out the window. Then I remembered we were on the tenth floor.

When I opened the door, the light caught me by surprise. I blinked until it was safe to open my eyes again, then gingerly walked through the hallway.

Jeff called, "I left a toothbrush for you in the bathroom."

His voice irked me. I went inside the bathroom and brushed my teeth. My eyes looked puffy and red. My light brown hair needed a trim, but at least it covered the bump on my temple.

I went into the kitchen, where the rain was louder because of the big window in the living room. The sky was overrun by one gray cloud that seemed to stretch all the way to Massachusetts.

"Eat," Jeff said. He was sitting next to a round, white

table, reading a big book about the Roman Empire. I never thought of him as a reader, but it wasn't like I knew him or cared to.

A plate with an omelet, vegetables, and cheese was waiting on the table next to a glass of orange juice. Without speaking, I sat and began eating. The omelet was cold but still tasted good, and the orange juice was fresh. I still preferred my morning Doritos than a breakfast made by Jeff.

"I see you managed to sleep," he said and put down the book. His plain clothes were gray, not the usual black. It was unsettling eating breakfast in his home. Up until yesterday, he'd been but a ghost lurking in the shadows, making himself visible when it was time to demand money and threaten to break my bones.

Jeff said, "It's already past noon. The taxi will be here soon."

"Fine."

He watched me quietly as I ate. When I finished, he casually said, "You're as smooth as a woman."

"What's that supposed to mean?"

"Just an observation."

I crossed my arms, feeling too exposed. "Well, I'm not."

"I'm not talking about your legs or your pits."

"I don't know why you're even talking about this."

"Just something I noticed." He shrugged. "You don't look feminine because of it."

"Good to know." I drank more juice, hating how easily he could press my buttons.

"I need you to understand something," he said. "It

will make your life easier if you do. Are you listening?"

"Yeah."

"There are two types of people who don't pay me back. The first type will probably pull through if I put enough pressure and give them a bit more time. The other type—people like you—will never get close to paying me back, and it's up to me to fix that." He held my gaze. "I usually kill people like you, Matt. That's the way it is. And yet here you are, very much alive thanks to the deal with Albert, the deal that yesterday you almost destroyed. So don't forget—not even for a second—how close you are to falling off the edge. Understand?"

I swallowed the growing lump in my throat and managed a quick nod. Despite being seated, it felt like I was going to fall.

"Good," Jeff said and leaned back in his chair. "Your clothes are next to the TV. The taxi should be waiting downstairs."

"Where does Albert live?"

"In Jeremy Hill Forest."

"People live there?"

"He does."

I went to pick up my clothes—now clean, although the back of my shirt had scratches. I got dressed, then Jeff came and handed me a small silver box.

"What's that?"

"A peace offering. Look at it later." He went to open the front door. "Call me when you get home."

I nodded and walked toward the entrance. When I was about to leave, Jeff grabbed my arm. "Don't screw up again. I mean it."

*

I've seen my share of Victorian houses, but Albert's house was in a different league with its two towers, wide porch, and Boston Ivy vines covering a large part of the walls. Since it was autumn, the leaves formed a brilliant orange, yellow, and red canopy. The American flag waved in the wind from one of the upper porches. I could only imaging how my shitty apartment must have looked like in his eyes.

"You know the guy who lives here?" the taxi driver asked.

"Sort of." I unbuckled my seat belt.

The driver whistled. "Must be loaded."

"Yeah, looks like it."

"I was told to come pick you up in about an hour."

I wondered if an hour would be enough to cause any permanent damage. "Try to be here on time," I said. "If I'm not coming out, can you please call the guy who ordered the taxi?"

He frowned at me in the rear-view mirror. "Uh, sure, I guess."

Once he drove off, I stood for a long moment in front of Albert's massive, isolated house. A tall cluster of pines blocked most of the sun's rays, creating an eerie atmosphere. The smell of dirt and rain brought back childhood memories of summer camping with my dad. We used to drive up north for the rivers and wildlife, sometimes as far as Maine. Dad wasn't big on camping, but he used to say my mom had loved New England's wilderness, so I should experience it as well.

"Are you coming in?"

Albert's deep voice startled me. I looked up and saw him in the double-hung window on the second floor.

"I'm coming."

The iron gate buzzed once I got close. I walked on the short path and knocked on the tall, wooden door. Looking around, it seemed as though the garden was well taken care of; there was even a small fountain with fish in it.

Albert opened the door with a smile. "Welcome to my humble abode." His clothes were less formal than yesterday, but they were still nice. His dark hair was combed to the side in a dorky fashion.

"Your house is not very humble," I said.

"Well, I suppose you're right. I found out about it from an article. A family used to live here." He sighed and walked inside. "A tragic affair, I'm afraid."

I followed him into the kitchen. "What happened?"

"Murdered. Throats slit. Happened on Christmas Eve."

The vivid mental image almost made me stumble. "That's sick. And you *moved here*?"

He opened the fridge to a bright glow that illuminated his face. "Why shouldn't I? I was the one who killed them."

I took a step back. "The hell?"

Albert laughed and shook his head. "Oh, your naivety is lovely. No, I did *not* kill the family who lived here. They moved away." He poured cold water into a glass. "Now, take this water and relax."

Still wary, I took the glass and drank. The entire kitchen was beautifully lit by the sun leaking through the windows.

Albert said, "Today we'll mostly run a few more minor tests to get a better understanding of your current physical state. I will also need your help with something else, but we'll talk about that later."

I nodded and put the empty glass on the table. "Listen, about what happened yesterday—I didn't mean to hurt you. You just caught me by surprise."

He nodded. "Apology accepted. In truth, I felt quite nervous myself, what with finally having a partner for my work. You might even call it a dream come true." He offered me his hand. "Let's say that today we're turning a new page in our partnership."

There was no way I was looking at this as a *partnership*, but I couldn't handle another dose of Jeff's anger. I shook his hand. "Okay."

He smiled, the excitement in his eyes making him look younger. "If you'd follow me, we can get started."

I went with him to the back of the house. Everywhere I looked, there was art, making it feel more like a museum than a house. I wasn't big on art, but I could tell when something was ugly enough to be very expensive.

"You live here alone?" I asked.

"I do. It can get lonely at times, but I prefer not to risk my privacy."

That was the second time he'd mentioned his privacy to me. I was tempted to ask, *what's the big deal?* Yet a part of me felt more comfortable embracing ignorance.

A big picture of a soldier with a flag in the background hung on one of the walls. The guy in the picture looked like a younger, slightly manlier, version of Albert. "Is that you?"

"Oh, no. Close enough. This is my twin brother, Henry."

"Is he still serving?"

Albert's posture stiffened. "Henry is somewhere in Afghanistan. They couldn't retrieve his body. He was captured and tortured to death, and the...people who did it took his body with them. I have videos they sent, of them trying to make him say horrible things about our country. But not Henry, not for those monsters."

I hated talking about death, especially after my dad died. I cleared my throat. "Sorry about your brother. He was a hero."

Albert nodded and patted my back. "That he was. And now it's up to me—up to us—to make sure our forces on the ground will not be subjected to these sorts of threats in the future. We will make sure no more families are forced to lose their loved ones."

I remained silent, wondering how I found myself with the fate of our troops on my shoulders. I could barely pay my electricity bill.

We kept walking further into the house until we reached a tall bookcase packed with old-looking books. Albert's expression turned serious, voice almost down to a whisper. "What you're about to see must only remain between us. I'm putting my trust in you, the same way I expect you to put your trust in me. Is that clear?"

I nodded.

He moved aside some books, revealing a little hole in the wall. It would have been impossible to notice unless you were deliberately searching for it. Albert slid the tip of his finger inside the little hole. Two seconds later, a mechanical voice said, "Please supply vocal confirmation."

"Albert."

"Confirmed."

He pulled his finger out as the bookcase started sliding silently to the side.

"It's like a movie," I said, torn between being impressed and freaking out.

"Oh, I didn't want it to be overly dramatic, but privacy is crucial here. There's only one way to enter my lab, and this is it."

Behind the bookcase, there was a regular-looking door. Albert opened it without a key, revealing a dim flight of stairs that led below ground. He stepped inside and I followed, my senses on full alert. The door closed by itself behind me. I tried opening it while Albert went down the stairs, but it was now locked. A small fingerprint scanner was attached to the door. I exhaled a tight breath and cautiously stepped down the stairs into a big, white lab.

"Damn. Is this all yours?"

"It is." There was pride in his voice. "It took me a long time to bring it to this state. The original house didn't have a secret underground lab, obviously."

I gawked at all the shelves with the medical equipment. There was a big examination bed in the middle of the room and a separate side room with a glass wall and a red mattress covering the floor.

"You'll get used to it," Albert said as he put on a white doctor's coat. "There's a bathroom over there if you need to use it."

"I'm fine."

"Then let's begin, shall we?"

He measured my height and weight, took samples of my hair and spit, and even scratched the side of one of my teeth for whatever reason. He followed that with generic medical questions before casually hitting me with, "How would you describe your mental state?"

The question was more loaded than a gun. "Pretty shitty, I suppose."

"Were you a happier person growing up?"

"Yes." There hadn't been many reasons not to be. Growing up without a mom could have cast a shadow over my childhood, but Dad had been more than enough.

Albert asked, "Have you ever thought about taking your own life?"

That one got under my skin and scratched my nerves. I reluctantly said, "I never hurt myself, but I thought about it after I had to shut down my dad's company."

"I see." He nodded while writing notes on his tablet. "Dark times tend to test our resistance."

"Yeah, I've been tested."

He put away the tablet. "Well, Matthew, no more intrusive questions for today."

I was about to tell him, again, to call me Matt, but he was going to keep calling me what he wanted to.

He said, "All we're missing is a blood test, but only if you haven't eaten in the last twelve hours."

"I have."

"Next time, then. I would now like your help with testing a cough medicine."

"I haven't been coughing."

"That's okay. Please lie down."

The bed felt hard and cold underneath my back. The sterile scent in the air made me uncomfortable. Growing up knowing my mom had died because of a reckless doctor had left a lasting effect, and it wasn't likely to change any time soon.

Albert said, "I will begin by causing you to cough, then I'll give you the medicine and monitor its effect."

"Is it dangerous?"

He narrowed his eyes, enough to transform his demeanor into something less friendly. "I don't appreciate these sorts of questions. What I choose to give you will not be questioned. Do you understand?"

"I didn't question you. I wondered."

He took a deep breath and seemed to be forcing himself to relax. "No harm done. But please avoid doing that again in the future. I know what I'm doing. Now, stay still."

He dripped a few drops of something into my mouth. I began coughing almost immediately as burning coals ignited in the middle of my throat. The pain became worse every time I swallowed, but I couldn't help myself from sucking down saliva to put out the flames.

"It burns," I croaked.

"That's good. It will be over soon."

He calmly watched me while I continued coughing myself to death.

"I need water," I managed to say while the pain started spreading down toward my chest.

"Not yet. It might affect the test."

He got up and peeked inside my mouth with a flashlight every few minutes. After the fifth time, he said, "Let's continue." He then dripped something cold and oily down my throat. The coughing stopped a moment later. The change was so drastic it felt as though I'd imagined coughing earlier.

Albert examined my throat and seemed pleased. "Feeling better?"

I touched my neck, still wary at the sudden change. "I think so."

"Then today was a success. If you feel any pain later, drink tea with lots of lemon. You might cough a bit of blood, but let it pass on its own."

I gawked at him. Cough blood?

He pulled out a white envelope from his coat pocket. "This is for you."

I sat up, took the envelope, and peeked inside. "This money is for Jeff."

"No, these 500 dollars are for you. The rest I will transfer directly to Jeff."

"He asked you to do that?"

"He did."

"Oh. Thanks." I shoved the envelope into my back pocket. I hadn't had this much money on me in a long time. With my shitty luck, I'd probably get myself mugged on my way home.

Albert needed to use his finger to open the door, but not his voice. When we walked toward the entrance, he said, "If you're not too busy, you can stay and watch TV with me. I bought a new one recently."

I couldn't think of many things I wanted to do less than hang out with Albert. "I have some things I need to take care of."

"Oh, well. Another time." He opened the entrance door. The taxi was waiting outside. "Thank you for your time and company." He sounded like I'd done more than cough for him. "I will see you again in a few days. Next time, make sure to fast for half a day for the blood test. This is mandatory. Please also remember that anything we did in my lab must not be shared with anyone else."

"Okay. Don't worry."

He smiled. "Enjoy the rest of your day, then."

*

When the taxi driver dropped me off in front of my building, it felt like I hadn't been there in over a week. Everything looked cleaner after the rain but having spent time in both Jeff and Albert's houses, my neighborhood now seemed way dirtier. The entire area was a failed attempt from thirty years back to make Hudson more modern. Now, all the streets south of Philbrick Street were occupied with unkempt buildings and broken promises.

I entered my building and climbed the stairs. On the second floor, the Broslavskiys were arguing inside their apartment. The door suddenly flew open as Bill was shouting, "It's your sister, you talk to her! It's not—oh,

Matt, haven't seen you in a while."

"Is that Matt?" Molly came to the door. She was in her sixties, small and stocky with long gray hair and a kind face. "How are you, dear?"

"Oh, you know me—same old."

Frowning, she nudged her husband. "Doesn't he look pale and skinny to you?"

Bill rolled his eyes. "He's fine. You think everyone looks skinny."

She shushed him. "You need some of my stew, dear, I can tell."

"May I?"

They both looked at me with obvious concern. I should have acted less eager, but a home-cooked meal sounded like a perfect remedy for my crappy mood.

Bill said, "Get the kid some food, Moll." He was a big guy with a heavy mustache, all gray like his short hair. He used to have a couple of stores around the area, but he'd sold most of them and only kept Abby's Corner, a furniture store.

Molly went back inside while Bill and I stayed in the hallway.

"How's things at the store?" I asked, knowing I'd need his help after Jeff had demolished what little I had.

"Work is busy, but I'm grateful. Thank God it's not so simple buying a couch on Amazon." He fixed his yarmulke and said in a lower voice, "You do look pale. There's also a bump on your head."

"I was clumsy, had too much to drink with some friends. You know how it is."

"I see. Remember that we're here if you need

anything."

"Thanks," I mumbled. Hearing his concern made me uneasy. Pity was always hard for me to digest.

To my relief, Molly returned quickly with the food. "Here you go, sweetie. I hope it's enough."

"It's more than enough. Thank you." I hurried up the stairs before they had a chance to ask more question.

*

The stew felt wonderful in my grateful stomach as I lay lazily on the couch, allowing my body to relax after the last chaotic twenty-four hours. I pulled out the money envelope from my pants pocket and carefully took out the bills, my heart doing a happy dance. Like a weirdo, I put the bills to my nose and sniffed them, half-expecting them to carry a special scent. They obviously didn't.

I put the money on the table and remembered the small silver box Jeff had given me. I pulled it out and peeked inside. Two well-rolled joints lay comfortably next to one another, waiting to be inhaled straight into my lungs. It wasn't enough to make Jeff any less of an asshole, but a gift from an asshole was still a gift.

I wanted peace and quiet while I smoked, but that would have been unfriendly of me, what with Caleb always offering me some of his goods. I took one of the joints and climbed out onto the fire escape. It was cold outside but bearable. The cold last night in the woods had been far worse. I shivered and pushed the memory away, convinced it would pop into one of my nightmares.

"Yo, Caleb. Come here."

He raised his window after a few seconds. The sunlight on his face made his eyes milkier than usual. "What's up, Matty?"

"I got me a nice something-something, if you know what I mean."

"Pussy?"

"What? No. Weed."

"Well, why didn't you say so?" He climbed out the window—something that wasn't easy for him—and sat on his side of the fire escape.

I took the first drag and then one more. I could already feel something pleasant happening behind my eyes when I offered Caleb the joint.

"Good stuff," I said.

He took a drag. "Yeah, sure is. How'd you come to possess a beauty like this?"

"Long story."

Caleb nodded, his eyes thoughtful. "It's just what I need in case they come after me tonight. I for sure wanna be high for that."

He was talking about the aliens again. They'd gotten hold of him when he was younger, and ever since then, he'd been expecting them to come back. He claimed they were the ones who'd messed up his eyes, but Bill said it'd happened while he was in Vietnam.

"You don't need to worry about some damn aliens," I said. "I'll kick their asses if they try getting near here."

"Ooh, you're a tough one, Brother Matt. I'd like to see you in action someday. But remember, whatever you do, be careful of their tails. Those things are deadly, believe you me."

"Dangerous tails. Got it."

He frowned, adding more lines to his wrinkled forehead. "Thing is, now they started following me in a police car!"

"Huh?"

He narrowed his eyes and whispered, "You didn't see the police car across the street?"

"Uh, nope."

"Oh, it's there all right."

"Well, maybe they're here to help you out with the aliens."

He turned his head and spat on the ground. "Ain't no cops gonna help me. I'd rather take my chances with *you*."

"Gee, thanks."

He chuckled. "By the way, how was the night out with your friend, Wreck-It Ralph?"

My mind went back to lying on the cold ground with Jeff's gun deep in my mouth. Not knowing if those were my last moments on earth. "It was fine."

Caleb twisted his lips but luckily dropped the subject. He brought out his newspaper and handed it to me with a pen. I flipped through the pages and found the crossword puzzles section. Caleb's eyes couldn't handle the small font, so it was my gig to read the wording and write down his answers. Even mildly high, he was sharp with his vocabulary, while I was struggling to make my handwriting readable.

About twenty minutes passed when my phone started ringing. I handed the newspaper and pen back to Caleb, then stumbled inside to see Jeff's number blinking on my phone. I'd forgotten to call him.

I sat on the couch and answered the call. "Hi."

"You're back home?"

"Yeah. Sorry for not calling." I forced myself to keep my voice even. As much as I hated and feared him, my well-being depended on his fickle mood.

He said, "What I tell you to do is not a request."

I pinched the bridge of my nose, hating being talked to like that. "I get that."

"How was your meeting with Albert?"

"Fine."

"Just fine?"

"I didn't shove him if that's what you're asking."

"Refreshing news. We'll have another go at you-know-what tomorrow."

"Tomorrow?"

"Is there a problem?"

I hoped for a day of quiet, but I didn't want to poke the bear. "No problem. When should I be ready?"

"Eight o'clock. We'll go to a dance bar."

"Which one?"

"Does it matter?"

"I don't want anyone I know to see me." I made sure to stick to my part of town in hopes of avoiding running into anyone I knew. Meeting Sharon had felt like scratching an open wound, and I preferred to avoid doing that again any time soon.

Jeff told me the name of the place, and I didn't recognize it, which was a good sign.

"Did he give you the money?" Jeff asked.

"He did. I thought you'd be keeping everything."

"I don't have anything to gain by having you starve or become homeless."

It was depressing to think how likely those two possibilities were. "Thank you."

The line went quiet for a few seconds before Jeff said, "Have a good evening, Matt. Bring your A-game tomorrow."

6

I was still mentally drained the following day and decided to take things easy. My only accomplishment was getting my laundry done. When Molly saw me on the way back, she offered to help with ironing.

Sitting next to the Broslavskiys' kitchen table, I ate a dream-like stack of pancakes with maple syrup while Molly made my clothes presentable. She and Bill had a nice apartment, maybe the biggest in the building. Once you got past Molly's obsession with little dolls and sculptures of angels, you couldn't help but appreciate how homey everything felt. There was a picture of their late teenage daughter, Abigail, on the wall, looking like a younger version of Molly.

"How have you been spending your days?" Molly casually asked while finishing one of my shirts.

I shifted uneasily in the chair. "I've been mostly working on different projects, but nothing I can talk about." I played with the sticky syrup on my plate.

"It's not that I don't enjoy having you around, but wouldn't it make more sense for you to spread your wings and move somewhere else?"

I was tempted to let her know my wings had been thoroughly clipped. "I like it here. It's my home." In truth, Hudson hadn't felt like home in a long time, and I doubted it ever would again.

Molly said, "As much as I love it here, I can picture you doing much better in Boston. Didn't your parents used to live there?"

"Yes."

"Got any other family members there?"

"Nope. My mom and dad were both only children. Seems to be a family curse."

"Oh, don't put stuff like curses into your head. Let's see…you could also move to New York. I do hate the noise, though, and the smell is dreadful. But there should be plenty of opportunities for a young man like you in the big city. I have a sister there…"

I kept listening with half an ear, feeling lousy that even Molly was trying to send me away. Her heart was in the right place, but since moving wasn't a relevant option, thinking about it was like salting an open wound.

"I always pictured myself living in a small town," I said as Molly began sailing too far with her New York propaganda. "My dad offered to pay for out-of-state college, but I wanted to stay close."

Her smile was warm. "I'm sure he appreciated it."

"He would've appreciated it more if I'd stuck around to help."

"What do you mean?"

I shook my head. "Never mind."

She eyed me suspiciously. "I have a feeling you've been carrying around too much baggage. Maybe it's time to throw some away. You'll feel lighter."

"It's not so simple," I mumbled and hurried to ask,

"How's it going with the magical ironing?"

Suspicion was still visible on her face as she slid my folded clothes toward me.

"Amazing. Thank you." I got up, eager to return to my apartment where I was safe from explaining my unstable existence.

Heading toward the entrance door, Molly called behind me, "Remember what I said—less baggage."

*

By the time Jeff came to pick me up later that night, I had jitters coming out of my ears. I tried to convince myself it couldn't go any worse than last time, but it most definitely could.

Jeff was wearing his trademark black clothes, but his shirt had a high collar that covered part of the snake tattoo. I knew better than to comment on that.

We drove in silence, and I gazed out the window at the full, bright moon. Thirty minutes later, we arrived at an open shopping complex that had seen better days. Different types of clubs and bars surrounded the big parking lot. I recognized where an old ice cream shop used to be years ago. *'Forget your problems with the best ice cream in all of New Hampshire!'* I could have used a bit of that magical ice cream right about now.

Considering it was a Sunday night, there were relatively a lot of people hanging around. Jeff pointed at a place that had the word *Fusion* glowing above it in blue neon lights.

"You ever been there before?" I asked.

"No, but I heard it's good. You ready to get the job

done?"

"I'm going to do my best."

He shook his head like I'd already failed and we were just wasting time.

We walked toward the club and were about to cross the road when I suddenly stopped and couldn't move a muscle. *Goddammit! This can't be happening.*

Jeff realized I wasn't walking next to him and turned around. "Come on."

I shook my head, limbs numb. He came back. "What's your problem?"

I walked back until I was out of the streetlight. "I can't go in. You see those guys over by the entrance? I can't be at the same place with them."

"Did they beat you up?"

"No. We used to be friends."

"I don't follow your dumb logic."

I rubbed my face, unable to stop the memories from playing in my brain. "When I found myself with no money, I asked my friends for help, but they acted like jerks." *How's it going in the granite business, Evans? Struck your first million yet?*

"I won't be able to talk with any girls with them around."

Jeff glared at me. "I didn't come here for nothing, Matt. Again."

With my heart beating fast, I glanced around and pointed at a different club. "What about this place? Looks cool."

Jeff snorted. "If you're into leather. The girls there will..." He scratched his chin and nodded. "Yeah, all right. We can go there."

I let out a sigh of relief. "Thank you."

He stepped closer and leaned into my face. "You'll find me something good tonight, won't you?"

"Yes. The best."

"But if you don't, what will I do then?"

Ice spikes poked my stomach at the thought of another failure. I took another glance at my old group of friends. Hell, simply standing in the same area made too many unpleasant emotions bubble up inside me.

I cleared my throat. "If I can't deliver, I'll help you out instead."

He scanned my face like he expected me to crack, but I kept my cool. He finally nodded and turned around. "Let's go."

*

It took me about five minutes to wonder whether I should have taken my chances with my old group of friends.

Jeff chuckled. "Told you so."

We were drinking at the bar, watching whatever the hell was happening around us. The women looked nasty, and the men looked even worse. There were people with pointy leather collars, and almost everyone had piercings or tattoos. Some were dancing, but with that kind of heavy metal music, you couldn't truly dance. Or speak. Or think.

I leaned closer to Jeff. "Maybe we should try a different place. I don't think these *ladies* are your type."

"Don't play games. Get to work before I start bleeding

from my ears."

"Fine." I took one last sip of beer and went over to the dance floor. The red lights made everyone look covered in blood. I caught looks in my direction from both women and men. An older guy with too much hair gel step in my way.

"My my, aren't you a lovely sight. All that's missing in a collar around your neck."

I forced a tight smile and tried to go somewhere else, but he blocked my way. "You don't need to play hard to get with me. Let's go to my place; I'd like to see you on all fours."

I scratched my crotch. "Listen, I have crabs, but if you don't mind, we could—" And off he went.

A couple more minutes passed of me strolling around like Alice in 'weirdo' land. People didn't respect personal space; I had my ass groped every two minutes. I was on my way back to the bar to get more alcohol in my blood when a woman stepped in my way. She was a tall redhead with big honey-colored eyes and round cheeks. The leather thing she wore made sure people wouldn't miss any important quality of her body. She seemed a few years older than me, and damn, she was hot. I loved redheads.

"First time here?" She had a southern accent but a subtle one.

"Is it that obvious?"

"Oh, it is. Keep walking like that and you might find yourself being dragged into the back room. Plenty of action's taking place over there."

I gawked at her.

She laughed, and I pretended not to notice the bouncing of her breast. "You're here by yourself?"

That was my opening. "I'm here with a friend. See that crazy guy over there?"

"Yeah…Is he your master?"

"No-no. It's not like that. We came here tonight hoping, you know, to meet a nice lady."

She snorted. "Here?"

"You seem nice enough." I gave her one of my smiles.

"Well, aren't you as sweet as sugar. Are you and your friend looking to meet a nice lady *together*?"

"Hmm…yes."

She looked at Jeff, who caught her looking. He was startled for a moment, but then raised his glass and gave a wink that seemed more like a mild seizure.

"You guys are from around here?" she asked.

"From Hudson."

"I've never been."

"Well, then you're missing out on…nothing really, other than my wonderful company."

Her smile was all red lips and white teeth when she leaned closer. I got a sniff of her rosy perfume. "I think your friend might be my type in bed, but you seem a bit…delicate."

"What? No, c'mon. Me?"

"I'll go check." She turned around and walked toward Jeff, who handed her a fresh glass of beer. She drank half of it in one go. Jeff stared at her like she'd stepped out of a magazine.

"Thanks. Name's Ruth."

"You don't look like a Ruth," Jeff said.

She scowled. "What the fuck is a Ruth supposed to look like?"

He blurted, "Less leather, probably."

She snickered and tilted her head at me. "Your friend here—what's your name, Sugar?"

"Matt."

"Your friend Matt is looking for a nice lady for you two to take home. Thing is, seems to me like he won't be able to handle the action. He might start crying, and that will make me feel bad."

"Matt? Nah, he's a tiger."

She eyed me. "Is he now?"

"The wildest guy I know. Kinky like you wouldn't believe."

My face heated up, but the red lights made it hard to tell.

Ruth smiled. "I'll take your word for it. Come here, Sugar." She grabbed my shirt and pulled me for a kiss with a lot of tongue and lips and more tongue. Then she moved to kiss Jeff, and it dawned on me that soon he and I would be having sex with the same woman. The taste of victory was bitter in my mouth.

7

We left the bar and walked toward the car. A guy was standing with his back to us, peeing on a wall. When he turned around, I sharply looked away. My entire body went cold, but I kept on walking.

"Evans? Is that you?"

Damn. I turned around. "Hey, Nick."

"My God, it is you! Where you've been, man?"

"I've been around."

Years of friendship flashed in front of my eyes. Camping in the woods when we both pretended to be brave while the coyotes howled in the dark. My first ever drive after I got my license. Nick sitting beside me talking about college and how we were going to leave Hudson to study miles and miles away.

"We thought you sold yourself to a circus or something." Nick came closer. I could easily smell the alcohol on his breath. "Come say hello to the guys. They'll go crazy when they see you."

I shook my head. "I need to go."

Nick looked past me at Jeff and Ruth. He was too drunk to hide his confusion. "Sure you don't want to come for a drink? My treat."

"I'm sure. Good night."

I turned around to leave, but he grabbed my arm. "Oh

man, guess what. Sharon's there as well! She'll *die* if I walk in with you." He started pulling me toward the club. "It will only take a few minutes. I'll give you fifty bucks for your time."

I shook him off. "I said I need to go."

He frowned like no one had ever said no to him. "What the hell? You want a hundred?"

"Fuck you."

"Hey, watch your mouth. Now my money isn't good enough for you? You were fine with it when you came begging like a hobo." He started laughing. "Remember that list? *Matt Evans's Special Rates*! We pissed ourselves when we wrote it."

My fist flew forward and smashed into Nick's face, catching him off guard and sending him to the ground. Nick looked up, eyes wide and his hand holding his jaw.

I opened my mouth to apologize, but couldn't get the lie out. Bastard had it coming. Nick's eyes suddenly narrowed. It was clear he was going to jump at me. I caught a sudden movement as Jeff came to stand beside me. "Think hard if you want to take this further."

Nick opened his mouth but ended up saying nothing. He got up and stumbled toward the club.

"Let's go before you cause any more drama," Jeff said and walked away.

*

"You okay, Sugar?" Ruth asked. She was sitting shotgun while I was in the back, staring out the window.

"I'm fine." I didn't know if that was true. A part of me hoped to someday bury the hatchet with my old group of friends, to have them reach out and apologize. Tonight, I'd burned that bridge to the ground.

Ruth and Jeff talked with each other during the drive. Ruth said she was a secretary and a yoga teacher. Jeff was, apparently, working in real estate. He sounded awkward talking to her, but his awkwardness gradually faded thanks to Ruth's natural chattiness.

Once inside the apartment, Ruth insisted we should all drink vodka. I needed to push Nick out of my thoughts and numb the pain in my hand, so I drank while those two started making out in the living room.

When Ruth said she was going to powder her nose, I tried my luck and told Jeff, "Listen, she's totally into you."

He put on jazz music and came closer. "What do you want?"

"I was just thinking you don't need me getting in your way. Three's a crowd."

He put his hands on my shoulders but without the familiar anger in his eyes. "We've gotten too far to start risking it. You did well up until now, but you could still screw this up like only you know how. I need you to relax and roll with whatever happens, okay?"

"Yeah, okay."

His lips stretched into a crooked smile. "I liked how you handled that guy earlier."

"I'm not sure it was smart to lose my cool."

"When a guy has a big mouth that needs closing, you help him out. Don't stress over it."

Ruth came out of the bathroom. "You boys haven't started without me, I hope."

Yeah, I just can't keep my hands away from Jeff.

"Not yet," Jeff said and gave me a final warning look.

Ruth had removed her high heels but still wore her leather outfit. When she got closer, Jeff moved to stand behind me and said, "I think Matt's afraid of you."

She sized me up and crossed her arms under her breasts. "I think so as well."

"I'm not."

"Maybe you should be." There was such intensity in her eyes, it turned my knees into jelly. Jeff put his hands on my waist, then slowly pulled my shirt over my head. Ruth was even closer now, placing her soft hands over my bare chest. It would have been nice if I wasn't painfully aware of Jeff standing so close behind me. He also took off his shirt, and now his warm skin was rubbing against my back.

Shivers ran through me when Ruth started kissing my neck, then continued traveling down until her lips and teeth reached my nipples, leaving me both numb and shaky. When Jeff started loosening my belt, it hit me that this was really going to happen with him tonight. He pulled down my pants and underwear, leaving me the only naked one between us.

Ruth started stroking my cock, her mouth still sucking on my nipple. I tried to ignore Jeff's warm breath on the back of my neck. Without saying a word, Ruth went down on her knees and put me in her warm mouth. Her lips were big and soft, and her tongue was... my God. It was a miracle my shaky legs could support me. I was completely hard by then, able to ignore sharing this intimate moment with another man. The vodka sure helped; I was light-headed, my senses foggy.

Ruth suddenly got up and put her wet lips to mine, making me taste my salty self on her tongue. She turned her head and started kissing Jeff, whose head was right next to mine. She switched from kissing him to kissing me like she was considering which meal to order.

Jeff said, "We should get the bed warm."

"Lead the way."

Jeff went first, then Ruth wrapped her hand around my cock and pulled me behind her. Inside Jeff's bedroom, she slowly removed her leather outfit and stood there in all her glory. I openly stared, soaking in every curve of her body like I needed to memorize it for a test.

She smirked. "Are you gonna do something or are you too used to watching porn?"

I was all over her in a heartbeat. My mouth couldn't get enough of her soft skin. Her hands didn't rest as well, exploring my body and leaving me hot with need.

Jeff went to get a condom. When he came back, I reluctantly moved aside to give him room, reminding myself this was about *his* pleasure. After rubbing his cock with lube, Jeff positioned himself between Ruth's bent legs and slid inside. She threw her head back and let out a deep groan, her fingernails digging into his back. I wondered if I should look away, but it seemed modesty wasn't welcomed in this room.

Jeff started thrusting into Ruth, his waist moving like angry waves. Between moans, Ruth said, "Matt, where's your dick at?"

I perched on my knees next to her face. She started sucking me, and every nerve in my body melted with pleasure. I toyed with her hair, loving the feeling of those red curls between my fingertips.

Jeff slapped my ass after a few minutes and said, "Your turn."

I put on the condom with a smile I couldn't contain. I hadn't had sex in ages, and Ruth was the kind of woman guys usually dreamed of. Jeff pulled out of Ruth and climbed off the bed, his face lit with bliss.

I asked Ruth, "May I?"

She laughed. "Oh my, such manners! It's like an old movie."

I didn't know which old movies she'd seen with threesomes in them, but I wasn't about to go in without asking. Still, I took her laughing at me as consent and slid myself inside.

God, I missed sex. There was almost no resistance as I pushed myself as deep as I could. She wrapped her legs around my waist and kissed me hard and deep.

Being so physically close to someone after all these months of isolation made every second more meaningful. It wasn't solely the physical act, but rather the feeling of sharing something intimate with someone. It made my skin transparent, my nerves exposed. I knew this intimacy was fake, but it filled an empty void inside me I'd almost given up on.

You fucked up too many times to deserve this feeling.

The familiar voice of self-judgment echoed in my head. I fought to silence it but failed. With my cheek resting beneath Ruth's chin, I shut my eyes as they began to sting.

Ruth gently stroked my hair. “Sugar?”

“I’m sorry.”

“It’s okay. Take it easy.”

I focused on my breath and let that guide me to mental safety. I was acting ridiculous, adding drama to what was supposed to be a celebration of sex.

“Drink.”

I opened my eyes to a blurry cup of water held by Jeff. I drank while Ruth kept stroking my hair, her other hand moving gently across my back.

“Sorry,” I mumbled. “I don’t know what happened.”

“No harm done. You’re up for showing me some more good time?”

I realized I was still hard inside her, and I needed more. I began to rock my hips, found my rhythm and lost myself in the movements of our naked bodies.

Ruth suddenly said, “Let’s try something different.”

I stopped moving and caught my breath. “Different?”

She looked at Jeff, her red curls stuck to her forehead. “Will Matt here go along with my wicked ways?”

He eyed me, not unkindly but with determination. “He will.”

She should have asked me that, but maybe she’d figured out something was twisted between us. She nibbled my lower lip and said, “Trust me on this. I want you to have fun.”

I kissed her damp neck. “I am having fun.”

“Oh, this is vanilla fun. Let me show you what *real* fun feels like. Lay on your back. No need for a condom now.”

I sighed and pulled out, threw the condom to the side, then gingerly lay with my back in the middle of the bed. The sheets were damp from sweat but carried a faint scent of rosy perfume.

Ruth sat beside me and asked Jeff, "You've got something to tie him up with?"

"Handcuffs."

"Bring them."

I raised my head. "Wait, what?"

She stroked my forehead "You just stay quiet and pretty."

Jeff opened his closet and came back with handcuffs. Even he seemed hesitant with this turn of events.

Ruth cuffed me to the head of the bed, not tight enough to hurt but enough to make it clear I wouldn't be going anywhere. Jeff came to sit on the other side of me. I felt vulnerable between them like I was about to be sacrificed with a dagger to my heart.

"Nothing for you to fear," Ruth said and ran her fingers slowly across my stomach. She and Jeff moved closer to my face until I could smell the alcohol on their breath. Ruth continued running her hands over my skin, soft fingers that made me shiver. I tried to relax and enjoy it, but when Jeff suddenly touched my balls, I hissed, "You mind?"

He whispered in my ear, "Killing the mood is the wrong move right now."

I caught the warning in his voice and forced myself to calm down. It was hard feeling like I was part of the experience since they were the ones making the decisions. But with Ruth's hands roaming my skin, and

Jeff's hand keeping me hard, I was able to let my guard down.

Ruth quietly said, "You're doing great, Sugar. And such a beautiful cock you have there."

I smiled. "You think so?"

"Are you fishing for compliments?"

"Sure am." I cleared my throat. "Say, can I come soon?"

"That's the plan." She played with my armpit hair, tugged at it gently. "But before that, be a sport and spread your legs."

"To...spread my legs?"

She whispered in my ear, "You ever had your hole played with?"

"My hole? You mean...oh, no. No way."

"A virgin, then. Thought so. You're gonna *love* it."

"I'm one thousand percent sure I won't. Listen, I like what we've done so far, but—"

She kissed me, hard and wet. If she thought a kiss would make me go along with her crazy head, she had no idea how stubborn I could be. But Jeff knew me well enough. He whispered in my ear, "Do what she says."

Ruth stopped the kiss and asked Jeff for the lube. My pulse quickly rose, and I was painfully aware of my cuffed hands and zero control over what was happening. "It's not a good idea."

Ruth chuckled. "Don't knock it till you've tried it. Now spread and bend your legs."

"Goddammit." I reluctantly did what she said. When she started rubbing cold lube on my asshole, I stopped breathing, feeling more naked than ever before. I wanted to shout at Jeff that this was not a part of the plan; I was there to help him get laid, so what the hell was I doing cuffed and spread like a turkey?

Ruth started circling my asshole with her finger, a slow and wet movement too alien for my brain to fully grasp.

"Deep breaths," Ruth said like I was having a goddamn baby. Then she pushed her finger inside.

"Fuck! It hurts."

"Relax your body and it will stop hurting."

I tried to unclench my asshole and not dwell on Ruth's finger being halfway inside my body. The pain was bearable, but the embarrassment was not. Ruth's finger slowly sank deeper, increasing the feeling of wrongness. But her pace gave my clenched muscles time to adjust to the invasion. Before I knew what was happening, the friction of her finger with my skin sparked deep pleasure in the middle of my groin. It was impossible to keep calm.

"There you go, Sugar. Nice and easy."

My hard-on was back, ignoring my brain. When Ruth twisted her finger inside me, sharp pain appeared, only to be quickly replaced with an even better sensation.

"I'm putting another finger in," she announced.

I raised my head. Seeing them both between my spread knees was unsettling. When Ruth started pushing another finger in, I bit down on my lip until she pushed it all the way inside. Her fingers slid in and out, firm movements that opened me up even more. The pain was there for a little while but gradually vanished. Waves of pleasure crashed against my consciousness as she played me like a piano. Electricity danced inside my waist.

When she made her fingers into a hook and twisted them inside me, bright stars exploded behind my eyelids. Without thinking, I pushed myself onto her fingers, opened myself up to this mind-blowing sensation that ought to be illegal. My precum dripped on my stomach. Ruth scooped it up and licked it clean while she held my gaze. The sexiest thing I'd ever seen.

Ruth asked, "You wanna shoot, Sugar?"

"God, yes. Please."

Jeff chuckled. I hated having him see me like this, this nakedness that was more than physical.

Ruth sharply twisted her fingers again. I moaned as my body shuddered from my toes to my scalp. Wherever she was pressing inside, it was the right spot to press.

With a teasing voice and a pinch to my nipple, Ruth asked, "You sure you're ready?"

"Yes. Ready. So freaking ready."

"What do you think?" she asked Jeff, who looked at my pleading face with a blank expression.

"Jeff, come on. You guys are killing me here."

"You seem alive to me." His eyes slid down. "Alive and dripping."

"Fucker. Please."

He finally nodded. "Let him shoot."

A minute later I came with a cry that echoed through every nerve in my body. Hot drops of semen landed on my stomach and chest as my butt cheeks clenched around Ruth's fingers. The feeling of relief was absolute, mind-blowing and liberating.

Ruth gently pulled her fingers out. I shook all over, the strain in my muscles becoming noticeable now that the adrenaline was fading. Right next to me, Jeff and Ruth went at it. I had nothing to do but look at Jeff pounding into her, making the entire bed shake. I was completely forgotten by then, and that suited me fine.

When Jeff climaxed, it sounded like Ruth did as well. They breathed into each other's faces, their intimacy making me uncomfortable.

Once Jeff pulled out, Ruth spread on the bed with a deep sigh. He kissed her pale stomach. "You're good?"

"Oh my, is that an understatement. Who knew Hudson offered such pleasures?"

Jeff went to bring the key and uncuffed me. We exchanged looks and I had no idea how to read his. It was clear something between us had changed tonight, yet it remained to be seen to what extent.

"Go take a shower," he said.

Walking to the bathroom wasn't easy thanks to my stiff muscles and the lingering sensation where foreign fingers had recently been. I stepped into the shower and let the water burn my skin and wash the stickiness away. I might have survived the craziness, but it hadn't left me feeling clean.

Back in the bedroom, Ruth was lying on her stomach with her eyes closed. Red hair spread around her head and on Jeff's hairy chest.

"She's asleep," he said when I entered. "Get in."

I thought of asking to go home, but it had ended poorly last time. I slipped into the bed and lay on my back next to him, the thick scent of sex still lingering in the air.

"Thank you," Jeff said.

I expected snowflakes in hell before I ever heard him thanking me. I pushed my luck and asked, "Will you give me some slack now?"

After a moment, he said, "We'll see."

8

The bed was empty when I woke up at around noon. My clothes lay folded on the nightstand next to the bed. I had a mild headache but nothing a strong coffee couldn't fix.

I got dressed and went into the living room, where Jeff and Ruth were sitting on the couch watching TV. He wore pants while she was naked, her head resting on his shoulder. They looked comfortable with one another, which sparked a pang of jealousy I didn't see coming.

"The sleeping beauty awakes," Ruth said when I came closer. Her skin was much paler in the light of day. "You feeling all right? Not too damaged?"

"I'm okay."

"You sleep like a baby, Sugar, even drool a little like one."

"I do not!"

They both snickered.

"Anyway, I need to go."

Jeff nodded. "Albert will be waiting for you tomorrow. A taxi will pick you up from your place at around one o'clock."

"Okay."

"Is this Albert a friend of yours?" Ruth asked. Her fingers—two of which had recently been inside me—

were playing with the dark hairs on Jeff's chest.

"He's a business partner," Jeff said. Even after last night, it was odd seeing him sitting to relaxed next to Ruth. It made me ponder on how easy it was to label someone as a specific type of person. I wasn't more fond of Jeff this morning, but I did acknowledge I didn't have him figured out like I thought I did.

"Okay," Ruth said. "See you around, Sugar."

I left them sitting on the couch and went to look for a bus on my way back to sanity.

Later in my apartment, I indulged myself with Jeff's second joint and invited Caleb to join. The high-quality weed helped push away thoughts of last night's craziness. I still didn't appreciate the way it all went down, but I was satisfied with the possibility of a less violent Jeff. If I was being honest with myself, I'd enjoyed being an object of desire. At this point in my life, I was willing to embrace any possible boost to my self-confidence, although I preferred it to be less intrusive.

"Those damn aliens are still out there," Caleb said while puffing out smoke. "Sitting in that damn car."

"Yeah, I saw the police car earlier. Must belong to someone who moved here."

He rolled his milky eyes. "Brother Matt, you're what is commonly known as *naive*. At least you've got the charm to make up for it."

"Much help it's given me."

Later that day, I did my round of collecting free local newspapers, then sat in my apartment and cut out coupons. This had turned into a sad hobby of mine during the last year. The coupons were usually for bread, cheese, and snacks, but I got lucky with one for a pair of underwear and one for towels. I shoved the coupons into my wallet and set out on a poor man's shopping spree.

*

After spending the following morning running and then grabbing a greasy steak bomb from a new deli, I was ready for the taxi at one o'clock. On the way to the forest, Jeff called. "Where are you?"

"On my way there."

"When you're done, tell the driver to drop you off at my place."

"Okay...is everything all right?"

"Just get your ass over here when you're done." He hung up.

What was that about? Maybe something to do with Ruth? Had she given him herpes? Damn, had she given *me* herpes? I pushed those thoughts away. Worrying about the meeting with Albert was enough for one brain to handle.

"God damn, this house is massive. I didn't know anyone lived out here."

I had a feeling I was going to go through this exact scene with every new taxi driver.

Albert greeted me at the door, looking fancy in a yellow button-down shirt and neatly pressed pants. "Matthew, nice to see you again."

"Thanks. You don't have to dress up every time I'm here."

He chuckled. “I was raised to dress nice whenever I have company. You may be my partner, but you are also my guest.”

“Okay, but I’m going to stick to my flannel shirts.”

He patted my shoulder. “You do seem to be fond of those. Now, please, come in. What an exciting day we’ve got planned!”

We started walking toward the back of the house when a sudden scream echoed through the hallway. I froze, a tight pressure seizing my chest. “What’s going on?”

His face flushed. “I can explain.”

Another scream, louder than before. Whoever this guy was, it sounded like he was dying somewhere in the house.

I raised my voice. “Where the hell is he?”

His shoulders slumped. “Follow me.”

I shrank away as he walked past me, then followed him at a safe distance. We entered a wide living room with a fireplace and more abstract art. When I saw where Albert was pointing at, my stomach dropped from embarrassment.

“I thought…”

“I know. It’s fine.”

He picked up the remote and came to stand beside me.

I asked, “What movie is this? Gross.”

“It’s not a movie, I’m afraid.”

On the screen, a naked guy was tied to a chair. His sweaty skin was covered with cuts and bruises. He screamed again when someone kicked him in the chest.

I flinched. "Is this…?"

"My brother."

"Were you watching this?"

"I was. It helps keep me focused. Do you want me to start it over for you to see?"

"You serious?"

He shrugged. "It might help you as well. We all need a motivational kick every once in a while."

Seeing a guy being tortured right before I was about to enter an underground lab wasn't what I had in mind when thinking of motivation. "I think I'll pass if that's all right." I had already averted my eyes.

Albert turned off the television. "I forgot it was on."

"That's okay."

"You think they're dead?"

"Who?"

"The monster who killed Henry. I was told they were, but I'm a man of facts, and I didn't get those." He shook his head with a sigh. "I guess I'll never truly know."

"I'm sure those bastards are six feet under."

He gave me a small smile. "Thank you, Matthew. Let's continue."

Once down in the lab, he asked, "You had a good night's sleep?"

"Yeah."

"Good. It's important you come here at your best. Now, let's get the blood test out of the way, and then we'll continue with—"

"Oh, damn."

"Pardon?"

"I forgot about the blood test. I ate like three hours

ago."

"You...ate." His lips turned thin. "I was clear with my request, very precise. I need you to work with me, not against me."

"I am working with you. I just forgot. Sorry."

He let out a deep breath, removed his glasses, then cleaned them with his shirt in quick and angry movements. I caught him mumbling, "So clear...I was so clear," before he suddenly shook his head and put on a thin smile that was downright spooky. "No harm done. But since you don't seem to be on the same page with me regarding the importance of my work—"

"I am."

"Don't interrupt. We now have no choice but to jump ahead into something more significant."

What the hell is happening? "You're taking this the wrong way. I have a lot on my mind these days, and I went running to clear my head, and then I was starving and—"

"Enough!" He pinched the bridge of his nose and took a deep breath. When he looked at me, the anger in his eyes was fierce. "What we're doing here is far more important than your childish need for a run. I thought you understood that. Now, remove everything but your underwear." He went to the bathroom while I anxiously took off my clothes. I hadn't seen this side of him before, and it made it clear I had no real grasp of whom I was dealing with.

Albert came back and handed me a bucket, then went to take a small bottle from one of his drawers. "Open your mouth."

I forced my jaw to move, stopping myself from asking what was in the bottle. A single drop slid down my throat, carrying with it a sour taste. My gag reflex kicked in as my stomach painfully cramped. Next thing I knew, everything I'd eaten that day came gushing out of my mouth and into the bucket.

"It would be better for you to have an empty stomach," Albert said in a flat voice. "Drink this water and take this mint." He took the bucket into the bathroom, where I heard him dumping the contents of my stomach down the toilet.

By the time he came back, my stomach felt less raw, but my fear had reached a new peak.

"Lie down on the bed," Albert said, avoiding my eyes. He then asked me to bend my knees and move my arms up and down. "You have full control over your limbs?" he asked.

"Yeah, usually."

"Answer with a yes or a no. Do you sometimes lose the feeling in one of your limbs?"

"No."

"Have any of your family members ever had a medical issue with one of their limbs?"

What does that even mean? "No."

"Good. Get up and follow me." He led me to the side room with the red mattress. "What will happen now is not something I planned on trying for a while, but it seems appropriate considering your newfound attitude."

I bit my lip because he wouldn't have liked what I wanted to say. Having both him and Jeff talk down to me was pushing my self-control to its limit.

Albert continued, "You will stand over there and walk slowly to the other side. During this time, I will release a small amount of gas into this room and that should affect your limbs. You'll be able to hear my voice from the speaker over there. Do not panic, and do not ignore my orders. Are we clear?"

"You're going to gas me? For forgetting to fast?"

"Stop acting like a child. Do you understand my orders or should I repeat them?"

"I heard you."

"Good. Go stand where I instructed you to."

I went to stand at the side of the room, my pulse going wild. I had goosebumps from the cold air on my exposed skin.

Albert closed the door behind him, and I made a mental note of the four-digit code he'd used for the panel on the wall. A loud *click* sounded, and a second later tight pressure filled my ears. I moved my jaw to unclog them.

"Do you hear me?" Albert's voice came out of the speaker.

"Yes."

"Wait for my order and then start walking. Slow steps." He went to stand next to the computer on the side of the lab and opened a folder on the screen. When he clicked on one of the files, three circles appeared. He moved the mouse to the left circle, which turned green once he clicked on it. From there he moved to one of the cabinets and took out a gas mask. Seeing him putting on that black mask while wearing his white lab coat was the stuff of nightmares. He went to stand by the glass wall, eyes small and foggy through the mask. An engine inside the wall rumbled to life.

"Begin walking."

I closed my eyes and took a deep breath, telling myself that nothing bad was about to happen since he needed me alive to help save the world. I opened my eyes and took a step forward, then another. By the third step, something felt wrong, like ants began crawling across my skin.

"Albert, I—"

"Don't stop."

Another step followed by another. The ants became frantic, digging their way underneath my skin. I didn't see them, but they must have been there since the feeling was too real to be a figment of my imagination. I opened my mouth to tell Albert to stop the gas, then my legs disappeared. I hit the mattress with full force, the awkward landing shoving the air right out of my lungs. It was pure luck I hadn't banged my chin on the ground. I turned to look at my legs, surprised to see them still connected to my body. I felt nothing below my waist.

"What the hell?"

"Relax, Matthew. Please try to—"

"Don't tell me to relax! What happened to my legs? Get me out of here!"

"I simply paralyzed you temporarily." His voice was so matter of fact, it infuriated me.

"Bring back my legs!" I slapped my thighs and pinched my skin, desperate to feel my legs were still alive.

"Soon you'll get your legs back. Try to reach the other side of the room."

"What? *How*?"

"Your hands are working, are they not?"

I smashed my fist on the mattress. "Get me out of here!"

"Do as I say, and then you'll get your legs back. No need to make a scene."

I wanted to hit him so badly, but I wanted to be done with this nightmare even more. With a grunt, I began crawling, my legs dead weight behind me. The muscles in my shoulders and upper back screamed with every inch of progress. What had seemed like a small distance a few minutes ago was now miles and miles. By the time I reached the other side, I gasped for air, skin slick with sweat.

"Good, Matthew."

"Fix this!"

"Soon. I will now run some quick tests." He stepped inside and quickly closed the door behind him.

If you hit him, he might leave you like this for hours.

Albert carried his tablet and a small bag. He took out a syringe with a small needle and sat down next to me. Without a warning, he stuck the needle in my ankle.

"Hey!"

"Did you feel it?"

"No, but don't—"

"Only address me when you feel pain, even the slightest. Other than that, remain quiet and let me work."

He poked all over my legs, but I didn't feel a thing. I

cringed every time the tip of the needle sunk into my flesh like butter, but it was like witnessing it happening to somebody else. When Albert finished with the small needle, he took out a syringe with a much bigger one. My mouth went dry as he casually slid it into my flesh. I was sure this time I'd feel something, but I didn't. Albert pulled the needle out, now smeared with my blood. Nausea hit my raw stomach hard, forcing me to avert my gaze.

A few nerve-wracking minutes later, I turned my head back to the sound of the bag being opened. I gasped. "What have you done?"

"It's only flesh wounds," Albert calmly said. "You've got plenty of blood left."

I didn't know what to say because my brain was trying to make sense of all the small wounds covering my legs and the thin rivers of blood dripping out of them. Once I got my legs back, this was going to hurt. I almost didn't notice what Albert took out from his bag, but when I did, down the drain went my fragile calm. "Don't touch me with that!"

"You won't feel a thing."

"It's a goddamn knife!"

"I don't intend to cut off any of your body parts."

"Oh, cool. No big deal, then."

"I'm losing my patience. You are here to help, not complain."

"Too bad. I'm done with this crazy shit. Bring back my legs and—" He cut me, a swift cut on my thigh. Time moved slowly in the seconds it took the blood to spill out onto the mattress.

I'm going to die in this lab.

"Damn it! See what you made me do." Albert hurried out of the room.

Dizziness hit my brain in a mighty wave. I rested my cheek on the mattress as I fought to breathe. When Albert came back, I couldn't open my eyes, feeling high in all the wrong ways. I heard him using some sort of spray, then the world slipped away.

*

"Matthew. Matthew, wake up."

I opened my eyes and yelped at the sight of a black monster.

"It's okay; I'm still wearing the mask."

I sighed and wiped the cold sweat from my face. The bright lights hurt my eyes. "My legs…"

"I cleaned the blood and closed the wounds."

My head weighed a ton. I couldn't even move it to look. "Give me back my legs."

"Can you try and crawl back to the other side?"

"What? No. Please, enough."

"Well, I wish you would at least try, but maybe we've done enough for one day."

Maybe?

He stood up and left the room, closed the door behind him and walked back to his computer. Through the blurriness, I saw a different circle turning yellow on the screen. The engine came back to life. This time I could smell the different gas, a bitterness that stung my nose.

"Try moving your toes," Albert said.

I tried. "I can't. It's not working!"

"It sometimes takes a minute. Concentrate and try again."

I focused all my willpower and managed to twitch my feet. The rest of my legs came back to me in a matter of minutes, accompanied by currents of pain deep in my muscles. A few drops of blood remained on my skin and the cut on my thigh looked like a thin, pale line.

"You can stand up now." Albert took off his mask and watched me with a stoic face. I carefully pushed myself up on my wobbly legs.

"Get yourself cleaned up in the shower."

I wanted to get the hell away from there, but I had sweat and dry blood on me. The small bathroom still reeked of puke, but I was only there to get a sense of cleanliness. When I finished showering, I dried myself off and stepped outside in my underwear, where Albert was working on his tablet.

"Please lie on the bed," he said without raising his eyes.

"I want to go."

He put the tablet on the table, looked at me, and crossed his arms. "I did something serious to your body, and I need to make sure you're all right. Lie down."

I also wanted to be sure I was back to normal, so I did what he said. He moved my legs and pinched my skin. It hurt, but after being paralyzed, I welcomed the pain.

"You seem to be fine," Albert said in a flat voice like I was already yesterday's news. "Get dressed."

While putting my clothes back on, I forced myself to keep my mouth shut, not trusting myself in those moments. My entire self-control was resting inside a fragile glass box.

Once I was dressed, Albert opened the door with his finger and walked me out. At the front entrance, he said, "I'm sorry today has turned out like this. At least I got a chance to test something I'd only been able to test on monkeys—and they poop a lot."

My God.

"Please remember to fast for at least twelve hours before our next meeting."

I managed a nod.

"Good. This is for you." He handed me a white envelope.

I should have thrown it at his face, but I'd earned every freaking dollar.

"There's your taxi. Have a good day and drink a lot of water. Orange juice would be even better."

Still dazed, I walked toward the taxi, promising myself to never set foot in this house again. I was done with this madness, completely done.

9

"Where to? Hey, where to?"

"What? Hmm..." I was about to give the driver Jeff's address, but I couldn't bring myself to deal with him right now. "Take me to Benson Park."

I'd walk over to Jeff's after I got a chance to cool down. Then, he and I were going to have a serious talk about what had happened in the lab and how it was never going to happen again.

Once at the park entrance, I went to buy a cup of freshly squeezed orange juice from a small food stand. Walking around the park, I remembered riding my bike over the squeaking wooden bridges with my old gang when we were kids. There wasn't a spot in the park where we haven't built a makeshift camp at one point or another. Nick and I used to fight over who would be captain, and at least in those meaningless conflicts I tended to win. It was hard to believe how different my worries had been back then. Hell, how different they had been a year ago.

I came across a small indie bookstore and bought a book about decision making, to hopefully learn about what I was doing so terribly wrong. I found a quiet spot on a bench next to a small garden where locals grew vegetables. Time passed and I embedded myself in the quiet and the book, oblivious to the world around me. Prickly currents swam across my legs every few minutes, more unpleasant than painful.

When someone sat next to me, I slid slightly aside and kept reading, eager to get past the lengthy prologue.

"Good book?"

I glanced up. Shadows from the trees' branches danced across the cop's face. "Mike?"

"Yep. It's been a while. Whatcha reading there?" He read the label. "That's a heavy read, man."

"Yeah, I was just passing the time."

I hadn't seen him since we finished high school. We used to be best friends up until third grade when word spread around town his dad was dealing drugs. My dad had forbidden me from hanging out with him, ignoring my protests. We'd stayed out of each other's way for years up until our fight over Lizzie Williams in high school. I couldn't even remember how it all started, but at one point he shoved me, then I shoved him harder and accidentally broke two of his teeth when he smashed against a door. I'd ended up dating Lizzie for a whole two weeks before realizing we had nothing in common. Up until we finished high school, Mike kept shooting me dirty looks.

"How've you been?" He narrowed his eyes. "You look pale."

"Yeah, I've been having a rough day. No, make it a rough year."

He nodded sympathetically. "Heard about your dad. These things hit you out of nowhere, huh?"

"Ain't that the truth." I leaned back on the bench. "So,

you're a cop."

He saluted. "Officer Johnson at your service. Been on the force for five years now, signed up right after high school."

He looked as though he worked out regularly, and I remembered him being a big deal in boxing competitions. His dark hair was cut military style, his beard well-groomed, emphasizing his high cheekbones. His wide nose and thin lips kept his face from looking handsome, but he had a toughness to him girls in Alvirne High School used to dig.

"You like being a cop?"

"Well, not much going on around our boring little Hudson. It's been almost a year since we had ourselves a good murder case, but at least it's a steady job. What about you? Still running your dad's company?"

I shifted uneasily on the bench. "Ran it straight into the ground. Thought I could jump in and fix everything."

"For real? That's gotta suck. I'm sure you gave it your best shot."

I looked away, the familiar sense of guilt growing inside me. "I don't know about that. My dad started a business from scratch, and I couldn't even keep it running."

"Was it doing okay when you took over?"

"Well, no."

He shrugged. "Then it's not your fault. Let it go."

It felt good hearing him say that, although it was easier said than done. "Thanks."

"Don't sweat it. I ran into Nick and the rest of your old

squad last week. They still seem tight. You're in touch with them?"

That one stung. "We drifted apart."

"Yeah, it happens." He glanced around and then back at me. "So...what have you been doing with yourself, other than being a bookworm?"

I've been going to this crazy guy's lab for money. Other than that, I've been helping a gangster get laid so he won't kill me.

"I'm currently between jobs. Taking it easy for a while."

"I hear you." He looked around again. "So, you're just sitting here reading?"

"Pretty much."

"Got no better place to be?"

"Hmm, no. I'm good."

Mike scratched his beard and leaned a little closer. "It's interesting hearing you say that, 'cause I was under the impression that right about now your ass should be over at Jeff Holden's apartment, not sitting here reading like a pussy." He looked into my eyes, his expression that of a cat who had caught himself a mouse.

I licked my lips, didn't want him to see me panicking. "You're working for Jeff?"

"I'm *working* for the police. Jeff's a good way to make money on the side. My wife has expensive taste. You remember Emily? I used to date her in high school. But let's get back to why you're here right now."

I cleared my throat. "I had a crappy day and needed to sit somewhere quiet for a while. How'd you know I was here?"

He smiled like he was about to happily pluck the wings of a butterfly. "I've been keeping an eye on you."

"What?"

"Didn't you notice my car in front of your crappy building?"

Caleb's aliens.

Mike took out a Marlboro cigarette and lit it, his nonchalant movements a sharp contrast to the uproar inside my brain.

"Jeff's paying you to spy on me?" I managed to sound calmer than I was. Despite being outside, I felt cornered.

Mike took a deep drag and exhaled two rings of smoke. "I guess you can say that. Seems like you're important to him for some reason." He gave me a dismissive once-over. "He's waiting for you right now, but you already know that."

"I'll go see him." I started to get up, but Mike grabbed my arm.

"Not so fast. We'll go together."

"Listen, I really needed to clear my head."

"Hey, man, I'm not here to judge. I'm just the guy who's gonna finish his smoke, then drag your sorry ass over to Jeff. It's all good." He chuckled and blew smoke in my face.

*

"You don't need to do this."

"But it's more fun." He cuffed my wrists behind my back.

"It's tight," I hissed.

"You're welcome to file a complaint. Let's go."

"My book."

"Jesus, you're annoying." He grabbed the book from the bench, then led me toward the park's exit. People openly stared like I was a criminal being brought to justice. I cast my gaze down and hoped Mike wouldn't lead me into a tree. At least his police car was parked close by. He opened the passenger door and shoved me inside, my hands still behind my back.

Mike got in and started the car after putting the seat belt around me. The heavy silence was broken a few minutes later by his phone ringing. He answered from the speaker. "Johnson."

"Listen to you sounding all manly."

Mike laughed. "Trish, is that you, babe?"

"You damn well know it. You finished playing cops and robbers?"

"Not quite. Still have something to do."

"Something boring?"

He glanced at me. "This time it's fun and nothing but fun. Can I call you later?"

"Sure, but I need to know if you're coming over tonight."

"You bet I am. Emily's visiting her bitch of a mom. I'm all yours."

"Oh, I like the sound of that. Talk to you later. Bye."

Mike said, "I'm gonna have myself some fun tonight, Matty boy."

"You're cheating."

He snorted. "Are you my priest?"

I looked out the window, anxiety bubbling under my skin. *All you did was sit and read a book. Keep your cool, and it will be all right.*

"You know, I'm feeling pretty good right now," Mike said.

"Good for you."

"I mean, I've been waiting for this kind of opportunity for years."

I frowned at his smiling face. "What?"

"Don't act surprised."

"I didn't mean to break your teeth."

"Yeah, whatever. My old man beat the shit out of me when we got the bill, but he was angrier about me letting some rich kid get me like that. *You let Richard Evans's son take you down? Are you fucking kidding me?*"

I remembered hearing what a total nutjob his father was. He'd gotten himself killed by doing something stupid a few years back, but I couldn't remember the specifics.

Mike said, "I planned on settling the score right after high school, even got my buddies to go along with it." He glanced at me, and I didn't like the spark in his eyes. "We were gonna shove you into my car and take you to Rangers Town Forest. I knew exactly which tree I'd tie you to and which baseball bat I'd use to break your knee." He shook his head. "But then you had to go on this...what was it, cross-country road trip?"

I nodded, feeling lightheaded.

"By the time you came back, my buddies weren't into it anymore. You were off the hook. But here we are now." He tapped my knee. "Got a hook nice and deep inside you now, huh, little fish?"

I sweated under my shirt, picturing having my knee

broken. "You always were an ass."

"Well, that may be, but now I'm an ass with a gun and authority, and that's a whole lot nicer."

Gray clouds overtook the sky as we parked in front of Jeff's building. Mike uncuffed me once we got outside. In the lobby, an armed guard sized us up, but he let us through. We walked into the elevator and stepped out onto Jeff's floor. In front of his door, Mike said, "Listen, I'm gonna put the cuffs back on. It will make me look more professional."

"We're right outside his door. Leave it."

He grabbed my arm and glared at me. "Turn around and—"

The door opened. Mike quickly let go of my arm.

"Mr. Holden, sir. I found him."

Jeff's angry expression made my stomach drop. He went to the kitchen and asked, "Where was he?"

"I was sitting for a bit at—"

"I wasn't asking you."

Mike smirked and closed the door behind us. "He was sitting at Benson Park, sir. I thought it would be best to see how long he was going to keep you waiting, but after an hour I figured enough was enough and went to fetch him. It wasn't easy, but I—"

"What? Jeff—"

He raised a warning finger at me and handed Mike a bottle of beer. "Go wait on the balcony. It's outside the gym."

"Sure thing."

Once it was only Jeff and I left, he told me to sit on the couch, then came to sit in front of me on the coffee table. Without any warning, he slapped me.

I jerked back. "Jeff—"

"Shut up and listen. Not far from here, there's a bigger shark than me, and it's him I have to answer to. Lately I've been too flexible with the way I handle my business, and it led to people running away with my money. Some I found easily enough, but some I haven't. Now the bigger shark wonders what's going on. Am I getting too soft? Did I lose my edge? You see where I'm going with that?"

"Yes." Jeff had a Jeff of his own. Knowing that sparked a sense of satisfaction deep inside me. *Do you wake up in cold sweat like I do? Did he fuck your mouth with a gun?*

He leaned closer. "Having you working with Albert is a crucial source of income, an income *you'll* make sure won't dry out any time soon. I wanted you to come here to let you know you and Albert will be seeing a lot more of one another, but two things happened since we last spoke."

"Listen—"

"The first one was Albert calling to complain about your cooperation. He said he isn't sure you're the right guy for the job anymore."

I held my breath in anticipation, but Jeff quickly added, "It took some convincing, but he's willing to give you another chance."

I couldn't believe this. Albert had made me paralyzed and cut me, *then* called to complain?

Jeff said, "The second thing that happened was you ignoring a simple order I gave you."

"If you'd let me explain what happened in that

goddamn lab, you'd understand why I needed to clear my head. I was going to come here right after, I swear."

He shook his head. "I don't need you to swear. I need you to follow my orders as though they were the words of God. Albert is a goose who lays golden eggs, and you're responsible for keeping this goose happy. Are we clear?"

I felt physically sick by that point. My hope of reasoning with him lay dead on the ground between us. "We're clear. Can I speak now?"

"Not if it's about Albert; it's none of my business."

"You're the one who's sending me there, so it damn well *is* your business."

He raised his hand to strike, and I quickly covered my face. "All right! Jesus. Can we at least speak about Mike?"

"What about him?"

I lowered my hands. "What's the deal with that?"

"Cops around this district are underpaid and bored. It didn't take much to have a few of them working for me on the side. You're not the only one I need to keep track of."

"I don't need anyone spying on me. I'm not running away."

"I have no way of knowing that. I had others who ran away, people with families and careers. You have none of that. And just so we're clear, if you *do* try to run away, I'll hunt you down and end you. You understand?" He looked straight into my eyes, didn't even blink.

"I…yeah, I understand. But does it have to be Mike?"

"You two have a history." It sounded like he already knew about it, and I had a feeling Mike had bent the truth to fit his narrative.

"That asshole has been out to get me for years."

Jeff shrugged. "A personal job has a better chance of success, and I can't take any risks with you."

"But he—"

"Enough. God, you're a handful." He stood up and called for Mike.

"He's screwed up in the head," I hissed.

"Good. Normal people aren't cut out for this." He glanced at his watch. "I need to go see Ruth."

"Ruth? Like a date?"

"Something like that."

Mike returned and gave me a disappointed glance. He probably hoped to find me bleeding.

Jeff told him, "It was smart of you to wait to see what he'd do."

Mike was practically glowing. "Thank you, sir. I've known Matty for years, so him acting like that was not at all surprising."

I jumped to my feet. "Shut your mouth and go cheat on your wife."

"Relax," Jeff growled.

Mike crossed his arms. "He was always like that, sir—shitty temper and a big mouth. Maybe he needs someone to teach him some manners. He lacks in the respect department, that's for sure."

Jeff eyed me. "That he does."

"You're seriously buying into his crap?"

"How is it crap? Mr. Holden told you exactly what to do, and you gave him the finger. That's disrespectful."

I took a deep breath, on the verge of losing it. "Can I go

now? I can't listen to this anymore."

Jeff was about to say something, but Mike interrupted. "He even asked me to lie and say I only met him on his way here."

I took a step toward him, seeing red. "You piece of—"

"As I said, sir, he was always up to no good. He even took money for sex from a girl he used to date, wanted to start a business out of it."

Rage claimed my body, overpowering my self-control. I jumped on Mike. We crashed on the floor, and I hurried to smash my fist into his face.

Jeff tried to pull me away, but I wasn't done; there was too much rage I'd been keeping bottled up. As I tried to get free of Jeff's hold on my shirt, my elbow accidentally smashed into his nose.

"*Fuck!*"

I looked around and saw Jeff covering his face. When blood started pouring from between his fingers, I knew I was screwed. "Jeff, I— "

Mike slammed his fist into my stomach. I rolled to my side, hissing in pain. If I hadn't puked so much at Albert's, I'd have done so now.

Mike jumped to his feet. "You okay, sir? Shit, doesn't look good."

Jeff hurried to the bathroom, leaving a trail of blood drops behind.

"You're not going anywhere!" Mike shouted even though I was still lying and holding my stomach.

"Don't let him go!"

"I won't, sir. Got him right in time." He could barely open his eye but had a victorious smile. With my mind clearer, it dawned on me I'd been played.

As I slowly got back to my feet, Mike whispered, "You did good, man."

"Fuck you."

"Looks like you're the one who's fucked. I'm so glad I'm not you right now."

From the bathroom, Jeff said, "Damn nose won't stop bleeding. Mike, there's duct tape in the right drawer in the kitchen. Tie him to the chair in the living room."

Shit. I hurried toward the bathroom. "Jeff, I'm sorry. Just—"

"Shut him up!"

Mike pulled me back. He got hold of my arm and bent it behind my back. I groaned in pain. "I can dislocate it in three seconds," he hissed and pushed me into the living room. "Put your ass on that chair and shut your mouth. Don't test me now."

I slumped on the chair, my body heavy and my thoughts swirling too fast. Mike went to the kitchen and came back with duct tape.

I didn't resist as he taped my hands and legs to the chair, painfully aware of the mess I was in. My head spun and I needed water badly, but Mike roughly put duct tape over my mouth before I could ask.

He whispered in my ear, "Not exactly tying you to a tree, but this will do for now. My old man would've been proud." He pinched my cheek, and I pointlessly jerked in the chair. Mike smirked and called, "Did it!"

I focused on steadying my breathing, but it was impossible with my mouth blocked and my head whirling.

Jeff came back holding a wet towel to his nose. He glared at me and went to take pincers and a small towel from the kitchen, then gave them to Mike. "Put the towel under his right hand. Do it to his index finger."

"Uh, do what?"

"What do you think? Take out his fingernail."

I stared at the pinchers with wide eyes, thinking it must be some kind of a sick joke.

Mike frowned at the pincers. "You want me to…?"

"You think you can work for me and not get your hands dirty?"

"What? No-no. It's fine. I just never…" He shook his head. "It's cool. I'll do it."

"I'm going for a quick shower. When I'm done, he better have one less fingernail." He hurried back to the bathroom and slammed the door behind him.

Mike exhaled and sat on a chair he took from the kitchen. He rubbed his face and looked into my eyes. "I'll try to make it quick." He took the pincers and stared at it like an alien thing. I half-expected him to have a change of heart, but his eyes filled with determination as he lowered the pincers close to my index finger. A sob escaped me; I couldn't hold it in.

"Don't start crying like a baby." He smirked. "I knew that bringing up Sharon would drive you crazy. Heard you stopped talking to everyone after word got out you were whoring yourself for greens. Didn't count on a black eye, though. Still, totally worth it. Here we go."

The pincers grabbed onto the tip of my fingernail. I didn't have long nails, so it took him a few seconds to get a solid grip. Then pain erupted, burning and sharp.

Needles of fire swam up my arm, burning between my bones. I sobbed and squirmed in the chair, hating that he was seeing me go through this.

"Calm down, goddamn you. I'm almost done. Just a bit more...there we go. Piece of cake." He left the fingernail on the towel where my blood was quickly soaking in. "Man, that was easier than I thought. Let's take out another one to surprise Jeff." He raised the pincers again and brought them close to my hand. I jerked in the chair, almost falling sideways.

"Don't lose your panties, I'm just messing with you." He went to the kitchen and took a bag of frozen vegetables to put over his eye.

Jeff came into the living room a minute later, his nose swollen but not broken.

Mike cleared his throat. "Oh man, I can't believe this loser did that to you."

I gave him the dirtiest look I could muster, once more furious at myself for falling into his trap.

Jeff wore nice clothes, so it seemed he was still going on his date. He came closer and examined my bloody finger. I couldn't meet his eyes, my anger making my vision blurry.

"You'll need to bandage it, Mike. What you need is in the bathroom."

"No problem. Listen, you have a minute? I think I have an offer for you." Mike came back to the living room and stood next to Jeff, still holding the frozen bag to his eye.

"You think you have an offer, or you have one?"

"I do, sir."

"Shut up with the *sir* shit. It's Jeff."

A stupid grin spread across Mike's face. He pointed at me. "Matt's a troublemaker; I believe you know that by now. I'm not sure what you two got going on, but I do know you need him to go to that house in the forest for money."

"Still not an offer."

"Stop paying me to keep an eye on him—I'll do that for free. In return, let me take over. I'll make sure he learns to behave, and you'll get peace and quiet from not having to deal with this loser." The way the words spilled out of his mouth made them sound rehearsed.

Jeff crossed his arms. "And your reward will be…?"

Mike glanced at me with contempt. "It's complicated."

I shook my head and tried to say "No" through the duct tape.

Jeff watched me with a blank expression, then told Mike, "I don't have the time or energy to handle this anymore. Make sure he learns his place. If he messes up, it's on you."

Mike lit up like a Christmas tree. "Yes, sir. Jeff. I won't let you down."

I tried to make it clear I wanted to speak, but I could only make muffled noises.

Jeff leaned his face in front of mine. "Whatever you feel like saying, keep it to yourself. I gave you more warnings than you deserve." With a softer voice, he added, "I have too much riding on this deal, and I can't have you risking it again. I'll keep an eye on Mike as well, but from now on, *he's* your voice of God." He held my chin. “No problems, no attitude, and no pissing off Albert. I mean it.” He straightened and went to the door. “I’ll give Albert your number, Mike. Promise him there will be no more problems.”

“I’ll do that. Nothing for you to worry about.”

Jeff opened the door and gave me one last disappointed look. “We’ll see.”

10

"Oh man, is this how winning the lottery feels?" Mike did a stupid touchdown dance in front of me.

I couldn't take it anymore. I tried getting myself out of that damn chair by pulling at the duct tape.

"Easy there, tiger. You'll only hurt yourself. I'll get you some water."

I stopped moving, badly needing to drink. Smudges of bright lights flickered in front of my eyes as the stench of my sweat reached my nose.

Mike called from the kitchen, "Jeff is one badass son of a bitch, no doubt about that. I don't know what's going on between you two, but he sure has your balls in a tight grip. Well, technically I have them now, and let me tell you, those little raisins fit right into my palm."

He came back with a bottle of water. "When I take the duct tape off, I don't wanna hear nothing about you being angry or whatnot." He tapped my cheek with the bottle. "Although I do hope you'll give me a hard time."

I was tied to a chair, and we were alone in the apartment, so giving him trouble was out of the question.

He ripped off the duct tape and wasn't gentle about it. I drank from the bottle he held to my lips, hating feeling so helpless. When I finished, he put the bottle on the floor and sat in the chair next to me.

"So...life's funny, huh?"

I cleared my throat. "Hilarious."

He leaned back and put his hands behind his head. "I can't believe I gave up the money from Jeff. If I'd known it would be so easy, I would've asked for a freaking raise."

I forced myself to stay calm and not bite back. It had been dumb to fall into his trap, but I wasn't about to search for another one to stumble into. "Can we talk? No bullshit."

He lowered his hands and leaned closer with an over-the-top frown. "Let me put on my serious face. What's on your mind?"

I needed to reach the part of him that wasn't evil, but I worried I'd be wasting my breath. "I know you don't like me."

He snorted. "I don't like your kind, Matty."

"My kind?"

"Rich kids with so few problems you had to come up with original ones."

"I didn't come up with anything, and I'm broke."

"Serves you right. How does it feel having your so-called friends turning their backs on you?"

He was talking about what happened when we were kids, when I told him I couldn't be his friend anymore. "I was eight, Mike. My dad told me to back off, so I did." It had been fifteen years since then, but I still remembered how angry I was at Dad, and how my stomach hurt when I had to tell Mike we could no longer be friends.

With his face blank, Mike said, "I get it. Daddy

couldn't have his little prince playing in the mud."

"It wasn't like that."

"Doesn't matter. Go on."

"What?"

He rolled his eyes. "You said you have something to say."

I recollected my thoughts. "You and I have bad history, but the shit I'm dealing with…you can't even imagine."

He nodded but remained quiet.

"I know I screwed up today, but this is crazy." I gestured with my head to my tied hands. The tight duct tape made my palms red and numb. "You're a cop. You've got to see how messed up this whole thing is."

He nodded again. "Pretty messed up, yeah."

"Right, so all I'm asking is for you to cut me some slack, okay?"

Mike scratched his bearded cheek. His bruised eye was beginning to swell. "I get what you're saying, but I'm not about to give up on this chance."

"I'm not…I'm not asking for that. I heard what Jeff said, but you don't have to be a jerk about it. Let's try—"

Without a warning, he slammed his hand on my bloody finger. I screamed, but he didn't let go.

"Stop!"

He squeezed harder, sending lightning bolts of pain straight through my arm. "Shut up and I'll raise my hand."

I had to bite my lip to keep myself from screaming.

"That's it, nice and quiet. You can take it."

Fog surrounded my senses. My heart pounded like

drums in my ears, and I was seconds from fainting. Then Mike finally raised his hand, igniting another spike of sharp pain, but at least I could breathe again.

He grabbed my hair and yanked my head up. "If I want to have more in life, I need Jeff on my side, and you're my express ticket to the promised land." He lowered his voice. "I'm not ending up living in the wrong side of town till the day I die. You understand?"

I nodded, feeling utterly spent. The pain from my finger refused to subside.

Mike said, "If Jeff Holden couldn't get you to behave, I know I've got my work cut out for me. Lucky for you, I'm a damn hard worker." He stood up. "Let's get you out of this chair."

"Thank you."

"Sure, man. What's the fun in beating you up like this?"

*

It was raining heavily when we parked in front of my building. Half the streetlights weren't working, and the few shops in the area were already closed.

Mike muted the radio. "I'll talk with Albert tomorrow and let you know when he wants you."

I nodded, my eyes stuck on the moving windshield wipers.

"How's your stomach?"

"You know the answer." He'd made me stand with my back to the wall before repeatedly smashing his fists into my stomach until my guts were about to explode.

"It will hurt more tomorrow," he said. "Fetch me the

plastic bag from the glove compartment before you go."

I opened the glove compartment and pulled out a cramped bag.

"Bring me one of the small packages from inside."

I took out a small black package and offered it to Mike, who twisted his lips and said, "Another one."

I kept my annoyance at bay and pulled out another package, just to have him ask for another one again. After the third one, he shook his head. "You know what, never mind, put them back."

"Jesus." I shoved the plastic bag into the glove compartment and slammed it shut.

"Nice." He smirked. "I now have your fingerprints all over packages filled with cocaine. If you're thinking of splitting town...don't. I'll make it look like you're a dealer who tried to sell drugs to kids."

"Asshole!" I tried to open the glove compartment, but he slammed it back, almost cutting my fingers off.

"Calm down! I don't trust you, and now I have insurance that you're not going anywhere." He grabbed my shirt and pulled me closer to him. "You hear what I'm saying? Answer me!"

"I hear you!"

He let go. "Hand over your ID."

"My ID? Why?"

"It will make it easier putting out a warrant for your arrest."

"Oh, come on."

He raised his fist.

I quickly took out my wallet and gave him my ID. He shoved it into his pocket, then lowered the window and pulled out a cigarette. “You can piss off now. I’ll see you soon.”

I got out of the car and trudged through the rain to my building, then struggled up the stairs while wheezing like an old man. In my bedroom, I slumped on the bed and put my face in my wet palms. I tried to calm the raging storm in my head, yet it kept growing inside me like a tumor.

I looked up at my closet doors. Those worthless things were always squeaking and driving me crazy, mocking me for not being able to afford a replacement. I jumped to my feet and pulled one of the doors so hard it broke right off and almost hit me on the way down.

I should have gone to Jeff straight away instead of going to that stupid park. I should have kept my cool when Mike tried to push my buttons. But most of all, I should have given up on Dad’s company instead of taking on that goddamn loan. He was dead, never coming back, so why the hell would he care about anything?

Every one of my organs was on fire. I bit down on my fist to try and hold it in. I’ve never felt such rage, like a living thing was crawling underneath my skin, threatening to swallow me whole.

The sudden taste of blood cleared my head. I stopped biting on my wounded hand before I could do more damage.

You’re losing it. Don’t let them win.

I drew in deep and measured breaths to untangle the knots in my chest. In the bathroom sink, I carefully washed my hand and splashed cold water on my flushed face, then took two Advils. Back in my bedroom, my escape folder peeked out from under a pile of clothes. I took it out and sat on the bed. Looking through the folder usually sparked a sense of optimism, but it failed to do so now.

My control over my life was slipping further away with every passing day, and it now seemed my escape window had been sealed tight. I had no way of knowing whether those bags truly contained cocaine, yet it seemed likely considering Mike's determination to have his way.

I hid the folder back in the closet and decided I couldn't handle my thoughts tonight. That meant I needed weed. I glanced outside the window at the unrelenting rain. There was no calling Caleb for help. I had an old half a bottle of whiskey lying around, which meant alcohol would be my temporary comfort.

I changed into dry clothes and moved to sit on the couch. I had no beverages to mix with the whiskey, so I drank straight from the bottle. The bitter alcohol swiftly swam into my brain thanks to my empty stomach. With every sip, my thoughts grew foggier and a lot more bearable, making me ponder on whether I should be drunk more often. The pitter-patter of the raindrops soothed me like a lullaby. Right when I was about to drag myself to bed, someone knocked on the door.

I froze and stopped breathing.

"Matt, you're there?"

Thank God. I clumsily put the bottle on the table. Getting up revealed the floor was covered with lumps and bumps. Maybe opening the door like this wasn't a smart decision. Thinking about decisions reminded me I'd forgotten my book in Mike's car.

I opened the door, and Bill said, "Sorry to bother you. Do you happen to have...?" He gave me a once-over. "You're drunk."

I sighed and leaned against the door. "I sure ain't sober."

"And you look like hell. What happened, son?"

Don't call me that. I tried to speak, but a sob escaped my mouth. Before I knew what was happening, I completely lost it.

Bill helped me reach the couch and sat next to me. The alcohol made it easier to let my frustration spill out in torrents, but I managed to calm down eventually.

Bill put his hand on my shoulder. "How much did you drink?"

I eyed the almost empty bottle. "A lot."

"Did you eat anything?"

I shook my head. "Fridge's empty."

"You have a woman downstairs who cooks for a battalion, and you let yourself go hungry?" The anger in his voice surprised me.

"It's my problem."

"All our problems are our own until we decide to share them with others."

I rubbed my face. "You sound wise, Sensei."

"What happened to your finger?"

Even with the haze of alcohol, I wasn't so far gone to start telling him about my messed-up life. "I was clumsy."

"Who did this to you?"

"I can't tell you that."

"Okay, then tell me how much you owe him."

"About a hundred grand." It was hard admitting how deep in shit I was even to myself.

Bill turned pale. "How...how were you able to—?"

"I don't want to get into this right now. It happened. I'm handling it."

"This is you handling it?"

"This is me after a shitty day, trying to stop thinking. Just...no thinking." I smacked my head until Bill grabbed my hand and lowered it.

"What are you going to do?" he asked, unable to hide the worry in his voice.

"I'll manage. I always manage." That was a lie, but I needed to hold on to it or I was bound to give up. I rubbed my eyes. "It's late. I'm going to sleep."

"It's eight o'clock."

"Well, it's late somewhere."

"Go to the police, Matt."

I snorted, although he deserved more than my drunken bitterness.

"I'm serious."

I massaged my temples. "I know you are, but it's not going to happen."

We sat in heavy silence for a long moment until Bill finally said, "Come to the store tomorrow morning. I need another set of hands."

I shook my head. "I don't want charity."

"Boy, I'm almost sixty years old and the furniture isn't getting any lighter. I need your help, and you need the money."

We both knew that what he could pay would not change a thing, but maybe working like a normal person would do me some good. I was starving for stability amid the chaos that had been unraveling around me.

I took a breath and tried to speak clearly. "A lot of stuff is happening right now, so I can't commit. But I'll come meet you at the store tomorrow morning."

"All right. I hope you'll remember that when you wake up. Come on, let me help you get to bed."

In my bedroom, Bill asked what happened to the closet.

"Earthquake," I mumbled and slumped on the bed.

"I see."

He took the blanket and tucked me in, made sure even my feet were covered. Before he left, I asked him not to say a word about this to Molly.

"I won't tell her." He turned off the light. "Except the part about your empty fridge."

"Good." I hugged my second pillow. "Remind her I love pasta."

"I'll do that."

I was asleep before he even closed the door.

Part Two
Down the Rabbit Hole

11

An angry headache wished me good morning. I forced myself to sit and was rewarded with a sharp pain in my stomach. I hesitantly lifted my shirt to the sight of nasty bruises decorating my skin. "Fucking Mike."

I struggled out of bed, stepped over my broken closet door, and slogged to the bathroom to brush my teeth and take a warm shower. Standing under the stream felt like swaying on a rocky boat, forcing me to lean with my palms against the tiles for balance. Once done, I stepped out of the shower and carefully replaced the bandage on my finger, then took an Advil and went to make a strong, bitter cup of coffee. With every vile gulp, my headache subsided until my brain transformed into a somewhat functioning organ.

I had a decision to make: crawl back to bed and dwell in self-pity, or get my shit together and stop acting like a goddamn failure. I drank more coffee and decided I'd been enough of a failure lately. It was time for a different tune.

I went to pick up my toolbox to reconnect the broken door to the closet. I used the opportunity to straighten the other door as well. There were a lot of things I could have done to make my apartment homier. When I'd moved here, I vowed this was a temporary arrangement, a setback I must endure before my bad luck finally runs out. Well, it was time to wake up from that fantasy.

I got dressed and decided to grab something to eat before heading to Abby's Corner. Walking downstairs, the door to Bill and Molly's apartment was slightly open. When I came closer, Molly popped out.

"Finally! I've been waiting for you." Her voice was overly perky compared to my mood.

"I slept like a corpse."

She sized me up. "Seems you drank like a sailor as well. Come in and have something to eat."

I followed her, my stomach making noises of encouragement. The apartment's signature scent of savory home cooking blessed my nose as I sat at the kitchen table.

"I need to go see Bill soon," I said as Molly stormed the fridge.

"Does that mean you're going to help him in the store?"

"I think so. But I'll need to make sure it's not charity."

"Oh, no charity, that's for sure. Lord knows what we'll do if he hurts his back, that stubborn ox. Any help you can spare, I'd be grateful."

After all the times Molly had come through for me, I wasn't about to let her and Bill down. "You can count on me."

"Wonderful. Now, tell me what you fancy, fish or chicken?"

"Well, I wouldn't want to offend either."

"Fish and chicken it is."

I ate faster than I could chew. It didn't matter that I'd just woken up and should have probably eaten something light—Molly knew my stomach by now, and she brought me the goods.

When I stepped outside with a full stomach, the sky was clear of clouds, but the smell of recent rain still lingered in the air. I made my way down Philbrick Street toward Abby's Corner, moving slowly thanks to the disaster-stricken area Mike had left behind. Some people eyed me suspiciously due to my weirdly slow walk and occasional grunts. At least the Advil was starting to kick in.

When I finally got to the store, Bill was talking with a customer about a table that never would have fit in my small apartment. I didn't want to bother him, so I strolled around among the furniture for a while. Many of them looked modern, but some were downright antiques.

"How's the head?"

I turned around. "Better. I drank a strong coffee, and Molly gave me a little something to eat."

"A little, huh?"

We both laughed. I felt awkward talking to him after he'd seen me break down last night, but it was also liberating to walk without my usual mask.

Bill said, "What do you think of my little kingdom?"

"It's wicked."

"Thank you. Now tell me what you really think."

I crossed my arms and gave it another look. "You need to keep the dust away from the furniture and also wipe the floor more often. Maybe think of putting the tables at the front instead of the chairs because the tables need more space, and it could be easier selling chairs after you sold a table."

He looked thoughtful. "Anything else?"

"Maybe change the light bulbs. This blue neon light works better in hospitals."

Bill watched me with a sober face, and I didn't know if I'd spoken out of turn. Being asked for my opinion wasn't common these days.

Bill eventually nodded and said, "Can you start today?"

"I...I think so. But I was serious last night about not being able to commit. Things might pop up, and I'll need to—"

"Whatever you can give is fine."

We talked about the salary, which was fair, and I offered to start with the dust before wiping the floor. Bill said to go ahead.

Cleaning gave me a chance to clear my head from thinking about the mess I was in. The old Motown songs playing in the background were also a nice distraction, and I found myself quietly singing along to some of the songs I recognized.

When Bill told me to take a break, I went outside to try my luck with Jeff. I desperately hoped that putting Mike in charge had been Jeff talking out of anger rather than using his common sense.

I went to a quiet alley where the air smelled like apple pie thanks to the Benson's Bakery close by.

Jeff answered impatiently. "Is this urgent?"

"Yes."

"Speak."

"I'm sorry about yesterday. It was an accident."

"Okay. Anything else?"

"About this crazy thing with Mike—"

"Let it go."

"What does that mean?"

"What I decided yesterday was a calculated decision, and I expect you to do as I say."

"But I'm not a child who needs babysitting, and he's mental!"

"Lower your voice."

I let out a tight breath. "He hit me after you left, although I didn't do anything wrong."

"That was his decision to make."

"Jeff, come on!"

"Listen to me. I need you for the long run, and as things stand now, I don't trust you to deliver. Mike will make sure you remember your commitments and feel the consequences when you forget. I don't want to hear any more about this." He hung up, and I had to go for a walk to steady my heartbeat. I stayed clear of walls since I was itching to smash my fist into one.

The store was much cleaner by the time we needed to close for the day. Before we left, Molly called to make sure I'd come over for dinner, and I agreed since my calendar was empty.

During the meal, Bill told hilarious stories about crazy customers he'd dealt with over the years. Molly filled in the parts Bill forgot, implying she must have heard these stories more than once. I later shared my initial ideas for the store, such as painting the front in a brighter, more welcoming color, and creating a Facebook page for us to use for campaigns. I wasn't an expert in that, but I was willing to learn.

"I have around fifty friends on Facebook," Molly proudly said. "That should be enough to get the buzz going, won't it?"

"Uh, sure," I said. "But we should maybe set a budget as backup."

By the end of dinner, I had Bill telling me to write down my ideas, and Molly giving me pots of heavenly food to fill my empty fridge. Walking up the stairs, my mood was surprisingly decent, like I had this newfound purpose. I hadn't had this feeling, or anything close to it, in a long time.

Opening the door to my apartment, I almost dropped the pots at the sight of Mike sitting casually on my couch.

"Shit! How'd you get in here?" I put the pots on the kitchen table, my hands unsteady.

Mike stood and came to the kitchen wearing his uniform. "You have an old lock on the door—it was easy to tweak it. And I already broke in last week."

"What?"

"Who do you think trashed your place?"

Heat rose underneath my skin. *He broke the Simpsons.*

Mike said, "I can see you're about to say something you shouldn't, so I advise you to take a breath and chill." He came closer. "Whatcha got there? Smells nice. Fetch me a plate."

"Breaking and entering is illegal."

"You don't say? I thought it was frowned upon. Good

thing there's a cop here to keep you safe. Where's my food?"

I sighed and gave him a plate and a spoon, hoping he'd be less of a jerk with a full stomach. He filled his plate and went to sit on the couch.

"Brought back your boring book," he said. "How's your stomach?"

"Great. How's your eye?"

He snickered. "Good one. Told the guys at the station I had a run-in with a drunk. Jesus, who made this? So good."

"My neighbor."

He winked. "You fucking her?"

That was a mental image I didn't need in my head. "It's not like that."

He shrugged and went on eating. I leaned against the wall, keeping a safe distance. Having him in my personal space felt like I'd been invaded.

"Why didn't you call before you came?"

He scowled like my question was out of place. "Well, because I didn't. You better get used to my surprise visits. Not like I'm gonna schedule an appointment with your highness. Oh, I had a chat with your buddy Albert earlier. Guy talks fancy, doesn't he? Anyway, he wanted to make sure you'd leave the attitude out the door from now on. I told him he got nothing to worry about, that I took it upon myself to sort you out."

I rubbed my face. "When should I go there again?"

"In a few days. He has some meetings out of town."

I breathed a sigh of relief. Having a few days away from that madman was a blessing.

Mike burped and patted his stomach. "Food was amazing. My wife's shit in the kitchen, but heaven forbid you tell her anything about it." He gave me a once-over. "Why are you standing over there? Afraid I'm gonna bite?"

"Yes."

"Well, man up and get your ass over here. Not like I'm going anywhere."

I went and sat on the couch, my body tense.

"Lift your shirt," he said. "I wanna see my work."

"You serious?"

The cold look he gave me was enough of an answer. I lifted my shirt, and Mike's lips stretched into a grin.

"Look at that. How are you handling the pain?"

"Advil."

"That's for kids. I'll get you stronger painkillers; you're gonna need them."

I lowered my shirt. "Why are you such a dick?"

"Calm down, princess. Let's keep this civil."

"I think we're past that by now."

"Then good thing we're leaving the thinking to me. Where were you earlier?"

"Working."

"Don't lie. You don't work."

"I do now, in a furniture store."

"Which one?"

I hesitated, but he could have found out anyway. "Abby's Corner."

"Down Philbrick Street? Yeah, I know the place." He scowled and scratched the stubble on his chin. "So...you just went and got yourself a job?"

He made it sound like I'd gotten myself chlamydia. "I need to work."

"You didn't ask me for permission. Did you ask Jeff?"

It took me a second to realize he was serious. "This whole mess happened because I *didn't* have a job."

"And working at that store will cover your debt?"

Hell no. "It's a start."

"Yeah, maybe, but you still need to ask for permission." He talked slowly like I was a child. "You heard Jeff yesterday—I'm calling the shots from now on."

I needed to be smart more than I needed to be right. "Listen, the job is for my neighbor. He and his wife helped me out a lot since I moved here, and I wanted to help them back."

Mike looked thoughtful before saying, "When Albert calls, you go. Doesn't matter what you have going on. You get that?"

"Yes."

"I'm still going to turn this into a lesson, so next time you'll know better." He leaned closer to my face. "Your days of freedom are over now, Matty boy. The fact that I'm not with you around the clock doesn't mean shit. I can lock you in here for days if I want to." He put his arm around my shoulders. Pressure filled my chest, but I forced myself to stay still. With his mouth to my ear, he quietly said, "I'll get an iron chain to tie around your neck, seal the windows and the door. Your entire life will be based on my decisions. Wouldn't that be fun?"

I sat numbly while the hell he was describing played like a horror film in my head. "I have a different definition of fun."

"You know I'm not bluffing, right?"

One glance at his cold eyes was enough. "I know."

He leaned back. "I won't lock you up, but I can always change my mind. Now, should we continue decorating your stomach?"

"Jesus, your sense of humor is so off."

He narrowed his eyes. "Who the hell's laughing?"

"Jeff didn't say I need to be your punching bag."

"Punching bag? I can use you as a cutting board if I want to. As long as I'll deliver you in one piece to Albert—and I will—I can do whatever the hell I want."

I didn't know if he was right or not. This mess didn't come with a guide, and it was pointless searching for logic when there was none to be found. I said, "Listen, I'm giving you zero trouble right now."

"So? I have a job to do."

"Yeah, being a cop."

He grabbed my jaw, nails digging into my skin. I clenched my fists and fought the impulse to hit him. "Don't go there, Matty—you won't win. Should we call Jeff and tell him you're giving me a hard time? That you're once again pissing on his orders?"

"No."

"You sure?" He reached for his phone.

"Stop! I'm sure."

"Then answer my question."

Any more bruises and I wouldn't be able to work the next day. I couldn't allow my work for Bill to start off like that. "Is there anything else...?"

He chewed on his lower lip. "Well, I do have my

leather belt."

I shook my head. "You gotta be kidding me."

"Hey, if you don't want the belt, handle the fists instead."

It was hard to believe I was debating how he should hurt me, but I didn't see a way out of it. "I need to be able to work."

"Are you asking for the belt?"

I exhaled. "Yes."

"All right, but don't expect me to play nice every time." He clapped his hands. "Enough talking. Go stand with your hands on the wall. Lose the shirt."

I stood up with a lump of dread in my stomach as he pulled out his belt. After taking off my shirt, I leaned my palms on the wall and anxiously waited, hoping he was merely trying to test me.

Then he whipped me. I choked, more from shock than pain.

"You're going to learn your place," Mike said, the belt tapping on his open palm. "I have too much riding on this gig, and I ain't taking any chances. The fact that I'm enjoying this is just the icing on the cake."

"Choke on that cake."

More whips followed, landing with enough force to leave no doubt about his desire to hurt. I moaned through clenched teeth but didn't give him the satisfaction of hearing me cry out.

By the time Mike stopped, burning lava and sweat covered my skin. He said, "Ride the pain."

"Shut up."

"Jesus, don't cry on me now."

"I'm not fucking crying."

"Good. If you want a reminder of how far things could've gone..." He came to stand next to me, took out something from his pocket and held it for me to see. I blinked as my brain caught up with my eyes.

"You're sick."

"I thought you might want it back."

I stared at my fingernail resting on Mike's open palm, still covered in dry blood. "Keep it."

"You sure?"

"God, I'm sure."

"All right." He put it back in his pocket. "Now tell me, what will you do next time you have a decision to make?"

I licked my lips. Sweat dripped from my forehead onto the floor. "I'll talk to you first."

"Huh? Didn't catch that."

"Then clean your dirty ears."

He punched me in the ribs.

I gasped but kept my palms against the wall. My mouth was going to get me killed.

"Let's try this again."

I fought the pain that was spreading throughout my side and said, "I'll talk to you before I have a decision to make."

"Be sure to remember that. Man, you're so red." He pinched my back. The sudden pain caused me to cry out.

"Don't be a pussy. I'm barely touching you."

"It burns!"

"Your old man never hit you?"

"No."

"Well, you always were a lucky prick. Just so you know, this could've been much more painful." He turned around and raised his shirt. Long-healed scars and burns covered his back. I looked away, lacking sympathy to spare.

He turned around and said, "One last thing."

My heart dropped. "What?"

"Stay as you are. I'm just gonna take a few photos of your back."

"No."

"It's your back, not your face. Chill."

I heard the camera on his phone working and quickly lowered my head, even though the camera wasn't aiming at my front.

"Why are you taking photos? Jeff asked you to?"

"None of your business."

"It's me you're taking photos of."

"But you belong to me now, and that includes your back. I might as well be taking photos of my car."

I stayed frozen in place, wanting to fight back but feeling too drained. What scared me the most was the certainty in his voice, how all of this seemed to make perfect sense to him.

Another two clicks followed before Mike said, "Okay, we had enough education for one day. Come here."

I let go of the wall and moved closer to him, my back still radiating heat.

He said, "I don't know when I'll stop by again, but you should expect me at any time." I flinched when he raised his hand, but he smirked and patted my cheek.

"Good luck with your new job. Try not to sink another business. I'll see you real soon. Promise."

12

It had been a long time since I last had a routine in my life. Working at Abby's Corner gave me back a schedule for my day and a welcome sense of significance. It wasn't a fancy job with great benefits and whatnot, but stepping into the store every morning filled me with the kind of energy I desperately needed.

I made sure to attend breakfast with the Broslavskiys every morning, where Bill and I would talk about what I should be focusing on for the rest of the day. I usually finished with the cleaning quickly and moved to work on my projects. I started with painting the front of the store to a more welcoming blue, then changed the light bulbs to a warmer color. When a regular client complimented Bill on the change, I smiled like a little boy.

My biggest project was taking photos of the furniture and uploading them to a Facebook page I'd created. I spent some of my time watching tutorials on how to set up social media campaigns, glad to discover it wasn't rocket science.

The first time the two cops came to the store it was around noon. Bill was out on errands and was supposed to come back soon since I wasn't yet ready to make sales on my own. The store was empty of customers and I was in the middle of arranging our new chairs, annoyed I couldn't find a good enough space for them.

"Can I help you?" I asked the two cops that entered. They were big, one due to muscles and the other due to fat. The muscled one had a pudgy nose that seemed to take a significant portion of his face.

"We're just looking," Muscles said and strolled around.

"Let me know if you need anything. We have a sale on the couches on the left side of the store."

They ignored me and kept walking between the aisles. I went back to fight with the chairs, considering moving one of the tables to the back to make more room. But that would require finding a new place for the three dressers currently at the back of the store. Bill was too keen on taking on new furniture, even when we clearly had no room for them.

I almost forgot about the cops until one of them was suddenly right next to me. I opened my mouth to ask if he wanted anything, but then I noticed the other cop standing on the other side of me. I moved my eyes between them, realizing they weren't there to buy anything.

"Jeff sent you," I said, aware of the trembling of my voice. "Or was it Mike?"

"We're not here to hear you speak," Muscles said.

"Then why are you here?"

The chubby one laughed. "You just told him to keep his mouth shut."

They took another step toward me, their chests pressing against my arms. I focused on keeping my cool although I wanted to run the hell away.

"We're not here to cause you problems," Muscles said. "Unless *you're* about to cause problems."

I shook my head, unable to speak even if I wanted to.

"Good," Chubby said and sat on an expensive chair. The buttons of his uniform struggled to restrain his gut. "I dunno how you've gotten involved with Jeff Holden, but you better stay on his good side. Man, this is one comfy chair. Makes my ass feel special."

Muscles said, "Maybe he'll give it to you for free."

It was a $200 chair. I remained quiet, afraid they would take it without permission. Bill would notice if a chair like that had gone missing, which meant I would need to add my own money to the register and pretend it had been sold.

Chubby started to wriggle his ass on the chair, making it squeak in a worrisome way.

"Don't break it," Muscles said, but in a tone that implied breaking it would be a hoot.

"I won't, but I'll give pretty boy here something to remember me by." He squeezed his round face and let out a fart that seemed to last forever.

Muscles laughed while I stopped breathing.

Chubby got up and winked at me. "Sniff it after we're gone. I can tell you're shy."

They started walking away. I let out a sigh of relief, but that allowed the stench to climb up my nose.

"We'll see you tomorrow," Muscles called from the end of the aisle.

"And the day after that," Chubby added.

They got out and left me alone in the store. I hurried

away from the smell, my anger quickly growing. This was my safe haven, the one place I didn't have to worry Jeff or Mike might ruin.

I wanted to go out and breathe fresh air, but a customer chose this moment to walk in. I swallowed down my anger and forced a smile on my face. "Can I help you?"

*

It was a Wednesday when my phone buzzed with the daily reminder I had set up. Bill was talking on the phone, ordering things I would later need to figure out where to squeeze.

I walked to the back of the store and slipped inside the small bathroom. There was an automatic air freshener there, but the room was so small that it smelled like a flower shop had exploded. I locked the door and leaned my back against it. I hated what I was about to do, but the one time I'd tried to pretend I forgot about Mike's order had ended badly.

I took off my shirt and placed it on the sink, then pulled my phone from my pocket and used it to take photos of the bruises on my torso and arms. Some were fresh and some were slowly fading. I sent the photos to Mike and waited until he sent back, "What about your thigh?"

With a grunt, I dropped my pants and took two photos of the bruises on my right thigh. He'd said they wouldn't interfere with my walking while he kicked me, but once they changed their color to blue and purple, walking became a painful affair.

I waited for Mike to send his okay before I got dressed and resumed working. Later that day, Bill pulled me aside while I was trying to move a table without involving excessive movements.

"What happened?" he asked, anger in his voice.

"What do you mean?" I tried to remember if I'd broken anything and didn't tell him. My first few days at the store had involved more than a few "*oops*" moments.

Bill said, "You can barely move without grimacing."

I opened and closed my mouth, caught off guard. "I'm fine."

"You're in pain and not for the first time. Tell me who's hurting you so we can do something about it."

My face grew hot. I had to look away from his eyes. "I'm handling it. Just let me get back to work. I won't grimace anymore."

"Don't turn this into a joke. Whatever is happening in your life, no one has the right to hurt you."

I began sweating under my shirt, worried he might fire me. "I'm working hard—you said that yourself."

"This has nothing to do with your work."

"Then I need you to understand that this is *my* life and I know what I'm doing."

"You don't look like someone who knows what he's doing. In fact, you look more lost as time goes by."

That one hurt. I felt like I was letting him down, and I was angry at him for making me feel that. "I need you to trust me," I said. "Or fire me if you can't handle it."

"I'm not firing you."

"Okay. Then drop it."

He shook his head. "It's like talking to a wall. I—"

A customer walked in. Bill gave me a final disappointed look and walked away.

I let out a tight breath. I would need to be more careful from now on or my relationship with Bill, both professional and personal, was bound to suffer. I just hoped I had it in me to pull it off.

*

It was over a week since I'd started working at Abby's Corner when Jeff stopped by. I suddenly noticed him talking to Bill about a chair and almost dropped my broom from shock. We made eye contact and my stomach did a flip before dropping to the ground. I couldn't handle being so close to him in a place I'd started to feel relatively safe.

Jeff's nose looked better with barely any swelling. His gray scarf covered the snake tattoo, but his entire demeanor remained intimidating; no piece of clothing would ever be enough to change that. He ended up making an order for a chair and signaled me to follow him as he headed out. I toyed with the notion of ignoring him, but the last time I ignored his order had ended catastrophically.

Jeff was leaning against his car when I stepped outside. "Want coffee?" he asked.

"I have coffee in the store. Let's get a smoothie over there."

"Those things are sugar bombs."

I stared at him until he reluctantly said, "Fine."

We walked to the juice place down the street. I ordered the extra-large, and Jeff ordered the regular.

We sat outside under a small heater hanging from the awning. It had been snowing for the last couple of days, but this morning it'd melted away.

Jeff asked, "You like working there?"

"I do, and I'm not quitting."

He narrowed his eyes. "Okay…"

"Sorry. I thought you might've come here to tell me that."

"I didn't." He drank from his smoothie. "You do more than clean?"

"Yes."

"Go on…"

I told him about the projects I'd been working on, feeling weird talking about them with someone who wasn't Bill.

"You have a good head for business," he said.

I snorted and shook my head. "Right."

"You can have a head for business and still not have the skills to run your own company."

"Yeah, maybe." I vividly remembered the chaotic days after I'd taken over Dad's company. All the meetings and reports, the fights with the suppliers and the bank. One mess followed another until I couldn't take it anymore and sold everything with a huge loss, gullibly believing that would be the end of it.

We sat quietly for a long minute, and it was getting awkward. I asked, "Why are you here? You could've checked up on me on the phone or asked one of your crooked cops."

He put down his smoothie. "I wanted to check that Mike hasn't been pushing too hard."

"He has."

Jeff shook his head. "You're working, and you look healthy."

"Healthy?" I clenched my fists. "Want to see my stomach? Or the marks from the belt on my back? My thighs are also a mess from the kicking session we had last time."

He looked surprised for a second, but his blank expression quickly returned. "Mike does what he thinks is right to get the job done. You should have done the same. Are you able to work every day?"

"Barely, but—"

"Then as long as you can still function, I'm staying out of it."

"He..." I lowered my voice, but it still trembled. "He comes to my place almost every day, sometimes in the middle of the goddamn night." I looked around to make sure no one was eavesdropping. "He hurts and humiliates me, do you get that? The other day he forced me to take a shower with freezing water, and when I couldn't take it anymore, he choked me until I passed out. I fucking did *nothing* wrong, but it didn't matter to him."

He exhaled slowly, clearly pondering over his next words. "You need to be afraid, or you'll end up making more mistakes."

"Oh, I'm afraid."

"Not enough." His dark eyes bored into me. "I'm sure that every time Mike shows up at your apartment, your balls get tighter and you think twice before opening your mouth. Am I right?"

I took a napkin and started tearing it apart. "Yes."

He leaned back. "That's how you should feel until the deal with Albert is complete."

I shook my head. "I can't handle being afraid all the time; it will drive me crazy." Hell, there were moments it felt it'd already had.

Jeff's voice was a tad gentler when he said, "You're tougher than you think, and this arrangement is temporary."

I let out an angry breath, exhausted from hearing him dismiss the hell I'd been going through. "Fine," I said. "You're right. I'm overreacting and Mike's a great normal guy. Everything's perfect." I went back to my smoothie, although it was tasteless in my mouth.

"Ruth says hello," Jeff said.

"Ruth? Are you two…?"

"We're getting there."

That explained why he hadn't told me to go with him to another club. I wanted to ask if she knew what he truly did for a living, but I pretty much knew the answer. "Good for you."

He nodded and looked somewhat uncomfortable. "It's still early stages, so everything can still go wrong. Sex's great, though."

"Did she use a strap-on?"

"Careful. And I said no to that."

I snickered. "Just the fingers, then."

"I'm pleading the fifth on that one. Are you dating anyone?"

"Me? God no." I had nothing that would be worth any girl's time. Even a one-night stand would be awkward considering the bruises I had under my clothes.

It was getting late, and I didn't want to keep sitting and talking like we were friends. I glanced at my watch, and Jeff got the hint. Once next to his car, he said, "Albert should be back soon. I hope the new Matt will be the one going to meet him."

"There's no *new Matt*," I said with a flat voice.

"You might not see it, but I do. Keep working hard, and don't take what's happening as the end of the world." He looked at the store behind me. "You're doing well."

He drove away, and I went back to drown myself in work.

*

Bill trusted me enough to let me close the store by myself, and I took my time since I had a solid idea of what was waiting for me back home.

Opening my door, I saw Mike lying on the couch, one hand behind his head and the other one holding a lit cigarette. He'd never directly said I should return home right after work, but it was clear I wasn't supposed to have a social life with him in the picture.

I took off my coat and hung it before saying, "I asked you to please not smoke in here."

Mike rolled his eyes. "I opened the window."

"You can use the fire escape."

"And you can shut the fuck up. Besides, it's freezing outside, and I ain't getting sick because of you."

It was stupid to try and talk sense into him. I took off my shoes and went to drink water in the kitchen, my body tense. I was used to his presence in my private space by now, yet it was impossible to predict how far he was going to take his twisted "education." I was tiptoeing my way between mines whenever he was around, feeling that my home was now a battlefield.

"You think you're smart, Matty?"

Something about the way he asked that sent a wave of unease through my body. "What do you mean?"

He blew smoke toward the open window as if that would prevent my apartment from smelling like an ashtray. "Come here when I'm talking to you."

I put the empty glass in the sink and hesitantly went to the living room. Mike wasn't wearing his uniform. His faded jeans had seen better days, and his white long sleeve shirt sat tight on his body. He sat up and blew smoke at me.

"On your knees," he said. "Good boy." He squeezed the cigarette butt out on a small plate, then tapped his feet. "My shoes won't take themselves off."

I hid the disgust from my face and removed his shoes, then pulled off his socks without waiting for him to tell me to.

He wiggled his toes. "That's better. Position one."

I put my hands behind my back.

He nodded his approval. "Now tell me, do you think you're smart?"

"No."

"Oh, I think you do. Got your head full of dangerous thoughts."

I'd learned to detect the subtle changes in his voice, and what I was reading now sparked an ominous feeling. "I don't think I'm smart."

He tapped my nose with his finger. "That sounds like a lie."

"I wouldn't have been in this mess if I was smart."

He scanned my face with narrowed eyes. The wheels in his head seemed to be spinning extra fast. "Well, you need to be pretty smart to put together something like this." He leaned down and pulled out something from under the couch.

When I saw him holding my escape folder, I couldn't breathe. I'd made sure to hide that folder better than before by covering it with extra clothes and bed sheets.

"It's not what you think," I said.

"No? Then why do you look like you're about to piss your pants?"

"It's something old. I forgot about it."

"You sure tried to hide it."

"Why were you looking in my closet?"

"Why?" He smacked my head with the folder. "Because I was looking for something like this! Couldn't you save this stuff on a computer like a normal person?"

I tried to steady my heartbeat but with little success. "Let me explain."

"What's to explain? You have escape routes here, bus lines, train stations...a freaking Ph.D. on how to run away." He shook his head. "You know what's gonna happen if I show this to Jeff?"

It would be the end of me. We both knew that. "I'll throw it away. I'll do it right now." I moved my hands to grab the folder, but Mike's palm flew like a bullet and hit the side of my head, rattling my brain. "Position one!"

Dazed, I returned my hands behind my back. "Listen, those things are old. I'm not running away."

He folded his arms, curiosity in his eyes. "Why didn't you run away? Before me, before Albert. I would've."

I was standing in front of a firing squad with nothing to lose by being honest. "I thought it would get better, that Jeff would cut me some slack and I'd find a good job. I didn't think he would take things so far, and I also didn't want to spend the rest of my life looking over my shoulder."

"I see." He looked out the window, his face unreadable. Every second of silence increased the pressure in my chest until he finally looked at me again. "I want to believe you, but what I have here…that's serious, you know?"

My throat seized up. I fought to say, "I swear to you that I'm telling the truth."

We stared at one another, and I was painfully aware of the power he had over me.

Mike finally said, "If I show this to Jeff, you're a dead man. If you're dead, my golden opportunity to move up in life will be buried with you. That's why we're gonna destroy this folder and forget you were ever dumb enough to make it. Okay?"

I nodded in relief. My body felt ten pounds lighter. "Thank you."

"Don't sweat it, buddy. We're on the same team you and I." He opened the folder and took out one of the pages before tearing it into shreds. "The first page will go inside you. The others I'll burn in the sink. Open your mouth."

"What?"

"Open it!"

He put the first piece of paper in my mouth and watched as I chewed on it before swallowing. My stomach cramped after more pieces went down my throat, and I almost threw up. Mike raised a warning finger. "What you puke, you'll eat again."

I forced the bile back down.

"Attaboy," Mike said when we finished with the page. "You're lucky I'm not feeding you this entire thing; you would've been shitting origami for a week."

He got up and went to the kitchen, took out all the pages from the folder, then put them in the sink. I watched motionlessly as he set fire to what I'd worked on for so long. It felt like he was burning more than paper.

The smoke made my eyes sting, but most of it went out the window. Mike poured water over the fire and came back to sit on the couch. "All right, it's done. No more talking about this." He leaned back while I was beginning to feel pain in my knees. "How'd you sleep?" he asked.

"Fine. Seven hours."

"Breakfast?"

"Eggs and vegetables."

"Lunch?"

"Chicken and potatoes."

"You took a dump?"

"I...yes. Once."

"Jerked off?"

"Not today."

"When?"

"Last night."

"With what?"

"Spit."

"Painkillers?"

"Took one this morning."

"No more than two a day."

"I know."

He asked me more questions, and I kept myself composed. This routine of interrogations about the stupidest and most private things in my life had become another thing for me to get used to. It was as though leaving marks on my body wasn't enough—he needed to leave them under my skin as well.

Mike pulled off my shirt once he finished his interrogation. "Let's see how you've been holding up." He ran his fingers across the left side of my chest. "Those bite marks are healing up faster than I thought. I've been sloppy."

I had learned to view Jeff's violence as a way to get a message across. Cause and effect. For Mike, it was a monster he constantly needed to feed. I didn't know how long I could withstand feeding his monster before it ended up swallowing me whole.

"And how's this one been treating you?" He pressed a bruise on my ribs. I hissed and fought to stay still.

He chuckled and took out his phone. I turned my head to the side. He took photos of my bruises, although I'd sent him the same photos earlier today. When I felt him raising the phone too high, I said, "We agreed—"

"I'm leaving your pretty face out of it. Relax."

I was once more tempted to ask why he was doing this, but I knew what he was going to say: *"It's just for me, and that's all you need to know."*

Once Mike finished, he leaned back with a smile of contentment. "I heard you had a visit from Jeff earlier. What do you think he told me after he talked to you?"

"Don't know."

He punched my chest. "Don't play dumb."

I cringed and took a breath. "He told you he was... satisfied."

"Satisfied with...?"

"The *new* me."

"That's right, buddy. He told me he saw a change in you." He stroked my cheek and lowered his voice. "I knew you were my express ticket forward. The rich kid's gonna help me get a new house. It won't be as fancy as where you used to live, but boy will I appreciate it like a freaking castle."

His eyes shone like a nasty thought was playing in his head. "I have big plans for you, Matty boy. Unlike my old man, I think big." He paused and shook his head. "If you'd have asked my old man about his future plans, he'd have stared at you like a dummy. If I learned anything from that asshole, it's to always plan ahead."

It wasn't the first time he'd mentioned having plans for me. It sent shivers across my skin every time. I reminded myself that he was nothing but Jeff's pawn, without any real say in the great scheme of things. Yet I couldn't stop myself from asking, "What plans do you have?"

He shook his head. "Tsk tsk. Nothing to worry your

head over. Just focus on making me look good in front of Jeff. You'll get another chance to shine tomorrow, this time with Albert."

Shit. "Tomorrow?"

"Yep. At noon." He leaned closer, the smoke on his breath making my nose itch. "I have a feeling Albert's gonna test you. That means that *I* will also be tested. You see where I'm going with that?"

"Yes."

"And what will you do?"

"I won't give him any trouble."

"That's right. Whatever Albert wants, you do." He ran his finger in small circles on my chin. "And if you happen to fuck this up for us, I'll go even harder on you." He lowered his voice and emphasized every word. "Maybe I'll arrange a nice surprise for your elderly friends downstairs."

It took me a second to grasp his threat, then my fragile calm shattered. I jumped forward, took hold of his shirt, and pushed him back. "If you ever get close to those people, I'll make you pay. They're not a part of this, you hear me?"

He stared at me with round eyes, but they quickly narrowed. "Get your hands off me."

I let go and went back on my knees, my pulse racing. I might've been powerless to stop his torments, but no one would hurt Bill and Molly because of me.

Mike yelled, "You feel like a man now? Huh?"

The anger in his eyes made it hard to speak. "I needed you to understand."

"Oh, you bet your ass I understand. I obviously can't

let you meet Albert with such crazy temper, so we're gonna speed up your education." He stood and cracked his knuckles in front of my face. "Let's move this to the bedroom. We're gonna add new marks to our collection. I'm going for blue ones this time."

13

I stayed in bed the following morning and tried to keep unnecessary movements to a bare minimum. A sense of gloom crept into my mind, taking over my thoughts and holding them captive. I tried to mentally escape by finishing my book about decision making, but it had turned out to be unhelpful.

In the last couple of months, I had adopted a morning routine where I would close my eyes and envision my life after this hell was dead and buried. A fresh start, far from the ghosts of my past mistakes. With every passing day, mentally escaping became harder than the day before. This morning, it was impossible.

When Mike came to pick me up, it was raining. Everywhere I looked, winter had stripped the trees of their autumn leaves, leaving them bare and depressing.

"Did you eat?" Mike asked while we drove.

"Albert told me to fast."

"Okay. You nervous?"

"I don't feel much of anything."

He eyed me but remained quiet.

When we stopped for a traffic light, Mike lifted my shirt. He stared at his "work" and said, "I was too rough on you last night. Try not to push me again, and I'll try to be more careful."

I didn't buy his act of remorse, nor his fake promise, but I was too drained to care. "Okay."

It had stopped raining by the time we arrived at Albert's house. He was waiting for us outside, wearing a yellow coat that was too big for his slim figure.

"You're telling me he's living alone in this huge house?" Mike asked.

"Yes."

"Jesus. Some people have too much money."

He got out of the car and hurried to shake Albert's hand.

"Nice to meet you, Officer Johnson."

"Mike's fine. We're all friends here." He put his hand on my shoulder. "Matt here is ready to do whatever you need him to. I've been working him extra hard lately, so everything should go smoothly."

Albert avoided my eyes and cleared his throat. "I'll need to check for myself if Matthew is ready to be a vital part of my work."

"Sure, take Matthew for a test drive." He pointed at Albert's house. "Say, you've got a GetSafe security system? I recognize their cameras."

"You have a good eye. Yes, everything here is under surveillance."

"You're using an external server?"

He scowled. "No, but maybe I should. I keep it all on a server in my office due to the poor internet connection out here."

"That's risky. Let me know if you need help with that. I know a guy."

"Thank you. I'll think about it."

"When should I pick up our troublemaker?"

"I don't have a lot of time today, unfortunately. We should be done in about thirty minutes. I hope you don't find me rude, but I would prefer it if you stayed here."

"Sure thing. Give me a call if he gives you a hard time; I'll come right away to sort him out."

I dug my remaining nails into my palms. Albert eyed me with puzzlement but kept quiet. We went inside, leaving Mike to wait in the car.

"Are you okay?" Albert asked once we entered his lab.

"I'm fine."

He scanned my face. "You look different."

It'd been over a week since I last saw him. Back then, Mike was nothing but an old memory. "Had a busy couple of days."

He crossed his arms and quietly said, "I'm not your enemy. I hope you know that."

I didn't know how to respond, so I remained quiet.

Albert said, "Well, at least Mike seems like a decent enough guy."

Heat spread throughout my body. I raised my shirt and watched as Albert's eyes grew big.

"I must be a pretty horrible person to deserve something like this from a *decent guy*."

He looked away with a tight jaw. "This is not my doing, nor is it my fault."

I let my shirt fall. "Tell me what to do. You said we don't have much time."

"Have you fasted?"

"Yes."

"Good. We'll start with the blood tests, then I'll need your ears for a short while."

Once he finished taking my blood, he dripped something cold into my ears. For a minute there, I just felt wetness in my ear canals, but that quickly changed into a growing and unpleasant buzzing sound.

Then I was deaf. I only fully noticed it when Albert said something without using his voice, only he probably did use it. In response to my confused and wary expression, he gave me a thumbs-up. I should've been freaking out, but I remained still, thinking that I'd either hear again or I wouldn't.

Sharp currents of pain gradually appeared deep in my ear canals, the feeling reaching as far as my jaw. I told Albert when it happened—although I couldn't hear myself speak—and he wrote it down on his tablet. After about ten minutes, he dripped something else into my ears. The pain subsided quickly, and my hearing got back to me in a matter of minutes, although an annoying buzzing sound lingered.

While we waited to make sure my ears were truly fine, Albert talked about his garden and his plans for it in the spring, even though New Hampshire's long winter was only getting started. Since being on his good side was in my best interest, I played along and pretended to care about his petunias and orchids.

At one point he asked, "Do you have a girlfriend?"

"No."

"Are you seeing anyone in a less committed manner?"

"You mean just for sex? Not at the moment. I'm not

much of a catch these days."

"Don't sell yourself short. And remember that our partnership shouldn't come in the way of your personal life."

There was that annoying word again. *Partnership*. It was also naive of him to think I could go on with my life with everything that was happening. Every ounce of energy I had went into surviving the deal with Jeff.

Albert checked my ears again and announced I was as good as new. At the entrance of his house, he said, "I wish I could give you the money like last time, but Jeff wants it all to go directly to him. I will be in touch about our next appointment."

Back in the car, Mike remained surprisingly quiet. I wanted to go work at the store, but I didn't have it in me to act normal while my body was in such pain. Not to mention Bill would easily tell how bruised I was, which would lead to another fight with no winners.

We suddenly stopped at a parking lot I didn't recognize. "Where are we?"

Mike turned off the engine. "We're going to eat. I'm buying."

"Why?"

"For fuck's sake, I'm buying you a burger, not a diamond ring."

I reluctantly got out and followed him inside. The place was decorated like it was still the '50s with red leather seats. Elvis played in the background, his deep voice swallowing the scattered sounds of conversation. The smell of fried food was heavy in the air. The elderly owner knew Mike, so he gave us free french fries and sodas with our burgers. I ate the french fries in silence after drowning them in ketchup.

Mike leaned back and drank his soda. "I used to work here in high school," he said. "Used to steal food to take back home. My old man made a daily list of things I should snatch."

"Okay."

After a minute of silence, he asked, "Are you all right?"

I shrugged. "It wasn't so bad today."

"Then what's up with the long face?"

"You're really asking me that?"

He raised an eyebrow. "Is someone forgetting his manners?"

I shook my head. "Sorry. Got a lot on my mind."

"Go on. I'm listening."

"No offense, but this ain't turning into a heart-to-heart."

"Because I'm part of the problem?"

"Yes." *And you don't have a heart.*

He nodded and leaned with his elbows on the table. "Sometimes it's important to put it all out there. Otherwise, you might explode, do something stupid."

Looking at him closely, it became clear what was happening. If I ended up hurting myself, Jeff would take it out on him. No longer would he have an "express ticket to the promised land."

"I think of killing myself," I said, and the look on Mike's face was priceless.

He lowered his voice. "What's this shit about killing yourself?"

I moved my drink between my hands. "My life's a mess. I tried convincing myself that someday I'll have a happily ever after, but I'm not buying it anymore." I realized that I wasn't only trying to scare him—I was also being honest with myself.

"Listen," Mike said and looked into my eyes, "I know I've been hard on you, but I'm not going to keep doing that forever, and Albert won't need you anymore one day. This whole thing is temporary."

He had a point, but 'temporary' felt like forever. It wasn't like a debt of one hundred grand would magically disappear after a few meetings with Albert. I rubbed my face, regretting opening up to him. "Let's not talk about this, okay? I need to mute my thoughts."

He snorted. "You should also turn down the drama, that's for sure."

"Don't act like I'm overreacting."

"Oh, please. You're such a whining bitch. I've seen people in worse states than you, so don't act like you're the world's biggest victim."

The waitress came with our burgers as I was about to make a mistake by answering him. I started eating, my anger draining the food of taste.

Mike suddenly said, "Just so we're clear, I can't make you not kill yourself—that's up to you—but what I can do is make sure your friendly neighbors end up paying the price."

I glared at him, barely able to stay still. "I told you not to—"

"Shut up. Next time you want to protect someone, don't make it obvious how much you care. That's stupid, even for you."

I forced myself to remain calm, but in my mind's eye, I shoved a fork through his eye.

We finished eating and got back to the car, then took the 102; a road I'd mostly avoided in the last year. I said, "Please drop me off over there. I'll take the bus once I'm done."

He shook his head. "You need to get some rest to make yourself less suicidal."

"I'm not suicidal. Drop me next to the cemetery."

He stopped the car on the side of the road. "You sure it's a good idea?"

"It's fine."

I got out and walked past the iron gate of Saint Patrick's Cemetery. The place seemed deserted for this time of day, probably due to the cloudy weather. I reached my parents' graves on a small hill overlooking nearby trees, feeling guilty for not visiting more often.

I'd picked out a simple gravestone for Dad but asked to add a quote from a song by Bruce Springsteen he used to love. The idiots had spelled one of the words wrong, but by the time I noticed, it had been too late.

"Hi, Dad." It was easier talking out loud when there wasn't anyone around. I never talked to my mom since I never really knew her. I sat on the soft grass and massaged the back of my neck. The conversation I'd had with Mike earlier was still nagging at my thoughts.

Coming to visit my dad's grave in the months following his death had been like picking at a bleeding open wound. The guilt I carried summoned dark thoughts of joining him in the afterlife. I wished to tell him I was sorry, needed him to look me in the eyes and grant me his forgiveness. I hadn't been there for him when his health suffered due to the dire state of the company. I'd known things were getting bleak, that he was handling it badly, but I didn't let this knowledge change my routine of college life.

The woman from the dean's office had come to get me during class with a grim expression. Sitting on a bench in front of the library, she told me Dad had died of a heart attack. It had most likely happened during the previous evening while he was working late, but he'd only been found once the cleaning lady arrived in the early hours of the morning.

Something nasty swirled in my stomach as the meaning behind her words sank in. I needed to stop breathing or I'd have ended up vomiting in the woman's lap.

The evening before I'd been at a frat party. Dad called at some point while I was dancing. I held the phone in my hand and watched his number on the screen, thinking it was weird getting a call from him at this hour. The entrance door was a few feet away, offering a quiet place to talk on the other side. I looked at the door, looked at the girl who was dancing in front of me, then slipped the phone back into my pocket. *Call you tomorrow, Dad.*

While the woman watched me with concern, I rubbed my face, waves of weakness hitting my body. In an instant, I understood what being alone truly meant. Dad was the only one I could call family, was my everything. His death had left me a particle floating aimlessly in space, with no connection to anything or anyone.

I looked the woman in the eyes and asked if she was sure, completely positive that Dad had died of a heart attack. She frowned and nodded.

And there I was, mere seconds after hearing my dad died, relieved from knowing he hadn't taken his own life. A heart attack was an event completely out of my control, which meant I was still a good person. Even though I'd left him alone on the battlefield, I couldn't possibly be responsible for someone's heart attack.

Looking back at the sick way my mind had reacted, I truly believed every bad thing in my life was well-deserved payback. I'd taken over Dad's failing company because I wanted his legacy to live on. But I couldn't make it work. Thinking of Jeff as my rightful punishment put me in a state of acceptance that was crucial to my conscience—perhaps even my sanity.

Facing Mike's brutality helped lessen the voices of blame that had been haunting me for the last year. I hadn't noticed it at first, but it gradually became apparent. By breaking me, he was also putting together something that has been broken for a long time. Acknowledging that twisted truth was painful, forced me to face dark parts of my soul I wished to leave uncharted. But I couldn't escape the truth the same way I couldn't escape my deal with Jeff.

Sitting in the cemetery and talking to Dad, my mind drifted back to when we used to sit in our backyard, drinking iced tea as I was talking his ear off. It was harder than usual talking to him now, but I needed to let him know what I was dealing with. I also wanted someone to listen and not cast judgment.

The sudden rain made me stop talking. I hadn't even noticed the gray clouds clustering above. I stood up with a grunt, put my hand on the cold gravestone, then hurried to catch the bus.

14

As soon as I walked in the door, soaking wet, Jeff called. I thought of ignoring him but couldn't bring myself to do so.

"How are you?" he asked when I answered the call.

I put him on speaker and threw my wet shirt on the floor. "Fine."

"You sure?"

"Does it matter? You made it clear you don't give a damn."

"I do give a damn, and now I'm hearing you're turning suicidal."

I should have known Mike would run and tell. "What if I am?"

"Only cowards take the easy way out."

I rolled my eyes and took off the rest of my wet clothes. "Compared to some of the things you've called me lately, *coward* might be close to a compliment."

"Matt."

"I'm not about to kill myself, all right? Things are crappy all around, and I said it to scare off Mike."

"I see." He was quiet for a few seconds. "Will it help having some time off from both Mike and Albert?"

My hand froze as I was about to grab a towel. "You serious?"

"Will it?"

"It most definitely will!"

"I'm giving you about a week. Use this time to take care of yourself, and don't think it means I won't be keeping an eye on you."

*

As my days of freedom passed, I began to feel healthy again, to gradually reclaim my old self. I worked non-stop at the store, keeping it spotless and well-organized. I even succeeded in making a few sales on my own. During the quiet hours, I got the store's Facebook page fully up and running, then set up campaigns for our top products. Molly's fifty Facebook friends hadn't been enough to create the buzz we were hoping for, shockingly.

"You should have been there, Moll," Bill said at Friday's dinner, right after he'd finished saying a Jewish prayer. "People showed up and knew *exactly* what they wanted before I even opened my mouth!"

"It's called advertising," I said and filled my plate with wonderful kosher food. "I'm sure you guys also had that in the '40s."

"Hey!" Molly raised a warning finger.

"My bad! I'm only saying it's no big deal."

"It *is* a big deal." Bill's voice turned serious. "You need to start giving yourself more credit where credit's due. You hear me?"

"Yes, sir." I looked at my plate, my face a few degrees warmer. I might've tried to play it cool but hearing him say those things made me glow deep inside.

Bill's good mood was also a result of my improved health. He commented on it after he'd seen me carrying heavy chairs into a van without struggling.

"Does that mean you took care of your problem?" he later asked.

The hope in his eyes sparked a sense of unease in my chest. I faked a smile. "Told you I got it covered."

The Broslavskiys invited me to join them on a road trip to hunt for furniture. There were events where people got rid of things they had lying around, and merchants let go of stock they didn't need.

It was a Sunday, and I liked the idea of getting out of Hudson for a while. It took us over two hours to reach Warners Pond in West Concord. The day was cloudy, but the forecast promised no rain until much later in the evening.

Bill and Molly knew many of the people there, and I wondered how much of the event was about buying things and how much about chatting. It didn't matter since the pond was beautiful and everyone seemed happy to be there.

Molly made sure to introduce me to her lady friends, telling them I was Bill's new partner and "As talented as the nice Jewish boy who invented Facebook." I smiled and put on my charm since it seemed to make her happy.

While the Broslavskiys were busy with their friends, I wandered around and asked for prices, then wrote down what I thought we should get. Bill joined me at some point and added things that seemed dumpster-worthy to me, but he insisted were diamonds in the rough.

"A fresh coat of paint and a nice touch of sandpaper are all these beauties need," Bill said in response to my skeptical stare. We needed to pay for shipment as well, and I wondered how much profit we were going to make when it was all said and done.

We were about to wrap things up and head back to Hudson when my phone started buzzing in my back pocket. I took it out and hissed, "Fuck."

Bill turned to me. "Pardon?"

I shook my head. "It's nothing. Give me a sec."

I walked away and stood under a tall tree, far enough to not be heard. With a deep breath, I answered the call. "Hi."

"You don't sound happy to hear from me."

"Must be a bad connection."

Mike snickered. "Yeah, must be. Where are you?"

"West Concord."

"What the hell for?"

"Looking for furniture to bring back to the store."

"Sounds thrilling. I hope you're not planning on staying there long 'cause tomorrow morning I'm taking you to see Albert. Vacation's over, buddy."

I rubbed my face. This past week had gone by too fast. Hell, it felt like I'd imagined it.

"You think I can maybe get one more—"

"I'll pretend I didn't hear that."

We hung up, and I felt the familiar bleakness slipping through the cracks of my mood.

"Matt, you ready?" Bill called.

No, I'm not.

"Coming."

*

When Mike picked me up the following morning it was clear he was in a bad mood and hadn't slept much.

"Everything okay?" I asked when we started driving. I was already edgy from seeing Albert again, so dealing with an angry Mike was less appealing than usual.

"Last night I found out my wife's been cheating on me. Stupid cunt."

I carefully asked, "Aren't you cheating on her?"

"Not the same thing."

I eyed him and decided it wasn't worth it. "Are you getting a divorce?"

He nibbled on his lower lip. "Don't know yet. We had a big argument, and she started crying and asking me to forgive her. I played it nice, man, did the whole '*you broke my heart*' act. We'll see how long I can play the wounded husband role. Anyway, how about you? Missed me?"

"You want the truth?"

"Oh, I know you didn't miss me. Would've been pretty weird if you did. You at least got a chance to rest and clear your head?"

"Yes."

"Good." He moved his hand and put it on my shoulder, started playing with my earlobe. Reminding me how easily he could do what he wanted. "To be honest, I'm a little bit nervous."

"Why?"

"You going to Albert after a week of zero education

sounds risky."

God, how I didn't miss his crap. "I'll behave. Don't worry."

"Obviously I'm worried. I have a feeling this past week has been a test. Maybe Jeff wants to check if my work has a lasting effect."

"You're overthinking it. He just gave me a week off; there isn't any test."

He chuckled. "This naivety is probably why you're in this mess." He moved his hand away. "Everything you and I do is a test; get that into your head. Wait." He glanced at me. "Are you planning on messing things up so I'll get in trouble with Jeff?"

"What? No."

"Matty...don't lie to me."

"I'm not planning anything!"

He tapped on the steering wheel with his fingers. "I shouldn't have let it slip that you were my ticket forward. Obviously you'd try to ruin it for me."

"I'm not!"

He started slowing the car until we stopped on the side of the road under a tall billboard for AT&T.

"Put your seat back."

"Why the hell for? I didn't do anything. Let's just—"

He pulled out his gun. "This ain't negotiation, simply a quick reminder of what will happen if you mess this up. Go on, you know the drill."

I moved my eyes from the gun to his face, realizing there was no point trying to talk him out of this. I'd hoped the last week had given him a chance to observe some humanity, but it clearly hadn't.

With a shaky hand, I unbuckled my seat belt and pulled back the seat, then lifted my shirt to expose my stomach.

"You heal up nicely." He sounded dissatisfied like I'd done that on purpose. He pressed the cold barrel against my belly button, then slowly leaned in on the gun. The sharp pain shot through me like an arrow, making me gasp.

Mike calmly said, "You have everything to lose if you screw this up, and doing that to fuck me over won't be worth it."

He put more pressure on my stomach, sending torrents of pain into my lower back. Cars passed us by as I shouted and panted, aware of Mike watching my every twitch.

He said, "I missed those sounds you make. I can listen to them all day. Now, swear you'll be a good boy today. Make a believer out of me."

"I'll be…I'll be a good boy."

He twisted the gun. The metal was about to cut my skin. Acid burned its way up my throat.

"You'll cause no problems to Albert. You'll do everything he wants."

"Yes. Fuck, I'm gonna throw up."

"So?"

"It's *your* car!"

He raised the gun and moved back. I held my stomach tight, fighting to keep my breakfast from gushing from my mouth. I looked down at the red scratches around my belly button. A few seconds more and I would've been bleeding.

We got back on the road and Mike happily whistled all the way to Albert's house. Once we parked, he turned to me with his familiar smirk, his bad mood gone now that the monster had been fed. "Go on. The doctor's waiting for his patient. I'll be waiting for you right here." He raised his gun and winked. "We both will."

I got out carefully and walked slowly until the pain eased up a bit. The forest was quiet, the wind barely a breeze between the trees.

When Albert opened the front door, I immediately sensed something wasn't right. His eyes looked puffy and his skin paler than usual. He seemed to be recovering from a bad hangover, but I couldn't picture him drinking so much. His smile looked forced when he said, "Come in, Matthew."

Once down in his lab, I asked if everything was all right. He leaned against the bed and crossed his arms. "I had a bad dream about my brother last night. Do you ever have bad dreams?"

"Yes." Was there any other kind?

He nodded. "Then you know they can be very unpleasant. In my dream, Henry had been angry at me for not helping him when those monsters..." He shook his head, eyes troubled. "It was very vivid, almost like a memory."

"He died far away," I said. "There was nothing you could've done."

"When he debated whether to stay in service, I told him staying would be a good opportunity to get a better retirement plan, and that a higher rank might open more doors for him in the future. He listened to my advice like he always had. I can tell myself I had nothing to do with his death till the end of time, but truth doesn't work like that." He sighed. "On top of that, this morning I found out my funding from the military is at risk. Someone decided to have a closer look at the books, and he didn't like that I was getting unsupervised support. I hope my contacts will be able to shift this attention elsewhere, but it's hard to say."

"Is supervision such a bad thing?"

He twisted his mouth like I'd said something dumb. "What people don't understand, they try to control. I can't have that." He cleared his throat. "Enough about that. Let's focus on the job at hand. Today we'll once more test the effect of the paralyzing gas on your body, and I expect you to keep yourself in check. Are we clear?"

I vividly remembered the sudden disappearance of my legs and the helplessness that followed. For a second, I thought of trying to convince him to do something else, but I could still feel the barrel of Mike's gun against my stomach. I exhaled and nodded. "We're clear."

He squeezed my shoulder. "Good. I knew I could count on you." He didn't move his hand. His eyes locked on mine, making me uncomfortable.

"Are we doing this?" I asked.

He blinked and moved his hand away. "Yes, of course. Remove your shirt and pants."

Once down to my underwear, Albert handed me the bucket and dripped the drops from last time down my throat. My stomach painfully cramped, feeling like a volcano was about to erupt. A few seconds later, I emptied my stomach into the bucket.

"Take this."

Still heaving, I took the mint from his hand and popped it into my mouth.

Inside the side room, I stood on the cold, red mattress, focusing on keeping my breaths steady and my heartbeat in check. Knowing what was coming somehow made it even worse.

Albert put the gas mask over his face after playing with the circles on his computer screen. "Begin walking."

The engine in the wall started humming, releasing gas I couldn't prevent myself from inhaling. Like last time, I managed to take a few steps before ants began crawling across my skin, then my legs disappeared. I crashed hard, only this time I blocked the main impact with my hands. The sense of not having my lower half messed with my brain, but I kept reminding myself it was only temporary.

"Begin crawling."

I used my arms to pull myself forward. It felt like carrying rocks to the top of a mountain. The muscles in my shoulders and upper arms heated up quickly, then turned into full-on fire by the time I reached the other side. The mattress stuck to my sweaty skin, itching like crazy.

"Crawl back to the other side."

Not even a second to catch my breath. Groaning, I awkwardly maneuvered myself around and resumed crawling. The other side of the room seemed alarmingly far, although I could've crossed it in less than five seconds by foot.

I didn't even reach the middle before Albert went back to his computer and clicked on a different circle that changed its color to purple. I held myself from asking about it, worried I might tick him off.

I was about to reach the other side when ants began crawling across my arms and back. "Shit," I hissed.

It didn't take more than five seconds for my upper body to get numb, then disappear completely. I had a moment of relief since the pain was now gone from my exhausted muscles, but panic swiftly took over.

"Albert, what the hell?"

He opened the door and stepped inside, carrying his bag and tablet. "I'm sorry for not warning you," he said through the mask and closed the door behind him. "A part of the experiment is to examine the surprise effect on your body. Sensors around the room are monitoring everything from your heartbeat to your body temperature." He sat next to me and took out a syringe with a long needle. "You're breathing too fast."

"I'm scared, okay?"

"You shouldn't be. I've tested everything before."

"On animals."

"Aren't we all animals?"

"Jesus."

"Think about using something like this on the battlefield. Winning without a bloodbath. Keeping our soldiers out of harm's way so no one would end up like Henry. One day you'll look back at this and feel proud of your sacrifices. Now, tell me if there's any pain."

I closed my eyes so I wouldn't have to look at the tools he took from his bag. Having been reduced to a head was too much to grasp. I felt the mattress against the bottom part of my neck, but below that laid a disturbing void.

A few minutes later, I opened my eyes in alarm when Albert stroked my hair. "You're a beautiful man."

What the hell? "Thanks. Are we done here?"

"Soon. Can I be honest with you?"

"I guess."

He let out a deep breath. It sounded louder through the mask. "I've been feeling lonelier than usual lately. I know it's a sacrifice I must endure for my work, but it doesn't make it easier. Do you sometimes feel lonely?" There was something weird with his voice, as if he was trying not to cry.

"I get lonely, but maybe we should talk about this later."

"What do you do to feel better?"

"I'm not the right guy to advise in the loneliness department."

"I'm not asking for advice."

It was ridiculous talking when I was but a head on a mattress and his own head was covered in a gas mask, but he seemed determined to have his way. "I like to run and go for long walks. I used to watch movies before Mike broke my TV. I talk a lot with my neighbors. Sometimes I have sex."

"I see. Sex helps you feel less lonely?"

"It can help for a while."

"Do you think it can help me?"

"Sure. Why not?"

He inhaled deeply through the mask. "I'm glad you said that. I thought a lot about whether it was the right thing to do, but I truly believe it can help me."

"Great."

"I promise you won't feel a thing."

"I won't…what?" I turned my head back as much as I could.

"I'm sorry. I know it's not professional, or even ethical, but I feel so deeply alone, and you are right here —my partner. Please, let me have this."

I couldn't feel my heart, but I knew it was running wild. "There's no way in hell you're doing that. I'm so freaking serious right now."

He stood up. "I give you my word that it won't hurt. In the future, you'll be able to forget it ever happened."

"The hell I'm going to forget this!"

"Please be quiet; I don't want to prevent you from using your mouth."

I raised my head as much as I could, straining the muscles in my neck. "It's not happening. *You're not fucking me!*"

He stripped off all his clothes and got down on his knees. Seeing his hard-on made this nightmare all the more real.

He said, "Your muscles won't resist, but I'm still going to use a lubricant."

I couldn't breathe, couldn't think. "Albert, listen to me. This was not a part of the agreement."

"You are here to help me however I see fit with my work."

"This is not about your work!"

"Getting this out of my system should help me focus better, and that will lead to better results." He sounded like he truly believed that.

I heard him pulling down my underwear. My pulse echoed through my ears. I focused my entire willpower into trying to move my limbs, but I might as well have tried controlling the Earth's rotation.

Albert pulled a lube bottle from his bag and rubbed some on his erect cock. I had no doubt that this image would haunt me for the rest of my life.

"Albert, you can still stop this. I won't mention it again, and we could—"

"Hush now. You've got nothing to fear."

"Damn you. *Help! Help!*"

"Stop acting silly."

He was right. Who was going to hear me down here? A heavy sense of defeat settled upon me. "What about... damn it, what about a condom?"

"No need. I did your blood tests, and I know myself. Nothing for you to worry about."

He climbed on top of me, his naked body covering mine. If he were heavy, I couldn't tell. Focusing my eyes, I noticed our blurry reflection on the glass wall. Seeing myself naked underneath him shattered something inside me.

"Please don't cry."

"Why? So you could convince yourself this isn't rape?"

He moved his head up and for a moment I allowed myself to believe I'd gotten some sense into him. Then pain exploded when he smashed his fist into my cheek. White flashes covered my vision as the metallic taste of blood filled my mouth. I spat and said, "Is this how you handle the truth?" My jaw burned, possibly broken. Currents of pain spread through my skull.

"I apologize. That…that was uncalled for. Now, please be quiet."

I stared at his reflection as he sank into me. With one movement of his hips, everything changed.

When he was fully inside, his entire body shook. A deep moan escaped his throat, crawling straight into my ears. Then came the thrusting, faster and faster. The sound of his waist smashing against my ass made me dizzy, made me want to pull my ears out.

I forced myself to stop crying but didn't turn my head. I kept staring at myself lying underneath his pale, sweaty body, my head rocking back and forth with the rhythm of his movements. He didn't say a word the entire time, just moaned and panted, his hands constantly moving across my skin, although I couldn't feel his touch. Saliva mixed with blood dripped from the corner of my mouth, creating a small, sticky puddle.

When Albert finally came, he let out an animalistic sound made more unnerving coming through the mask. His breath was heavy as he gently stroked my head. "That was beautiful. Thank you. I'm sorry for ejaculating inside you. I promise you again I don't carry diseases."

I didn't answer, my mind blank.

He stood up, his pale feet inches from my face. "I'll bring something to clean you up and then bring back the movement to your body. Good as new. How does that sound?"

I licked my lips, tasting blood. My cheek and jaw were swelling fast. "It sounds like a rapist who's trying to play it cool."

I expected him to hit me, but he got dressed instead. I shut my eyes as he began cleaning my asshole with napkins from his bag, grateful I couldn't physically feel the shame.

Albert got up without a word, then left and closed the glass door behind him. His face was flushed as he took off the black mask, his eyes avoiding me. When he went back to his computer, I expected him to activate the gas that would bring me back my body, but he didn't. I lay for another twenty minutes while he worked on his computer like I wasn't there.

I wondered whether I'd strangle him to death once I got my hands back. Maybe he wondered the same, and by leaving me useless, he was giving me a chance to cool down.

Lying like a corpse, my thoughts were a scattered puzzle. I had been fully aware of every horrific second, yet I hadn't felt a thing. It left my mind in disarray. I wondered if I could push the memory into a dark drawer in the back of my mind, to let it stay forgotten until the end of time. Somehow, I was doubtful.

When Albert decided enough time had passed, he released the other gas by clicking on a different circle that switched its color to yellow. He'd told me earlier I'd feel no pain, but the first thing I noticed was the wrongness inside me. Even if I hadn't been aware of what took place, this feeling would have made things crystal clear.

"I have other things to do, Matthew. Please get up." He waited outside the open door like he was holding an elevator for me.

I pushed myself up, which made the wrongness inside me feel more noticeable. The dry blood on the corner of my mouth was itching, but that was negligible compared to my throbbing jaw. It was hard to walk on my shaky legs, but I hurried to grab my underwear and stepped outside the room.

"You should consider taking a shower," Albert said.

I stood in front of him and looked into his eyes, failing to find any sign of remorse. I pictured myself lunging at him, pounding his face until he was unrecognizable. But the last time I'd allowed myself to lose myself to fury, it came back to haunt me.

Albert cleared his throat. "Go clean yourself before you end up doing something you'll regret." There was a trace of fear in his voice but also a warning.

Despite the dark thoughts swirling in my head, the feeble voice of logic kept me from exploding. I walked to the bathroom, washed Albert from my skin with boiling water and soap. Ignoring the small mirror on the wall, I dried myself off and stepped out into the bright lab.

"I left a painkiller for you on the counter," Albert said with his back to me.

I took the painkiller and was barely able to drink it down with my bruised jaw.

Walking toward the entrance of the house, we

didn't speak, the silence eerie. It felt like I was walking automatically, my brain incapable of coherent thoughts.

At the front door, Albert began speaking, but I ignored him and walked away.

The door slammed behind me.

15

"Christ, you look like crap. Your cheek's all swollen. *What did you do?*"

Sitting in Mike's car, I numbly stared ahead, my breath unsteady. "I need to see Jeff." It was hard to speak. I wished the painkiller would start working.

"We're not seeing Jeff until you tell me what's going on."

"It's between me and him."

He slammed his fist on the dashboard. "Don't give me that shit; you know you're mine as well. Fuck, I knew you were gonna mess this up for me!"

I clenched my fists. "Take me to see Jeff."

Mike shook his head. "Nope. Not if you're not gonna tell me what for. I'll take you home and milk the truth out of you the old-fashioned way."

"Don't." I pinched the bridge of my nose, trying to collect my scattered thoughts. "He...he forced himself on me."

"What the hell does that mean?"

"You know what that means!"

He cleared his throat and said, "Wasn't that a part of your deal? I mean, I don't really know what you're supposed to do over there, but I sort of figured sex was a part of it."

I felt sick hearing him say that. "Sex wasn't a part of it. God, why would you even think that? What happened shouldn't have happened, and I-I..."

"Take it easy. I'll call Jeff. You want me to tell him what happened?"

"No. Just tell him I need to see him right away."

"Yeah, I'm on it. Wait here. Take this." He gave me a bottle of water, and I drank as he got out of the car. He came back a minute later and said, "He's not home."

"I need to see him. I can't—"

"He'll be home in about twenty minutes. We're going there now."

I could finally breathe better. "Thank you."

"Does it hurt?" Mike asked after we started driving. The rain was pouring heavily, but it was still early so the road was easy to see.

"It hurts in my jaw."

"I mean...you know."

I had a sudden flashback of Albert thrusting into me, his deep moans right next to my ear. *That was beautiful. Thank you.* I shook my head with a shudder, tasting bile. "It's complicated."

Mike glanced at me but remained quiet.

It had stopped raining by the time we reached Jeff's building. "He should be there by now," Mike said. "You ready?"

"No." *What if he'll refuse to listen?*

"Well, we're already here. Let's go before the rain starts again."

*

Jeff stared at me for a long moment before letting us inside. He told me to sit on the couch, then sat next to me. Mike went to stand close to the kitchen and crossed his arms.

"How's your jaw?" Jeff asked.

"Hurts."

I flinched when he touched my chin.

"Relax." He tilted my head carefully to the side. "It doesn't look broken, but it will take time to heal." He let go. "What happened?"

I rubbed my face, the side that wasn't bruised. The gravity of this meeting sat heavily on my chest, knowing the ramifications could change everything. "I didn't want it. I told him no."

"You need to be clearer."

I focused my thoughts, determined to get the words out. "He used gas on me, made me crawl when I couldn't feel my legs. Then he made me paralyzed from the neck down. He came inside the room and started talking about being lonely, how I was his partner. He asked me about sex, then took off his clothes, and—"

"Okay. I understand."

"I told him to stop, but he wouldn't listen. He said it would help him with his work. I just lay there like a corpse, and he...shit!" I put my face in my hands, every nerve in my body on fire. I needed to reach into my brain and remove those images because carrying them around would slowly poison me.

Jeff asked, "Did you two argue before that happened?"

I raised my head. "Argue? No."

"Did you say anything that might've pissed him off?"

"What?"

"You have a big mouth, Matt. Try to remember if—"

"I didn't say anything to him!"

"All right. Calm down." He took a breath and let it out slowly. "I'm sorry you had to go through this."

The honesty in his voice was encouraging. "We're on the same page here, right? I'm not going back there."

He looked down at his hands, his shoulders stiff. "It's not so simple."

My blood boiled in an instant. A buzzing sound filled my ears. "Our agreement was *not* about sex. I'm not going back there."

He remained quiet, still avoiding my eyes. The meaning behind his silence became clear, and my heart sank. "You're going to make me go back there."

"I'll ask for a few days off for you, but—"

I jumped to my feet and hurried toward the door, unwilling to sit there and debate whether I should go back to a psychopath.

Jeff said, "Come back here."

I ignored him and opened the front door, but Mike pushed hard and shut it. "He didn't say you can go."

I growled, "Get your hand out of my way."

"Enough," Jeff said. "Come here, Matt."

I waited to be sure I could control myself, then slowly walked back to him.

He put his hands on my shoulders. "I'm sorry about what happened."

"Thanks. It means the world."

"Manners," Mike murmured close behind me.

"I need you to let go of what happened, to move on."

I shook my head. "I can't move on. He'll do it again."

"He might. But you survived this time, and you'll survive again. Breaking up the deal isn't an option at the moment, so I'm telling you again—your job is to keep him happy. Too much is riding on this."

I looked into Jeff's eyes, reminded that for him I was nothing but a means to an end. "You're forcing me to go back to a madman." I couldn't bring myself to say the word *rapist*. "You don't even give a fuck. God, I hope that someday someone will put a bullet in your head and that—"

"On your knees! Position two." Mike stood next to me, his warm breath on my face.

"It's none of your business," I hissed.

"*You are* my business."

I debated whether I could take him down before Jeff stopped me, but that wouldn't solve a thing, just open another battlefront.

Mike grabbed my arm and squeezed. "Calm the hell down and get down on your knees. Position two. *Now*."

His words had a direct route to my brain, cutting through my rage. I sheepishly sank to my knees and put my hands behind my head.

Mike blurted, "Sorry about that. He had a long day."

Jeff went away for a few seconds and came back with a small silver box. I only took it once Mike allowed me to stand up.

Jeff told Mike, "Take him home and make sure he eats and gets some rest."

Without saying another word, Mike and I left. By the

time we got inside the car, exhaustion sank into my bones. I wanted to crawl into my bed, to shut myself from everything and everyone. It took me a few seconds to notice Mike hadn't started the car. He stared at me with a deep scowl.

I asked, "What?"

"You're really asking me what, you little shit? How could you talk to Jeff like that?"

"I'd plenty of reasons."

"Doesn't matter. You acted like I've taught you nothing."

"Oh, give me a break. This isn't about you."

He grabbed my shirt. "Watch your mouth. What you do reflects on me, don't you get that? When you lose it in front of Jeff, it's *me* he'll get mad at." He shook his head. "I should fucking break your bones right now."

"Then fucking break them and shut up already!"

His eyes grew wide, and I realized I was about to cross a dangerous line. Yet I didn't let fear overpower me. I stared him back in the eyes until he finally looked away and started the car.

*

"You don't need to come with me," I said as we climbed the stairs.

"Just keep walking."

Inside my apartment, Mike took ice from my fridge, wrapped it in a small towel, and told me to put it on my cheek. He then took out some of the food Molly had given me and heated it up.

"I'm not hungry," I said.

"He said you eat, so you eat."

We ate in silence. I took small bites, but it still hurt.

Mike finished first and said, "Take tomorrow off from work. I'll come by early to check up on you, then we'll go for a run."

"A run?"

"I stopped running a while back, so now is as good a time as any to get back into it. It will also help clear your head."

There wasn't enough land in New Hampshire to clear my head. "Fine."

I finished eating, and Mike got up and took our dishes to the sink, where he washed them with soap. I stared at his back with a frown, too tired to comment.

Mike turned around. "You okay staying here alone?"

"Yes."

He dried his hands on a towel. "Maybe call someone to come hang out."

I shook my head. "Not gonna happen."

He watched me closely before saying, "All right. Just don't do anything stupid. I mean it."

I nodded, too drained to freak him out like last time.

After he left, I took a shower and stood under the hot stream with my forehead resting against the tiles. I tried to trick my brain into thinking of happier things, but it was a waste of time. When I realized an hour had passed, I got out and faced my reflection. The side of my face was swollen, not a bruise that would soon heal. Bill would see me like this, Molly as well. More lies. At least with Mike's better-concealed bruises I had a chance to pretend they didn't exist.

I got dressed and climbed out onto the fire escape with one of Jeff's joints. The air smelled like rain and the street was quieter than usual. I took the first puff and held my breath to enhance the effect, then slowly released the smoke.

A few minutes later, Caleb opened his window and stuck his head out. "What you've got cooking, Matty?"

"Come here and check."

He got out carefully and sat on his side of the fire escape. I passed him the joint. Before putting it to his lips, he asked, "What's wrong with your mouth?"

"You can see my bruise?"

"I can hear you speak."

"It's no big deal."

"Umm. Sounds to me like that cop had another go at you."

I stared at him, momentarily lost for words. "How... how do you know about that?"

He blew out smoke and gave me back the joint. "Wicked good stuff."

"Caleb..."

"I have myself some mighty fine ears, mind you. When both our windows are open, I can hear him talking shit and hurting you. Every time I want to go over there and whip his ass, but I don't think it'd be wise. Besides, if you let him do that in the first place, I'm sure you have your reasons."

I let out a tight breath, shame growing inside me. I wanted to ask if he thought less of me, but I didn't trust him to be honest.

I asked, "You ever feel like somebody up there decided

you're going down, no matter what?"

He pondered on my question and finally nodded. "I've been known to feel like that from time to time. Doesn't mean it's true, though. Doesn't mean other folks don't have it worse than me."

"Well, tell them to give me a call; I'll make them feel a whole lot better. Anyway, at least now you know that police car wasn't here for you. No aliens."

He snorted. "Like they'd ever use something so obvious. No, man, *ice cream trucks*—that's where those motherfuckers at! Playing that stupid-ass music in those stupid-ass pink trucks. Keep an eye out for me, will ya?"

I blew out smoke. "Yeah, I've got your back."

He pointed his finger at me. "And I've got yours, Brother Matt. Don't you forget that."

16

I was pulled from sleep by a hand touching my back. Every nerve in my body shrieked in alarm. I sharply turned around and sent my fist toward Albert, hitting his face. He yelled, his voice higher than usual.

I blinked the blurriness away, and my heart dropped at the sight of Mike. He looked at me with murder in his eyes, leaning against my closet and holding his jaw.

"I thought you were Albert."

He glared at me for a long moment before lowering his hand. "Forget it. Good thing you hit like a chick."

I pushed myself up to a sitting position, my heart gradually settling down.

Mike sat on the bed wearing sports clothes. "How do you feel?"

I ran a hand through my messy morning hair. "Had a hard time falling asleep, but I think I'm okay."

"Good." He pulled a note from his pocket. "Here are some support centers' numbers, if you need someone to talk to."

I hesitantly took the list. He had written down the names and numbers of three places. The names mentioned 'sexual assault' and 'domestic violence'. I felt uneasy thinking of the types of people who turned to places like these for help. *Am I one of them?*

"Uh, thank you."

"No biggie. Keep in mind they might try to convince you to file a complaint—something you're not about to do, *right*?"

I nodded at his less-than-subtle warning. "Don't worry."

"Good boy. By the way, the missus and I made up."

I put the list aside. "You've forgiven her?"

"Yep, after a long negotiation." He leaned closer with a sly smile. "From now on she'll be ready to do anal once a week and let me spend three evenings away with the guys. I'm gonna be spending most of the time inside Trish, but Emily doesn't need to know about that. So, overall, it's pretty sweet."

"That's cool." It wasn't, but I had enough problems of my own. "You want to go for a run?"

"Sure do. You usually run in Merrifield Park, right?"

I remembered he used to watch me when I wasn't aware, waiting for me to make a mistake so he could step in and take over my life. "That's the only park I don't need to drive to."

"Cool. And once we're done, we'll have a nice education session."

I was suddenly fully awake. "Why?"

"Why?" He grabbed the back of my neck. I could see the little capillaries in the corner of his eyes. "Don't you feel it, Matty? Your fear's almost gone. I can't smell it no more." He sniffed my neck. "Nope, can't smell it at all. Looks like yesterday you found out there are scarier things in the world than me." He shook his head with mock remorse. "I can't let it stay that way."

"I'm still scared of you."

"Even if that's true, after the way you acted yesterday —"

"You know why I acted like that."

He stroked my head like he was calming down a child. I kept my fists clenched underneath the blanket. "I know what you've been through, and that was why I let your little tantrum slide yesterday. But you made me look bad in front of Jeff, and I ain't letting it happen ever again."

*

The sun was high in the sky, spreading a fake sense of warmth.

"Stop looking so miserable," Mike said as we reached the start of the track. "You're bringing down my mood." He tightened his shoelaces. "Man, I'm so pumped for this. Are there any hot chicks running here?"

"Don't know."

He rolled his eyes. "All right, let's go."

Running had become my mental and physical escape in the last year, but sharing it with Mike tainted the experience, made me feel like running inside a cage. I was also aware of the likelihood of this being my last run for a while, assuming Mike was about to resume his education sessions.

I glanced to the side when I heard Mike panting. He was obviously rustier than he thought. His ego wouldn't let him run slower than me, and my hatred caused me to run even faster.

Luckily for him, his phone started ringing and saved

him from a possible heart attack. He halted and gasped heavily, relief across his flushed face. I stopped a few feet ahead and wiped my damp brow.

"It's Jeff. Hold on."

Unease ran through me, an ominous feeling in the middle of my chest.

"Hi, Jeff. What's up?" Mike watched me while Jeff answered. "Yeah, I'm with him now...what? No, he's doing fine." He lowered his voice and turned around, but I could still barely hear him say, "Between you and me, I think he might have overplayed this whole *rape* card...you know how he is."

I shouldn't have been surprised by anything Mike said or did, yet I found myself stunned.

Mike said, "When does Albert want him? Tonight? You mean the entire night? I see...he's not gonna like it...yeah, don't worry, he'll be good."

Despite the cold, my skin caught fire. My pulse throbbed in my ears at the thought of being locked in that lab for so many hours.

It will never stop. It will just get worse and worse.

Ever since Jeff had knocked on my door in the middle of the night and shoved his deal down my throat, my life began slipping faster into chaos. I kept waiting for the exit sign to appear, but it never did.

The sudden understanding of what I must do—what I should have done a long time ago—filled me with adrenaline. With purpose.

It ends now.

I took a quiet step back while Mike kept talking with his back to me, oblivious to what he'd unintentionally set into motion. Knowing I was about to put my life on the line, I took one last step back, then turned around and ran like hell.

*

"Matt! What the hell?"

Icy wind smashed into my face and screamed in my ears, but I could still hear him trying to catch up with me.

"You don't want do this! Stop!"

He sounded farther than he had a few seconds ago. The curve of the track provided a temporary cover from his line of sight. I noticed a small, almost unseen turn to the side. Without a second to think, I took the turn and dashed through oak trees and thick bushes, barely dodging the branches and logs.

I slowed as I got close to leaving the park, then crouched between the bushes and listened closely. The tree branches rustled, sending my heart sprinting, but it was only the wind. Minutes passed and it seemed Mike didn't know where I was.

I let out a deep sigh and sank to the ground with my back against a tree. I had more sweat on me than skin. The realization of what I'd done began sinking in, spreading hot dread in the pit of my stomach.

I leaned my head back and tried to calm myself down. *A plan*. I needed a good, solid plan because I wasn't about to turn full-on Tarzan and start living in the woods. I needed to check which bus would get me as far away from Hudson. Almost everyone in town owned a car, so public transportation wasn't something to blindly rely on.

I didn't have my phone with me, but that wasn't necessarily a bad thing since Mike might have had a way to track it. It was also possible that soon every one of Jeff's crooked cops would be on the lookout. God, I was losing it. My chest hurt.

Go back and ask for forgiveness. It's too much for you to handle.

I shook my head and slapped myself to shut down the voices of doubt. "That's not helping," I said out loud. "Focus. Focus."

I had my wallet with me, which held my credit card and one hundred bucks, but my credit card was maxed out, had been for months. I had about three hundred bucks in my apartment, hidden in the kitchen. Going back was risky, but it wasn't far. If I were Mike, I'd first scan the park before moving on to other locations. *But what if he was already in my apartment?*

The fire escape. I could try using it to check for Mike through my bedroom window. I remembered leaving my window a little open this morning. Going back would also give me a chance to grab my parents' photo album.

I came out of the woods and straight into the busy street, scanning in a frenzy everything that crossed my line of sight. The streets seemed overly wide and exposed as I ran through them like a target in a shooting range. Mike's police car was parked in front of my building, but there was no sign of him around. I hurried to where the fire escape hung in midair.

"Goddammit!" I remembered the stairs being lower,

close enough so I could jump and grab the bottom part, then haul myself up. But they were way too high, and even the ones on Caleb's building were out of reach. *Caleb*. If he were home, I could try to reach my apartment from his side of the fire escape.

Without a second thought, I entered Caleb's building, hurried up the stairs, then knocked on his door.

"Who's there?"

Thank God. "Caleb, it's me, Matt."

"Brother Matt?"

"Yes."

He opened the door and stared at me with a frown. I've never been in his apartment before. "Matt? Look at you looking all tall. Were you like this yesterday?"

"Yeah, probably. Let me in, okay?"

He took his hand out of his robe and gestured me inside. "My nose tells me you went running."

He had a nice apartment, with a big carpet in the living room and about a thousand music albums, all vinyl. A song by Nina Simone was playing in the background.

"Sorry to bother you. Can I please use your fire escape to get to my apartment?"

"Forgot your key?"

"Something like that."

"Isn't there a safer way?"

"There isn't."

"Well, go ahead, then. No falling, you hear?"

He showed me to his bedroom, and I carefully climbed onto the fire escape. As I remembered, my window was slightly open. I tried looking for any movement inside, but my window was too dusty. I carefully lifted one leg over the railing, not liking the creaking sound my weight caused. I didn't have a fear of heights, but I wasn't a fan. It took some maneuvering and flexibility, but I was eventually able to reach the other side. Before raising my window, I listened for any sounds but heard nothing.

"Is someone there?" Caleb asked from his bedroom, lines of concern on his brow.

"No. It's just..."

"Oh, I hear you, Matty. Do what you must. We all got our aliens."

"Yeah, I guess we do." I raised my window, then carefully squeezed inside and tiptoed toward my bedroom door. I was about to go into the living room when my phone started ringing from the kitchen, causing me to yelp in surprise. I forced myself to relax and stepped into the living room. Mike's number blinked on my screen. The call ended after a few seconds, revealing five missed calls from him.

I went to the cabinet and pulled out the hidden three hundred bucks, which suddenly felt like a pitiful amount. I needed to quickly pack a bag and grab my parents' photo album, but before I had a chance to do any of that, angry footsteps sounded from outside the front door. I took a shaky step back, hoping I'd only imagined the sound. Then Mike banged on the door.

"You there, Matt?" He sounded short of breath. "Matt!"

I didn't make a sound, didn't move a muscle except anxiously glancing at the cabinet with the photo album. Opening those old doors would make a noise I couldn't risk making.

Mike started messing with the lock. As quietly as I could, I returned to my bedroom and hurried toward the window. I had one leg out when Mike stormed into my apartment.

"Matt!"

Shit. I pushed myself out the window, my body a shaking mess. Caleb was already back inside. There was no way I was risking going down the rusty flight of stairs with Mike so close. I stood with my back to the wall, as far away from the open window as I could. My heart pounded with a hammer against my chest. I glanced around, hoping to find another way down, but there was none.

Mike stomped around my apartment, calling my name. When he reached my bedroom, his heavy breaths sounded alarmingly close. I wasn't religious, but I found myself praying for whoever was willing to listen to not let Mike see me.

"Fucking bastard," he grumbled, right before the springs squeaked when he sat on my bed. It sounded like he was dialing on his phone. I wasn't surprised to hear him say, "Jeff, you got a minute? Yes, it's urgent… listen, that little fucker ran away…that's why I needed to hang up…yeah, I looked everywhere in the park… I'm at his place right now, and he hasn't been here… well, the door was locked, and his phone is still in the kitchen…no, he's not hiding in the bathroom…what? The window? It's open."

The springs squeaked again, and God was giving

me the finger. I looked down as Mike got his upper body through the open window. He noticed my legs immediately and slowly shook his head as we made eye contact.

"Good thinking, Jeff, I got him right here...you should see the look on his face...come here, you piece of—"

That was as far as he got. I kicked his face and heard his nose breaking. He fell back inside with a cry of pain.

Caleb was suddenly at his window, eyes wide with panic.

I hissed, "Get inside and close your window. You didn't see me."

In less than two seconds, he was gone.

Mike kept moaning inside my bedroom—the sweetest sound to ever reach my ears. I stormed down the stairs and once at the bottom, pushed the bolt that should release the ladder. "Damn it!"

Nobody used this bolt in ages; it was covered in rust. I tried kicking it, but it didn't budge.

"Matt! Don't fucking run from me!" It sounded like he was climbing out my window.

The hell with this. I turned around, grabbed the cold railing, then carefully lowered myself until I hung in midair.

"Matt!"

I let go and awkwardly hit the ground, lost my footing and crashed on my ass. My ankles were sore but didn't feel broken. I pushed myself carefully to my feet.

"You're a dead man!" The stairs squeaked and shook as Mike dashed down.

I began running, didn't dare to look back. The

only way was forward because the other way offered nothing but hell.

Part Three
A Little Life

17

"I run a respectable business. I hope that's clear."

"Yes, sir." It wasn't, but I was too exhausted to care.

"All right. You're paying for three nights?"

"Yes. And can I please have a room with a window to the parking lot and a back door?"

"The rooms don't have back doors."

"Oh. Just the window, then."

The manager eyed me like he was considering telling me to take a hike. I couldn't blame him for being suspicious since I'd shown up in the middle of the night wearing sports clothes, asked to pay in cash, and had a nasty bruise on the side of my face. I probably wouldn't have rented myself a room.

"One last thing," the guy said from across the messy front desk. He seemed to be in his fifties, overweight with a round, tanned face that was as smooth as his bald head. Small and faded scars decorated the back of his hands. A cigarette pack peeked from the breast pocket of his worn-out army coat. I noticed a silver star framed on the wall. "I take the privacy of my guests seriously, but I don't take lightly to them bringing in their...clients."

"Um, okay. I don't have any clients."

He sighed and tapped impatiently on the counter

with his thick fingers. "I'm talking about guys coming here and paying for your time."

"My time? Oh no-no, I'm not…I'm not doing that kind of stuff."

He stared at me as if he had a scanner for rent boys, then finally nodded. "All right. Had some issues with these sorts of things in the past. Thought to make it clear."

"It's okay. Do you serve breakfast?"

"Sure do. I'll also send someone to sponge your back."

I chuckled. "I'll take that as a no."

"Where's your luggage?"

"What? Oh, I travel light."

"You mean empty handed."

I kept my mouth shut.

He rolled his eyes, then finally walked me to my room on the ground floor. I'd be able to see the parking lot and the road from the room's big window, although I'd have no means of escape other than the front door.

It was freezing outside, and I tried hard to stand still without shaking too badly. It had taken me more than a three-hour bus drive to find myself in this small and deserted motel. The sign I'd passed on the side of the road said, *"Welcome to Grafton! Home of 819 happy Vermonters."*

I'd changed two buses on my way here. The last bus had driven past interstate 91, and then I was no longer in my home state.

The man said, "This room has a bathtub. If you prefer —"

"A bathtub is wicked. Thank you."

Still hesitant, he handed me the key. "I won't be having anyone come looking for you, will I?"

"For me? No. No one." Unless Jeff's influence ran deeper than I thought. I asked, "Do you have stores around here?"

He pointed to the south although all I saw was darkness. "About a twenty-minute walk down the road you'll find a small shopping center. My brother runs the burger joint next to the main entrance. If you tell him you're staying here, you'll get a discount."

"Thank you. I'll check it out tomorrow."

He nodded. "Well, you have yourself a good night." He gave me a once-over. "Looks like you had a long day."

Try a long year. He left, and I stepped inside the warm room. It was small but clean with patterned wallpaper of faded red squares. When I sat on the bed, the mattress felt solid with no noticeable lumps. I slumped on my back and let the air slowly leave my lungs. It felt like I'd been holding my breath for hours.

I wanted to get a hot shower and wash the dry sweat from my skin, but I ended up falling asleep in my dirty clothes.

*

I awoke with a scream to cold hands wrapped around my throat, squeezing tight. With my eyes wide open, it took me a moment to remember where I was.

Calm the hell down. They don't know where you are.

I rubbed my neck, still feeling those cold hands choking me. With a grunt, I crawled into a ball, not sure if I was ready to face the new day. The quiet around was absolute—my rapid breath the only sound I heard.

Having no distractions allowed stressful thoughts to flood my brain. If Mike had gone ahead with his threat and framed me for those cocaine bags, I might've been a wanted man right now. Yet it was his threat to hurt Bill and Molly that worried me the most. I needed to remind myself that as much as I hated Mike, he was anything but stupid. Hurting innocent people in a small place like Hudson would not go unnoticed, and wouldn't be worth the risk now that I was no longer in town.

I pushed myself out of bed and peeled off every smelly piece of clothing from my skin. I needed to find something clean to wear, fast. Looking at my reflection in the mirror, the bruise on my cheek looked a little better, but it was still noticeable.

Someone had left a sealed toothbrush in the cabinet under the sink. I used it while the water ran in the tub, wondering whether I'd be able to squeeze through the small window above the toilet in case of danger. It didn't look hopeful.

I slipped into the bathtub. Lying motionless in the hot water spread a sense of ease across my body, but my brain refused to settle down. Despite my successful escape, I didn't have enough money to support myself, nor did I have a plan for my next move. I'd also left my parents' photo album behind and was sure I'd end up regretting it for the rest of my life. My rent had been paid for the next five months, but knowing Jeff, I doubted my apartment would stay in one piece for long.

I ducked under the hot water when the thoughts became overwhelming. If it hadn't been for my lungs demanding air, I would have stayed down there for hours. With my head above the surface, I decided I was far enough from Jeff and Mike, at least for the time being. Still, I needed to lie low, maybe dye my hair. A beard would also help, but that would take longer.

I came out of the bathtub and into my dirty clothes, then stepped outside into the cloudy day. Walking down the road past vast fields of wheat, I felt far away from civilization. The few passing cars stopped to ask if I needed help. It boded well for local hospitality, but also made it clear I was a strange bird around these parts.

The shopping center wasn't impressive, but it had what I needed. There were no big brands, only local shops with names like "Lily's Magical Gardening Tools" and "Trevor's Home Supplies." Most stores had signs for "BUY LOCAL!" hanging proudly. Between the two main walls of the structure, a big handmade poster said, "Don't miss out on Grafton's Chili Festival!"

I walked into a small clothing store and collected clothes that weren't too expensive, although it was annoying paying state taxes after I was used to the New Hampshire way of things.

Feeling famished, I went to eat a burger with extra everything. The owner gave me a discount when I mentioned where I was staying, but when he tried making small talk, I found myself mumbling and dodging his questions like bullets.

I decided to go ahead and get my hair dyed. If I was going to make this work, I couldn't afford to take any risks. The woman at the hairdressing salon thought I was joking when I asked to dye my hair. "You don't touch a color like yours!"

"Still, I need it black."

With a little smile and a wink, she asked, "Are you going undercover?"

"I need it for a role I'm about to play." That was the first thing that came into my mind, and for the next thirty minutes I did my best to handle the tsunami of questions she threw my way. Once she finished, I stared at my reflection, lost for words. The black color made me look like somebody else, and I needed to remind myself that was the whole point.

Back in my room, I stuffed my dirty clothes in a bag and changed into something clean, then lay in bed and let myself relax. It was my first day as a fugitive, and I had yet to screw up. Still, I couldn't postpone deciding on my next move. Even though this motel wasn't expensive, I'd soon be left without any money.

I didn't have a clear destination in mind. Maybe Boston which wasn't so far, or maybe even California for the killer weather. But I couldn't afford to travel all the way to the West Coast, and hitchhiking sounded like a solid recipe for ending up dead in a ditch.

I yawned and turned around on my stomach. Golden light shone through the curtains, covering everything in a peaceful glow. If I were still in Hudson, right about now I would've been making my way home from work, where Mike would've been waiting for another session of his screwed-up notion of education. *Remember to make me hear the pain, Matty, or I'll need to go harder.*

I began drifting toward sleep when a knock on the door jolted me up. *They're here.* I stopped breathing and stared anxiously at the door, expecting it to fly open.

"Hmm, hello?"

I breathed a sigh of relief at the sound of the manager's voice. Still fighting jitters, I carefully opened the door halfway.

The guy frowned. "You dyed your hair."

"What? Oh, yeah. I…um, wanted something different."

"Well, it's different. You got what you needed from the shopping center?"

I opened the door a bit more and peeked outside. Nobody else was there. The sunset painted the sky in deep orange and red. "Yes, thank you. Your brother gave me a discount on the burger. It was delicious."

"The secret is the Richard's BBQ Sauce. They make it upstate." He crossed his arms. "Listen, I don't know what you've got going on these days, but I have a friend who's been looking for help with his fields. He can pay in cash, and you'll also get a semi-warm lunch."

"You mean like taking stuff out of the ground and putting seeds inside?"

"That pretty much sums it up. Maybe he'll even let you drive a tractor and honk the horn. Not something you have a lot of experience with, I reckon."

"Not really."

"Well, he could still use another set of hands. We're expecting a week without snow, and that's a good time to get some work done before the next blizzard."

I opened my mouth to decline since I was ready to keep moving further away from Hudson. But thinking I could simply start fresh with the amount of money

I had was naive. Getting paid in cash sounded like an opportunity I'd be stupid to turn away. Before I had a chance to second-guess myself, I asked, "When can I start?"

He blinked in surprise, probably expecting me to refuse or ask more questions. "You can start tomorrow morning. Tom will come to pick you up at six. Got a number I can give him?"

"Uh…no. Lost my phone."

He raised an eyebrow. "How unfortunate. I'll give him the number of your room in case he needs to talk to you."

"Great. Sorry, but I didn't catch your name yesterday."

"It's Hank."

"Thanks, Hank. I appreciate it. Say, mind if I use your computer for five minutes? I left kind of in a hurry—"

"You? No…"

I laughed, which helped ease some of the tightness in my chest. "There's someone I want to send an email to, letting him know I'm all right."

"You can call him if you want."

"I think an email would be better." Talking with Bill would be too much for my nerves, and I didn't want to hear the concern in his voice, nor the disappointment.

Hank agreed, and once in front of his computer, I logged into my Gmail account and put in Bill's email. I wrote that I was okay and needed to disappear for a while. With unsteady hands, I suggested that he and Molly should try keeping a low profile for a few weeks, maybe go visit Molly's sister out of town. I also asked Bill to tell Caleb I was okay, then ended the email by thanking him and Molly for everything they'd done for me. Mostly for giving me a sense of family in the last few weeks.

I had a fist-sized lump in my throat when I sent the email, knowing I was taking the coward's way but not feeling strong enough to handle it differently.

Back in my room, I slumped on the bed and closed my eyes, soaking in the peaceful silence. I wasn't sure whether taking on that job was a good idea, but leaving was always an option if things didn't work out. Nothing was holding me back anymore. No Jeff, no Mike, and no crazy-ass Albert.

18

"What's wrong with your hands?"

I looked up. "What?"

"You've been looking at them funny." Steve came closer. The sun was high in the sky, and we were both smelly and covered in dirt. Even during wintertime, it wasn't hard breaking a sweat when you were outside working your ass off.

"It's nothing," I said and lowered my hands.

Steve smiled through a whole lot of freckles. Tom had only recently started assigning us to the same fields, which was a nice change since most of the other guys were grumpy and unfriendly.

Steve said, "You've got the hands of an office guy. Not used to blisters and cuts?"

"Nope, 'fraid not."

His voice went dramatically low. "Those are a warrior's hands now. Nothing to feel ashamed of."

I snickered. "No shame."

Although it'd only been a couple of weeks since I got here, my hands were changing, and maybe so was I. The first couple of days of working at the fields had been hell, but after my body had gotten used to the new daily challenge, I found myself embracing it. My mind was calmer while I worked, my thoughts less hectic.

"You work hard," Steve said. "Maybe even too hard."

"Meaning?"

"Oh, you know. Taking a break now and then won't kill ya. You're making some of the guys look mighty lazy."

"Well, some of them *are* mighty lazy."

He chuckled. "True that. Don't know why old Tom is keeping them around. Anyway, just letting you know what I heard. Don't let it bother you or nothing." He bumped my shoulder with his fist. "You're leaving less work for me, which makes you my new favorite person."

I nodded. "Honored."

"You're not from around here, are ya?"

"Ohio." I didn't even know why I chose Ohio of all places, but once I said that to Hank a few weeks back, I needed to stick to the lie. My major mistake was being upfront about my real name. When I'd told it to Hank on my first night in town, I didn't expect to stay for more than a few days. Now it was too late to do anything about it, but at least my name wasn't unique in any way.

Steve asked, "How's Vermont been treating you?"

"Mostly giving me blisters."

He laughed. It felt nice making someone laugh.

"You're from a bigger town?" he asked as he helped me lift a bag of fertilizer to the back of a truck.

"I think all towns are bigger than this place." I jumped down from the truck and landed in front of him. I was taller than him by about a head.

"True that," he said. "So, why come here? Grafton

ain't exactly filled with opportunities last time I checked."

We were moving into dangerous territory, but I needed to get used to answering those types of questions. "I just felt like having a fresh start somewhere new. This place happened to be on my way."

He scratched the back of his head. "Well, I can't picture myself living anywhere else, to be frank." He raised his hands to the sides. The gloves were too big for his thin hands, which made him look like a cartoon. "This is home, you know? But hey, people here are super friendly, even to strangers with blisters. Give it some time, you might like it here."

"Thanks. I'll do that."

I thought he was going to leave, but then he asked, "Got plans after work?"

I hesitated. It was a simple question, but somehow it made me feel like I was put on the spot. "Well...no, no plans." I usually watched TV in my room or went for a run. My social life was non-existent, and it suited me well.

Steve said, "We're going for a swim after work in Saxtons River. Water's cold as fuck, but once your balls get used to it, it's fun."

"Sounds cool. Enjoy."

"Wait, what? I'm asking if you wanna come."

"Oh. Hmm, who are you going with?"

"Some friends. All from around here."

"Wouldn't they mind me joining?"

"Huh?" He sized me up. "You seem harmless enough. Got lice?"

"No."

"Then why would they mind?"

I had no answer to that. I also had no real reason not to go, so I agreed.

Steve patted my shoulder. "Cool. I'll come pick you up later. Keep working those hands, office guy."

*

I shivered as my poor balls transformed into ice cubes underneath the water. Four of Steve's friends had joined us, and they all seemed fine with having me tag along. Despite the cold, I couldn't deny how beautiful the river was. The trees bent so far over the riverbank, it seemed they were leaning in to take a sip. We had about an hour of daylight left, with deep shades of gold already covering the sky.

I did my best to settle into the conversations around me while being careful not to volunteer extra details about myself. I couldn't help being jealous seeing how at ease those guys were with one another. It was something I used to take for granted, then one day it was gone.

A red pickup truck drove on the dirt road and parked close by. Two girls got out. I stopped swimming, my feet barely touching the ground.

"Isn't the water too cold for swimming?" the curly-haired blond asked. Her red sunglasses covered half her face. It sometimes felt fashion in Grafton was stuck in the '60s.

"It's plenty warm!" Steve called back, and we all tried to keep a straight face. "Matt, this blond beauty is my girl Amber. The other weird-looking one is Blue."

The weird-looking one rolled her eyes. She was beautiful in a way that made me openly stare as her light-brown hair blew in the wind. Both girls stripped to their bathing suits, then dove in.

Amber shrieked. "Steve! This is so freaking cold! My ovaries are gonna stop working and we'll never have babies."

"Woman, I don't want no babies!"

"Steven Davis Roberts, you take that back!"

Blue swam casually toward me. She had three small and lovely beauty marks under her left eye. Instead of introducing myself properly, what came out of my mouth was, "Aren't you freezing?"

"I like the cold. Keeps me focused."

I forced my eyes to look at her face and not slip to what lay beneath the lucid water. "Nice to meet you."

Her arms sent little waves my way as she kept floating. "Likewise. I heard about you."

"From Steve?"

"Uncle Hank."

"Motel owner Hank?"

"That's the one. All charm and grace."

I laughed, knowing how far Hank was from being those things. I noticed that the others had swum farther away from us. It sounded like Amber was still talking about babies.

I asked, "Is Blue your real name?" Talking to her reminded me of how long it had been since my last real conversation with the opposite sex.

"Blue's my real name, yes. My mom loved that Joni

Mitchell album. She split town when I was twelve, so I can't stand listening to it."

"Sorry about that."

"Nah, there are other good albums. So, what's your story?" She looked straight into my eyes.

"Me? No story."

"We all have stories."

"I think I'm rewriting mine these days."

"A better story than the old one?"

It better be. "I'm aiming for a better one, yes."

She swam around me in a circle, her movements elegant and quiet. When she stopped in front of me, she asked, "Is this just a stop on your way to the next chapter?"

I thought I'd become accustomed to dodging personal questions, but she kept me on my toes. "I don't know about the next chapter yet. I'm here for now, working with Steve."

"My condolences."

I smiled. "He's all right."

Like he knew we were talking about him, Steve suddenly called, "Yo, Matt, show her your blisters!"

"Jesus," I mumbled, hoping the cold would prevent my face from flushing. I quickly asked, "You from around here?"

"Born and raised. I lived for a while in New York, but there were way too many buildings."

"I'm also from a small place, but I guess it seems bigger now in comparison. Anyway, it's nice in Grafton."

"It is. Maybe a bit nicer *now*." She winked so quickly I

didn't know if I imagined it. Then she swam away, and I thought to myself this girl would be trouble, but I still hurried to follow her.

*

"Get away from me! *Get off!*"

"Matt! Matt!"

I opened my eyes to a man looming above me. His face was covered in shadows and his warm palm was on my chest. My blood froze. I opened my mouth to scream.

Light exploded, burning my eyes and making me sharply look away.

"It's me," Hank said.

I moved my face back toward him. The light came from the lamp next to my bed. Hank stared at me with wide eyes, his breath whistling.

"What happened?" I asked.

"Goddammit." He wiped his face and sat on the bed. "I thought someone was killing you."

I looked around me, beginning to understand what had happened. The moonlight shined through the open door, which was now slightly broken.

I sat up, focusing on taking proper breaths instead of trying to speak. *What could I even say?*

After a long moment of silence, Hank asked, "Do you remember what you dreamed about?"

"No."

"Matt."

Albert had been on top of me, but he was bigger than in real life, bigger than Jeff. His weight squashed my bones. My lungs were on fire. Both of us were naked and this time I was able to move my limbs but couldn't push him away. I screamed at him to stop, but he wouldn't listen. *You are my partner.*

"I didn't mean to wake you," I said, staring at the wall in front of me. I tried to keep myself composed, to not show him how deeply embarrassed I felt.

"I was already awake." He stood up and frowned at the door.

"Did you try knocking?" I asked, still confused on why he'd felt the need to break his own door.

"Try? I knocked like crazy, but you kept screaming."

Damn it. "I'm sorry. I'll find another place to stay tomorrow."

The anger in his eyes scared me. For a second, I thought he might hit me. "When I want you out, I'll make it clear." He looked back at the broken door. Parts of the wood lay scattered on the floor.

"I'll pay for it," I said.

"No."

"I'm not asking."

He scratched his chin. "Pay me back with work. Take over the front desk for a few hours tomorrow. We'll call it even."

"You sure?"

He nodded and picked up one of the wooden pieces. "You have a gun?"

"A gun? No."

"You ever used one?"

"No."

Hank let the wood fall. "We'll need to take care of that. Try to go back to sleep. I'll work on your door tomorrow."

"What do you mean by *take care of that*?"

He walked toward the open door. "When you might end up in a battle, you come prepared. There's no other way."

*

"How's that?"

Blue frowned at the shirt I was holding. "It's very green."

"I'm not color blind. Should I try it on?"

"You should try putting it back on the rack."

I sighed and returned the shirt. We've been shopping for over two hours, trying to renew my "redneck wardrobe," as Blue called it. So far, I only bought two new shirts and one pair of jeans. Blue vetoed most of the things I picked, making me think I could have bought a hundred shirts by now if I were shopping on my own. Luckily, there were only three relevant clothing stores in town, and we were now in number three.

"How's that?" I asked and pulled out a yellowish polo shirt.

"Ooh, now we're getting somewhere."

"It's sort of dorky."

"It's mature without looking too posh."

I went to try it on. When I came back, Blue gave me a thumbs up.

I watched myself in the mirror. The shirt was a bit tight. My biceps seemed bigger, which wasn't a surprise considering how hard I've been working. Blue snickered next to me, making me realize I'd been flexing like a douche.

"Sorry," I mumbled.

"Hey, if you got it, flaunt it."

"I'm not sure how many occasions I'll have to wear this."

"Fridays at the creek."

"I'll be wearing a jacket or a coat."

"Spring will be here eventually." She looked out the window at the snowy world outside. "I hope."

"Fine. I'm buying it."

Barbra welcomed us with a smile at the register. She was wearing a red puffer coat although it was plenty warm inside the store. "How's your dad and uncle Hank?" she asked Blue.

"Dad's into fishing this month, which is better than last month when he was into motorcycles. And Uncle Hank...well, we're still working on a hobby for that one. How's George and that damn knee of his?"

Barbra sighed like she was tired of the topic yet eager to talk about it extensively. "It hasn't gotten much worse, thank God, but the device I bought online didn't help at all. Between you and me, I wonder if all those five-star reviews were genuine. Who can really tell these days? Anyway, this damn weather sure ain't helping matters."

"I hear you," Blue said. "Give me some of that global warming in January and I'll throw you a party you'll never forget."

Barbra turned to me. "And how have you been settling in?"

"Taking it one day at a time, ma'am."

I gave her cash for the shirt, which she took with a coy smile. "May I just say, you two look mighty handsome together."

Without missing a beat, Blue said, "And with that new shirt we bought him—my goodness."

I quickly said, "We're just friends."

Barbra raised both eyebrows in confusion.

I cleared my throat. "I mean, we look separately handsome. Not together handsome. You know?" *Words, why are you betraying me?*

"Oh, I see." She sounded disappointed like she'd lost a bet on us. In truth, it wouldn't have surprised me if there were a bet like that going on around town.

Barbra said, "Well, who knows what the future might hold?" She winked at Blue—unsubtly—and I pretended not to notice.

I've only been living here for about a month or so, carefully rebuilding myself by keeping a low profile as much as possible in such a small but nosy town. Dating was not in my cards since I could find myself needing to flee with no warning. I also liked Blue too much to bring her into my messy life.

I grabbed my bag, and we made our way outside before things could get any more awkward.

19

"Fucking Victor," Steve mumbled for the fifth time in the last ten minutes.

"Let it go," I said and shoveled dirt aside. The rain earlier had made it easier to dig but also easier to sink ankle-deep into the ground if I wasn't careful.

Steve said, "He's just sitting there like a bag of potatoes, smoking with his buddies. Homer Simpson would've been proud."

I chuckled, loving the Simpsons reference. "They're taking a break."

Steve snorted. "A break from their previous break? I'm so hungry, I'm about to give you a bite."

"I'm delicious."

"Ha! Gross. Anyway, we could have been out of here by now, that's all I'm saying."

He was right. It was getting late, and we didn't have enough daytime to finish everything we needed, not to mention the temperatures were dropping fast. I was supposed to go out to eat with the guys, and my stomach didn't approve of the delay.

The sound of laughter made me lose concentration, and I accidentally threw dirt at Steve.

"Watch it, man!"

"Damn, sorry."

More laughter. Victor and his two friends were looking at us from the back of a truck, enjoying the show. I made eye contact with Victor, who was my height but probably twice my weight. When he blew a kiss in my direction, I had enough.

"Mind giving us a hand, Victor? And how about you two clowns?"

That shut them up. Next to me, Steve whistled.

"Big mouth," Victor called back and spat on the ground. "Keep working. Almost done, no?"

"We could've been done an hour ago if you would've done your part."

"Did enough. Work fast. Are you the boss man now?"

"If I were the boss, your ass would have been long gone by now."

He jumped down from the back of the truck and started walking toward me, his movements measured and confident. The guys working around us stopped to watch. Half of them were also Hispanic, but there was no love between them and Victor.

A voice in my head urged me to flee. The last time I'd been in a fight, it ended with Mike getting a free pass to torment me.

"If you were boss, I was gone, huh?" Victor stopped in front of me, close enough to throw a punch. He reeked of sweat, dirt, and cigarettes.

"You're lazy," I said, my voice slightly trembling, "and you make your friends act lazy as well."

"You need to watch your mouth, stranger. Dangerous things are coming out of it."

"Just get back to work. We're all tired."

He poked his gloved finger into my chest. "I think you need to learn how to shut your pretty mouth."

Before I could reply, Steve said, "Man, you eat like a pig and never stop yapping. What do *you* know about shutting a mouth?"

Laughter erupted behind me, momentarily easing some of my stress. It seemed as though the rest of the guys had moved closer, but it remained to be seen whether they would help in case of a fight. When it came to things like this, grown men were still kids in a playground.

"Be quiet, little one." Victor spoke to Steve but was still looking into my eyes.

I could read him easily, the back and forth going on in his head as he debated whether it was worth it to fight me. A part of me wanted him to. Despite the likelihood of getting my face smashed, I itched to fight back. To stand my ground.

One of Victor's friends came closer and put his hand on Victor's shoulder. My Spanish was far from great, but I could understand enough to know he was trying to calm him down.

Victor raised his hand to shush his friend, then spat on my shirt. No one spoke. This was clearly my turn to react. Before I could decide what to do, Victor's friends dragged him away.

I let out a tight breath as Steve clapped. "My hero! We could've handled him easily, though."

I snickered as the rest of the guys went back to work. "I don't think your jabbering would've helped much."

"Shows how little you know. Anyway, I'm ordering

the burgers tonight."

I grabbed the shovel. "Yeah?"

"I'm not paying for yours, just don't mind ordering it for you."

"Idiot."

"Oh, you're right!" He put his palm over his heart. "I shouldn't stand in the way of you and your favorite burger girl. Silly me."

"Nothing's going on between us."

"Listen, I've known Blue since we were in Charlotte Brown's kindergarten, and let me tell you—she gets what she wants, and what she wants is a nice dose of Matty-loving. What's the big deal, man? She's dope. But don't tell her I said that!"

Is this a new shirt?

Yes.

Why do you need a new shirt?

For work.

That's not it. You're trying to impress a special someone?

No.

Don't lie to me. I think you're planning on sticking your dirty cock into somewhere you shouldn't.

Mike—

You don't fool around without my say so. Now throw this shirt before I cut your cock off.

I shook my head, the memory like rotten food in my stomach. "It's not the right time."

Steve frowned. "You're waiting for a full moon or something?"

"Nope, but it's still not happening. Let's get back to work before I start eating this dirt."

"Always so mysterious," Steve mumbled under his breath.

I pretended not to hear and kept on shoveling.

*

The endless fields soaked in the silvery moonlight outside my room. The world felt peaceful so late at night, but inside my head, a storm was raging.

I was leaning with my elbows on the wooden railing, focusing on the steady flow of air into my lungs. My nightmares weren't new by any means, but the last one had possessed a level of reality that felt more like a memory than a dream. I could still feel Jeff's cold hands slowly choking the life out of me; his dark eyes filling my vision like the last thing left in the world while Mike was yelling from the shadows, *"Kill him, Jeff! End the motherfucker!"*

Frustration got the best of me, and I kicked the wooden railing with a grunt.

"You break it, you fix it."

I sharply turned around. "Jesus, you trying to scare me to death?"

"You'll survive. Another fun night?"

That was what Hank had started calling the nights I walked around, unable—or unwilling—to sleep in my room.

"Fun like a root canal."

He came out of the shadows wearing his worn-out army coat and stood next to me, a lit cigarette in his hand. "Want one?"

"I don't…yeah, okay."

He raised an eyebrow in surprise and gave me a cigarette. I inhaled deeply, my lungs warming up. We stood in silence for a while, the silvery fields like an endless ocean.

Hank said, "Good thing I didn't put another guest next to your room."

"Why?"

"Waking up to screams isn't everyone's cup of tea. The last guy asked to move."

Despite the cool air, my face got warm. "Sorry."

"Not your fault, and I've plenty of rooms within a safe distance."

"Do you want me to move out?"

"Don't be thick. We already went over this."

I nodded and took another drag. My cold breaths blended with the smoke.

"Heard Tom's been riding you hard this week," Hank said.

I wanted to be left alone with my sour mood, but Hank was bad at getting the message. "It's all right."

"I also heard about your fight with Victor."

I sighed. "People around here have big mouths."

"Nah, we're just bored as fuck. What was it about?"

"Nothing special."

"He didn't like you telling him to go back to work, huh?"

I chuckled despite myself. "It's like you were there. Maybe you should fill me in."

He let out a smoky breath. "Tom let him go from what I've heard."

"Bullshit."

"That's the rumor."

"Who did you hear it from?"

"Tom."

I frowned. "So how is that a rumor?"

"Well, I guess it's not much of a rumor, then."

I felt a sudden pang of fear. "Is he going to fire me as well?"

"What the hell for? You told a lazy man to work."

I nodded and took another drag of my cigarette.

"You always had these 'fun nights'?" Hank's voice sounded more serious than usual. Ever since he'd burst into my room about a month before, we hadn't directly talked about it.

"Not always," I said. "It comes and goes."

"You talked to anyone about it?"

"Like a shrink?"

"For instance. It helped me plenty after I'd retired from service."

"I don't need a shrink; I'm handling it."

"That's debatable. We'll go tomorrow to the shooting range."

"You have time?"

"I always have time for shooting. You're keeping your friend in a safe place?"

"Hid it under my mattress."

"Good." Hank threw the dead cigarette on the ground in front of us, which was odd considering it was his place. The motel was still mostly deserted this time of year, but come spring, farmers from across the country should be coming to attend local farming conventions.

Hank asked, "You think whoever you ran away from

is still after you?"

His directness caught me off guard. "Why do you think I—?"

"No reason for a midnight snack of bullshit, kid. Gives me heartburn."

I watched the tall wheat slowly swinging at the rhythm of the wind. "I don't know what he's doing. I'll know for sure when he's either dead or when he's caught me."

He put his hand on my shoulder and squeezed gently. It was an un-Hank thing to do. "For what it's worth, you probably found yourself the last place anyone would bother looking."

I gave him a sideways glance. "You think so?"

"I love Grafton, but you don't need to be a genius to realize it's on nobody's radar."

I nodded, feeling a little better.

He moved his hand away. "I know the local sheriff. He's a drunk who cheats on poker nights, but his heart is in the right place. Let me know if you want to give him a visit and ask for help."

It was a tempting notion, but overall useless. I had no proof of what had taken place in Hudson, simply my word against theirs. Even if I ended up leading the police into Albert's underground lab, it was simply a lab in a weird location. No bodies swinging from the ceiling or brains floating inside glass jars.

"I'll take a pass on the sheriff thing for now. Thanks anyway."

I was about to head back inside when Hank asked, "When you left Ohio, did you get closure from what you left behind?"

I thought about it and shook my head. "No. Things happened quickly that day."

"Well, maybe that's why your brain is still stuck in the past."

"Maybe." I still thought a lot about Bill, Molly, and Caleb. The way I'd left was a mess. I only checked my email once since I sent Bill the update about my escape. His answer was short, but he'd written what I hoped he would: *Focus on taking care of yourself, Matt. Molly and I will be okay. When you feel it's safe to reach out to us, we'll be happy to hear from you.*

Hank yawned and patted his belly. "I'm heading off to bed. You should do the same."

"I'll try." I took one final drag of my cigarette, then threw it next to Hank's cigarette butt. He smacked the back of my head. "Don't litter."

"You did the same!"

"I'm allowed. Pick it up and go catch up on your beauty sleep." He walked away, whistling to himself.

I rubbed the back of my head and went to collect our cigarette butts.

20

My name is Matt Evans. I was born and raised in Hudson, NH. I'm currently living—hiding—in Grafton, VT. If you're reading this document, it means I'm probably dead.

I will try to give you as much information as I can, but I won't be able to write here the circumstances of my passing since I won't be aware of them until the end.

What I'm about to write might seem made-up, but every word is true. I'll try to be as detailed as I can to help with your investigation, assuming you'll bother investigating this. If not, maybe I'll get some peace from writing things down.

It all started a year ago when my dad died…

*

"You boys worked well today," Tom said, "excluding the incident with the tractor and the cow."

Steve jumped to his feet. "That cow was suicidal, I'm telling you."

Tom gave him an impatient glare. "Nevertheless, looks like it's going to snow tomorrow, so you can all take the day off. Matt, stay a minute."

"Me? Yeah, okay."

The rest of the guys left the trailer with Steve telling anyone who was willing to listen about his lack of fault in the cow incident. I sat in the chair in front of Tom's desk, my stomach tight with hunger. "Did I do something wrong?"

Tom arched his gray eyebrows, fingers tapping on his cowboy hat. He and Hank had been friends since they were kids, but while Hank had let himself go by eating junk food and sitting at his desk, Tom looked younger, with a solid build and tons of energy. Steve had said he has Native American blood but warned me to never call him 'Chief.'

"Why do you think you did something wrong?" Tom's voice was deep like it was coming from the center of his body. It made even the less important things he said sound meaningful. Talking to him one-on-one made me nervous. This job was the most stable thing in my unstable life.

I said, "Always expect the worst and all that."

He nodded like he understood my meaning. "Well, this time it's the opposite. I'm offering you a promotion. Nothing too fancy, but I need a right-hand man to run this show with me. Spring's around the corner and there's a whole lot of work coming our way. Is a promotion something you might be interested in?"

I sat straighter, trying not to show how surprised I was. I had only been working there for two months, and no one had ever offered me a promotion before. "Some of the guys have been here much longer," I said.

"I'm not choosing based on seniority; I'm choosing based on ability and work ethic. You're good in both departments."

My commitment to my work was mostly due to the

mental escape I got from hard labor. There were days I got to bed so exhausted, my sleep turned into a dreamless coma.

Before I had a chance to second-guess myself, I went with my instincts and said, "I'll take it."

Tom nodded and granted me a rare smile. "Good. Now, I know I've been paying you in cash, but it might be time for you to tell me your social security number and sign on some forms."

Oh hell. Why couldn't anything be simple? I knew I was lucky to be working undocumented, but even after all this time, I couldn't risk it.

"Tom, I appreciate the offer, but if it means that—"

"Is it such a big deal for you?"

I looked down at the small cuts decorating my hands. I was proud of those cuts, had earned each and every one. "Yeah, it is."

"Care to share why it's such a big deal?"

I shook my head, unable to meet his eyes.

He sighed. "I guess we'll need to keep our mouths shut about this, won't we?"

I raised my eyes. "You sure?"

He waved his hand dismissively. "Half the people here don't even have social security numbers."

I nodded, grateful and relieved.

Tom gave me a ride back to the motel. He had a way of gripping the wheel with both calm and confidence, or perhaps I was too used to driving with Steve who didn't believe in sticking to one lane. People recognized Tom's black pickup truck and honked.

"It's like you're a movie star."

He chuckled. "I've been providing steady jobs to the community for a long time. That's being valuable, not popular. Be good to Grafton, and it will be good to you."

"I hear you."

When we reached the motel, Tom asked, "You like living here?"

"It's enough for now."

"Hank must be better company than I thought."

"He grows on you."

Tom unbuckled his seat belt. "I think I'll invite myself to one of Hank's famous bitter coffees. You have yourself a good evening, Matt. My headaches are now yours."

"Bring them."

In my room, I took a hot, well-earned shower. Laboring nine hours a day, you end up getting used to smelling disgusting, but I wasn't staying like that longer than I had to.

Drying myself in front of the mirror, it was hard to imagine I was the same man I'd been before. After my beard became decent, it was way too light brown to have any logical connection to my dyed black hair, so I went for a buzz cut. The most welcomed change was the lack of bruises on my skin. I could once again watch myself in the mirror without feeling a sense of defeat.

I stopped at the front desk on my way outside. Tom had already left, and Hank was watching TV with a jar of M&M'S resting on his belly.

Without so much as looking in my direction, Hank said, "You said yes."

"Yes to...?"

"The promotion. Tom's been looking for the right guy for a while. You up for the job?"

"I think so. I mean, yeah, I'm up for it."

"That's the spirit. I had a good feeling about you."

I snorted. "You thought I was a prostitute."

"Doesn't mean I thought you were a lazy one."

We looked at one another and laughed.

"You'll remember to be here by ten?"

"Yes." I took a brown M&M. "Tom gave us a day off tomorrow, so I can give some extra hours tonight."

"Two extra hours would be nice. You're meeting up with your buddies?"

"Yep. Some food and beer for this hard-working man."

"Don't get anyone pregnant."

"Not making any promises."

I stepped outside and began walking toward the shopping center. After more than three months in Grafton, I still couldn't find any better alternatives for grabbing dinner and a cold beer. The few places closer to the town's center put on the 'Closed' sign at around seven o'clock, so they were useless to us during weekdays.

It felt as though Grafton was hidden inside an invisible bubble where you'd be surprised to run into someone you haven't met before. I once more found myself debating my current living situation. If I was going to set roots here, I'd need a permanent place to live. Hank gave me a discount on the room and a part-time position filling in at the front desk, but living for months in a motel had raised questions I was getting tired of dodging.

I was the last to arrive at the restaurant, but the guys waited with their orders. It was only recently that I'd begun feeling more natural around them, less like the new guy who was being evaluated. I told them about the promotion, and they called for a toast.

A few minutes later, Steve said to me, "Look at you climbing up the ladder, Matty. A few months ago you were looking at those blisters like you got the plague or something."

"I still don't like blisters."

Steve moved closer while the others talked among themselves. He'd tried fixing his hair, but those curls were having none of that. He said, "I'm happy for you, man."

"Thank you. Um, did you want that promotion?"

He looked thoughtful as he nibbled on my french fries. "Well, I wouldn't have given old Tom the finger if he'd offered, that's for sure. Also, Amber would've given me some slack about all the *you need to earn more money* bullshit. But let's face it, I won't be good at telling people what to do and bossing them around. You, on the other hand...I think you'd turn out to be a mighty fine asshole."

"Screw you. You're fired, and you're paying for my dinner."

"See? You're a natural!" He cleared his throat and lowered his voice. "Does that mean I can count on you to stick around?"

He'd asked me that from time to time, wondered if I was going to leave as suddenly as I'd appeared. I took one of his onion rings. "Now that I can tell you what to do, I'm going nowhere."

"That's my boy! You're coming for Saturday's dinner, right? Mom's making her notorious meatloaf."

"Wouldn't miss it."

"Cool. Oh, incoming, Matty. Don't blush."

Blue approached our table. God, she was a sight. Even in her pinkish waitress uniform she managed to look elegant. When she wasn't working here, she ran her own small business for graphic design. I'd seen some of her work and told her she should consider doing it full time.

She reached our table. "What are you guys celebrating? Steve finally hit puberty?"

"Hey!"

"I've been sort of promoted," I said.

She crossed her arms and raised an eyebrow. "You're getting more money for more work?"

"Yes."

"Then you've been promoted, not *sort of*." She squeezed my shoulder, sending warm currents down my arm. "We're fresh out of champagne, but the next round of beer is on the house."

"Hear! Hear!" Steve called.

I was the first to leave because of my shift at the motel. Blue walked me out, and I waited while she had her daily cigarette.

"Isn't it funny," she said and lit the cigarette, "how the one who's always blue between us is *you*?"

We were sitting on a bench outside the shopping center. The moon was huge in the sky and the night was cold but luckily not windy. The air around here carried an earthy scent I couldn't get enough of, even after all this time.

"I'm all right," I said, "just got a lot on my mind."

"You're worried about the promotion? Tom's not known for easily trusting people, so you should see his offer as a compliment." She cleared her throat. "However, it might be time for you to find a place of your own. One might think you're not a serious man, what with you living like a nomad."

Without thinking, I blurted out, "I'm not sure if this place is far enough."

She blew out smoke and frowned. "Far enough from where?"

I rubbed my face, knowing I'd said too much. "Never mind. Forget it."

She snorted. "There you go again, being all dark and mysterious."

I bumped her leg with mine. "Isn't that why you're here? To unravel the mystery?"

"I'm mostly here because you might be good in bed." She eyed me and laughed. "Oh my, even with so little light I can still see you blushing."

Hearing her talk like that made me think of Ruth, and that made me think of Jeff. I shook my head. *Not now.*

"You okay? I was just messing with you."

"Yeah, I'm fine." I was used to her odd sense of humor, but it still caught me off guard from time to time. "I need to head back. Don't want to be late on Hank."

"Oh, Uncle Hank won't mind. Say you were protecting me from harm."

"I think you can take care of yourself better than most people, including me."

She stood up. "I appreciate the confidence."

I was taller than her by a significant margin, but she seemed taller when she looked me straight in the eyes. The moonlight illuminated the left side of her face, emphasizing the three small, lovely beauty marks under her left eye.

"See you Friday night by the creek?" she asked.

"Yeah, I'll be there." Those weekly events were the closest we got to partying around here.

"Have a lovely night," she said and held my chin. "But don't do anything foolish like hitting on another girl, you hear?"

"Roger that." I kissed her cheek like I usually did when we said goodbye, then I was heading back toward safer ground.

Walking by myself on the familiar dirt road, feeling the night's breeze on my face and thinking about my promotion, I should have felt good—hell, I should have felt great. Instead, I walked fast with my eyes to the front, worried of what might be lurking between the clustered trees on the side of the road.

I had common sense on my side, telling me to stop acting like a child. But common sense wasn't enough to make me stop seeing blurry movements at the corner of my eyes, or stop my ears from hearing Jeff's angry voice carried by the wind.

It would pass, I once again told myself as the lights from the motel appeared up ahead. People didn't go around their entire lives imagining things or waking up screaming. Those things ought to have an expiration date, and I was more than ready for my demons to expire once and for all.

*

I threw a log into the bonfire and watched the flames devour it. In the background played a Taylor Swift song people at the party seemed to dig.

I was sitting lazily on a folding chair after eating two greasy burgers. Despite the commotion close by, I struggled to keep my eyes open. Tom wasn't deliberately trying to wear me down, but he was more than happy to drop a shitload of assignments on my still greenhorn head. "Your shoulders are broad enough to handle the load," was what he'd said, and me looking all worried hadn't helped change his tune.

At least I'd gotten a chance to play boss, and it was nice realizing I wasn't a total disaster at it. Last time I'd been someone's boss, it'd ended with Chapter Thirteen. I'd expected more hard times from the rest of the guys, some of whom had been working with Tom for years. But after a few days of awkwardness, they'd gotten accustomed to the new way of things.

Up ahead, Blue was talking with some guys who were lamely trying to make a pass on her. I didn't need to dig too deep to realize I was jealous. I toyed with the notion of marching over there and asking her to dance. But then what? Going out? Dating? Bringing her into my unstable life was unfair, although I was feeling mighty tempted while watching her laugh at some other guy's joke. Hell, I could be funny. I could be freaking hilarious.

I moved my gaze away before I was caught spying like a creepy teenager. I didn't even know most of the people at this party because they were from nearby towns like Windham and Chester. Steve had insisted I come along, and he seemed to know almost everyone here.

I stretched my legs forward and closed my sleepy eyes, enjoying the fire's warmth. Blue laughed again, her voice far away in the darkness behind my eyelids. I heard footsteps approaching but ignored them and kept slipping into peaceful unconsciousness. I'd been so exhausted lately that I could fall asleep anywhere and anytime.

The footsteps moved closer and stopped right behind me. Something cold and hard pressed against the back of my head. I jolted and opened my eyes.

"Stay still. Don't make me shoot you."

Panic spread throughout my chest, squeezing my heart. "How'd you find me?"

"I'm a good hunter, and you're good at being prey."

Hearing his voice after all this time was enough to turn my blood cold.

Mike said, "We're gonna go for a nice walk you and I, then I'll put you in my trunk and drive us back home. Easy peasy."

My breath came out in uneven gusts of air. "Leave me alone."

He put his hand on my shoulder and whispered in my ear, "You know I can't do that. Get up and come along quietly before this turns ugly."

"I'll kill you before I let you take me back."

Mike's laughter echoed around me. "You sure talk the

talk, I'll give you that. I spent months looking for you. Good thing I haven't given up, huh?"

"I'm not…I'm not going back." My voice was thin, lacking vigor.

"It's cute you think you have a say in that." Mike moved in front of me, wearing his uniform. I tried lifting my fists to hit him, but fear incapacitated me. The party was still going strong close by, where dozens of people weren't aware of Mike aiming a gun at my face.

"You ready to come quietly?"

I tried to catch somebody's eye, but no one was goddamn looking. "I'm not going with you."

"If you really wanted to disappear, you'd have gone further than Vermont. I mean, come on, Matty, it's like you were waiting for me to come catch you." He smiled and nodded. "I see what's going on…you missed my education, didn't you?"

"Shut up."

"Ooh, looks like I hit a nerve, but we can discuss it later over a nice cup of tea. Now get your ass up. Time to get you back home."

"You won't shoot me here."

"Oh, please. I'll shoot you right between the fucking eyes. Everyone will piss their pants and run away while I slip away from here. I'll need to call Jeff to tell him you put up a fight, but he said I should *try* bringing you back alive." His voice went low. "Get up and turn around. Walk slowly into the woods over there with your big mouth shut."

"Mike—"

He unlocked the safety and pressed the barrel against my forehead. The cold metal sent goosebumps down my face and neck. I took a deep breath and nodded, believing he was truly going to shoot me. I didn't want Blue or Steve to see my dead body.

Mike moved the gun back but kept it aiming at my face. I stood up slowly with my muscles stiff, then he turn me around and pressed the gun against my lower back. Someone at the party laughed and another one let out a drunken howl. I kept my eyes to the front, worried any sudden movement would end up with a bullet piercing my spine.

It would only take us a few steps to disappear from everyone's line of sight. Mike must have parked on one of the dirt roads close by. We'd be back in Hudson in a few hours, leaving my new life in the rear-view mirror.

He pushed me forward with the gun, his other hand tightly gripping my shoulder. We began walking slowly, the darkness gradually swallowing us like an endless mouth. The ground was damp from recent rain, making our steps soundless.

Walking deeper into darkness, the cold air began creeping up on me. The sounds of the party faded like an old memory. I thought about faking a fall, then use the opportunity to pry the gun from Mike. But I was more likely to end up dead.

Mike said, "We're getting close. Keep being good. It will be warmer for you in my trunk."

"Fuck you."

I felt the barrel of the gun easing up the pressure on my back, then blinding pain exploded as he slammed the gun on my shoulder blade. I dropped to my knees with a cry of pain.

Mike calmly walked in front of me and raised my face with the gun. It was too dark to see his face, but I could picture his mean smile like we were in a well-lit room. The sounds of the party were long gone by now.

"You'll never learn," he said.

I rolled my shoulder to speed the blood flow to the growing bruise.

"Tell me what I want to hear," he said.

"What?"

"Don't play dumb."

"I'm not saying it."

"Don't be like that. Say that you belong to me."

He'd made me say those words time and time again. Made me shout them out to make the pain stop. But even with a gun aiming at my face, I couldn't let those words out of my mouth. I spent months trying to rebuild myself just to have it crumble around me in minutes. I was going to hold on to what little dignity I had left for as long as possible.

Mike moved his hand and pressed the gun against my forehead. "Say it, or I'll blow your brains out."

I kept my mouth shut, knowing he wouldn't risk aggravating Jeff.

"That's how you wanna play it?" He sighed like I'd let him down. "Guess I'll be heading home empty handed."

I heard his finger slowly squeezing the trigger. Before I could open my mouth, he shot me.

*

Consciousness hit me like a slap in the face. The echo of my scream rang in my ears as I stared into Steve's wide eyes.

"Where is he?"

"Where's who?"

I opened my mouth to say Mike's name, but before I could get the word out, I noticed everything was quiet. All around, people stood and stared at me.

"It's okay, man." Steve crouched down and squeezed my shoulder.

I was still sitting on the folding chair in front of the bonfire. A minute ago, I was deep in the woods having my brain blown out of my skull.

"You had a bad dream, that's all."

I buried my face in my hands. *This can't be happening.*

"Is he all right?" someone called.

The sputtering fire sounded loud. For the first time tonight, there was no music. God, why didn't someone put the music back on?

"He's fine!" Steve called back. "Nothing to see here. Put the music back on before I start singing."

I kept my face in my hands, not daring to raise my eyes and look at all those faces. It took them about five more seconds to bring back the music, and those seconds stretched forever. I took a handful of deep breaths and slowly raised my head to meet Steve's worried eyes.

"Sorry about that," I mumbled.

"Nothing to be sorry for."

"How long was I screaming?"

He scratched his head and looked away. “Oh, uh, what’s time anyway?”

“Christ. That long?”

“Listen, the party was already dying, but now everyone’s got something new to talk about.” He tapped my shoulder. “You’re a hero!”

I heard someone coming and turned my head to look.

“I leave you alone for ten minutes and that’s what you do to get my attention?”

“Ease off, Blue. My boy here is still shaky.”

“I’m fine.”

“You’re pale as a ghost, man, so obviously you’re not *fine*.”

“Here.” Blue offered me a cold beer. I took it and drank a mouthful, hoping it would help stop my body from trembling so badly.

“Can I bring you anything?” Steve asked. “Maybe take you back to the motel?” I hated the way he looked at me, like I might break without supervision.

“Go back to the party,” I said. “I’m all right.”

“Fine, but we’ll head back soon. And I’ll be keeping my eyes on you, Blue; keep your hands away from my boy when he’s fragile.”

Blue sat next to me on another folding chair. “Piss off, Steven.”

I chuckled. He hated being called that.

Once Steve left, I exhaled and tried to force my body to relax. Some people still snuck glances in my direction, but most seemed to have gotten back to a party mood. For months I’d been trying to blend in and not draw attention to myself, but tonight I’d royally fucked everything up.

"Sorry," I told Blue.

"Last time I checked, we don't get to control our dreams—or our nightmares."

No, I wanted to say, but we *can* control where we fall asleep. Considering how often I had nightmares, I should have been more careful. Letting my guard down was a privilege I had yet to earn.

"Want to talk about your dream?" Blue asked, making an effort to sound casual.

"No."

"Okay. Just remember that if nightmares were real, they would have been reality, not nightmares."

I rubbed my fingers on the cold bottle and said, "They can feel identical sometimes."

She gave me a sideways glance. "Why do I have a feeling that what happened here wasn't unusual for you?"

I moved uneasily in my chair. "Have you been talking to Hank?"

"About your nightmares? No. But if he noticed, then tonight wasn't a one-time thing."

"I don't want to talk about it."

"There are people you can talk to."

I shook my head. "I'm handling it, okay? It's temporary."

"Did someone hurt you?"

"Blue!" I never raised my voice at a woman, and Blue was the last person I could imagine yelling at. A couple of people glanced at us. I rubbed my face. "I'm sorry."

She patted my leg. "It's fine. I was out of line."

"You should go back to the party. I won't cause another scene."

"I'm fine where I am."

"I don't want pity."

"Oh, let it go, Matty. I'm sitting with a friend and looking at the fire. No drama."

I sighed and stretched my legs forward, still feeling like a jerk. "Fine. No drama."

"Well, no *more* drama."

The girl knew how to make me laugh.

*

"Nothing like starting your day with the sweet sound of a firing gun, am I right?"

I gave a polite nod but remained quiet as the owner of the shooting range unlocked the big iron entrance door. I was the first customer there and hopefully would be the only one for the next hour or so.

It was a Saturday, and I should have been enjoying the chance to sleep late. But I was still edgy after the fiasco last night at the party. Having dozens of strangers suddenly thinking I'm crazy was the last thing I needed. Grafton was small enough for gossip to travel faster than light.

The owner opened the door and stepped inside. I waited for him to turn on the lights before I entered, then I needed to wait again for his computer to start. He used the time to share an old story about his and Hank's military days. I was usually fine with lending him my ear, but this was not one of those times.

The moment he registered my cash payment, I

walked into the shooting range and stopped at my usual spot on the far left. The smell of gunpowder lingered in the air from the previous day. It felt thick in my throat like I could swallow it.

Once both my ears and eyes were protected, I pulled out my gun and stared at it. I did that from time to time; held it tight to absorb a temporary sense of security.

I raised my gaze toward the paper target. My heart was steady, my body calm. Yet underneath my skin restlessness stirred. I raised my arm and released the safety on the gun. The world began to narrow, its borders blurry. The only thing remaining was the paper target straight ahead, ready to face my rage. This morning, I had plenty of rage to spare.

Say that you belong to me.

I fired at my demons again and again and again.

21

"Listen, all I'm saying is that you were the one who dropped that ball, so don't go blame it on me."

Steve's face turned hilariously red. "You threw like a fucking girl, Trevor! Anyone would've dropped that ball."

Blue cuffed the back of his head. "Watch it."

"You were also there. Tell me it wasn't his fault."

Blue twisted her lips. "Your game was a bit off that day, T."

"Ha! Justice served."

They were going on and on about a football game that had taken place in their last year of high school. Watching Steve getting so hyped about something that was a permanent scar on his ego was giving me a hell of a good time.

We were sitting at Marta's, drinking milkshakes. The place was so pinkish, it'd made my eyes hurt the first time I stepped inside. But when it came to sweets, old Marta was in a league of her own.

Trevor owned the only hardware store in town. He'd invited us out to celebrate a new store he was about to open in a town north of Grafton. He was also my running partner from time to time. Having a local joining me opened a new world of secret routes I never would've found on my own.

Trevor nudged me with his elbow. "As a neutral participant, who do you believe in all this?"

I put down my vanilla milkshake and made a thoughtful face. "Well, I'm working with Steve every day, so I'll be the first to admit his motor skills are a mess."

Blue and Trevor both laughed, while Steve looked at me all hurt. I added, "But seems to me like it wasn't his fault back then, so I'm with Stevie on this one."

"Damn right you are," Steve said and threw a straw at Trevor.

My phone rang. I answered the call and leaned sideways. "Yeah, Hank?"

"The guys want to move poker night an hour earlier."

I glanced at my watch. "Should I leave now?"

"A minute from now will also work."

I snickered. "You know they're gonna wipe the floor with your ass, right? Your poker face is a joke."

He snorted. "So little faith. See you soon."

I hung up. "Got to go, guys. Early shift at the motel."

"Want me to stop by later?" Steve asked.

"Nah, no need."

"Well, at least leave me your shake, man."

I slid my half-filled milkshake to Steve, who grabbed it with a smile.

"Enjoy my herpes," I said.

"Oh, I will."

Blue walked me to the door. "Do you really need to have two jobs, Matty?"

Her question caught me by surprise. I loved having

two incomes and not having to worry about money. I would probably appreciate a stable income for the rest of my life. "Well, if I can manage it, why not?"

She played with her necklace, something I'd seen her do when she was uncomfortable. "Might be nice for you to have some time off every once in a while. Seems like you always have a shift at the motel or something extra to do for Tom."

"But I still make time for you guys."

She twisted her lips. "I guess."

We both knew what she meant. It was true I'd been trying to keep my time with her less private since my temptation was becoming an ever-growing challenge. I reminded myself I was doing this for her; keeping her away from a mess she had no business being dragged into.

I kissed her cheek. "Have a good night. Keep an eye on Steve for me with all this sugar."

I got out and started walking toward the motel. The town center was almost deserted by now, with most places already closed. I walked past Southern Pie Cafe where they made the best triple berry pie in the world. Local bands would come to play there occasionally and Steve, Trevor, and I made sure to attend every time.

I was tired but not enough to have a problem handling a few hours at the front desk. It mostly involved warming up the chair at these hours, but I appreciated the downtime and extra money.

The cold air caressed my neck, reminding me I'd left my scarf at Marta's. I was too close to the motel to turn back now, so it was best to ask Steve to bring my scarf to work tomorrow.

I was about to take out my phone when lights from a driving car appeared behind me. I moved to the side of the road, hoping I wouldn't get mud on my boots. The car slowly drove past me before stopping fifty feet ahead. I wondered if they wanted directions or whether it was someone who knew me. By this point, almost everyone in town knew who I was.

The door of the passenger side suddenly opened. Someone big got out, but it was too dark to tell who he was. I stopped walking, unable to ignore the nervousness growing inside my chest. I was used to being edgy about most things, but nighttime tended to intensify the feeling.

I was about to give myself the usual *calm the hell down* talk when I got a glimpse of the baseball bat in the man's hand. Despite the dark, I'd seen Jeff enough times to recognize his broad shoulders.

Panic hit my body, dropping my heart to the ground. In an instant, I turned around and dashed back. Another car door opened behind me, followed by the sound of feet hitting the ground and running toward me.

Why the hell did I leave my gun at the motel? I could have ended this once and for all.

The wind whistled in my ears as I ran, swallowing the sound of pursuit. My jeans were too tight, preventing me from reaching my maximum speed. My leather boots were also not helping, but it was a two-minute run back to Marta's, where Steve and Trevor should still be sitting. I was going to reach them on time, yet I was petrified of what this meant for my future in Grafton.

I caught a glimpse of people walking up ahead, not looking in my direction. I opened my mouth to call for help when something hard hit my right shoulder. I lost my footing and crashed on the ground, hurting my knees and scratching my hands. When I looked up, the people up ahead were gone. Despite the pain, I forced myself to stand, too close to safety to give up now.

I took two steps but didn't get a chance to catch enough speed when someone smashed into me from behind. The ground met my knees and palms again, the impact raising a cloud of dust that found its way into my lungs.

Coughing, I turned around, ready to tackle the one who'd brought me down. I got a glimpse of movement right before a foot collided with my face, rattling my brain and throwing me into darkness.

*

Pain echoed through my skull as I gradually regained consciousness. I could tell I was inside a driving car by the movement of my body. The bag over my head made it hard to breathe and impossible to see. Warm blood stuck to my forehead; its metallic scent strong inside the stuffy bag. I tried to move my hands and realized they were tied behind my back with a zip tie. I was lying sideways, my head resting on something relatively soft. It took me a few seconds to realize my head was on somebody's lap. I tried to straighten but was shoved back down.

They didn't block my mouth. I licked my parched lips

and said, "Jeff? Where are we going?" I waited but he didn't respond. "Damn you, answer me! Mike?"

Silence was again my answer. If I was going to end this night with a bullet in my head, I wasn't going out without a fight. I tried once more to push myself to a sitting position, and the guy who held me smashed his fist into the side of my head.

The car suddenly stopped. Maybe we were already back in Hudson and I'd been out for hours. When the back door opened, the guy moved me from his lap, then roughly dragged me out. I stumbled and fell on the ground.

Even out in the open, there wasn't enough air coming into my lungs. "Take it off!"

Two sets of hands dragged me across the ground, then dropped me on the wet grass. They slowly circled me, the sound of their footsteps marking their location. I tried to stand, but a kick to my ribs sent me back down with a grunt.

The sound of a baseball bat tapping on an open palm made acid swirl in my stomach.

"Take it off! I can't fucking breathe! Take—"

One of them roughly pulled the bag off my head. The cold air hit my lungs, leaving me dizzy. I moved to sit and shook my head to sort out my blurry sight.

The massive guy in front of me became clearer until I could tell who he was. I stared at him, my mouth hanging open as my brain caught up with my eyes. I let out a deep breath. "Thank God."

"What?"

I looked up at Victor's big head blocking the moon.

"I thought you were somebody else. Wait." I looked around. The other guy there also looked Hispanic. "Is it just the two of you here?"

Victor crouched down, puzzlement on his round, hairy face. "You can take us both?"

I shook my head. "Not what I meant. Did...did Jeff send you?"

Victor frowned at the other guy. "You kicked him too hard in the head."

The other guy shrugged and said something in Spanish, causing Victor to laugh.

"I didn't mean for you to lose your job," I said once my heartbeat settled.

His eyes hardened before he slapped me. "You told Tom. Snitch."

I shook my head, my ear ringing. "I didn't! It was somebody else."

"Little Steve?"

If he had gone after Steve, I would have broken his face, although I had a feeling it really was Steve who'd told Tom. "Not him. There were other people there and they were all pissed off at you. Come on, Victor, let me go."

He snorted. "Just like that?"

"You want to hit me some more? Go ahead, I can take it."

He shook his head, eyes tired. "I needed that job, man."

The vulnerability on his face surprised me. "I didn't mean for you to lose your job. I'm sorry it went down like that. I have money in my wallet—take it."

He spat on my face. "Don't want your gringo money."

I wiped his spit on my shoulder. "There's got to be other places where you can find work."

He glanced into the distance, worry lines on his brow. "This is a good place."

"Yeah, I hear you."

He stood up and kicked dirt while cursing in Spanish. I lay back on the wet grass, still feeling an ache in my brain from the kick.

"You gonna tell anyone about this?" Victor asked.

I raised my head. "No."

We looked at one another for a long moment. I wondered what had been his plan. Beat me up and leave me bleeding? Kill me?

Without a word, Victor nodded to his friend, who came to free my hands while I moved to sit.

The guy said something in Spanish to Victor, who responded with a nod. Without a warning, the guy smashed his fist into my chest, sending me flat on my back. Another punch followed, right into my guts.

Victor laughed. "You offered."

I groaned and tried to catch my breath, cursing my big mouth.

Although he spat on me earlier when I offered him money, Victor pulled my wallet from my pants and took all the money I had there.

"I need it more than you," he said and handed me back the empty wallet.

They drove me back to the motel, and neither of us said a word as I got out and made my clumsy way toward the reception area. When I opened the door and the bell above rang, Hank called, "Where the hell have you—oh shit. Come here and sit down."

I slumped in the chair next to the front desk. "I'm all right."

"Should I call an ambulance?"

"No."

"Who did this? The one you ran away from?"

I was too tired to make up a story. "I thought it was him, but it was Victor."

"Victor? That fucking—"

"He thought I got him fired, tried to get even. It's fine now. Don't tell anyone about this, okay? And sorry about poker night. If you go now—"

"You came here bleeding, and you think I'm gonna go play poker?" He went angrily to the back office and came back with a first aid kit.

I sat quietly while he cleaned and bandaged my cuts. I had enough experience to know that how I was feeling now was nothing compared to how I'd feel tomorrow morning.

"How's your sight?" he asked. "Any blurriness? Bright spots?"

"No."

"You might still have a concussion."

"I know."

He went to make me a cup of tea, then set it on the table.

The bell above the door suddenly rang. Blue stepped inside, holding my scarf. "What the hell happened?"

"I fell."

She shifted her gaze to Hank, who said, "Victor got

him."

"Hank."

"I keep no secrets from this one."

Blue walked inside and leaned her face close to mine. "Well, it could've been worse, I suppose. Victor could've broken you in two."

"Thanks for the vote of confidence."

"Go play poker," she told Hank.

"He might have a concussion."

"I know. Don't worry."

Hank got up, looking pleased with the chance to go lose his money. He gave Blue a quick hug before walking out into the night.

"I can keep myself awake," I said.

"Am I such bad company?" She sat on the big chair behind the reception desk and put my scarf on the table.

She was anything but bad company, but I was still feeling edgy and couldn't count on my willpower. Before I could reply, she took off her boots and put her legs on my lap. "At least do something useful while we're waiting to see if your brain explodes."

I hid a smile and began rubbing her pale feet. Her toes were dangerously close to my crotch, but for now I had things under control down there.

Blue took out her phone and put on Tracy Chapman's 'Fast Car,' which was her favorite song. "Are you in pain?" she asked.

My head was throbbing and my knees were killing me; the scratches there deeper than I'd thought. "I can handle pain."

She raised an eyebrow, waiting for me to elaborate.

"I'm not getting into this now," I said.

"Will you ever?"

"Maybe when it's less fresh."

"Then it happened recently."

I gave her a look.

"Fine. Forget it. My turn." She moved her feet off my lap and came to stand behind me. When she put her hands on my shoulders, I flinched.

"I'm not about to strangle you. Take a deep breath and relax for once."

I opened my mouth to say it wasn't a good idea, but the way she worked my tangled muscles was heavenly. I sighed and gave in, letting her press and squeeze wherever she wanted. After a while, I leaned back and felt Blue's breasts against the back of my head. She dug her fingers deeper, causing me to gasp.

"Too painful?"

"It's perfect."

"I've never felt so many knots in one back. You've been carrying heavy loads."

We both knew she wasn't talking about physical loads.

Her fingers slipped beneath the collar of my shirt, rubbing the upper part of my chest. I wanted her to go lower, wished to feel her fingers on every part of me.

She leaned her face next to my ear. "You're shaking, Matty."

Was I? "I'm sorry."

"You're spending too much time being sorry."

"Sorry."

She snickered. "I can also never tell what you want."

I want my new life to stop being shackled to the demons of my past.

I said, "Right now, I just want a friend."

She leaned her head down and kissed the top of my head. "You got it."

"You want to play poker?"

"Haven't you suffered enough?"

I laughed. "Famous last words."

We played cards until the early hours of the morning, and it was embarrassing how many times she kicked my ass. Yet I wouldn't have had it any other way.

22

Another month passed and spring was beginning to make an appearance. The days became warmer while the fields turned greener. It was the first time I got to experience Grafton outside of winter, and it felt like discovering a whole new town. Spring also meant more guests staying at the motel. I helped Hank however I could, but I was short on free time.

Bob Dylan was playing on the radio while I was doing paperwork in Tom's trailer. We both hated paperwork, but he was the one paying, which left all the paperwork for me to enjoy.

The sudden sound of Tom's phone ringing jolted me up. He had driven to a different field earlier and I wasn't expecting him back for at least another hour. I looked around and found his phone on the desk under some papers. I checked who the caller was in case it was someone who worked with us. The picture of the man who was calling wasn't of anyone I knew. After taking a closer look, a sense of remorse crept under my skin. The man on the screen looked so much like Bill, they could have been brothers.

I tried not to think about him and Molly too often but was met with little success. As the call went to voicemail, my mind drifted back to Hudson and my time with the Broslavskiys. They had helped keep me sane, and I'd turned my back on them when I fled.

I rubbed my face, feeling like the world's biggest disappointment.

You know they're still worried.

I had a new phone these days and could easily check the Facebook page I'd opened for Abby's Corner to see whether Bill was still updating it. I remembered explaining to him the different settings, and him acting like I was explaining how to fly a plane. But he'd gotten the hang of it eventually.

I took out my phone and searched for the store. The first link was to Abby's Corner's Facebook page. I clicked on the link and waited for the slow connection to show mercy. The page finally loaded, and the first thing that struck me was the cover picture. Instead of the one I'd taken of the store, the cover was now a black background with white text. *Business is Closed.*

"The hell?" I didn't dare scroll down for a long minute. Fear took hold of my body as the voice inside my head kept saying, *whatever happened, it's your fault.*

I let out a deep breath and forced myself to scroll down. The feed was packed with posts from people who were sorry for what had happened, but none of them wrote what made the store close down.

Frustrated, I typed the name of the store in Google and found one news story. After three minutes, I knew all about the fire that destroyed the store a few days after I'd gotten the email from Bill that assured me everything was okay. No one had been injured in the fire, but the photos of devastation told a story my mind struggled to digest. I could easily identify the few furniture that survived, could remember moving them around the store to make room and keeping them spotless for potential buyers. The article didn't say what had been the causes of the fire, just that the matter was being investigated.

I leaned back in the chair and stared at the wall. My body was numb, my brain blank. When I shut my eyes, all I could see was fire.

The trailer door opened sometime later, throwing me back to reality.

"Damn, I knew I forgot it here. Had any calls? Matt, you okay?"

"W-what?"

Tom sat on the other side of the table and took off his cowboy hat. "What's wrong?"

"Nothing."

"Let's try this again. *What's wrong?*"

I rubbed my face, drained to my core. The words coming out of my mouth were not the words I thought I'd end up saying. "I need to go back home."

I realized I was not at all surprised. I'd tried convincing myself for months that Hudson was a part of my past, destined to eventually fade away like an old memory. But running away had turned out to be what I'd feared—a constant battle to keep myself together, of looking over my shoulder in dread. Time hadn't been my healer because I never took care of the wound.

I had no way of knowing what going back to Hudson after all this time would mean. Maybe it wouldn't give me the closure Hank once said I clearly needed. But I had to at least try. My conscience, not to mention my sanity, was worth the risk.

"You need to leave *now*?" Tom asked, concern in his voice.

Going back now wouldn't fix the chaos I'd left in my wake, but I couldn't stay here like everything was all right. I'd done that when Dad's company began facing problems, and I wasn't repeating that mistake.

I stood up, determination pumping adrenaline into my blood. "I'll try to come back as fast as I can, but if I can't…" I offered Tom my hand.

He frowned. "What do you mean *if you can't*?"

My days of naivety were behind me. I knew that going back, even after all these months, would be dangerous. "I won't promise you something I'm not sure I can keep."

It looked like Tom was about to say something, but the determination in my eyes must have made him reconsider. He sighed and shook my hand, discomfort on his face.

"Let me know what's going on with you once you're back home," he said.

"I will if I can." I wanted to tell him that my hometown wasn't very far, that I could get back here in less than a day. Only I couldn't bring myself to promise something that wasn't fully in my control to keep.

Tom gave me a stern look. "Go back home and do what you need to do. Come back here when you're ready."

With that, I walked away.

*

Hank was sitting behind the front desk, reading a magazine about cars. He raised an eyebrow when I came in with my backpack. “School’s out early?”

I stopped in front of his desk, although it felt more like *our* desk. “I need to go back home.”

He closed the magazine and leaned back, his hands on his stomach. “Did you think it through?”

“I have. I need to get my closure.”

He narrowed his eyes. “If it’s because of what I said that night—”

“It’s not. We both know I’ve been keeping one foot out the door ever since I got here. I want…I want to be here for the long run.” Saying those words felt like the most honest I’ve been with myself in a long time.

Hank slowly nodded. “I knew you had the hots for me.”

I chuckled. “Damn it. You see right through me.”

He cleared his throat. “When should I expect you back?”

“It shouldn’t take more than half a day, but I can’t say for sure.”

“Last time I checked Ohio wasn’t so close to Vermont.”

Shit.

He shook his head. “Doesn’t matter. You have your gun with you?”

“Yes.”

“Loaded?”

“Yes.”

"Take my car."

"The bus is fine."

"Don't be a brave fool. At least ask Steve to take you."

I shook my head. "Can't do that."

"Well, you always were the thick sort."

"There's one more thing."

He seemed hesitant to listen. "Go on."

"I saved a file on your computer, something I've been working on during my shifts here. You'll find it under my name."

"What will I find on this file?"

"Something I don't want you to look at for the next two months. If you don't hear from me—"

"Hold on now—"

"If you don't hear from me, please send this file to the Sheriff."

I had little faith that this would change anything, but I'd written down everything that happened since my dad's death and up until my escape from Hudson. If something would end up happening to me back home, I hoped that somehow someone would be able to investigate and settle the score.

I said, "I need your word that you'll ignore that file for the next two months." I hated putting him in this position, but I trusted him to do right by me.

He rubbed his face. "You're killing me here. Yeah, all right. You have my word. Did you let your friends know you're leaving?"

"No. Only Tom and you. I'm planning on getting back here in less than a day. No need to make a big deal out of it."

He nodded. "That's more like it. Now get your ass out of here. See you soon."

*

It was the middle of the day, the sky so bright it seemed more white than blue. Gazing at the vast fields and scattered farmhouses, I felt at home. The feeling was bittersweet since it meant Hudson had truly become a part of my past, about to be buried for good.

I had been waiting at the bus station for the last thirty minutes, on my phone a list of buses I could take to quickly get away from Hudson. I had mapped out routes to Londonderry, Windham, and even as far as Boston. My final destination would be Grafton, but I wasn't about to get picky about it in case of trouble.

A red pickup truck slowed down until it stopped in front of me. Blue came out wearing a yellow dress that seemed to be custom-made for her figure.

I stood up. "Hank told you?" I should have known he wouldn't keep it a secret from her.

"He might've let it slip. What's the deal?" She came closer, hands on her hips, still looking taller than she was. The beauty marks under her eye stood out under the sun.

"It's complicated."

"Give me the children's version, then."

I shoved my hands into my pockets. "I need to return home to get my closure, otherwise I'll keep feeling like I don't belong here." *Or anywhere else.* "I also left behind something important, and not having it close is driving me crazy."

Blue nodded, her eyes thoughtful. "In that case, go and have your closure, as long as you remember your way back."

I smiled. Her standing under the sun in that yellow dress was a sight I wanted to carry with me for as long as possible. I cleared my throat, knowing I must be honest with her once more, although it hurt me every single time. "I'm still not the right guy for you, Blue. I have stuff I'm dealing with, and I think I've been dealing with them wrong."

Blue crossed her arms. "I didn't say you're the one, but I still like you well enough. And don't think it's that hard-to-get act that's fueling my interest—I have more class than that. Maybe once I know you better, I'll figure out you're nothing special and move on. Maybe I won't."

I nodded. "Fair enough."

She quietly asked, "Will the cause of your nightmares be where you're going?"

I hesitated, but there was no point pretending. "Yes, but I'm not planning on running into them."

"You need a gun? I can get you one from Dad."

I shook my head. "I have my own."

"You know how to use it?"

"I do." I had no intention of going willingly to settle the score with Jeff or Mike, but I wasn't about to let them hurt me again.

My bus was getting closer. "I need to go. Thanks for saying goodbye."

"Let's call it *see you later*."

"All right. See you later, Blue."

Sitting on the bus and looking at the world passing

by, I realized I'd forgotten to kiss her cheek.

Part Four
Closure

23

"Are you all right?"

"What?"

"You look a bit pale. Are you feeling well?"

I forced a smile. "I'm fine, just a bit nauseous."

"Well, maybe an apple will help. Here you go. Oh, that's my stop. Feel better, dear." The old lady left the bus, and the driver took off again. Hudson was less than an hour away, and with every new mile, my anxiety intensified.

The apple was juicy and sweet, more so since I hadn't eaten today. A few minutes before arriving in Hudson, when no one was watching, I took out my 9mm Beretta Nano gun. I could breathe better when I held it close. Knowing how willing I was to use it was proof enough I was coming back to Hudson a different man.

The last stop was at Nashua. From there I needed to take another bus to reach Hudson and my old neighborhood. I got off on Philbrick Street, surrounded by familiar stores and restaurants. It'd been four months since I left, yet it might as well have been a moment.

I tried to move but couldn't, worried each step from this point on would be wrong.

The sooner you start, the sooner you'll finish.

I started walking, avoiding making eye contact with anyone. After a short walk deeper into the neighborhood, there it was. What used to be Bill's beautiful store was now nothing but debris. Most of the remains had been removed, but there was no sign of renovation. Like what had happened would remain a gravestone in the middle of the street.

For a long moment I could do nothing but stare, a hollow feeling nesting in my chest. I didn't start that damn fire, but I might as well have. The thought of speaking with Bill and Molly was suddenly overwhelming. I had dozens of things to say to them, but nothing that could undo what I'd caused.

I hurried to the nearest bar. It was almost empty at this time of day. A Sinatra song played in the background. I sat in front of the bartender and ordered a beer, looking to feel more relaxed, not wasted. The bartender served me but didn't leave. I gave him the I'm-not-about-to-tell-you-my-life's-story look, and he narrowed his eyes.

"Don't I know you from somewhere?"

I moved uneasily on the stool. "Don't see how. I'm not from around here."

"Oh." He shrugged. "You just remind me of someone I used to see around."

"Not me."

"All right. Can I get you anything else?"

"No. I need to get going. I'll finish this outside."

I hurried back to the street, took a couple more sips, then threw the bottle in a nearby trash can. I was almost at my old building when I decided to see Caleb first since he was supposed to be the easier part of my visit. Once on Caleb's floor, I knocked on his door, nervous as one could be.

"Who's there?" His grumpy voice made me smile.

"It's me, Caleb. Brother Matt." Silence was my only response for a long minute. Then came the sound of his footsteps before the door slowly opened, but only halfway. There was more gray in his hair than I remembered.

He watched me with a deep scowl. "Is it really you, Matty?"

"Yeah. Can I come in?"

"You better well get yourself in here, so I can kick your sorry ass! Where the fuck have you been?"

I stepped inside, and he locked the door behind me. His apartment was how I remembered, filled with music albums. I sat on the couch and he sat in front of me, looking at me with suspicion.

Before I could open my mouth, Caleb yelled, "I thought you were dead, man! That's no way to treat an old fucker like me."

While other older people had no problem talking about the hardship that came with aging, Caleb wasn't like that. Hearing him mentioning his age and sounding hurt was like a punch to my gut. I put my fingers to my eyes and took a deep breath.

"Matt—"

"Give me a sec." After a few moments, I was stable enough to speak. "I don't know how much of the story you want to hear."

"Enough to understand why you took off like that.

Wasn't very friendly by my standards."

"No, it wasn't." I leaned back on the couch. "Okay, I'll give you the main points." I told him a guy I owed money to had forced me to help a crazy scientist, then brought in a crooked cop to keep me in line. Caleb knew about Mike from the times he'd heard him beating me, but now I was finally able to explain why I'd put up with it.

"I couldn't take it anymore," I said. "I needed to get away and start somewhere fresh before I snapped, or they killed me." I looked at my hands while I spoke. Seeing the look on Caleb's face would have made it harder to let it all out.

When Caleb finally spoke, the pity was clear in his voice. "Oh, Matty. I'm sorry, man."

"Not your fault. This is all on me."

"Nope. Uh-uh. This is life giving you the finger, which happens to good people sometimes. But come on, you should have split town way before that shit went down. Why'd you let it get so fucking far?"

He was asking what I'd been asking myself for months. "I thought that I could handle it, that it would get better. Only it didn't."

He let out a deep breath. "Until you couldn't take it no more."

"Yeah."

We sat in silence for a while, my story lingering in the air between us. I finally asked, "Did Mike come to see you after I left? The cop. Did he give you any trouble?"

"Oh, he sure did. He and some of his friends kept coming by to ask if I heard from you. I sent them on their merry way and told them to go help old ladies cross the street instead of asking me dumbass questions!"

"Are they still coming here?"

He massaged his chin. "Hmm, nope, not for a while. It's been more than a month since the last time."

Good. I knew they wouldn't be looking for me forever, definitely not in Hudson.

"Is there a special lady in your life, Matty?"

I opened my mouth to say no, but that wouldn't have been the truth. "I think there's someone. Maybe after I finish my business here, I'll be man enough to do something about it." That thought carried a nice, warm feeling, and I found myself holding back a smile.

Caleb leaned forward. "Is she preeettty?"

I chuckled. "She sure is, and tough. She'll tell you exactly what she thinks, won't try to sugarcoat it or nothing."

He clapped. "Sounds like you should go back and bring her flowers. Nothing that might have spiders, though. Girls don't like no spiders."

We talked some more like old times, but it was getting late. "I need to get going."

Caleb's shoulders slumped. "I feel that it's our last goodbye, man."

"Face to face, it probably is." I didn't want to promise him I'd come visit because once this day was done, I wanted—no, needed—to leave Hudson behind me once and for all.

"Well, good." Caleb pointed his bony finger at me. "After the shit you've been through, I don't want you spending another minute here. You hear me?"

"Loud and clear. Thanks for—"

The knock on the door made me stop talking. My heart skipped a beat, although it was simply a knock on the door, nothing to lose my cool over.

I asked, "Are you expecting anyone?"

"Nope. Not many people stop by to say hello these days."

"Maybe I should—"

Another knock. "Police. Open up!"

I jumped to my feet and wrapped my hand around the barrel of my gun, but I couldn't use it on cops.

Caleb got up and hissed, "Use the fire escape like last time."

How did they know I was here? Goddammit, this couldn't be happening.

"Open up!"

I ran on tiptoe toward the bedroom, a storm of thoughts in my head. I would need to get the hell away from Hudson, didn't matter the destination. I knew this part of town well enough to keep a low profile for a few hours until sundown.

I lifted the window in Caleb's bedroom as fists pounded against the entrance door. I carefully climbed on the stool by the window and slipped to the other side. I had two legs on the fire escape when a voice stopped me dead in my tracks.

"Don't move. Hands where I can see them."

He was standing right next to me, leaning against the wall. If I hadn't been in such a frenzy, I would've noticed him before I got myself completely out of the apartment. I raised my hands and stared ahead at my dusty window.

"How'd you know I was here?" I didn't get a good look at him, but I remembered Muscles' voice, although I hadn't heard it since the last time he and his partner had come to Abby's Corner.

He said, "We made sure people around here knew we were looking for you."

I closed my eyes, furious at myself. "The bartender."

"Called us right after you left. Oh, what do we have here? Nice gun. I'm gonna keep it. Now come along quietly. There's someone who's been waiting to see you."

24

"Then the idiot gave me a night shift, on my goddamn birthday!"

"You're kidding me. After you asked—"

"After I asked for a day off, that's right. Can you believe this crap?"

They had been talking non-stop for the last hour, ignoring my presence at the back of the police car. After they cuffed me, we drove outside of town on Bush Hill Road, past Wood Mills Lumber where a friend of my dad used to work years ago. We'd taken a turn on a narrow dirt road between tall white ash trees until we stopped in the middle of nowhere. The way they drove without discussing the destination made it clear they had this planned out in advance, and all that was missing was for me to make a wrong move.

I thought about trying to reason with them, but they had proven to be assholes during every one of our past encounters.

Lights suddenly appeared from behind. I craned my head back and saw another police car getting closer, then parking in front of us. Mike got out, the sight of him bringing back the fear I had fought for months to free myself of.

The two cops got out as well and slammed the doors

behind them. I didn't hear their words, but I caught echoes of their laughter. After a few minutes of me stewing in dread, they opened the door and pulled me out.

"You sure it's okay leaving him alone with you?" Muscles asked.

Mike sized me up. My kick to his face the day I escaped had left a small bump on the side of his nose. "I can handle him."

"Should I leave the cuffs on?"

"Yeah, but leave me the key."

"All right. Enjoy."

They entered their car and drove away, raising a screen of dust in their wake. When I turned around to face Mike, his fist collided with the side of my face. I lost my balance and fell to the ground, my face pounding in agony.

"Get up. On your feet!"

I spat blood from my torn lip and pushed myself up with a grunt.

"Well look at you. I thought they were pulling a prank when they called me. Nice beard you've got there. Makes you feel like a man? Hey, eyes on me."

I spat more blood and raised my eyes. "Where's Jeff?"

"Oh, he's coming. You can bet your bottom dollar he won't miss this for the world. But you and I have enough time for a friendly catch up." He came closer, crunching leaves with his boots. "You have any idea how hard it is to stand here and not break you to pieces?"

"I had to run."

He shook his head. "You *chose* to run, right after you broke my goddamn nose! And guess who was left to pay the price?" He grabbed my face and squeezed. "That's right, you little fuck. He had a couple of guys beat the shit out of me after you ran. Christ, I can't believe you came back."

Mike's phone started ringing. He put his hand on my shoulder and pushed me down on my knees. "Hi, Jeff...yeah, I got him right here and he's not going anywhere...I'll send you our location...see you soon."

He sent our location and crouched down next to me. "What do you think will happen now?"

"We're gonna order pizza and chill."

"Funny. More likely he's gonna kill you."

I looked into his eyes and saw that he meant it. Honestly, it wasn't hard to figure out.

Mike stood up and went to lean against his car. He pulled out a cigarette and lit it. "If I were you—and thank God I'm not—I'd be pissing all over myself. Jeff was so mad when you ran away, I thought he was gonna kill me." He blew out smoke and shook his head. "Can't say I blame you, though."

A spark of hope flickered in my chest. "Mike, you can still make it right."

"Oh, can I?"

"Let me go. You won't ever see me again."

"You mean letting you split?" He rubbed his chin, eyes thoughtful. "You'll need to give me a shiner, otherwise Jeff won't buy it."

"Okay."

"Then what?"

"I'll run to catch a ride out of here."

"And if you decide to come back?"

"I swear that you'll never see me again after today."

He chuckled. "You're something else, man. Never see you again? If I let you go, I won't be seeing *anything* ever again. So no, nice try, but you're staying right here on your knees like the bitch you are."

"Fucking psycho."

"What was that?"

I looked away and kept my mouth shut.

"Yeah, thought so."

I debated whether it would be worth it to try and run. I could smash into Mike when he wasn't looking, tackle him to the ground, then run to hide between the trees. I glanced around me. The trees weren't clustered enough to provide a decent cover, and with my hands cuffed, I wouldn't be able to get very far.

Mike kept smoking while the cold crept up on me. I had my jacket on, but the temperature was dropping fast.

The sound of a car getting close cut through the silence, pushing my fear to a whole new level.

Mike came closer and hissed, "Don't say anything that might tick him off. Tell him what he wants to hear and promise to do better. You hear me?"

I nodded, knowing in my heart that Jeff already knew how he wanted things to play out. He parked his BMW next to us and got out, still wearing black.

Mike cleared his throat, his back stiff. "Hi, Jeff. Been a while."

Jeff ignored him and came to stand in front of me. His

head was completely shaved. His small dark eyes didn't blink as he held my chin and brushed his thumb against my beard. "That's a nice look."

My mouth was too dry for words. My heart was trying to escape my chest.

Jeff said, "I had people looking all over for you. Just last week, I thought to myself you'd be one of the few who got away. But that doesn't seem to be the case." He let go of my chin and slowly paced around me, a hawk circling a rodent. "You came back to settle the score?"

"No."

"You had a gun."

"For protection."

"You know how to use it?"

"Yes."

"Do you have the balls to use it?"

"I do."

He watched me closely. "Did you see my face when you fired that gun? Pictured my brain exploding?"

Knives were hidden behind his words, ready to cut. I remained quiet.

He raised his right hand and held it for me to see. My mouth slowly opened in shock.

"Your actions had consequences."

I stared at his palm. The middle finger was completely gone, the cut so clean it seemed like he wasn't born with five fingers.

"I'm sorry," I said, and a part of me meant it.

Jeff paced around me again. "I had to make up a story for Ruth. I'm still dating her."

"That…that's nice."

He suddenly stopped in front of me, as tall as a building. I caught him clenching his fists a second before my cheek exploded. I crashed on my side, my face on fire. The scent of wet soil filled my nose right before Jeff kicked my stomach.

I wheezed, “Stop. Hear me out.”

He used his feet to turn me on my back, then step on my chest with growing force. I heard the bones in my chest crack as I struggled to suck in air. My sternum was about to snap.

Jeff suddenly raised his foot, allowing me a second of relief before kicking my thigh. With a yell, I turned on my stomach and tried to crawl away. It was pointless, but the primal part of my brain took over. Jeff grabbed my ankles and dragged me back. Little sharp rocks scraped my cheek. More kicks followed, landing on every part of my body. By the time the beating stopped, every inch of me was pulsing with agony.

“Pick him up and uncuff him,” Jeff said, his voice barely audible through the ringing in my ears. “You two follow me.”

Mike was careful when he took off my cuffs and pulled me up. I blinked to clear the storm of bright flickering lights from my sight.

“We’ll go slow,” Mike said.

“I can’t move.”

“You better try.”

Jeff took something from the back of his car and walked into the woods. I grimaced as blood trickled from the cut in my eyebrow into my eye. Mike wiped the blood away, but more drops followed.

Every step felt like a fresh punch, and I badly needed water. Mike and I clumsily followed Jeff deeper into the woods, the pain forcing me to stop every few feet to catch my breath. Rays of light shone through the trees, but sunset already loomed in the sky.

Mike and I stopped walking when we reached Jeff, who turned around to face us. Seeing the shovel in his hands sent a wave of weakness through my body.

Jeff held the shovel in front of me. "Do it on the spot over there."

"Please listen—"

"No. Get to work or you'll shovel with a broken leg."

I took the heavy shovel and stared at it. My brain tried to grasp what was happening, but there wasn't much to figure out—I was about to dig my own grave. I glanced at Mike who was avoiding my eyes and making it clear he was staying out of this.

I could have tried to smash the shovel on Jeff's head, but in the state I was in he would've seen in coming.

The ground was damp enough for me to push the shovel in without putting too much effort, but that was only the upper layer. I carefully took off my jacket to allow my arms more movement.

Jeff went to sit on a rock about three feet away while Mike leaned with his back against a nearby tree. No one spoke, and the only sounds came from the shovel hitting the ground and my moans of pain. With every lift of the shovel, the soil felt heavier, my muscles more strained. By the time I dug a hole past my waist, daylight was quickly fading.

Jeff told me to stop, then crouched down next to the

hole. He took away the shovel and put it on the ground next to him.

I said, "You don't have to do this. I won't run away again." Going back to the way things was would be hell on earth, but at least I'd be alive. I looked into Jeff's eyes. "I had to try to get away from this."

"I know. You might not believe it, but I *am* sorry for this. Still, I can't back down."

All I had left was honesty. "I don't want to die."

He shook his head. "Enough. You're only making it harder for yourself. Lie down."

Mike took a step closer. "Jeff, don't...don't you think he sort of learned his lesson? I mean—"

Jeff shut him up with a glance. Mike went back to lean against the tree, eyes to the ground.

"Lie down," Jeff said again, his voice more tired than angry. "I won't tell you again."

My body was in such pain, it made lying down on the ground a momentary relief. The hole was cramped, barely allowing movement to my arms and legs. The air felt thick down here, carrying the earthly scent of damp soil.

Every bad decision I'd made following my father's death raced through my thoughts, haunting me for the last time.

Metal scraped against the ground from above, then a pile of dirt landed on top of me. I expected Jeff to shoot me, but he was going to bury me alive.

"Jeff, don't do this."

"What I'm doing is your fault. I gave you a way out."

"I tried!"

"You failed."

More dirt kept landing from above, covering my lower body completely. I wished to pass out, to not be aware of the ground swallowing me whole.

"This is wrong," Mike said. "He learned his lesson, man. C'mon!"

"Shut up! Both of you can fit in there."

"Jesus, I can't watch this."

Dirt kept raining down. Some went into my mouth and I spat it out. I thought about pushing myself up and trying to get out. I was bound to fail, but that could make Jeff shoot me instead. Never did I think I'd be so desperate to get shot. Yet I couldn't move; panic seized my muscles and held me down.

The dirt kept piling up, covering my torso as well as my lower half. I could barely breathe as my lungs got squashed underneath the growing weight of soil.

"Jeff, I'm begging you. I'll do anything you want."

"You said that before."

I squeezed my eyes shut a second before dirt landed on my face. It reached my mouth, my nose, my ears. I shook my head in a frenzy, unable to move my hands to wipe my face. My breath came out in feeble whistles as heat spread throughout my chest. I sucked in as much air as I could and yelled, "I'll go to Albert whenever he wants!"

"That worked out great last time."

My head started spinning, a sense of vertigo that quickly grew stronger. "It won't…it won't be the same."

"It's always the same with you."

The next pile of dirt went straight into my mouth. I

didn't have enough saliva to spit it out and my nose was already too clogged for air to come in. I forced the dirt down my throat and swallowed it until a bit of air swam into my burning lungs.

"Albert can do...do whatever he wants."

"Enough, Matt."

I heard the shovel hitting the ground again. The fire in my lungs had begun spreading throughout my torso and up my neck. With my brain foggy and consciousness fading, I murmured, "I'm worth more to you alive."

The next rain of dirt completely covered my face. Emptiness grew inside my chest as the last traces of oxygen vanished from my inanimate lungs. Once every cell in my body accepted the inevitable, all traces of fear scattered.

A shred of thought cut through the silence in my brain. *This is dying.*

Something moved above me, rattling the thick layer of dirt. The weight began to shift right before a hand grabbed my shirt and yanked hard.

My face got out of the ground and fresh air rushed into me in desperate, hungry gulps. My senses sharpened, bringing awareness to the aching in my chest and ribs. I coughed the dirt out of my mouth and shook my head to get it out of my nose and ears. My lower half was still covered in too much soil for me to move my arms and legs, but all that mattered was breathing. Nothing ever felt better than the air swimming down my body.

"I'm not interested in words," Jeff said, his voice

barely audible through my heavy breathing and ringing ears. “Others before you gave me empty promises.”

“I’m not...” I coughed. Dirt was still in my throat and stuck to the inside of my cheeks. “I’m not making empty promises. Send me to Albert. You’ll get your money back.”

He remained silent for a long, stressful moment, then said, “There are worse ways to die, Matt.”

I couldn’t think of anything worse than what had just happened, but I nodded to his threat—no, his promise.

He used the shovel to lift dirt from my lower body until I was able to move my limbs. Everything hurt when I pushed myself up and grabbed the edges of the pit, my legs barely supporting my weight.

Jeff raised my chin with dirty fingers. “Every breath you take from now on is a gift from me. Every day you wake up is because I let you live. Don’t ever forget how you felt in that hole because I will make it even worse if you betray me again.”

I managed to nod, believing his every word.

25

They gave me water, and I drank until my throat stopped feeling like a desert. I used some of the water to wash my face and hair, but dirt remained underneath my clothes, mixed with my sweat. I pulled off my shirt and used it to wipe away what I could from my skin, but the shirt quickly turned into a filthy rag.

Jeff put the shovel in the back of his trunk and came back to tell Mike, “I’m going to see Ruth. Take him to my place.”

Before driving away, he took my wallet and phone, then gave Mike a key and the code for opening his apartment.

Mike moved to stand in front of me while I was leaning against a tree, still appreciating the uninterrupted flow of oxygen. With a wrinkled nose, he said, “You’re going to get dirt all over my car.”

I was dealing with too much pain to worry about his car. “I cleaned what I could.”

“Just try not to move too much. You think you might have a broken rib?”

“It feels like they’re bruised.”

“All right.” He looked around. The sun had already disappeared behind the trees, leaving very little light. “Let’s get out of here.”

The drive to Jeff's apartment passed in heavy silence. So many parts of me were bruised, I was a lump of pain trying not to break. I numbly watched Hudson settling down after another day of regular people living regular lives. Funny how one world could crumble while others were left unaffected.

When we reached Jeff's building, the guard let us into the elevator without asking questions. I could feel his eyes following me as I stumbled forward, looking like I'd rolled around in the mud like a pig.

Jeff's apartment seemed different, mostly due to the new wide couch and black carpet which covered the entire living room floor. Ruth must have made some adjustments.

I'd hoped to never set foot in this place again after losing so much of myself between these walls.

"Go take a shower," Mike said as he opened the fridge and grabbed a beer. "I'll put something on your cuts when you're done."

I took off the rest of my dirty clothes in the bathroom and stepped into the shower. The hot water washed away blood and dirt until the current turned lucid. By the time I stepped outside with a towel around my waist, I felt somewhat better, although the pain was still another layer of skin surrounding my body.

"Yeah, I'll be back soon...just need to finish something first." Mike was talking on the phone in the living room. I came closer while he stood with his back to me, facing the window. "Yeah, don't worry, it will be all right...the doctor said you'd feel like this because of your blood pressure...what? Sure, I'll bring it when I'm back...extra ketchup...see you soon." He ended the call and turned around. "Emily's pregnant."

It took me a second to remember Emily was his wife. The thought of Mike reproducing was unsettling, but I still said, "Congratulations."

"Yeah, thanks." He hesitated before saying, "I don't think the baby's mine. She got pregnant the same time I was busy with you, and she was busy screwing around. She said there was no way it wasn't mine, but I could tell she was lying about them using a condom." He shrugged. "Nothing for me to do about it now. Anyway, Jeff called while you were in the shower. I told him I needed to go, and he said to cuff you to his bed. You're gonna give me a hard time?"

"No."

"Good." He scanned my body. "You're going to look like a truck hit you by tomorrow."

It felt like that. Standing was causing havoc to my ribs and legs. In the bedroom, Mike took Jeff's cuffs from the closet and cuffed my hands above my head to the bed frame. He went to bring some band-aids and put them on my face, elbows, and knees. When he finished, he removed my towel and covered me with a blanket, then sat on the bed.

After a long minute of silence, I said, "Go be with your wife."

Mike cleared his throat and quietly said, "When you were in that grave, I almost pissed my pants. I was sure he was gonna bury you." He shook his head. "But now I'm thinking it might have been better for you to have died in those woods. Get this shit over with, you know?"

My skin turned cold. "I don't want to die."

"You know you're going back to Albert, right? I'm sure he's got big plans for you."

He knew how to make his words feel like punches. "It doesn't matter." I meant it. After staring death in the face today, I didn't want to see it anytime soon.

Mike shrugged. "If you say so. It's your shitty life after all."

Anger lit inside me. "Did you do it?"

"Do what?"

"Burn down the store."

He narrowed his eyes like he needed to remember. If my hands weren't cuffed, I would have jumped on him.

"No," he finally said. "It was somebody else."

"I don't believe you."

"It was me who came up with the idea after Jeff sent those guys to beat the shit out of me. I was sure he was gonna send them again once it became clear we couldn't find you, so I offered to do something that might get your attention." He frowned. "You didn't come back after the fire, though."

"I found out about it today."

"Oh." He nodded with a small smile. "Then it did work."

"Fuck you!"

He slapped me. "Watch your mouth. I have no problem kicking your ass when you're tied up."

"You have no problem doing pretty much anything, it seems."

"Are you seriously blaming me for this? I warned you that those two would suffer if you ran, didn't I?

You chose to let them deal with your mess, so don't go acting like you're the victim in all of this. That fire was a lot more your doing than mine."

"Whatever helps you sleep at night."

He snorted. "You sure got a set of balls on you. I should've broken them a long time ago."

"You can go now."

He stood up. "All right. I'm out of here. You know how to bring out the ugly in me, that's for sure. If I'm getting you back, I don't know how I'll be. Right now I still feel bad for you, but that might change." He ran his fingers across my bruised ribs. I saw the monster stirring in his eyes, demanding to be fed. "Hell, I feel it changing already. It's messed up, isn't it?"

"Yes."

"Well, I'm being honest with you; you deserve that at least. Oh, almost forgot." He shoved his hand into his pocket and pulled out his phone.

I numbly stared at the ceiling as he took photos of my bruises from different angles. He might have taken photos of my face as well, but it didn't matter.

"Good ones," he said and winked. "Catch you later, Matty boy. Welcome home."

He turned off all the lights before leaving. The darkness swallowed the room, leaving narrow strips of moonlight shining through the closed blinds. Yesterday, I'd gone to sleep many miles away from here, in a bed that wasn't mine but in many ways was. I had shifted so quickly from one life to another, it didn't feel real. Lying in the dark, it dawned on me that everything in my life had changed once more.

*

I woke with a start to the sound of a door being closed. I looked around in confusion. This was not my motel room. Realization trickled into my consciousness, forcing me to remember where I was and why my hands were cuffed. Pain quickly rose across my body.

Jeff stood with his back to me after probably putting his clothes in the closet. The soft amber light coming from the hallway illuminated the snake tattoo wrapped around his torso. It almost looked like he had been born with that tattoo, the snake growing with him.

Jeff turned around and our eyes met. “Are you in pain?” he asked.

“Yes.”

He left and came back with a white pill and water. I was surprised when he took off the cuffs, something I was sure would not happen until tomorrow at least. My arms felt stiff. I must have slept for a few hours.

I took the pill with the water while Jeff turned off the light in the hallway, casting everything into darkness. He climbed into bed and lay next to me. We were both under the same blanket, his warmth reaching my skin.

He said, “Ruth will come here tomorrow morning. I let it slip that you’re here, and she wants to say hello. She thinks you were away for a family crisis. When she sees your bruises, tell her you were in a fight. One wrong word and we’ll be having a problem.”

“Okay.”

A few more seconds of silence passed before he asked, “Did Mike hurt you?”

"No. Are you going to put him in charge again?"

"I'm not sure yet. He failed last time." He turned his head toward me. "But so did you, and I still gave you a second chance. Or was it a third chance? A fourth?"

I sighed quietly. "What about Albert?"

"I'll talk with him tomorrow."

"Maybe he found someone else."

"He didn't."

I turned around with my back to Jeff. Lying on my side hurt, but it was easier for me to fall asleep like that. For the first time in ages, I longed to face the nightmares of my subconscious instead of facing what reality had in store.

In the darkness of the room, Jeff said, "Tell me why you came back."

"Because I'm an idiot."

"Matt."

It took me a few seconds to be able to speak. "I found out about Bill's store today. I wanted to apologize to him and Molly for dragging them into this." I didn't want to tell him about the constant nightmares, about sensing him and Mike lurking in the shadows, watching my every move. Nor did I want him to know that coming back to Hudson was supposed to give me closure so I could finally move on.

"I'm sorry it came to this," Jeff said. "The money they got from the insurance should be enough."

"It doesn't make you any less of a monster. Bill and Molly loved that store. They weren't a part of this."

"Then it wouldn't have brought you back."

His truth stung. I didn't want to think about that any

longer. The guilt would always be a part of me, eating away at my conscience.

I asked, "Did you trash my place? I have a photo album there."

"Your place is how you left it. What's in the album?"

"My parents when they were young. I wanted to take it with me."

"To where you lived for all these months?"

"Yes."

"Tell me about that place."

"I don't want to." Pressure formed in the back of my eyes and deep in my throat. I tried collecting myself before I ended up losing it.

Jeff said, "Tell me what you've been up to. It will make it easier for you to understand that it's over now."

Without going into the specifics and mentioning names, I reluctantly told him about the last few months. By the time I finished, he'd already fallen asleep, and I didn't know how much of my story he'd heard. It didn't matter. Jeff was right; I needed to understand that what I had in Grafton was over, and there was no going back.

26

I was lying at the bottom of a grave, half my body covered in wet soil. I tried calling out to Jeff, but every time I opened my mouth, my throat sharply clenched. Dirt kept falling from above like angry raindrops. I tried kicking myself free and managed to get most of my body out of the ground. Then something happened—I wasn't sure what—and I was drowning once more.

My lungs burned, pointlessly struggling to suck in air. Something moist and slimy crawled across my hands. I wiped it away and saw that the ground was filled with worms, all crawling toward my face.

I cried again for Jeff to stop and was relieved to finally hear my voice. It sounded small and distant, but it was better than not having it at all. The worms were now crawling freely on my skin, some have already reached my neck.

I called out to Jeff with everything I had, but the dirt kept on falling.

*

"Matt! Wake up, Sugar."

My eyes flew open. I blinked and shook my head, my heart beating like it was trying to win a race. "Ruth?"

"Yeah, hon. You scared the shit out of me with all this

yelling. What the hell were you dreaming?"

"I don't remember," I lied and looked around, half-expecting to see worms crawling on the bed. I wiped sweat from my face and moved to sit, grimacing from the pain in my ribs. A bit of sunlight shined through the closed blinds, but the room was still dim. I looked again at Ruth, who was still redheaded and beautiful. She wore regular clothes, a sweater, and jeans. Last time I'd seen her she was either in leather or naked.

"Sorry if I startled you," I said.

"That's okay. As long as you're all right." She smiled. "Oh, how I love your beard. You look like a lumberjack."

"Thanks. Where's Jeff?"

"Working out. He asked me to leave you alone, but I heard you screaming like you were dying." She scanned my body, looking a bit nauseous.

"I was in a fight."

"You don't say. Did you win?"

"No."

"Well, it takes a big man to admit he failed." Ruth moved closer and squeezed my chest. "You've been putting on some muscles, I see. Very sexy. Is there a special lady in your life?"

"What? No, no special lady."

"Well, it will come when you're ready." She winked. "You're one of the good guys, I can tell."

She was dating a gangster, so her sense of judgment was obviously lacking.

"Maybe go grab a quick shower, Sugar. You still look a bit out of it."

"Yeah, I'll do that."

"Good. I'm working on some nice breakfast for you boys."

God, I was starving. I carefully got out of bed and walked naked to the bathroom.

Once done with the shower, I was greeted by my reflection. I thought I'd grown used to seeing myself bruised from my days with Mike, but what I was seeing now was on a whole new level. I closed my eyes and braced my hands on the bathroom countertop, trying to convince myself that being alive was enough for now. It had to be enough.

I brushed my teeth with the same toothbrush I'd used months ago, then decided to use Jeff's shaver to trim and fix my beard. When I stepped outside, Jeff called from the living room, "You have clothes on the bed."

I went to the bedroom and saw a pile of clothes. It took me a moment to realize they were my old clothes, the ones I'd left back in my apartment. Was he there this morning?

I got dressed, every movement sparking needles of pain. My old shirt felt tight around my upper body, yet I felt weaker than I ever felt before.

In the kitchen, Ruth was making something that smelled nice while Jeff was sitting on the couch reading a book.

"Oh no! What happened to the manly beard?" Ruth asked.

"Was getting itchy."

"Looks better like this," Jeff said and came closer. I took a step back, half-expecting him to punch me. Only he wouldn't do that in front of Ruth, and me acting scared might have looked weird in her eyes.

"Can we eat?" Jeff put his hand on my back. I didn't know if he was trying to calm me down or sending me a warning.

Ruth made an omelet and a salad. I was luckily able to survive the meal without being an active participant. Once we finished, Ruth gave Jeff a long, wet kiss, then kissed me on the cheek before leaving for work.

Jeff and I moved to sit in the living room. I was nervous from being alone with him, unsure of what to expect. Less than a day ago he'd tried to bury me alive, and now we were sitting in his living room after sharing breakfast. I didn't even try to make sense of it.

Jeff said, "I got the photo album you mentioned."

I was relieved, but it felt hollow by this point; a pitiful consolation prize. "Thank you. Where is it?"

"Somewhere safe. I'll let you have it once I feel more confident about your behavior."

All I could do was stare at him. I'd told him something personal, and he was now using it against me. *He was about to bury you alive, so how is this a surprise?*

"It's safe," he said. "I hope you don't think that one night has made the last four months meaningless."

I mumbled, "I don't think that."

"Okay. Go to the balcony. I'll get you another pill and something to smoke."

I hadn't smoked weed in ages, careful to always be alert and ready to flee at any sign of danger. Evidently, there was no reason to be alert anymore.

I went to the balcony through the gym, my steps

awkward and slow. Sitting outside, I lazily watched my hometown spread peacefully before me. Trees had started to bloom with the coming spring alongside the Merrimack riverbank.

Jeff came and gave me a white pill, then handed me a joint. We sat and watched our town for a while, passing the joint between us. Once I finished, Jeff pulled out my phone. I eyed it suspiciously. "What's that for?"

"You left a job yesterday. Only fair to let them know you're not coming back."

My mouth went dry. "I don't know what to say."

"You'll figure something out."

I took my phone with unsteady hands. "I'll write Tom a text."

"No. I want to hear you say the words. *You* need to hear yourself say the words."

"Does it have to be now?"

"Yes. Go on."

"Not fair," I mumbled and searched for Tom's number, ignoring the ten missed calls I had.

Jeff's voice rose. "Fair? You owe me about one hundred grand, and that's when I'm not counting your interest for the last four months. Make the call and leave that part behind you."

I took a deep breath and dialed Tom's number, telling myself that dragging this any longer won't make it easier.

"Hi, Matt." Tom sounded relieved.

I licked my dry lips. "Hi."

"Are you still back home?"

"I...yeah, I am."

"You took care of things?"

I rubbed my itching eyes. "Tom, listen, I'm not coming back. Stuff happened, and I need to stay here."

He stalled before saying, "Would giving you another month help?"

"No." A lump formed in my throat, and no matter how much I swallowed, it kept growing. "I'm sorry. I messed up, and now I need to handle it. But it will be okay."

"Then why are you crying?"

Was I? Damn, I was. I cleared my throat. "Can you please tell the guys I'm not coming back? To Hank as well. Tell him…to remember what we talked about when I left. I still want him to do that."

"I think you should talk to them yourself."

"I can't."

Jeff got up and moved to stand behind me, put his hands on my shoulders.

Tom said, "Listen, whatever mess you've gotten yourself into, I'm sure it's not the end of the world. Let's meet and see if we could—"

"No." I wasn't getting him involved like I'd done with Bill. Otherwise, Tom would come to his fields one morning to find them turned into ash. "I need to go. Thanks again for…you know."

"No need to thank me. I'm saving your job for one more month. You take care."

I hung up and instantly started sobbing.

Jeff rubbed my shoulders. "You did what you had to do."

"It hurts."

"Consequences usually do."

He moved his hands away and took my phone. I wiped my eyes as he clicked and scrolled. A bad feeling grew in the pit of my stomach.

"What are you doing?" I asked.

"Insurance."

"What does that mean?"

He did something else on the phone and then put it in his back pocket. "I'm not taking any more chances with you."

My pulse rose. "What did you do?"

He moved to stand in front of me. "I sent myself the numbers of those you were in contact with. It will be easy tracking them down."

I shook my head, fists clenched. "Don't do this."

He put his hand under my chin and raised my head. "I'm not doing anything. You start behaving as you should, and they'll go on living their lives like you never existed. You mess things up again, and I'll get to them."

"I won't let you hurt them."

His eyes narrowed. "Let it go."

I jumped to my feet, lifted the small glass table next to me, then hurled it with a scream to the side of the balcony. Rain of glass splashed, missing me by inches. I glared at the mess I'd made, my heart running wild.

Jeff moved behind me. I ready myself for pain.

"Feeling better?" His voice was flat.

"No."

"I'm not planning on hurting those people. Their safety is on you."

I rubbed my face, completely spent. "I want this all to

stop."

"Give it another year; that's how long it should take you to pay me back. Then you'll be free to go on with your life."

I turned to face him. "A year?"

"Give or take. It's up to you more than it's up to me."

A year. Could I survive this for a year? God, I hoped I could. I looked around. "Sorry about the table."

"Clean it later. Now go get some rest. Mind where you step."

I did what he said because that was the easiest thing to do.

*

In the following days, I mostly kept myself high. Life was better like that, made more sense. I stayed in the apartment the entire time, keeping myself busy with TV and some of Jeff's books. When I wasn't doing that, I sat for hours pondering death. In the endless darkness behind my eyelids, I strangled Jeff in his sleep until his body stopped twitching. I hit Albert so hard I broke his face, scattering his precious brain across the floor. I used Mike's gun to shoot his legs, then followed him as he tried to crawl away. By the time I shot his head, every part of his body had a bullet with my name on it.

I wondered how deep this darkness would permeate into my soul, and when it would eventually consume me.

*

About a week after I'd gotten back to Hudson, Jeff woke

me up with my parents' photo album in his hands. Relief filled me as I saw that old thing in one piece.

Jeff sat next to me and handed me the album. "Show me," he said but in a tone that implied I could refuse.

We sat shoulder-to-shoulder as I went through the photos. When I'd been a kid who was finally coming to terms with his mom's death, I became obsessed with this album. Discovering it had been like finding a hidden treasure chest. I'd made my dad tell me every detail he could remember about every single photo.

We were getting to the end of the album, and there were early photos of me.

"You were a cute baby," Jeff said.

"I was in a commercial when I was two."

"Commercial for what?"

"Toilet paper. A woman played my mom, and she was looking for me around the house. When she found me, I was all covered up with pink toilet paper."

Jeff chuckled. "I need to find that online."

"It's not there anymore; I checked a few years ago. Dad used to make fun of that until I started high school. Every time we went grocery shopping, he called me the Toilet Paper Expert and asked me to choose the best kind."

I didn't know why I was talking so freely, revealing private parts of my past. Maybe I needed to remember I had a life before this hell, and I might have one again when it was all said and done.

"Do you have family albums?" I asked, not sure I could even imagine him as a kid.

"No. My parents weren't the taking-photos type."

"Where are they now?"

He cleared his throat. "Dead. My dad got involved with the wrong kind of people. My mom found herself in the crossfire."

"Oh. Is that why you...?"

"It started with me seeking revenge like a dumb fuck. Then it somehow turned into what I do. Some things you don't get to quit when you feel like it."

"Can't you quit now?"

"No. What's done is done." He got up. "Meet me in the living room."

I could tell by his voice something was up. Once I entered the living room, Jeff said, "I ordered pizza."

I sat opposite him on the couch. "I guess I'm going back to Albert."

"How'd you figure that out?"

"You gave me back my album and you're ordering pizza. I know how to read you."

"You do, huh?" There was some amusement in his voice, as much as Jeff could be amused.

"Yes." I folded my legs on the couch. "You're not very complex."

He shook his head. "Oh, that mouth of yours."

"When should I be at Albert's?"

"Tomorrow morning. You'll spend the night there."

The entire night? I held my fear at bay. "Okay."

"About Mike...he's out of the picture for now. I hope for your sake you won't give me a reason to change my mind."

It wasn't only for *my* sake. Blue, Steve, and the rest were also a part of this now. Remembering that kept me determined to see this deal through.

I asked, “Can I go smoke?”

“You should start smoking less.”

“It helps me relax.”

“You’ll end up addicted.”

“Fine.”

Annoyed, I got up and took two steps before Jeff said, “Wait. Take one from the drawer.”

“Thank you.”

27

The car shook on the dirt road in Jeremy Hill Forest. The low fog made it feel like we were driving on top of a cloud, but also made it hard to see the road. I looked out the window and focused on inhaling and exhaling. *A year. It will only take a year.*

Albert's house looked the same as I remembered: big and beautiful, surrounded by untamed nature. Nothing to imply what took place beneath ground.

Jeff parked in front of the iron gate. "I'll pick you up tomorrow. Whatever it is he wants to do, go with it. As for what happened last time, don't bring it up."

"Okay."

He scanned my face. I could tell he was worried. We both had a lot riding on the outcome of this meeting, yet it was on me to see it through.

"Go on," Jeff finally said. "Oh, remember to take the pills he has for me."

"Pills for what?"

"None of your business. Just remember."

I got out of the car and into the profound smell of nature. Albert buzzed me in and then opened the front door. My muscles tensed at the sight of him, heart beating faster. He seemed a bit skinnier than the last time I'd seen him, his posture stiff.

We stared at one another for a long moment until he said, "I didn't think I'd see you again."

"That makes two of us."

He cleared his throat and put his hands behind his back. His gray sweater seemed new. "Last time you were here, I was out of line. I should…I should have maybe handled it differently."

That was a messed-up version of an apology if there ever was one. "We don't need to talk about it."

He nodded. "Fair enough. And now that you're back, what should I expect?"

"I'm here to do what you want."

"As you were before."

"I don't know what more to say. Try me out, I guess."

He nodded and his posture became less stiff. "I like your little beard."

"Thank you."

"Well, come in. We've got so much to do!"

He led me down the stairs and into the bright lab. I stood motionless by the entrance, staring at what I'd tried so hard to forget. All I could think was, *I'm not supposed to be here.*

Albert's computer screen was showing the circles that controlled the gas. I turned my gaze to the side room where I was once made to crawl and bleed, to lose a part of myself to somebody else's desires.

"Matthew. Matthew."

"W-what?"

"You look pale. Go sit on the bed. You want water?"

"Yes."

I forced my legs to move and sat on the bed. Albert

returned with a glass of water. “Here you go. And before I forget, I should give you the pills for Jeff.” He opened one of his many drawers, then came back and handed me a small, white envelope.

I gave him the empty glass and shoved the envelope into my pocket. “What do they do?”

“I’m probably not supposed to tell you this, but one pill will make you weak for a few hours. Two will make you sick for a day or two, and three might cause a heart attack. Any more than that and it’s sure death. Bring them straight to Jeff, okay? They are serious.”

Jeff was probably planning on using them on people who owed him money, so yeah, they were rather serious.

“You still look shaky,” Albert said. “I can give you something that will make you calmer, but I’m afraid it might be dangerous with the anesthesia.”

“Anesthesia?”

He crossed his arms. “You will need to be unconscious for the next few hours.”

I focused on my breathing and tried to keep my voice natural. “Can you please explain?”

“Of course. I need to try a substance that should ease the pain in the abdominal cavity. Different types of infections could occur there, and I believe I found a way to handle some of them. These types of infections usually heal with time, but some could get dangerous without the right treatment, mostly in poor countries. Selling this patent will earn me enough money to not have to worry about funding for a long time.”

“But…I don’t have an infection there.”

"True, but that could be easily arranged. I need to create the symptoms, not the full infection. For now, it should be enough."

"Will it hurt?"

He smiled and gently squeezed my shoulder. I flinched and he quickly removed his hand. "It will not hurt at all. When you wake up, you'll feel absolutely fine."

"Why do I need to be unconscious?"

"Well, I will need to perform a simple surgery on you, so being awake is not an option."

The word sounded alien. "Surgery?"

He waved his hand dismissively. "It's not as dramatic as it sounds. You might end up with a small scar on your abdomen, but that should be almost unnoticeable." He clapped. "So, let's get started. Please remove your clothes and lie on the bed."

I couldn't help but think about my mom. My dad had never told me the specifics of her passing, only that she'd gone in for a simple operation and never came out due to malpractice. I grew up dreading doctors, so having Albert acting so eager to cut me open brought back the fear I'd been carrying with me for years.

"Do you have all the things...I mean, that hospitals have? Do you have the right equipment?"

He twisted his lips in annoyance. "Obviously my lab can't be as equipped as a regular hospital—that would be ridiculous. But I do have the essentials. Now, please remove your clothes and lie down. Time is ticking."

I couldn't move. My body and brain were at odds. I had an ominous feeling I was about to end up dead.

"Have you ever done this before?" I asked.

"What do you mean?"

I licked my dry lips. "Have you ever used anesthesia on someone? Have you ever performed this sort of surgery?"

"I know what I'm doing."

"Well, if you haven't done this before…"

He shook his head. "And here I thought I'd get you back with more brain and less mouth."

"I'm not trying to be stubborn, but this is surgery we're talking about, and—"

"Enough. Just stop talking. I need to be at my best right now, and you questioning me isn't helping. Remove your clothes and lie on the bed. Don't say another word."

I could barely take a proper breath as I took off my clothes. The thought of trying to escape crossed my mind, but I couldn't risk the safety of my friends in Grafton.

Lying on the bed naked, a blanket covering my lower half, I noticed Albert moving from place to place looking disoriented. He brought an oxygen mask and placed it on my face.

"Take deep breaths," he said.

The right side of the mask didn't fully cover my face. What I was inhaling got mixed with regular air.

"Albert, you—"

"Quiet. It will all be over soon. Relax."

I tried speaking again, but my words came out as mumbles. I wanted to raise my hands and fix the mask myself, but my limbs were gone.

Darkness quickly followed.

*

Fog floated inside my brain, tickling my senses. The cool air on my skin made me feel somewhat aware, yet I wasn't truly conscious. Like experiencing the end of a dream in the seconds before waking up.

A Beatles song played in the back of my mind, although I didn't like the Beatles. John Lennon's voice sounded both far and close, coming from everywhere at once. Without warning, I dove once more into unconsciousness, lost myself in endless space. A sudden cold feeling in my lower stomach pulled me back—although I didn't know where *back* was.

Some sort of cream was being rubbed on my skin; the feeling too real to be an illusion. Shreds of thoughts slipped through the fog. My argument with Albert, the mask he'd placed on my face so he could perform surgery on me. With the memory came a troubling realization of what was happening.

Alarmed, I tried to wake up, but I couldn't move any part of my body, not even my eyes. *My God. This cannot be happening.*

I hadn't imagined the Beatles before; Albert sang along to one of their songs as he massaged my abdomen with the cold cream. When he suddenly stopped touching me, I didn't know whether it was a good sign or not. I had no idea how long I'd been unconscious. Perhaps the surgery was already over, and he was rubbing the cream to soothe the cut. It didn't feel like I'd been cut, but I didn't have a lot of experience with waking up from surgeries.

The sudden sound of metal tools being moved appeared close to my ear. No sound in the world was ever more chilling.

Albert came to stand beside me, his shirt rubbing against my arm. He was still singing along to 'Across the universe' by the Beatles, sounding relaxed like he was about to do laundry rather than surgery.

Something cold and sharp touched my lower stomach. I stopped breathing, alarm bells screaming in my ears. *Don't do this. Don't—*

A straight cut across my skin brought the fire of hell into my body. I screamed inside the cage that held me captive. Warm blood poured down my skin. *Too much. There's too much blood.*

Albert kept singing next to me, didn't skip a beat. He touched me close to the cut. By the way he positioned his hands, I could tell he was about to spread my skin open. Knowing my mind was in danger of shattering, I gathered my feeble willpower and gave it everything I got. It felt like I was killing myself in one last bloody battle, and all I had to show for it was a weak moan that barely escaped my throat.

Albert stopped. His hands moved away, replaced with his warm breath on my face. "Matthew?"

Thank God.

"Matthew? Can you hear me?" He lifted my eyelids. The bright light stung. Albert's blurry face floated above me.

One more try. Give it one more try.

This time my attempts didn't work at all. I couldn't

even manage a moan or a twist. Albert moved away and resumed his position next to my waist.

In the darkness of my mind, I yelled in frustration. It was like being in the hole in the ground again, only this time I couldn't even beg for mercy.

Albert's hands were back on my skin, resting firmly on both sides of the still-bleeding cut. *Oh, God, please don't do it.*

Pain the likes of which I never felt before erupted when he spread my skin open. Acid scorched the center of my body. A supernova exploded behind my eyelids.

As the cage inside my mind finally shattered, I opened my mouth and screamed.

*

"Damn it! Try to stay still."

"It burns!"

"Don't move or you'll bleed more." Albert hurried to wipe the blood and used a spray to seal the cut on my abdomen. It stung like a hundred bees.

"Take deep breaths."

"I can't. Fuck, it hurts!"

"Don't move! I'll help with that." He hurried away as waves of pain kept hitting my stomach. I wasn't sure how long I could stay conscious, wasn't sure I even wanted to.

Albert came back holding a syringe. "Lie still." He stuck the needle into my arm and injected me with whatever was inside. After about two minutes, the pain slowly subsided. My breathing grew steadier, but my heart refused to settle down.

"How long have you been awake?" he asked while cleaning the blood from my skin.

"I felt you cut me. I was awake before that, but I couldn't move."

He exhaled. "My God."

"I'm thirsty."

"Thirsty? Right, of course." He hurried outside the lab and came back with a glass of orange juice and chocolate. I drank and ate what he put in my mouth, my senses gradually sharpening.

When Albert finally spoke, he sounded weary. "I have no idea how this could have happened. I'm sorry, I truly am. I'll let you rest for a while. Is it warm enough in here?"

"Yes, but—"

"Then get some rest." He went to the door and turned off the light. "Your cut will be fine as long as you don't move too much. The shot I gave you should make it easier for you to fall asleep. I need...I need to go think for a bit." He left and closed the door, leaving me in complete darkness.

*

The shot was strong enough to make me slip into a dreamless sleep. When I woke up, Albert was standing next to me, looking refreshed. He smelled like soap, the color back in his cheeks.

"Are you feeling better?" he asked.

"I think so." I tried moving my hands and was relieved to discover I could control my limbs completely, although it still didn't feel as natural as it should. I raised my head and examined the cut on my stomach. It didn't look as big as I'd feared, but the skin around it was red.

"It itches," I said.

"That's a sign of healing. And it's a good thing we stopped before the operation could go any further." He cleared his throat. "Was it the oxygen mask? Did I put it wrong?"

"Yeah, I tried to tell you that."

He shook his head. "I also must have removed it too fast."

"I don't know. Listen, it clearly didn't work. Can you call Jeff to come pick me up?"

"Pick you up? What on earth for?"

The surprise in his voice made me want to punch him. I looked him straight in the eyes. "I was awake while you cut me open. I felt *everything*."

"And I feel awful about that. Now that I know—"

"No. Whatever it is you want to say—don't. Not today."

He crossed his arms, jaw stiff. "Listen here. I had a long talk with Jeff when you came back, and he was clear about the way things will work from now on."

"Albert, you don't know what it felt like."

He stroked my hair. "I believe you that it was horrific. But I never promised that your part in this would be risk-free."

I shook my head from his touch. "You said I wouldn't feel a thing."

His eyes hardened. "I'm doing my best here. There are always risks when you're trying to create something new, something groundbreaking. Remember that what we're doing here is bigger than both of us—you must understand that."

He started walking around me. My pulse rose as he lifted the oxygen mask, then flicked a switch on the gas tank. "We've already started. I'll work on the other side of your abdomen." He came closer, voice soothing. "This time it will work, I promise. Put your head down and relax. It will only take—"

I grabbed his hand when he was about to put the mask on my face. "I said no."

"Let go of me! You're forgetting your place."

"We're not doing this today."

"Jeff will hear about this."

"Fine. Tell him. But you get that mask the hell away from me. I'm serious." I let go of his hand because I would have hurt him otherwise. Facing Jeff was petrifying, but letting Albert cut me open again was plain insanity at this point.

He glared at me with flushed cheeks, then closed his eyes and took a deep breath that seemed like a sign of acceptance.

I put my head back down. The thought of leaving the lab and breathing fresh air gave me much-needed peace of mind. I would need to wait for Jeff to arrive, and that made me realize I didn't know what time it was

I caught Albert moving in the corner of my eye. Before I knew what was happening, he quickly leaned down and put the mask on my face.

I had a moment of utter shock, of not believing he did that after I'd been so straightforward with my refusal. I stopped breathing and tried to push his hands away, but he painfully pressed the mask onto my face. My lungs fought for air but giving in would have meant losing consciousness. I reached for the cart next to my head but couldn't get a grip on anything big enough to have an impact.

"Stay still!" Albert yelled and pushed the mask down harder.

My lungs were burning coals inside my chest; I had to breathe and put the fire out. My hand finally wrapped itself around something solid. I lifted whatever it was and hit Albert in the face.

He screamed and let go. I threw the mask away, but some gas got through in the last second, enough to bring back the fog around my senses. I pushed myself to a sitting position. My head weighed a ton. Down on the floor, Albert was still screaming. I shook my head to make the dizziness go away, but it only worked partially.

When I was able to focus on Albert, I covered my mouth to hold back a gag. He was holding his cheek, blood pouring from between his fingers. I had cut him a few inches under his eye. All I could think was, *Jeff is going to kill me.* My legs were jelly when I put them on the floor. I grabbed the bed firmly and managed to keep myself steady. "Albert?"

"Bastard. What have you done?" He was half-sobbing and half-yelling.

"I told you no, but you—"

"Shut up and give me the spray!"

I was tempted to refuse, but this had already gone too

far. I went to get him the spray and some towels. When he removed his hand from his bleeding cheek, I had to look away. The cut wasn't deep, but it was ugly. If I had aimed an inch higher, I'd have taken out an eye.

He used the spray and growled in pain.

"You should go see a doctor," I said.

"Don't tell me what to do." He pushed himself to his feet.

I went to lean on the bed because my head was spinning non-stop. I was aware of my nudity, but it felt negligible all things considered.

Albert took a step toward me while pressing the towel against his cheek.

"I want to go," I said.

"You'll go when I say we're done. Lie down and be quiet."

"I'm not letting you operate on me again."

"Oh, I have other plans for you." There was spite in his voice, ringing loud and clear in my ears. I remained standing, unsure of what to do. The cut in my stomach started to hurt again. I shouldn't have been moving so soon.

Albert suddenly went to one of his cabinets and pulled out a corded phone. I haven't seen one of those in ages. He dialed angrily and after a few moments, said, "Jeff, it's me."

Fucking fantastic.

"No, everything is not all right...Matthew is still causing problems and not cooperating...he even cut my face open! Yes, I am dead serious...I am talking to you now with a cut on my face, caused by that unprofessional clown you promised wouldn't cause any more problems! Come over here and pick him up... what? Well, you said that last time, and the time before that, but it's clear you've been made a fool...see you in an hour...goodbye."

He hung up, and we both stared at one another. The cut on his cheek looked red and swollen, but it wasn't bleeding anymore.

With my throat tight, I said, "Why not tell him what really went down? About how your failed surgery had —"

He raised his hand. "Enough. I didn't tell him that because it's none of his business. Now get on the bed. An hour is enough time for me to move forward with my work."

"Your work is shit."

"What's that?"

I shook my head as another wave of dizziness hit. "Forget it."

"Say what you want. Go on."

"I was awake while you cut me open. That speaks volumes on how shit your work is. You need help. None of what you're doing will bring your brother back."

Albert took a step toward me, face flushed and eyes wide. I knew I could take him down in case of a fight, but something about the rage in his eyes left me doubtful.

"Do as I say," he hissed. "Get on the bed and shut your filthy mouth."

"I'm not getting on this damn bed, and you should look at yourself in the mirror; you're losing it."

"If I am losing it, it's only because of *you*. Listen carefully, you unprofessional buffoon. I'll create tumors inside your body. I'll make you feel pain for days—no, weeks. I'll make you wish you were dead. Do you—"

I shoved him, causing him to crash on the floor. "You're fucking crazy! Let me out of here!"

He looked up and shook his head. "I won't take orders from a nobody like you."

Rage took over my thoughts, flooded my veins. I never felt like this before, had never been so determined to hurt someone.

I'll make you wish you were dead.

I had no plan when I roughly pulled Albert to his feet, but one glance at the side room was enough to change that.

*

"What the hell are you doing? Let go of me! You can't—"

I threw him on the red mattress, then hurried out of the room and closed the glass door behind me. I had a good enough memory to remember the four-digit code that controlled the door. I locked him in and rushed to the computer where the familiar circles were still on the screen. They looked like a game for kids, completely harmless. One click had been enough to turn me into a defenseless lump of meat all those months ago.

Albert pushed himself to his feet, yet to notice me standing next to his computer. I put my palm on the mouse. "Do you remember the first time you gassed me? How I passed out after you cut me?"

Albert straightened and froze when he saw where I

was standing. "Get away from there!" His voice came out of a speaker above my head.

"Remember the second time?" My throat tightened, but I needed to say those words. "You were lonely, you said, and I was right here, your partner, so you paralyzed and fucked me!"

He put his palms on the glass wall. They left sweaty handprints. "You don't want to do this. I'm sorry for what happened, but you agreed to this deal."

"I didn't have a choice!"

"That's not…that's not my concern. Come over here and let me out. I paid good money for you, and it's clear I haven't gotten my money's worth. Let me out, and I'll let you go. Whatever Jeff decides to do, that's on you."

I shook my head. "You have zero regrets."

He watched me for a long moment before saying, "I have two regrets when it comes to you. The first one is giving you another chance after you ran away; you're clearly too self-destructive to be any help to me." An ugly smile stretched across his face, looking more unnerving due to the cut. "My second regret is not fucking you more when I had the chance. It's the only thing you're good for."

Rage tainted every part of my body. There was freedom in hating someone so profoundly, a lack of reason to hold back. I moved the mouse and clicked on the circle that should paralyze him from the neck down.

"No!"

I took a step back. "Seems like I'm also good at using a mouse."

"Idiot, what have you done?" There was terror in his

eyes, but I was past caring. Whatever might happen to me after today, at least I put up a fight.

The engine in the walls began to grumble.

"You fool!" Albert fell to his knees, then crashed on his side. He mumbled, "There's an order to the way you release...release the gas." Something was wrong with his mouth; it was twisting in a way it shouldn't. His face turned the color of ash. His eyes grew so big, it seemed they were about to pop from his skull.

"Albert? Why are you—"

He opened his mouth to speak, and a gush of blood splashed out.

"Shit!" I clicked on the circle that should stop the gas, but nothing happened. "Come on!" From the speaker above my head, Albert sounded like he was suffocating, his throat filled with liquid I could only assume was more of his blood. I kept clicking on the mouse in a frenzy until my vision finally filled with yellow. The humming of the engine grew quieter. Another minute passed until it stopped working completely. Silence took over, leaving me aware of my heavy breath.

I slowly turned my head to the side, immediately noticing the growing puddle of blood around Albert's body. Even on the red mattress, it was easy to spot.

A frantic voice in the back of my mind urged me to do something, but I had no idea what to do after killing someone.

28

I sat silently on the floor, staring at Albert's body and half-expecting him to wake up and put an end to this nightmare. Even in death, he was stubborn.

I needed to come up with a plan, but my mind was a blank piece of paper and I had no pen to write with. Looking at the locked door leading back to the house, it was obvious I was screwed. The only way to open that door would be to use Albert's finger, and that meant opening the glass door and pulling him out.

Jeff must have been out there by now, getting angrier by the minute. I pushed myself up and carefully got dressed, then walked over to the side room. With a deep breath, I entered the code and opened the door, removing the last barrier between me and the man I'd killed.

If you start thinking about it now, you'll lose it. Get out of there first.

Walking inside, I tried to avoid stepping in the puddle of blood around Albert's body. I'd never seen so much blood in my life. It was like a scene from a low-budget horror movie, only I could smell it all, this profound and metallic scent.

I leaned down, took hold of his shirt, and started to pull him out. He was heavier than I expected, and with my lingering dizziness, it was impossible to drag him for more than a few feet. Panting, I let go to catch my breath. Then the phone rang. I jolted from the sudden noise, unsure if I was ready to face Jeff. But it wasn't like I had much choice. I went to pick up the call. "Hello?"

"What happened?"

I leaned against the wall, my legs unstable. "I messed up."

"I wouldn't be standing out here if you hadn't."

"It's bad."

"Spill it out already. And where's Albert?"

I exhaled slowly. "He's dead."

A few seconds of silence passed before he said, "Repeat yourself. Be very clear."

I tried to focus my thoughts. "He was operating on me, cutting my stomach, and I woke up in the middle."

"Jesus."

"And then he wanted to do it all over again! I tried to talk him out of it, but he's crazy." *Was*. "We got into a fight, and he...God, it was an accident, I swear."

His breaths sounded deep and measured. "You sure he's dead?"

I glanced at Albert, lying in a pool of his own blood. The gas must've caused his veins and arteries to explode. "I'm sure."

"Goddammit. Where are you?"

"In his lab. It's underground. I need to use his finger to unlock the door."

"The hell?"

I told him that entering the lab required Albert's fingerprint and voice confirmation, but exiting only required his fingerprint. At least I hoped it still worked like that, or I was going to rot down here.

I said, “I need to drag him up the stairs to use his finger for the door, but he’s too heavy.”

“He’s not a big guy.”

“I know, but the damn gas he hit me with is still messing with my head.” Even standing still, there were moments when the edges of my vision blurred out like I was looking through water.

Jeff said, “You need to get out of there. Is there a knife around?”

“A knife?” I looked around and saw the cart with all the creepy equipment Albert had planned to use on me. “There are knives in here.”

“Take one and cut his finger off.”

“You can’t be serious.”

“You killed a man, but cutting a finger is too much for you?”

Hearing him say it like that, plain and simple, was like a punch to my gut. It wasn’t something my mind was ready to wrap itself around. “I’ll wait a bit.”

“I’m standing here in the middle of the fucking forest, Matt. Cut his finger off now, or you’ll wish you stayed there.”

I rubbed my face. *This is really happening*. “Is there a right way to do this? I mean, should I…Christ.”

“Don’t lose your shit. You’ll need to cut through the bone. Try doing it with one strong cut. Don’t let things get messy. You know which finger you need?”

“Yes.”

“Go on, then.”

I went to pick up what seemed like the sharpest knife, then returned to the side room and crouched next to Albert, careful not to let blood touch my pants. I knew which finger I needed because I'd seen him use that finger before. I held his hand by the sleeve of his coat and placed his palm facing the mattress.

Here we go. One more step toward insanity. How'd you like the scenery?

Once I had the knife pressed against his skin, I looked away and started pushing down hard. The skin tore easily, but once I reached the bone, I needed to lean in with my full body weight. When something finally gave in and the knife connected with the mattress, a sudden burst of relief hit me. Then my stomach flipped. I let go of the knife and ran to vomit in the bathroom. My muscles felt like rags when I pushed myself back to my feet. I flushed the toilet and washed my face and mouth, then went back to pick up the phone.

"I did it," I said, my voice hoarse.

"Good. Will the door close once you leave?"

"Yes. It closes automatically after about a minute. Then the bookcase moves back to cover the door." It had been months since I last saw that in action, but everything that had happened to me in this place was tattooed on my brain.

"Okay," Jeff said. "Make sure it's happening that way before you leave the house. Wipe your fingerprints from any place you might have touched; wet toilet paper should be enough for that. And try to check for keys to lock the main door once you're out."

"Okay." Hearing someone else guiding me was a

blessing.

"Leave the finger behind. Everything connected to him must stay buried in that lab."

I hung up and went to look for the keys in Albert's pockets, but I couldn't find them. Maybe they were up in the house. I used wet toilet paper to wipe off everything that might have had my fingerprints on it. I also thoroughly washed the knife I'd used to cut off Albert's finger.

Once done sabotaging evidence, I grabbed a small towel and used it to pick up the finger from the floor. A sharp broken bone stuck out from the open cut. I gagged and looked away, then carefully walked up the stairs and put the tip of the finger on the scanner. The three seconds it took the door to start moving were nerve wracking.

I placed the finger on the floor and kept hold of the bloody towel that now held my fingerprints. Without looking back, I left the lab for the last time.

*

"Give it to me."

I handed Jeff Albert's keys, which I'd found in the kitchen. I also gave him the towel with Albert's blood.

It was getting late, with maybe another hour of light remaining. Breathing fresh air was reviving, but standing in front of Jeff in the middle of nowhere almost made me wish to be back in the lab.

"Did the bookcase move like you said?"

"Yes, and I wiped my fingerprints from everywhere I touched."

He looked past me. "There are security cameras around the house."

"What? Dammit." I forgot about those. They must've recorded me entering and leaving. "Can we break them?"

"It won't matter."

I scratched the back of my head and forced the wheels in my brain to speed up. "Wait. During one of the times I was here, Mike talked with Albert about the security, said he has a friend who's an expert."

Jeff looked thoughtful before nodding. "Get in the car. You have blood on your shirt; take it off and hold on to it."

"You're going to call Mike?"

"Get in the fucking car," he growled and walked away.

Sitting alone in the car, it hit me how drained I was. Now that the adrenaline had left my system, I was running on fumes. I looked down and saw that the so-called stitches from the spray were holding up, but the area still looked red and a bit swollen. I eased my head back and stared ahead at the dirt road cutting a path through the tall trees. My thoughts began to scatter, leaving my brain vacant.

A police car suddenly appeared from the other side of the road. I caught a glimpse of Mike driving while next to him sat a guy with long hair. They passed me by and parked close by. After a minute, I heard the muffled sounds of their voices.

Looking at the fading light outside, it dawned on me I must have been sitting in the car longer than I thought. In the rear-view mirror, Jeff was talking with Mike's friend and pointing at the house.

A knock on the window made me jump. Mike signaled me to lower the window, then said, "Hi, Matty. Jeff and Scott are taking down the cameras. Once they're done, I'll stay with Scott to check inside. Albert must have had a place to store all the videos. Even if he put them on a cloud service, Scott should be able to hack it and delete everything."

He looked at me like I was supposed to respond, so I said, "Okay."

He watched my face closely. "You look pale. Hold on a sec."

When he came back, he handed me a bottle of water and an energy bar. "You sure he's dead?" he asked. "We can't reach him down there to check."

I took a sip of water, realizing how dry my throat was. "Nobody can reach him; you'll need his finger and his voice. And yes, I'm sure he's dead."

"Is it true what Jeff told me? Did you wake up while he was cutting you?"

"Yeah."

"Oh, man. That's extreme. At least you got him back. Try not to overthink it."

Not overthink it? He sounded like I'd accidentally run over a cat.

Jeff and Scott came back as I was finishing the energy bar. Mike went to talk to them. "He's in shock. He shouldn't be here."

"He's fine."

"I'm serious, Jeff. You guys can leave. Scott and I will take care of this."

They kept talking and I zoned out and pondered on whether I was in shock. It wasn't like a headache when you could easily tell, although I was anything but normal.

Jeff entered the car. I felt him watching me while I was staring ahead. Without saying a word, we began driving. The car rocked on the dirt road, the front lights cutting through the mist. After about twenty minutes, we parked in a small parking lot surrounded by stores. Ironically, in front of us was a Life Is Good store. The sign in the window read, "Spring SALE! 50% off on all NEW arrivals!"

Jeff said, "I'm buying food. Stay here."

I rested my head against the window as he got out. People walked across the parking lot, the sound of their voices not nearly enough to distract me from thinking. I could still hear him suffocating, smelled his blood and felt the cutting of his finger. I tried to make sense of it all, but there was no sense to be found.

Jeff came back with bags that smelled nice and put them on my lap. I peeked inside and saw Chinese food. It was odd that he'd bought us food, but I didn't have a blueprint of how things should go from now on. I was an extra in my own horror film.

Once inside Jeff's apartment, he took the food and started putting plates on the table. I stood near the entrance, feeling out of place and disoriented.

"Eat," Jeff said without looking at me. "Leave the shirt on the floor. I'll get rid of it later."

I pulled off my shirt and left it on the floor, then went to sit at the table and scooped noodles onto my plate. As my mouth gotten used to the taste, I became more aware and attuned, as if someone played with the stations in my head.

"You need a doctor for the cut?" Jeff asked, still avoiding looking at me.

"I don't know. Should I?"

"If the pain's not too bad, let's wait and see."

I took more food, although my stomach started to cramp. When I finally lowered the fork, I realized I'd begun to shake. I tried to force my body to stay still, but my nerves grew a mind of their own. My chest got tangled, my lungs tied together in a tight knot.

"I'm not feeling well."

Jeff looked up from his plate. "Take deep breaths."

"I can't. I…fuck, I killed him."

"You did. Feeling sorry now won't change that."

"I didn't say I was sorry." I rubbed my aching chest. "I think I'm having a heart attack."

"Jesus Christ, it's not a heart attack. Go to the balcony. I'll bring you something to smoke."

I hurried to grab a clean shirt and stepped out onto the balcony. The fresh air flew straight into my chest, easing up the knots. The sight of Hudson all peaceful and picturesque made me angry. This town was filled with clueless people living their lives like the world was sane. I wanted to go house to house and give everyone a reality slap.

Jeff came and handed me a joint. I inhaled it so deeply, even my legs were getting high. I closed my eyes as the thoughts in my head gradually eased their attacks. When I finished the joint, I was blissfully high.

"Better?" Jeff asked.

"Yeah." It was a fake kind of better, but I cherished it. I debated how to explain to Jeff the chain of events that had led to him covering for murder. How I had every intention to see this through until all hell broke loose. Something told me that meant shit to him, and I should save my breath.

Jeff turned to look at a spot in the distance, his jaw set and shoulders stiff. "Go take a shower and wait for me in the bedroom."

"I...yeah, okay."

I carefully washed my cut and watched as the skin around it became redder. I had no idea how strong the seal was and whether it would suddenly open.

I turned off the water and put on my sweatpants, then went to wait in the bedroom. I should have been terrified, but the weed kept my fear at bay.

When Jeff came into the bedroom, we stood facing one another for a long time. Despite my hatred toward him, the disappointment in his eyes stung.

He closed the door behind him and took a step toward me. I remembered the night he banged on my door and told me that Albert would be my salvation, my last chance. How he later shoved a gun down my throat in the middle of nowhere. How he sent me back to a rapist because a deal's a deal.

Without warning—although some things didn't require warnings—he shot his fist into my chest with full force, sending me stumbling on the bed. I fought to breathe as he pulled me back up and smashed his fist against my temple, filling my vision with smears of bright lights. More pain followed, a storm of fists and kicks that reached everywhere but the cut on my stomach.

As the blows continued to land, merciful stillness filled my chaotic brain. No drug in the world could have been so kind.

Jeff stopped and took a step back, but I grabbed his leg. "Is that all you've got?"

He growled, "Don't push your luck."

I spat blood on his pants. "Fuck you."

The beating continued. By the time he had enough and walked away, pain was my new state of being. I wanted to thank him for making everything right inside my head, but I passed out before I had the chance.

29

The next time I opened my eyes was to a hand stroking my shoulder. A blurry figure sat on the floor next to the bed.

"You're alive," Mike said.

I blinked the blurriness away and licked my torn lips. "Am I?"

"Afraid so."

I was lying on my stomach, one hand touching the cold floor. Even lying still, the bruises on my body made themselves known once I was fully conscious. "Is Jeff here?"

"You're mumbling. Try again."

"Is Jeff here?"

"No. He went out for some errands and asked me to keep an eye on you. You look like shit, Matty."

"Yeah? I feel fantastic, though."

Mike snickered. "That's the spirit. Can I bring you anything?"

"Water."

He went to bring me water and held the glass to my lips as I slowly drank.

"Thanks," I said and put my cheek back on the damp pillow. As long as I didn't move or take deep breaths, the pain was bearable.

Mike said, "We took care of the cameras and the recordings."

I was too drained to feel relief, but I still said, "Okay."

He scanned my face. "Jeff sure let you have it this time. Did you plan it?"

"What do you mean?"

"Did you plan on getting rid of Albert?" He watched me with genuine curiosity.

"What happened was an accident."

"I see." He shrugged. "Didn't look like it, though."

I tilted my head to have a better view of his face. "You saw what happened down there?"

"What? No. I'm talking about the video of you leaving the house with a bloody shirt, looking normal and not trying to call someone for help."

"I called Jeff." That wasn't true; Albert was the one who'd called him.

"I'm talking about the police or an ambulance. The logical thing to do would have been to call them."

I mumbled, "Nothing that what went down there was *logical*."

"Well, that might be hard to explain. Luckily for you, all evidence is gone. Looks like Albert's gonna stay down there until he's nothing but a skeleton."

When I'd left the lab for the last time, I thought about who would go down there to look for him. He was a loner, and he'd once said that he—and only he—had access to his lab. So yes, Albert would probably rot down there, surrounded by the inventions he'd been so obsessed with.

Mike stroked the back of my neck. "I told you this

yesterday and I'm telling you again, don't overthink this. You fought back because you feared you'd end up dead, didn't you?"

I hesitantly nodded. I'd mostly fought back because of revenge, but that only came *after* he'd threatened to hurt me more.

"So that's that," Mike said, "survival."

"Why are you telling me all of this? This whole giving-a-damn-about-me act isn't believable."

"So now I'm a bad guy for trying to cheer you up?"

"I don't need you to cheer me up." Speaking was draining what little energy I had. "You can go. I won't go anywhere."

"All right. I have better things to do than sitting here staring at your fucked-up face. But before I go, there's something you should probably know. I'm telling you this because I think you had enough shit in your life, so maybe it's time for you to catch a break. Are you listening?"

"Yes."

"Jeff's about to pimp you out."

A sharp pain stabbed at my chest. "What are you talking about?"

"You, sex, money."

"Cut the crap, I'm not in the mood."

"Does it sound so crazy considering Albert's out of the picture because of you?"

Yes, I wanted to say. *The craziest thing to ever come out of your filthy mouth.* But as much as I hated admitting it, it didn't sound completely crazy.

"You took out the golden goose, Matty. That's a whole

lot of money Jeff's never gonna get because of you. And to be clear, what I'm talking about won't happen in Hudson. It's sunny Mexico for you."

Mexico? "Why there?"

Mike leaned closer, his breath carrying a faint scent of cigarettes. "Because your white ass is gonna sell well over there."

"You're lying."

"I'm not saying I have it all figured out; he didn't talk to me about it directly. I reckon it will start off with an auction, then you'll be shifted over to the lucky winner. From then on, a part of the money will be sent directly to Jeff. Now, to be fair, he might tell them to send you back here once he made enough money from whoring you out, but it will be way easier for him to simply forget about you." He stroked my head. "Here it is, Matty, my gift to you—honesty. Sorry I didn't use nicer wrapping paper."

No matter how hard I tried telling myself that he was trying to mess with my head, I had a deep and sickening feeling he meant every single word. It also explained why I was still alive now that Albert was out of the picture.

I asked, "How do you know about this?"

"Like I said, he didn't talk to me about it directly, but I heard him talking with other people and the picture was pretty clear."

"You could be wrong."

He snorted. "I could also be a Disney princess, but I ain't. Go ask him about it if you want, but he'll probably deny it to spare himself the drama." He moved closer until his mouth floated above my ear. "I'm giving you an advantage here, man, a card he doesn't know you have. You can do nothing until you wake up one day to a group of Mexicans waiting for a good time, or you can do something about it before it's too late."

My breath turned heavy, pulse hammering. "I can't escape. He'll hurt people I care about."

"Yeah, escaping again would probably be pointless. Guess you'll have to kill him."

It was getting to be too much. A headache grew in the center of my head. "I'm not some cold-blooded killer. What happened last night—"

"Yeah, whatever. Listen, you're about to lose what's left of your pathetic little life, and it's up to you to try and stop it. Not like me and the guys at the station will be busting our balls trying to catch whoever ended him. He might be good money now, but people could start to snoop around one day, and that would mean trouble."

"Then why don't *you* do something about him?"

He snorted. "You little bitch. Can't take care of your own mess. You know what, maybe someday one of us will decide to do something about him, but by then you'll be a regular in whichever whorehouse you'll end up in. You won't even care about Jeff anymore, what with all those lovely gentlemen you're gonna spread your ass cheeks for."

I stopped myself from biting back. "Can you…?"

"Yes?"

"I had a gun when I came back. That cop took it. Can you get it back for me?" I envisioned what it would feel like blowing Jeff's head off and finally escaping his claws. It left a pleasant feeling inside my chest, making me believe I could truly pull it off.

Mike shook his head. "I ain't getting involved."

"Then what the fuck do you expect me to do?"

"Calm down. I ain't giving you a seminar on how to get away with murder. Use your brain. It's only the two of you here, and he doesn't suspect you. You're not going to get a better chance." He stood up. "Anyway, this is your mess to handle. I did my good deed of the day. Adiós, Chiquita."

He left, leaving behind what felt like poison in my veins.

Violent thoughts rushed through my brain, demanding to be heard. Failing to sabotage Jeff's plan would mean a one-way ticket to hell, of constantly wishing I'd done something while I still had the chance.

I dragged myself out of bed and went down on all fours, didn't even bother trying to stand. By the time I found my pants in the bathroom, my body was in agony, sweat covering my skin. Panting, I fumbled through the pockets, not believing I could catch a break. Then my hand closed around the small envelope containing Albert's pills, and I almost cried in relief.

Dragging myself back to the bedroom, I told myself I wasn't about to do anything drastic until I could be positive Jeff was planning on sending me to Mexico. That was what I kept telling myself once I was back in bed and the pills were safely hidden underneath the mattress. Only deep down, I feared it might have already been too late.

*

Jeff mentioned the pills the first time he talked to me after the beating. I stared at the ceiling and said that Albert hadn't given them to me. Jeff called me a failure and stormed out.

I slowly got my strength back as the days crawled by. The cut on my stomach turned into a thin, pale line. Every time I ran my fingers over it, my mind traveled back to the moment the knife had cut my skin and the madness that followed.

I was relieved when Jeff chose to give me the silent treatment since it lowered the chances of him suspecting my intentions. In truth, my intentions weren't something I allowed myself to fully contemplate on. They were possibilities floating in the back of my mind, disturbing but nonetheless comforting.

I heard Jeff talking on the phone in the living room late one evening. It was almost impossible to understand his words from the bedroom, but I was able to catch my name. I got out of bed, opened the door quietly, and listened as Jeff said, "He'll do what I tell him to, that's not a problem...he needs more time to heal... be ready to set everything up."

The conversation ended about a minute later. I remained standing outside the bedroom, my brain clogged with ominous thoughts.

"What do you want?"

I didn't notice him until he was right on the other side of the hallway. "We need to talk."

"Make it quick."

"What happens next?"

With a blank stare, he said, "You're paying me back, that's what happens next."

"As a whore?"

He narrowed his eyes. "Little birds have been talking."

"That's not an answer."

"That's all you're going to get at this point."

"I didn't mean to kill him."

He shook his head. "You don't mean many of the things you do, but you still end up doing them. Now I need to minimize my losses."

"It can't just be about money."

"But it is. You should be smarter about this by now. Focus on getting your strength back." He began to walk away.

"It's my goddamn life, Jeff!"

He stopped but didn't look at me. "It may be your life, but it's *my* decision. I'll try to do right by you, all things considered."

Every response I had would have sounded cynical, so I turned around and closed the bedroom door behind me.

30

When I was nine, my dog was bitten by a fox and got rabies. Dad had taken him to three different vets, but all had given us the same fatal news: Milo was beyond saving, and we should hurry to say our goodbyes.

I was devastated. Milo was barely more than a pup, and in my child's mind the six months we'd spent together were a lifetime. I pleaded with Dad to spare Milo, to not kill him like he'd done something wrong. I had been the one who walked with him where I shouldn't have, who let him run into the bushes where he'd probably gotten bitten by that damn fox. Milo shouldn't have paid for my mistakes.

Dad had given me as much sympathy as one can expect from a dad, but I was as stubborn as one can expect from a child. When his patience dried out, he looked me in the eyes and said, "That dog is dangerous. He might hurt you even though he wouldn't mean it."

"I don't care."

"*I* do. This is not a situation where both you and Milo can come out alive and well. We need to decide who is more important, and the answer is simple."

"Yes," I said. "Milo." But I knew that wasn't true. For the first time in my life, I felt the consequences of my actions, the crushing weight of wrong decisions.

Milo was as good as dead.

*

I woke up in alarm the following day to Jeff shouting from the living room. I forced my heart to settle down and listened to him say, "You can come over in a couple of days...what's the big deal? Ruth, listen to me, I'm not hiding anything...no, there's nobody else! For fuck's sake, you think I have time to date another woman?"

Christ, he did not just tell her that.

"No, I didn't mean it's a question of time—I don't *want* to date anybody else."

I pulled the blanket over my head—not that it did much good. Jeff shouted some more before ending the call. The angry sound of cabinets being slammed followed. He was drinking; I was sure of that.

He had told Ruth that she could come over in a couple of days, which meant whatever Jeff had planned for me was about to go down.

My skin turned hot as my brain was overrun with thoughts about decisions and repercussions. How specific moments in time could alter the course of your entire life.

Time passed until I was jolted back to awareness by the sound of footsteps approaching the bedroom. I pretended to be asleep as the door creaked open. Jeff's heavy breaths reached my ears while he remained standing by the entrance. After a long, stressful moment, he said, "You're awake."

I sighed and lowered the blanket. His flushed cheeks and puffy eyes made it clear he was drunk. I'd seen him drink before, but never to such an extent.

Jeff stumbled inside and slumped on the bed with a grunt. “Dating’s fucking hard.”

I wasn’t going to get a better shot at prying him for information. “Yeah, it usually is. Maybe you should let her come over. Why wait?”

“None of your business.” He rubbed his face. “She deserves better than what I can give her.”

“She likes you.”

He snorted. “She doesn’t know me.”

“She likes what she does know.”

“That’s not enough. Not for the long run.” He pinched the bridge of his nose. “Fuck, why is everything so complicated?”

Seeing him with his guard down was unsettling, made him unpredictable. But I needed to press on before I lost my chance. “You should invite her over for dinner tonight. I’ll help you cook.”

He shook his head. “You don’t know how to cook. You’re useless.”

“Then we can order something. Why can’t she come over?”

“I just said it's none of your fucking business.”

“You sure about that?”

“What?” He shook his head. “You talk too much. Always talking.” He turned toward me, made his fingers into a gun, and held it to the side of my head. “I should've buried you in those woods when I had the chance.” He pushed his fingers against my skull. I groaned as pain spread down my jaw. “You’re like a curse. I can’t escape you.”

I readied myself for more pain, but he sharply moved his hand away and got up. "Wait here until I call you. It's time to end this shit." He wobbled out of the room.

I rested my face in my palms. A dark vision invaded my thoughts, of a different bed in a different room in a different country. Men would come to have their way until I'd remain nothing but an empty shell filled with filth.

Jeff had been right about one thing. It was time to end this shit.

I pulled out the pills from underneath the mattress. They looked harmless, like pills you might take for a headache. It was absurd to think how much I had riding on them. I shoved the envelope into my pocket and watched the shadows on the ceiling while waiting for Jeff to call for me. After about an hour, I heard my name.

My legs were steady as I walked toward the living room, my heart as well. The calm covering my senses felt surreal like a spell.

Jeff was sitting on the couch, looking spent but no longer drunk.

I said, "I need coffee. What can I get you?" I looked out the window, not trusting myself to make eye contact.

"Nothing for me."

Wonderful.

"Let me make you a cup. I have a feeling it's going to be a heavy talk."

He leaned back on the couch, ran a hand over his shaved head. "Fine. Make mine black."

I opened the cabinet and started making his coffee. My hand was still surprisingly steady as I took out the envelope. For a long moment, I stared at the small pills that held the power to change my life.

Jeff cleared his throat impatiently from the living room. I shook my head, took a pill and dropped it in the boiling cup. Then another pill and another and another. Four pills. Was that enough? I put another one in because screwing up wasn't an option.

The pills disintegrated immediately. I had no way of knowing if they affected the taste or whether the coffee would sabotage their effect. I was taking my first steps on no man's land, with no map to guide me.

I placed the cup in front of Jeff and went back to make one for myself. I took my time, hoping it would give him a chance to drink. When I got back to the living room, he'd already taken a few sips, but it didn't seem enough.

I sat in front of him in the chair I'd been twice tortured on.

Jeff looked pale, black under his eyes. "I'm going to talk straight with you." He took another sip. I hadn't made it too hot so he wouldn't have to wait. "We have a corpse rotting in an underground lab, and I don't have a way of getting rid of it."

"The tapes are gone, and I didn't leave my fingerprints around the house."

"On paper, yes, we seem to be in the clear. That doesn't make you any less of a screw up." He shook his head and blinked a few times. "Anyway, what's done is done. The simplest thing to do would be to kill you, but I'm not about to do that—hell knows why." Another sip of coffee. He cleared his throat like something was bugging him there. I watched him closer than I ever watched anything in my life. "There's only one way for you to pay me back in a time frame that won't last for years." His eyes bored into mine.

If I didn't know what he was about to say, I'd have been shitting myself with fear by now. "Go on," I said.

"I got the name of someone who can help us. He'll set up video recording equipment in your apartment, then open a chat room for you. You're going to jerk off and stuff until you get people to pay for private chats. That should take about six to seven hours of your day." He coughed. "Other than that, you'll meet clients a couple of times a week through an agency. The clients will all be women, which is less profitable, but I'm assuming will cause less drama. Those women will mostly want you to take them out, show them a good time. Some will want sex. I think you can handle that. You'll keep half of the money, and if you manage to find a better paying job, you'll be able to pay me back that way." He rubbed his face, looking a lot paler now, almost gray. His eyes were reddish. "Matt, wake up. What do you think?"

I blinked. My chest hurt because I forgot to breathe. "What about Mexico?"

"Mexico?" His eyes hardened. "You think I'm going to send you on a goddamn vacation?"

Oh, God.

I put my face in my hands, feeling like I was falling. Jeff started coughing heavily, and his breaths came out in whistles. When I raised my gaze, it was the first time I ever saw fear on his face.

"Jeff—"

"How'd you do it?"

"I'm going to call an ambulance."

"With the pills from Albert?"

"Y-yes."

"How many?" He leaned back and rubbed his chest like he had a rash there. His shaved head was slick with sweat.

"Let me call an ambulance."

"Matt, *how many*?"

"Five."

He remained quiet like I'd used a foreign language, then an ugly laugh escaped him. "No…no need to call an ambulance; they won't make it in time."

"What can I do? Tell me!"

"Stop crying. When you kill a man, you don't cry. Show me this respect at least." He leaned forward and let out a deep moan while his shoulders shivered. When he raised his eyes to look at me, they were glassy and couldn't focus. "Listen…listen to me. You need to lay low for a while. Christ, that hurts."

"Should I—"

"Quiet! I'm telling you to lay low because they don't know you're back. They don't even know your name. Keep a low profile and you should—goddammit—and you should be fine."

"You were supposed to send me to Mexico!"

He leaned back, his chest moving fast like something underneath the skin was about to explode. Thin blue veins appeared underneath his eyes. With a crooked smile, he said, "I can't believe the shit that's coming out of your mouth sometimes."

Those were his last words to me. About a minute

later, he began smashing his fists into his chest, fighting to let air get in. I had no way of helping him, of taking back what I'd done. I gave him the dignity of not looking away, of witnessing him fighting for as long as he could.

I vaguely remember sitting there for a long time, staring at Jeff looking asleep. A cold feeling spread inside my chest. A small voice in the back of my head said, *you can't stay here.*

I managed to convince my body to stand, but before I could take one step, dizziness seized my head. The room began to spin and the floor quickly faded.

Next thing I knew, I knew nothing at all.

Part Five
Redemption

31

The knock on my door came as I was listening to the weather forecast on the radio. The weatherman promised sunny days throughout the week and advised the listeners to *"Go out with your families to enjoy nature!"*

I shut down the radio and hesitantly opened the entrance door. Ruth was standing on the other side, red hair framing her pale, round face. She seemed relieved to see me, but I couldn't bring myself to speak.

It was the fifth day since I'd left Jeff's apartment for the last time. The only people who came to see me were Bill and Molly. They came over every day to bring me food I didn't want to eat, but I accepted it anyway since that was their way of helping. Our reunion had been filled with questions I couldn't answer and shame I could barely contain.

Ruth said, "You know how hard it was to find you? I ended up tracking down that cop Jeff knew. He gave me your address."

I moved aside so she could come in. My apartment was clean because I didn't do enough to make it unclean. I mostly lay in bed or sat on the fire escape with Caleb, who got the hint about my mood and didn't press for conversation. Late at night, when sleep would elude me, I went to sit in the park until morning.

"You look too skinny. Are you sick?" She went to sit on the couch.

"I was sick for a while."

"Oh. Have...have you heard?"

I didn't have it in me to play dumb. "I heard."

"Why weren't you at the funeral? There were barely any people there. I didn't know anyone."

"I was sick and didn't have your number." Both things were technically true.

She took a deep breath and released it slowly. "I still can't believe this. A heart attack? He was fucking healthy! Ate all this green shit, worked out. Goddammit."

"I'm sorry." My vocabulary felt basic. Hearing she thought it was a heart attack had released some of the tension I'd been carrying. I didn't know what people would think the cause of death was, and I had been expecting the police to come arrest me any day now. I wouldn't survive an interrogation; I was getting less than two hours sleep each night, and my appetite was almost down to nothing. They'd break me like a twig. Only they hadn't come, and now Ruth was telling me it was a heart attack.

"It's all so weird." She massaged her temples. "I tried talking to people at the funeral, but they acted like there's nothing to say."

You don't want to hear what they have to say, I stopped myself from saying. Maybe she did love him, so letting her know the kind of person he'd truly been would have only hurt her more. It also didn't feel as though I had the right to tell her the truth considering I was the reason she was now in mourning.

She leaned her head back. Her eyes looked tired, but her red hair was still wild and beautiful. "I sometimes wonder if I even truly knew him."

"You knew what he chose to share with you. What you felt comfortable knowing."

She should have sensed something wasn't right between Jeff and me. Even though we'd pretended to be friends when she was around, she must have picked up on our weird dynamic and preferred to ignore it.

"I think you should let it go, Ruth. Move on."

She looked like she was about to hit me, then looked like she was about to cry. I should have maybe sat next to her, comforted her. But that would have made her feel welcomed, and I wanted to be left alone.

She did leave after a few minutes. It was awkward again when she stood by the door because it seemed she was expecting me to say something like, "Keep in touch," and I had no intention of doing so.

When she left, it felt as though another chapter had been closed and left behind.

*

There were no nights nor days. Time tangled into itself, becoming meaningless. I was a hollow shape lying motionless in bed, lacking desires or goals. Existing rather than living.

My ribs sharpened underneath my skin as the void inside my stomach grew. My sleep was shallow and offered little comfort. I was slipping away from myself, wondering how this journey might end.

Maybe I already knew.

*

A strong knock on the door pulled me to awareness. I wondered if I'd imagined it, then Mike called my name. I wanted to ignore him, but he would probably mess with the lock.

Did he come to arrest me? How long has it been since I killed Jeff? Two weeks?

I rubbed the sleep from my eyes and went to open the door. The surprised look on Mike's face made it clear how much I'd let myself go.

"You look like shit," he said. "When was the last time you ate?"

I moved aside to let him in. "When I was hungry."

He went straight to the kitchen and opened the fridge. "The chicken and rice still look edible." He put the pot on the table, then filled a plate with food before warming it in the microwave. He was wearing his uniform, beard well-groomed.

"I'm not hungry," I said.

"Yeah, you're past that by now. You'll get hungry again once you start eating." He took out something from his pocket and put it on the table. "Your ID."

I forgot he had it. It felt like years had passed since the day he got a free pass to torment me. "What about the drugs?"

He shook his head like I'd said something dumb. "There were no drugs. Like I was gonna drive around with cocaine in my glove compartment."

I was too tired for anger. I'd also suspected it was all a bluff.

When the microwave beeped, Mike took out the plate and put it on the table. "Eat."

"Why are you here?"

"First you eat, then we'll talk. I'm not going anywhere until you finish this plate."

I wasn't much of a match for him when I was stronger, but now I had zero chance of throwing him out. With a sigh, I sat at the table and forced food into my mouth. The first bites tasted odd on my rusty taste buds. My stomach rumbled loudly, and by the time I finished eating, painful cramps took over. Yet I also felt a small burst of energy hitting my body like an old rusty engine had been awakened.

Mike went to sit on the couch. "Seems like being a murderer isn't working out for you so well."

I went to sit next to him, his bluntness failing to leave a mark. "Seems like it."

"How'd you do it?"

I hesitated, but Mike had been a part of everything that happened. "Pills. Albert gave them to me. I was supposed to pass them over to Jeff, but I kept them hidden."

"Where are those pills now?"

"Down the drain."

He scratched his chin and nodded. "Okay, that was smart."

"What would've been smart is not listening to you."

"Oh?"

I looked him in the eyes, my anger quickly rising

to the surface. "You said he was going to send me to Mexico, but he planned something else, something I could've lived with."

"Then why'd you kill him?"

"He told me that after I gave him the pills. There was nothing I could do by then."

"And if there was a way?"

It took me a moment to understand his question. "I didn't want to kill him. If you hadn't gotten that thing about Mexico all wrong, everything would've been different." That thought was a ghost haunting my dreams.

Mike put his hand on my shoulder. "I'm guessing that jerking off in front of a camera and occasionally hitting some pussy isn't such a big deal, all things considered."

"Yeah, I would've managed. Wait." I moved his hand away. "How'd you know about that?"

He smirked and shook his head. "Always too naive for your own good."

I watched his face, the arrogance he couldn't, or wouldn't, hide. "You tricked me."

He leaned closer. "I didn't want him killing you, so I pitched him an alternative."

"Then why the hell did you lie?"

"After I helped you guys take care of the security cameras at Albert's, Jeff wanted me to get more involved in his work. You show a guy like that you're good at solving problems, and suddenly there are more problems need solving. Thing was, after the night he almost buried you alive, I decided that as a father, I didn't need this shit in my life. But you know there was no going back with Jeff." He lowered his voice. "I'm grateful to you, Matty. You took care of that problem for me. I had no idea you'd pull through and manage to make it look like a heart attack." He stared at me like I'd cured cancer. "Brilliant job, man."

In my head, I threw him on the floor and beat him to a pulp until his face was nothing but blood and bits of brain. But I wasn't as stupid as I was weak.

"Get out."

"Oh, c'mon. You wanted him dead more than me. With both him and Albert out of the picture, you should be out celebrating, not slowly dying in here."

"We all deal with killing people differently. Get out."

"Don't be an ungrateful shit. I gave Jeff another option instead of putting a bullet in your head."

"But you told me something different! You didn't give me a chance to take the other option."

"I just told you it was getting to be too much, and I have a family to think of. So yeah, I changed my mind and told you about Mexico. Wasn't the nicest thing I ever did, but that's life for you."

"Thanks for the reminder. Now leave me alone."

"Can't do that."

I rubbed my face, exhausted to my core. The food I'd eaten wasn't enough to erase weeks of neglect. I decided to go back to my bedroom and try to ignore him until he'd eventually leave.

I stood up, but he grabbed my wrist. "Sit down."

"I can't be next to you anymore."

"We're gonna talk. Let's keep this civil. You know how I can get when I'm not civil."

I reluctantly sat back down. He put his palm on the back of my head. “You look pale. Come here, lie down.”

“No.”

“I won’t hurt you.”

I almost laughed at how twisted that statement was.

He put pressure on my head. I wanted him to have his say and leave, so I let him lower me until I lay on my side, my head on his lap.

“You took what happened way out of proportion,” he said in a soothing voice. “It’s not like you killed two saints.”

“Doesn’t matter.” I shut my eyes and let the truth spill out. “I don’t feel like being alive anymore. It seems pointless, all of it.”

“You’re finally a free man.”

“Freedom shouldn’t come at such cost.”

“True, but having you dead won’t make anything better, simply make the two nice people downstairs feel bad for the rest of their lives. You want that?”

I hated how well he knew me. “No.”

“Good. I’m glad you said that.” He stroked my head, the feeling both wrong and comforting. “You’re gonna get your strength back one step at a time. I’ll help. You can’t do this on your own.”

“I don’t want anything from you.”

“It’s not about what you want; it’s about what you need. I’ll make sure you eat and do some exercise. You’ll start feeling better in a few days.”

Talking about feeling better with the man who’d tortured me was a dose of surrealism I could barely fathom. I wondered if Mike had grown a conscience, but it wasn't the apocalypse, so that was unlikely. It didn't matter, though. I was aware of my declining health and my lack of mental ability to fight it. I was sinking to the bottom of the ocean, and it was so quiet and peaceful down there, I had forgotten to swim back up.

A weak voice in the back of my mind urged me to give it one final try before giving up. Mike was the kind of asshole who wouldn't go easy on me.

"Okay," I said. "I'll try."

"Good." He moved his fingers gently across my forehead. "Let me sort you out, then we'll see money coming in."

I opened my eyes. "What are you talking about?"

"Shhh. It's okay. We don't need to talk about it now."

"Mike, I'm weak, not dumb. Tell me what the hell you're on about."

"All right, let's have this conversation now." He waited a few seconds before saying, "You're going to do what Jeff wanted you to, but you're going to do it for me. Nine hours on a video chat, five days a week. Other than that, you're gonna work for an escort agency. You and I will split the money evenly. I'll give you a few days to get stronger, but then it's time to work."

I moved to sit and shook my head. "You really are mental. God, the crap I had to listen to you say for all these months. Get out. I'm serious, *get the fuck out!*"

He raised a finger. "You need to cool it."

"I didn't escape Jeff just to deal with his cheap clone."

"I'm nobody's clone."

"Get. Out."

He shook his head. "You always underestimated me."

I rolled my eyes. "If you're about to start a heartwarming monologue, give me a second to throw up."

"No monologue, but I didn't come here without being sure I'd get you to agree."

"You were wrong."

"Say no to me and you're going to prison."

His threat sent a jolt to my heart, but that was what he wanted; for me to succumb to fear. "You're full of shit. If you had something on me, I would've been in prison by now."

He sighed like he was disappointed in me. "You want me to give you the full show? Fine, here we go." He took out his phone. "What I'm about to show you is not only saved on this phone, so you can throw it out the window for all I care."

He held the phone to my face. It took me a few seconds to realize what I was seeing. I never noticed the camera inside the lab. It seemed to have been located on the far left, high enough to capture most of the space below. I watched myself pushing Albert into the side room, then locking him in. I wanted to tell Mike to stop the video, but I was paralyzed. I watched myself standing naked next to the computer, talking to Albert who was locked in the glass room. There was no sound to the recording, which made me seem even crazier without any context. The video showed me activating the gas, and what followed was as dark and brutal as I remembered.

"Enough." I looked away.

Mike put the phone back in his pocket. "Sorry about

that, but you chose to be stubborn." He lowered his voice. "Once I send this video to the right people, this whole thing will start crashing down on you. Even if you run, you'll never have a moment's peace."

Every nerve in my body trembled. A sharp pain grew in the center of my head. I forced out a tight breath and said, "I'll tell them about you. About how you messed with the cameras around the house and about your connection to Jeff. Even about how you knew I was being experimented on and didn't do anything to stop it. Shit, you drove me there!"

He shrugged off my threat. "You can say whatever the hell you want. At the end of the day, it's *you* on that video, and my so-called involvement is nothing but your word against mine—and you're a murderer." He moved closer and put his arm around my shoulders. I should have pushed him away, but numbness took over my body.

He said, "A long time ago, I mentioned having big plans for you, do you remember? I knew there were better ways to get money out of you, and Jeff was a fool not to see it sooner. Why do you think I took all those photos of your bruises? People paid for those."

I tasted bile. "You're sick."

"I'm a businessman, and I was nice enough to give you a few weeks of peace. But it seems you used that time to rot in here. Did you think you were simply gonna pick up from where you left off? No, man, it doesn't work like that."

I rubbed my eyes, hating how deep his words cut.

He stroked my back. "Agree to my offer and let's shake

on it. I won't back down."

I knew him well enough to believe that. It felt like I was back facing Jeff and his nonnegotiable offer to be Albert's lab rat. But now I had even less to lose than before, which left Mike with fewer cards than he thought.

I said, "I won't spend more than six hours on a chat and no more than four days a week."

"What? That's nothing."

"*I'm not a goddamn slave*. And no meeting men."

"But they pay more."

"No. Men."

"Jesus, all right. As long as you behave, you'll only meet with women. Six hours on the chat, four days a week. Do we have a deal, then?"

I stared at the floor, the words stuck in my mouth as I began processing what I was about to agree to.

"Oh, come on, Matty. It's not the end of the world. Besides, you *need* me."

"I don't need you."

He bumped my leg with his. "You don't even sound convinced. Look at me as your redemption."

I tilted my head at him. Something about that word sparked a warm feeling inside me. "Redemption?"

"That's right, Killer. Those two may have deserved what you gave them, but it doesn't make your hands any less bloody." He leaned closer. "I remember those looks in your eyes whenever I was done educating you. They were brief, but I know how to spot bliss when I see it."

"Shut up."

"I'm not judging you; it's you who did the judging."

My eyes itched—no, they burned. I wanted to burst out of the room and escape him, yet my body was a lifeless rock. I reluctantly accepted the truth of his words because I'd known what was happening between us, what I'd been secretly getting out of his brutality.

Now I was slowly killing myself in this apartment, unable to cope with what I'd done.

"Hit me," I said.

"Huh?"

I cleared my throat. "You're my redemption, aren't you? My magic pill to make everything better. Go on, I want to feel it."

He moved away. "Hold on now. I'm not about to treat you like I did before." He winked. "I need you in top shape to make all those women happy and generous."

"Hit me."

"No."

I spat at his face.

He jolted back. "You're crazy!"

"I hope the baby isn't yours."

He growled and punched me in the face, threw me on the ground. By the time he stopped kicking, I lay flat on my back, bruised and moaning. He stood above me with his feet on my chest, eyes blazing. "Is this what you wanted? Huh?"

A sense of peace flowed through my body, calming my thoughts and making them bearable.

"Yes, it is."

32

The room smelled like lavender thanks to the burning candles scattered around. I could see stars through the skylight, floating above in endless black.

The woman—Tamara, I think—had put on Michael Bolton before I got here, and the same cheesy songs were playing on repeat for the last two hours. I glanced at my watch, making sure to be discreet about it, and saw our time was almost up. I needed to get going although Tamara felt nice beside me. The smell of our drying sweat mixed with lavender.

I had yet to find the right way to end a meeting that was all about sex and money without making it feel cold. Although these things were rarely just about sex, as I'd discovered first-hand in the last few weeks. Sex was often forgotten in favor of companionship, of putting the lonely to rest with a make-believe love affair utterly absent of true emotions.

Sex was also the easy part, with clear expectations and outcomes. Everything else tended to get messy. This night had luckily been solely about sex, and Tamara was now resting with her head on my chest after almost two hours of getting her money's worth. At least I hoped she did. The tip at the end would be my honest review because money never lied—it just made you do dumb mistakes that could ruin your life.

"Is it time?" she asked in a sleepy voice.

I made a show of checking my watch, then made a sound of disappointment. "Yeah, seems like it."

"Dammit. I hate time. It never works your way."

I tilted my head and kissed the top of her messy hair, knowing this would make her hug me closer and rub her leg against my limp cock. Everything could become predictable with time; you just had to look closely for patterns, then learn how to set them in motion and react accordingly.

"I had a great time," I said and partly meant it, remembering other meetings that hadn't ended well for different reasons.

"You're just saying that."

"I'm not." My fingers touched the side of her right breast, causing her to shiver.

"I want to see you again." She sounded both stern and hesitant, like this was a first date rather than a business deal.

I knew she'd want us to meet again. It was usually easy to tell. "You sure? I mean, you don't need to pay for sex."

She raised her head and kissed my cheek, her warm palm on the other side of my face. "You're a wonderful liar, or in need of glasses."

I didn't insult her with another lie.

Once we were both fully dressed and the lavender candles were almost out, we stood and stared at one another in her dim bedroom. Michael Bolton refused to shut up in the background. My time here was officially over, but I knew these final minutes were crucial since this is when regrets tended to replace the thrill.

Tamara took a step toward me, rest her palms on my chest. Even close to sixty, she seemed powerful and sharp. Based on the framed diplomas on the wall, I assumed she was a professor. I made sure not to look directly at the photos of her husband hanging on every wall.

Tamara raised her head for a final kiss, and I made sure to move my tongue the way she liked. When we broke the kiss, she slipped a bill into my waiting palm. I didn't verbally acknowledge the tip, just gave a quick nod.

While waiting for my taxi outside, I glanced down at the one-hundred-dollar bill and felt nothing as I slipped it into my pocket. What was there to feel?

*

I was sitting on my bed in the middle of a video chat when my phone started blinking in the corner of my eye. More than twenty people were watching me live—a new record in the month I'd been doing this. The little chat window buzzed with comments, but the requests for private chats held the best money opportunities—and the most extreme demands.

I didn't glance at my phone because this was not the time to lose my concentration. My shift was about to end, and I needed to get this part right. Once I finished and drops of semen covered my chest and stomach, I said goodbye to whoever was watching, promised to be back tomorrow, then logged out. My balance showed

I'd made over three hundred dollars, which was decent even after Mike's cut.

My body felt stiff from sitting on the bed for so many hours. I stretched and went to take a hot shower, then got dressed and grabbed my daily joint. I was starving but there was still time until my dinner with the Broslavskiys. Molly had promised lasagna, and I had promised to leave an empty plate.

Sitting on the fire escape, the setting sun felt wonderful on my skin. Summer was finally here, and it was warm enough to make the air sweet and inviting. Running in the park was once again a journey through different shades of lively green.

I looked at my phone and frowned at the unfamiliar number. Few people knew my current number, and the only person who usually called me was Mike. Even the agency went through him for setting up appointments.

I took a drag from the joint and called the number back. After four rings, I heard, "Matt?"

I dropped my joint, which landed three floors down.

"Matt? You're there?"

I wasn't. My brain was suddenly back in a town I'd left behind, the sharp shift leaving me dizzy. "Blue?"

"Oh, jackpot. I knew I'd get it right eventually. Couldn't your parents have given you a less generic name? Anyway, are you okay?"

"I'm…Christ, how'd you get my number? I told you I was from Ohio." Hearing her voice instantly flooded my brain with memories I'd tried to block. I hadn't planned on calling her, knowing I wasn't the same man she and the rest had grown to know back in Grafton. I did, however, plan on calling Hank in the coming days to tell him not to send the file I'd saved on his computer.

Blue said, "Yeah, Ohio put me off track for a while, but I got help from an ex who knows how to get things done."

"He's a criminal?"

"Joshua? Don't be silly. He's just good with technology." She took a breath. "So...how are you?"

I had no idea how to begin answering that, but I settled for as much honesty as I could. "My life is complicated. It was bad for a while, but I think I'm doing better."

"Mind if I ask why you took off like that?"

I exhaled and said, "I got involved with someone I shouldn't have. When I met you and the others, I was running away from him. Coming back home for closure turned into the biggest mistake of my life. Now this guy...he's out of the picture, but I'm still dealing with things I can't walk away from."

She stayed quiet for a while, and I was worried I'd scared her off. "Blue?"

"I'm glad you're doing better."

"Thank you."

"I also wish you'd have shared what was going on with you back then. I probably wouldn't have been much help, but I would've listened."

"I know. I'm good at being smart in hindsight. Hmm, how's everyone doing?"

"Steve and Amber are getting married next week."

"Holy shit! No way. When did he pop the question?"

"A few weeks back. They found a good deal on a small

wedding hall, so they decided to go ahead and do it, those crazy kids."

"That's so wicked." I remembered him talking about it non-stop during our morning rides when all I wanted was a few more minutes of sleep.

Blue said, "So, you've got plans for next Thursday?"

"Me?"

"No, the other guy I'm talking to right now."

I rubbed my face, trying to take control of my thoughts. "Going back is tricky. The way I left..."

"No one will give you a hard time. They'll just be happy to see you. Plus, I need a date."

"A date?"

"Well, I simply cannot go by myself to Grafton's most exclusive event of the season, now can I?"

I could ask for a couple of days off. Mike was fine with this sort of thing as long as I gave extra hours on other days. I could make it work, but did I want to?

"Blue, I'm still not the right guy for you."

"Well, look at you getting ahead of yourself. I only need a date for the wedding and prefer a gentleman who happens to be photogenic."

I snickered. "I'll do my best."

She sighed dramatically. "In this day and age, that's all a girl can ask for."

Sitting outside after we hung up, my mind buzzed with rare and pleasant thoughts. I shouldn't have allowed myself to succumb to silly optimism, but I couldn't help it. A nice feeling spread throughout my body from thinking of seeing my friends from Grafton again. It was a part of my life I cherished but knew I must leave behind. Now it seemed I might be able to slip back in, although partially.

The sound of a window being opened pulled me back to reality. Caleb stuck his head out. "Nice to smell you, Brother Matt."

I chuckled. "Your nose is a bit behind, I'm afraid. I dropped my joint on the ground."

He scowled. "Ain't that the saddest story ever told."

"It sure is up there."

"Care for some quality company?"

"Always." I watched him struggle to climb out the window, and a pang of unease ran through me. I opened my phone and created a reminder to get him a better stool to climb on.

"You feeling all right?" I asked as he sat down on the stairs, a little short of breath.

"Hanging in there." He looked into my eyes. "It's not easy turning forty, let me tell you."

I laughed. "Yeah, must be rough." I decided to share with him what'd happened. "I had a call with Blue earlier."

"Blue?"

"The girl I told you about a while back. The one from Vermont."

"Oh, I remember. You called her?"

"She called me."

"Ooh, that means she fancies you."

I shrugged. "It's still complicated."

"Then be a man and uncomplicate it."

"Not so simple."

He slapped his knee. "Since when is anything good

also simple?"

He had a point. Maybe I was overcomplicating something that had enough complications for a lifetime. I learned to expect the worst to happen, to be on my guard in anticipation for things to break. I wondered if I had it in me to rewire my brain.

"It's nice out here," Caleb said with a sigh. "No need for two working eyes to feel the sun going down. Makes everything feel okey-dokey."

I closed my eyes and embraced the warmth across my face as a gentle breeze fluttered my hair. "Yeah, I hear you."

33

"Remember what I said: moving to the fifth gear could be a hazard. Put as much pressure as you need and don't let her push you around."

"Her?"

Bill raised a warning finger. "Don't you start."

"Wait!" Molly hurried out of the building with a small basket. "Some snacks for the road."

"I'm going to a wedding; there's gonna be food."

"That will start hours from now."

She'd always enjoyed giving me food, but ever since my drastic weight loss, she'd made it her mission to ensure it would never happen again.

I took the basket and kissed her cheek. "Thank you."

"You're going to stay there for a few days?" Bill asked. He looked better these days, thanks to a new regime of working out and eating healthy. Getting the insurance money for the store had set him up comfortably, but I still felt a wave of guilt every time I walked past Abby's Corner's resting place.

I said, "One night should be enough."

"I'm assuming you're going to drink."

"Yeah, probably, but I'll crash on a friend's couch."

He nodded, eyes stern. "Make sure to do that."

"Oh, you're so handsome," Molly said as I put the

basket in the car.

"Mighty dashing," Bill said.

I ran my hands down my new suit. "I do clean up nicely."

Molly said, "Now go stand together you two so I can take a photo."

"Those damn photos again," Bill muttered, but we both did what she said. I put my arm around his shoulders and smiled while Molly fought with the camera on her phone.

I thanked them again for the car and promised to send a message once I reached Grafton. Then I was on my way to a place I never thought I'd see again.

*

"You'll be all right. Take deep breaths and let's get in there. They'll finish all the food!"

I shook my head, feet glued to the ground. We stood outside the small wedding hall, far enough to not get noticed by anyone.

"I can't. They'll all be there: Tom, Hank, Trevor... everyone."

"Well, Steve's a popular guy."

I let out a tight breath and looked at Blue. She was so beautiful in her black dress. Her hair was pulled back, revealing two golden earrings. "I don't think I can do this."

She raised her head and gave me a look that was all business. "Listen, I get it. Maybe seeing all those people at the same time is a bit much, but going one by one won't be any easier." She put her hands on my shoulders. "We're already here, looking all nice and fancy. Seeing you will make Steve so happy he'll shout, *my boy's back!* all across the hall. And yes, people will probably ask what happened, but you'll only tell them what you're willing to share." She lowered her voice. "And I will be right there, making sure no one's pushing too hard."

"Promise?"

She twisted her lips. "I might need to pee at some point, and talk to some friends, and maybe—"

I kissed her; it had been way too long coming. She tensed for a moment, making me worry I was out of line, but then her lips relaxed and she was all in. The inside of my body melted while our tongues got better acquainted.

When we stopped to breathe, Blue raised a warning finger. "This better not be about buttering me up to let you bail."

"No, ma'am."

She fixed her hair. "Good. Now, we should go inside before I drag you over to my place and forget I'm supposed to be a lady."

I kissed her lips, my anxiety finally under control. "God forbid."

Near the entrance, we were greeted by cheesy music and the sound of people talking. I took one final breath and opened the door.

Tom and Hank were the first ones I saw, talking and eating next to the buffet. Hank's cheeks were flushed from drinking. He was laughing at something Tom had said when suddenly our eyes met. Tom turned his head as well, and both of them stared at me as if I'd landed from the moon. I hesitantly raised my hand to wave when Steve's voice cut through the noise. "Matt!"

I looked around and found him making his way through the crowd, elbowing his guests out of the way. Next thing I knew, he pulled me into a hug that shoved all sense of dread out of my body.

"Fucking bastard."

"I'm sorry."

"You better be!" He let go and scanned my face, his wild hair caged under too much hairspray. "Are you all right, man? No bullshit."

I nodded and couldn't hide my smile. It was so good seeing him. "I'm doing better."

"Good. Blue, my boy's back!"

She gave me a knowing look.

"Congratulations," I said.

"You better congratulate Amber 'cause she's about to snatch the hottest guy in town."

Blue looked around. "Oh yeah? Where's he hiding?"

"Ha ha." Steve gave her a quick hug, then turned to me. "We'll catch up later, Matty—now we drink." He turned around with his arm around my back. "Somebody give us a drink, goddamn you!"

*

"Looks exactly how I left it," I said as I scanned the room that used to be my home. It felt like years had passed since I'd last been here.

"Hate to break it to you, but all the rooms look the same."

I chuckled and turned around. "Nah, this one's special."

Hank was leaning on the wooden railing outside my old room, blowing smoke into the warm night air. I went and stood next to him.

The wedding had been fantastic with no drama I couldn't handle or questions that dug too deep. When it ended, I took a ride with Hank for some one-on-one time.

"To be honest, I didn't think I'd see you again," Hank said. "Was close to reading that file you saved. You can bet your ass I cursed you every single day for making me wait."

"I know, but it was for the best." Having the police come after Jeff would've most likely ended up with me being charged with murder. I had the biggest motive imaginable written on that file, including my connection to Albert and the whereabouts of his underground lab.

"Can you delete it?" I asked.

"With pleasure."

I leaned forward and rested my arms on the railing. "I missed this place," I said, meaning more than just the motel. My connection to Grafton and its people had been tugging at my soul ever since I left.

"Grafton has been known to grow on people, although it's easy dismissing it as just a tiny dot on the map."

"Good thing I was broke back then."

He gave me a once-over. "This suit you're wearing seems expensive."

"I'm getting by."

We exchanged looks, and he dropped the subject.

"Are you a free man, Matt?" he asked instead, which wasn't a less loaded question.

"In a way. More than before, at least."

"There's a whole lot you're not telling me, and I can't say I like it."

"I know. But I am doing better." I looked him in the eyes. "No bullshit."

He nodded but didn't look convinced. Maybe because *I* wasn't entirely convinced. But I needed to believe this to be true, needed to remember how damaged I'd been after Jeff's death.

"How's that gun of yours?" Hank asked.

"I lost it."

"Did you use it?"

"No."

He nodded, relief on his face. "Good."

We stayed in silence for a while, coyotes howling in the distance. Hank broke the silence by asking, "Is this a one-time visit?"

I opened my mouth to say I didn't know, but I ended up saying, "I'll come back soon." I hadn't been in Grafton for more than a few hours, but I already felt more at home here than in Hudson.

A car was coming close. A few seconds later, Blue's pickup truck emerged from the shadows. She stuck her head through the open window, her hair blowing in the wind. "You ladies had enough time to catch up on your gossip?"

"Were just getting to the juicy parts," Hank said. "Are

you sober enough to drive?"

"Ask me tomorrow."

"Young lady—"

"I'm fine!" She winked at me. "You coming?"

"Jesus," Hank mumbled. "I don't need to see this."

"I'll stop by tomorrow to say goodbye before heading back," I told Hank and walked toward the car.

"Give a few hours at the front desk while you're at it."
I laughed and waved him goodbye.

*

Two months after Steve's wedding, I was lying in Blue's bed, her head resting on my chest as her fingers gently moved across my stomach.

"You'll love it there," she said in a sleepy voice. "Champlain is the prettiest lake in the world."

"Yeah?"

"Well, at least in northern Vermont."

"You used to go there with your parents?"

"Every summer, up until Mom left. Haven't been there in over ten years."

"Sure you don't want to go to a motel? Maybe Hank can help us get a good price."

"You think all motel owners know each other?"

"I know they do, through their secret society."

She snickered. "No motels this time. It won't be the same unless it's full-on camping. Worried about bears?"

"What? I am now."

She nibbled on my nipple. "I'll protect you from the bears and wolves."

"Wolves as well?"

"They might scare off the bears."

"I'll pay to see that."

I slowly moved my fingers over her bare hip. She wasn't ticklish, so I enjoyed her smoothness with no interruptions. This intimacy came with a price when my mind would occasionally hit me with flashes of other women in different beds, waiting to get their money's worth. I became good at blocking those images, but the constant battle was exhausting.

Blue's bedroom was dark, and a nice summer breeze flew in through the open window and danced on my skin. I loved sleeping in her house where the mornings were filled with the sound of birds and the smell of nature.

My apartment back in Hudson has turned into a place of work, and not the kind of work I enjoyed being surrounded with throughout the day. My conscience gave me hell every time I thought about what I was keeping a secret from Blue. Sharing how I was making money would have ended everything, and I wasn't willing to risk the best thing in my life, regardless of how selfish that made me.

My phone suddenly rang.

Blue raised her head. "Who's calling you at this hour?"

I didn't need to check to know who it was. I tried to stay calm as I gently moved Blue away. "Must be a friend who had too much to drink. I better take this outside."

She yawned. "Can't you call him back in the morning?"

The phone stopped ringing. It was 1:00 a.m. and I

could have called Mike later, telling him I'd been asleep when he called. But my deal with him included being available around the clock, and I couldn't risk ignoring him.

"I better call him back." I turned on the night lamp and quickly grabbed my pants and shirt.

"You think it will take long?"

"No. I'll be right back, but you should go to sleep." I went barefoot downstairs and stepped out into the dim backyard. Past the white picket fence, the world seemed endless, the vast fields bathing in the moonlight. I didn't realize how much I'd missed this place until I got it back.

My phone started ringing again. I leaned my back against the tree in Blue's backyard, then took a deep breath and answered the call. "Hi."

"Hi, buddy. Sorry about the hour, but a lucky lady's waiting. Order a taxi to—"

"I'm not home."

"Oh. Where are you?"

"In Vermont."

He cleared his throat. "I must've missed the message you left me about that."

"It's a short visit."

"Doesn't matter. You've been going there way too often lately, and since when do you not tell me about this in advance?"

"I didn't think you'd mind." That was a lie. I'd chosen to take the risk instead of facing a refusal. He had refused my requests twice in the past month, and I was running out of excuses to tell Blue. I said, "I'll get back first thing tomorrow."

He snorted. "Little fucker. You don't have enough chat hours this week, and you've only met with half the clients the agency has set up for you lately."

"They kept setting up meetings at the last minute, and—"

"So what? We told them you were the guy to call for any last-minute gig."

He told them that. "They started setting up way too many meetings."

"You sound like it's a bad thing. You're popular. More money."

"Listen, going on about it now is pointless. Let's meet tomorrow and talk."

"Talk about what?"

I kept my voice low and said, "About our arrangement. I'm not bailing on you, but it's getting to be too intense." I let out a nervous breath. "I might be able to get a job from the man I used to work for in Vermont. It will pay less than what I'm making now, but I'll give you most of the money, so it shouldn't matter."

"Why the hell would I let you do that?"

"When Jeff told me about this deal, he promised I could find a different job as long as it wouldn't hurt his cut."

"That was nice of him, but I ain't Jeff, and I don't want you doing anything else."

His refusal proved what I'd suspected—this was about control more than it was about money.

"I need to head back," I said. "Let's talk about this

tomorrow."

He remained silent for a long time, and I thought the line might be dead. "Mike?"

"You're going to listen to me now, listen *real* good."

I exhaled slowly, knowing I was heading toward trouble. "What is it?"

"I know where she lives."

Sharp pressure hit my chest. I hissed, "Watch your mouth."

"If you think I won't get her out of the way, you're a fool."

Flashes of Bill's burned-down store filled my vision.

Mike said, "You're breaking up with her tonight and coming back home. Then you're gonna work your ass off, and I do mean it literally because you're going to meet with men as well."

"No."

"What's that?"

"I said no."

He snorted. "No isn't an option here, Killer."

A ringing sound grew in my ears. Breaking up with Blue would mean losing everything I'd managed to rebuild. I couldn't let him take that away from me. "I'm not breaking up with her."

"Yeah, keep telling yourself that. Best to do it tonight 'cause tomorrow you're going back to work. No more Vermont."

"Not gonna happen."

"Here you go again, forcing me to be the bad guy. Maybe your girl and your neighbors should start a club for people who got hurt because of you."

I closed my eyes and tried to grab hold of the growing storm inside me, but it was futile. Once we were on a path of Mike threatening to hurt Blue, I had little left to lose. I yelled at him to take back his words, and he responded by yelling louder, his threats like blows. I pictured him hurting Blue like he used to hurt me, and that vision broke something inside me I'd been barely keeping together.

My body was on fire, but it was out of my control. I screamed at him, throwing words that made no sense because nothing was making sense.

Lights came on in Blue's house at some point, and it dawned on me the line had been dead for a while. The realization should have made me stop, but it did nothing to put out the fire.

I kept on screaming.

34

The first thing I noticed was the soreness in my throat. It felt like someone had rubbed sandpaper against my vocal cords. I looked around through bright blurriness and couldn't understand what I was seeing. It looked like a hospital room, but I had no idea how I got here. I tried moving my hands but couldn't.

"What the hell?" My hands and legs were tied to the bed. *Is this a nightmare?* With my messed-up head, nothing would've surprised me.

"Matt?" Blue got up from a chair and came closer. She looked exhausted, her hair unkempt.

"Where am I?" I tried to move my hands again, but the bindings were too strong. The sterile hospital smell reminded me of Albert's lab, and my panic intensified. "What's going on? It's not funny!"

"Relax, Matty. It's for your own protection."

"Huh? Protection from whom?"

She narrowed her eyes like she was trying to decide if I was pulling her leg. "Protection from *you*."

"That's ridiculous."

"Don't you remember last night?"

Unease tingled underneath my skin. "Last night? I… I'm not sure."

She took a step closer. "We were in bed when you got

that phone call. You—"

"Wait. Give me a moment."

Images and sounds came alive and began filling the gaps in my memory. I remembered getting the phone call from Mike, then the rest of the pieces fell into place.

"Damn." I closed my eyes and leaned my head back.

Blue put her hand on my shoulder. "I heard you shouting. You didn't stop when I tried talking to you, then you passed out. In the ambulance you said some things but nothing that made much sense."

"I..."

"It's okay." She sat on the bed. I tried to move my head because crying in front of her was embarrassing, but I couldn't use my hands to cover my face. She forced my head on her chest and whispered words I could barely hear. When I finally managed to get hold of myself, she gently wiped my face.

"I'm sorry," was all I was able to say.

"Tell me what's happening."

I shook my head. "I can't."

"I don't need to hear everything, just enough to understand. I deserve that at least."

She was right. I shut my eyes and allowed fragments of the truth to spill out. Enough for her to understand that bad things had happened and now someone was using my actions against me, making me do things I didn't want to do.

Then came silence, long and painful. I waited for her to leave because she couldn't possibly handle the mess that was my life.

Blue let out a deep breath before finally saying, "You

should go to the police."

"I can't do that. This guy *is* the police. And he...he knows where you live. I dragged you into this mess, so I'm not risking anything with him."

"I'm not afraid."

"Then good thing I'm afraid for the both of us."

"What is he forcing you to do?"

I shook my head, unable to let the words bleed out of my mouth. "Don't ask me that."

She scowled and tugged at her necklace. "Are you hurting anyone?"

"No. It's nothing like that. Just please don't ask me about it, okay?"

She hesitantly nodded. "There's nothing you can do?"

It was frustrating not being able to make her understand how strong Mike's hold on me was. How deep my fear of him ran. I said, "He's smart, always seems to be a step ahead of me. He has proof against me, and I..." I had nothing. Mike had a video recording of what I'd done, and I didn't have anything that incriminated him. But *why?*

I leaned my head back, thoughts swirling in my brain.

"Matt? Are you okay?"

Almost to myself, I said, "I can also get proof."

"How are you going to do that?"

I closed my eyes and focused. I'd need strong enough proof to make Mike back off for good. Anything less wouldn't be worth the risk. I opened my eyes. "You mentioned your ex a while back, the one who helped track me down."

"Yeah..."

"Can he help me set up recording equipment and hide it?" What I was using for my chat videos was too noticeable.

She nibbled on her lower lip and nodded. "I think so. But where?"

"In my apartment, back in Hudson."

"Okay. I'm calling him now."

"Wait. After you call him, I don't want you involved in this."

She put her palm on my cheek. "Of course. I'll just wait at home, cleaning and cooking dinner while thinking of my favorite soap opera."

"I'm sensing a touch of sarcasm."

She smacked my shoulder. "You bet your ass you're sensing it. I'm calling Joshua and then we'll get to work." Determination was written loud and clear on her face.

Having a plan filled my body with adrenaline, yet the thought of failing and ending up worse than today tainted my fragile optimism. This was my last chance to regain my freedom, but I wasn't sure I was strong enough to face the coming war.

*

Going back to Hudson with Joshua and Blue to help save my life was not how I'd envisioned Blue's first visit to my hometown would be.

When we got to my building, I asked them to wait in the car, then hurried up to my apartment. I couldn't let them see the video equipment in my bedroom. Only when all evidence of my work was hidden, I asked them to come up.

Blue didn't comment on my apartment, but I could tell she was watching closely, maybe trying to gather more pieces of the complicated puzzle that was my life.

Joshua set up the new recording equipment on the table between the kitchen and the living room, then hid it underneath old newspapers. He was kind enough to act professionally without asking questions, or maybe Blue had warned him about that in advance.

Once they both left, I called Mike and told him I was back in town. I'd also called him the day before from the hospital and told him Blue and I were done. No more Vermont.

He came to my apartment and immediately handed me a list of names and numbers. "Those are new clients you're going to meet in the next couple of weeks."

I scanned the list. "These are all men."

"You're a sharp one. I told you I'd be letting the agency know your ass is now open for business. Got a problem?"

I did, but I had a bigger problem I needed to focus on. "Okay."

"You sure? No drama?"

I slipped the list into my pocket. "I'll do it."

He scanned my face with a raised eyebrow, clearly expecting a fight. "Well, good. I was told those guys are regulars. Mostly married men who are looking for a good, discrete time. You'll get back to women in a few weeks if you behave."

I nodded, barely listening, hoping my anxiety wasn't showing.

Mike took his jacket off and put it on a chair. "You know I'm not trying to be the bad guy, right? We had an agreement, but you decided to piss all over it."

"I only asked for fewer hours or another way to make money."

He took a step closer and put his palm on the back of my neck, making me lean closer to him. "It's too early for you to ask for anything. Not too long ago you were slowly rotting in here. I gave you a second chance, probably saved your life. You don't get to decide how to pay me back. Do your job, earn us more money, and it won't be long before I let you date again and take longer breaks."

His promises were hollow, words I knew not to trust. "Okay."

He came even closer. "It's not easy for me to say, but I'm grateful. You're making life a lot easier for me now with the baby on the way. All in all, we make a good team you and I."

"Pimping me out is not a partnership."

"Sure it is. You're a prime stock and we're letting people enjoy you for money—it could've been worse. When you have doubts, keep in mind the alternative; you'll get a lot more action in prison."

Instead of letting his words cut, I hoped they would keep on coming for the recording.

Mike went to sit on the couch and put his legs on the table.

I asked, "Is this your night off?"

"Yep. Free as a bird."

"I'm bringing something to lighten the mood."

He smirked and kicked off his shoes. "Yeah, let's do that. I've been a fucking slave for Emily all week. It's time for some downtime."

I brought him a beer, then opened the window and lit a joint for him. He hesitated before inhaling, but eventually shrugged and took a deep puff. I usually made my joints light, but this time I put in as much weed as possible.

Mike blew smoke toward the window and then handed me the joint. I held it close to my mouth and waited for him to finish checking his phone before passing it back to him.

"She cried when you dumped her?" he asked.

"What?"

"The girl from Vermont."

"Yeah, it was tough."

"It's for her own good. No offense, Matty, but you shouldn't be getting involved with anyone at this point. I made a mistake when I let you play without supervision." He took a sip of beer. "Dumping that girl is the best thing you could've done. Since I care about your well-being, it's my responsibility to point it out."

"Thanks for having my well-being at heart."

He chuckled for almost ten seconds, indicating the weed was working.

"I dreamed about them yesterday," I said.

"Them?"

"Jeff. Albert."

"Was it a wet dream?"

"Christ."

"I'm kidding!" He smoked more. Despite the open window, the air in the room turned misty. "Let's not talk about those two. I'm trying to keep my spirit up, what with Emily's transformation into a cow. I don't need to think about two corpses."

Damn it. I couldn't miss this opportunity.

"I think that talking about it could help me move on." There was no point adding that *he* was the only one I could talk to about this.

He rolled his eyes. "Fine. Go on. What did you dream about?"

I'd been rehearsing what to say all day, but the words now clung to my tongue. "The way they died. What happened before that."

He nodded. The thick smoke floated between us. I was getting lightheaded without actively smoking. "That was a bad time for you, no doubt. You were stupid to run and even more stupid to come back. Still, you need to leave what happened in the past. You're building something better now."

"I don't see how I'm building something better."

"You're working and making money, aren't you?"

"It's dirty money."

"Doesn't matter. You do what you need to do. And if you want me to keep my mouth shut about your little murder spree, you better stop looking at it as dirty money and focus on making those clients happy."

At any other time, those words would have hurt, but now they were the most beautiful music that could have reached my ears. "Maybe you're right." I looked down at my hands. "Not like I have a choice."

"Nope." He took a final puff before throwing the joint out the window. "No choice at all." He leaned closer to me and said, "You think I'm dumb, Matty? After all this time, you still think that?"

"I don't know what you mean."

"The weed, the beer, the small talk. I can see right through you."

I didn't have enough air in my lungs to speak. All I could do was stare at him.

"You think that making me high and friendly will make me forget about your little tantrum the other night?"

I was too relieved to care what he'd do about that.

He watched me closely and said, "Since you've been cool about working with men, I'm gonna let what happened slide. You can make it up to me by paying for an Uber; ain't no way I'm driving home like this."

After he left, I hurried to check the recording, half expecting it to not have worked. But it was all there. I lay down on my couch and savored this rare feeling of accomplishment. The war wasn't over yet, but at least I was going in well armed.

When I called Blue, she answered immediately. "Are you okay?"

I haven't been this okay in a long time. "Blue, we got him."

35

Mike's wife went to stay at her mom's this weekend, so I knew I'd find him alone.

Anxiety pulsed underneath my skin as I walked toward his house. The sun was about to set, but the air was still warm. The houses around were mostly one story high, with many needing a fresh coat of paint. Kids played outside, running after one another on the open front lawns. I kept walking until I reached Mike's house. It was smaller than the other houses. The police car was parked outside, and the TV was playing by the sound of it.

Standing in front of his door, the pressure in my chest reached its peak. There was only one outcome I could live with, and I wasn't leaving until I got it.

I knocked on the door. After a few seconds, the sound of the TV stopped, replaced by approaching footsteps. The door opened, and Mike stared at me with wide eyes.

"You better have a good reason for this," he said.

"I do."

He gestured me inside. I looked around, surprised that someone like Mike could live in a normal house. He might have been a man's man, but Emily sure put her womanly touch everywhere. I could imagine them arguing about the pink vase next to the TV.

A picture of Mike and Emily on their wedding day hung on the wall. On the living room table stood a half-empty bottle of Budweiser next to an overflowing ashtray.

I turned around and Mike was in front of me, our faces almost touching.

"Explain yourself," he said. "Make it good."

"We need to talk. Can we sit?"

He nodded. "Go on."

I sat on the couch and Mike sat next to me, his shoulders stiff. Simply by being in his house, I was changing our dynamic, and it was clear he didn't approve.

"Speak," he said. "Then I'll decide what to do with you."

I ran my tongue across my dry mouth. "A couple of days ago you were in my apartment."

"Yeah..."

"We talked."

"And?"

"I recorded everything."

Confusion spread across his face. Before he had a chance to speak, I said, "I have a video recording of you talking about what happened with Albert and Jeff, and how you've been using it to make me...you know." I forced myself to keep looking him in the eyes. Bowing down to him was rooted into my DNA by now, so standing up to him felt like fighting against a law of nature. "I'm not planning on using what I recorded. As long as you keep what you have on me to yourself and leave me alone, I'll do the same."

"You think..." He cleared his throat. "You think that what you have on me is even close to what I have on you? You can't be that dumb. I mean, I have a video of you killing a guy, then leaving him to rot. You have a video of me smoking weed, drinking beer, and talking shit. Pretty different, don't you think?"

I expected him to choose this route. "You're right. If you tell on me, I'm screwed. But having a video of what happened in the lab popping up out of nowhere, and having you on record talking about the same event... that's too much of a coincidence. It's been months since what happened with Albert, and you didn't report any of it, which makes you an accomplice. You know I have enough to take you down with me. With the baby on the way—"

"Shut up about that."

"I want out. I'm done."

He looked away, foot tapping on the floor. This was him calculating his next move, measuring the odds of getting what he wanted. The tapping on the floor became faster, and it was getting obvious the math didn't add up for him.

"I want to see what you recorded," he said.

Another thing I was prepared for. I took out my phone. "I have a backup of everything." I played him the video, which clearly showed his face as he spoke about what he knew and what he was forcing me to do. When he looked away, I put the phone back in my pocket.

"You thought about this all by yourself?" he asked.

"Once I realized you'd never let me go, it wasn't hard to figure out I needed to stop you. Luckily, you love to hear yourself talk."

He snickered and stood up. I hesitated but stood as well.

"Looks like I taught you well," he said in a flat voice. "Probably too well."

I remained quiet, feeling some of the tightness in my chest loosen.

He sized me up. "So that's that, huh?"

I nodded. "I'll be leaving in the next couple of days."

"Going to that girl of yours?"

"Yes."

"She gives good head?"

"Goodbye." I walked past him toward the door.

"Has she ever heard you cry and beg?"

I kept on walking.

"How about all those videos of you playing with yourself? Did you let her see them? Should I show her?"

"Only if you want Emily to know you've been cheating."

I had my hand on the doorknob when he shouted, "Hey!"

I turned around in time to see his fist moving, but not fast enough to dodge. The side of my face exploded with pain. I lost my balance and fell on the floor, blinding lights filling my vision.

"You're such a big shot, huh?"

His voice sounded muffled through the ringing in my ears. I pushed myself up on all fours, knowing I must escape before he lost it completely.

"Now you're calling all the shots, is that it?"

I was about to stand when Mike grabbed the back

of my shirt and yanked hard. I slammed onto my back with a cry of pain.

His face loomed above me, covered in bright, flickering spots. "You couldn't keep on being a good whore, huh? You just had to cause drama."

"Stop."

He crouched down. "Stop? No, you don't want that. You *need* me."

My spine throbbed with burning pins. "I don't need you."

He grabbed my face, his nails digging into my cheeks. "I'm your redemption, your savior."

"Fuck off!" I pushed his hand away and got a punch to my guts in return.

"Man, I missed educating you."

I turned on my stomach. Despite the pain, my sight slowly sharpened, enough to start pushing myself toward the entrance.

"Where do you think you're going, buddy?" He kicked my ribs. I screamed and rolled on my back.

He's going to kill me.

"You love that, don't you?" He leaned down. "All you need is some tough—"

I sent my hand and grabbed his crotch, squeezed with all the force I had. He screamed and fell on the floor. I pushed myself up, got hold of his head, then smacked it on the floor. His eyes turned glassy. It was almost too easy losing myself and breaking his skull, but I wasn't so far gone.

I got up and wobbled as I tried reaching for the door. Staying there any longer was sure to end with one of us dead, and the odds were not in my favor.

Mike suddenly grabbed my ankle and pulled, sending me knees-first onto the floor. I yelled and turned around to see him lunge. He landed on top of me and hit my face twice before I managed to smash my fist at his throat. He choked and fell on his side, struggling to breathe.

My face was a lump of pain, blood pouring from my nose and lips. I couldn't bring myself to stand as gravity glued me to the ground. Then Mike jumped on me again.

I lost count of the times he hit me and the times I was able to hit him back. At one point, we were like two drunks who could barely move but didn't have the sense to stop fighting. We broke the living room table and the pink vase. He tried using a chair to hit me with but couldn't lift it. I pulled his wedding picture off the wall and hurled it at him, missing my target but smashing the picture into little shards of glass.

The staggering pain paled in comparison to the satisfaction I got from finally fighting back. I could tell he didn't expect me to last for as long as I did, but pain was a monster I'd been forced to tame.

When it was finally over and neither of us could stand or move, we lay next to one another on the floor, panting and bleeding.

"Fucking crazy," he mumbled. "Couldn't stay down."

I coughed. "You should've let me go."

He laughed with little air. "And miss all the fun?"

I knew I should use this opportunity to drag myself out of the house, but my body refused to cooperate.

"You need me," Mike said, sounding like he truly

believed that.

"I don't need you. Not anymore."

He dragged himself toward me, and before I could figure out what was happening, he held a piece of broken glass to my neck.

"I think it's called a plot twist," he said and put pressure on my neck.

"Do it," I said.

"Don't test me."

"If that's the only way to get rid of you, just do it."

He cut me, a sharp pain that numbed all other sensations in my body.

Then he threw the glass away. "I have enough cleaning to do without getting rid of a corpse." He lay his head down next to me.

"I'm done," I said. "You need to understand that."

He was quiet for a while, our heavy breaths echoing between us. A few drops of blood trickled down my neck, but the cut wasn't deep.

"Don't come back to town," Mike finally said. "If I see you again, I'll kill you. You hear me?"

"Yes."

I tried to move, but a sharp pain ran down my spine and stopped me.

Mike snickered. "You'll remember this education session for a long time."

"I'll forget you faster than you think."

"Forget?" He moved his hand and put a finger against the side of my head. "I'm already living there, Matty, and I ain't going away."

I groaned and pushed myself to my feet before his

words got a chance to spread more poison. Gravity tried to pull me down, but I didn't let it. With my vision a blurry mess, I stumbled forward and managed to reach the entrance.

Then I was gone.

EPILOGUE

We have the weirdest dog alive. Twenty cars might drive by our house, but only the red ones will cause Sam to bark. He also only eats chicken and beef, never pork. When Bill and Molly met him, they said he must've had a good Jewish upbringing before we got him.

Blue is working inside the house on a new website she's designing. I'm sitting on the porch, preparing a marketing plan and a budget for a potential new client. My work at Abby's Corner gave me the confidence to pursue this line of work. My current project is a joint one with Blue. Landing this deal will help us get new stuff for the house.

Sam barks, and when I raise my head, there it is—a red car.

"You're something else, Sam."

Blue comes out and stretches. She's wearing one of my flannel shirts, her hair tied in a tight ponytail. "All done."

"Did it turn out okay?"

"Are you implying there's another option?"

"No, ma'am." I move to give her room on the swing. I built this swing myself, my subtle way of leaving a mark on a house that was now partly mine.

I still wake up sometimes expecting to see the peeling walls of my old bedroom, to hear the buzzing street outside my window. Yet I don't allow myself to dwell on memories from Hudson when I can help it. At this point in my life, the bad memories overcome the good.

"You're almost done?" Blue asks and pats Sam on the head. He loves her like crazy, but he only tolerates me. Maybe because he knows I know how weird he is.

"I'm done," I say. "I'll let you make it pretty later."

"Okay. Let's take care of dinner."

I put the laptop aside and get up, not worried someone might try stealing it in Grafton.

We have a good workflow in the kitchen, knowing what the other might need and when to get out of the way. It takes Blue about ten minutes to casually say, "Susan called to remind us of your appointment. You're going, right?"

I sense something hidden in her voice. "Did I talk in my sleep again?"

"What? No. Not really." She shrugs. "Maybe a bit."

I turn my back to her and start cutting more tomatoes, although I've already cut plenty.

"Sleeping next to a psycho every night can't be easy. She's afraid of you."

"Shut up."

"Matty?"

I shake my head. "Not you. Forget it." I try to lighten my tone. "I remember my appointment with Susan. No worries."

"Look at me."

I sigh and turn around. "I'm fine."

She crosses her arms and looks at me like my skin is transparent.

I say, "I asked you to wake me up when you hear me talking."

"It only lasted a few seconds."

"What did I say?"

Her posture stiffens. "I don't remember."

Now it's my turn to give her a look. We can both read each other too well by now. In truth, it offers more problems than solutions.

"You were talking about a grave," she says, a slight tremble in her voice. "About being buried."

I suspected as much. Last time I woke her up was by screaming, "Don't cut me!"

I open my mouth to apologize, but she won't accept it. I settle for saying, "Just wake me up next time, okay?" Because we both know there will be a next time.

She nods and continues preparing the food. The air in the kitchen feels tenser.

When I started seeing the therapist, I told her some of the things that had happened would always be private and she should find ways to get the general picture without pushing. In retrospect, I should have sought help sooner, but I allowed myself to believe my newfound freedom would be enough to keep my demons at bay.

"This pasta's gonna turn out so good," Blue says as she sets the table.

"Shouldn't I be the one giving the final score?"

"You think you're gonna score my cooking? Have I taught you nothing?"

We sit at opposite sides of the table, with Sam standing next to Blue. He knows she'll sneak him food under the table. We talk about my fishing trip with Steve this coming weekend. He's the worst fisherman in all of Vermont, his patience as thin as a piece of paper. But we both enjoy our time alone together, so I give him the benefit of the doubt.

Caleb calls after dinner and we chat while I'm doing the dishes. This time the aliens are stalking him in a FedEx truck, but he doesn't sound overly concerned. We finish the call after he promises to join Bill and Molly on their next monthly visit.

Blue and I head off to bed relatively early. Our friends tease us about being an old couple, but it's not like there's much to do around town.

Blue falls asleep quickly, but I remain awake next to her. Sam is snoring softly at the foot of the bed.

My thoughts are loud and restless in the darkness of the room. I'm considering quietly moving into our spare room to avoid having Blue face another night of me talking in my sleep. But if she wakes up to find me sleeping in another room, she'll spill a bucket of cold water on my head. Again.

I'm not the only one currently awake. Mike's voice is crystal clear in the back of my mind. *"You're about to mess this up, buddy. Give her time and she'll figure out she deserves better—you know she does."*

My fists are clenched tight underneath the blanket. I try to deflect my thoughts, but it's no use.

"You miss my education, Matty. You need my redemption so bad. Go on, give me a call and let's stop

pretending. I can fix you in no time."

His words are knives I must dodge. They cut deep at times, leaving wounds that darken my mood for days.

I close my eyes and focus on the air flowing in and out of my body, the rise and fall of my chest. There are ways to push him back, methods I've learned to master. But they are far from guaranteed.

To my relief, I'm able to shut him out tonight, to drown him in my subconscious where he can do less harm.

Before sleep claims me, I remind myself to be grateful. I've reached a point where I can better control my fears and insecurities. To forgive myself for the road I took and the pain it brought.

If the ghosts of my past ever return to settle the score, I'll give them hell. But they are not here tonight, and despite it all, I know I'll find my peace.

The End

ACKNOWLEDGMENTS

Writing this book has been a crazy journey. It took me over seven years of writing, rewriting, editing, and second-guessing myself until I gathered the courage to put this story out there. If you're reading these words, that means I have completed my journey and you, my reader, have finished it as well.

Thank you.

Since we are living in a time of fewer physical borders, I took full advantage of that. I met a wonderful woman from Australia online, and for months she advised me on everything from structure, to language, to character development. Thank you, Diana, you are one of a kind.

Through Fiverr.com I reached dozens of beta readers who helped shape my story into what it had become. Thank you to Stephanie, Matt, Jamie, Michaele, Nicholas, Bianca, Simona, Ash, Nikki, Karl, Amanda, EJ, Whitney, and anyone else I might have forgotten.

If you feel like reaching out for any reason, please do so, through avshenerbooks@gmail.com

Leaving a review would be greatly appreciated.

Thank you,
A.V. Shener.